THE WRATH OF THE IUTES

The Song of Octa
Book Two

JAMES CALBRAITH

FLYING
SQUID

Published July 2021 by Flying Squid

Visit James Calbraith's official website at
jamescalbraith.wordpress.com
for the latest news, book details, and other information

Copyright © James Calbraith, 2020
Cover photo: Oleksandr Zamuruiev, Peter Lorrimer via Shutterstock

This book is a work of fiction. Names, characters, places and incidents either are products of the author's imagination or are used fictitiously. Any resemblance to actual events or locales or persons, living or dead, is entirely coincidental.

All rights reserved. Except as permitted under the U.S. Copyright Act of 1976, no part of this publication may be reproduced, distributed or transmitted in any form or by any means, or stored in a database or retrieval system, without the prior written permission of the publisher.
Fan fiction and fan art is encouraged.

WESTERN BRITANNIA, c. 460 AD

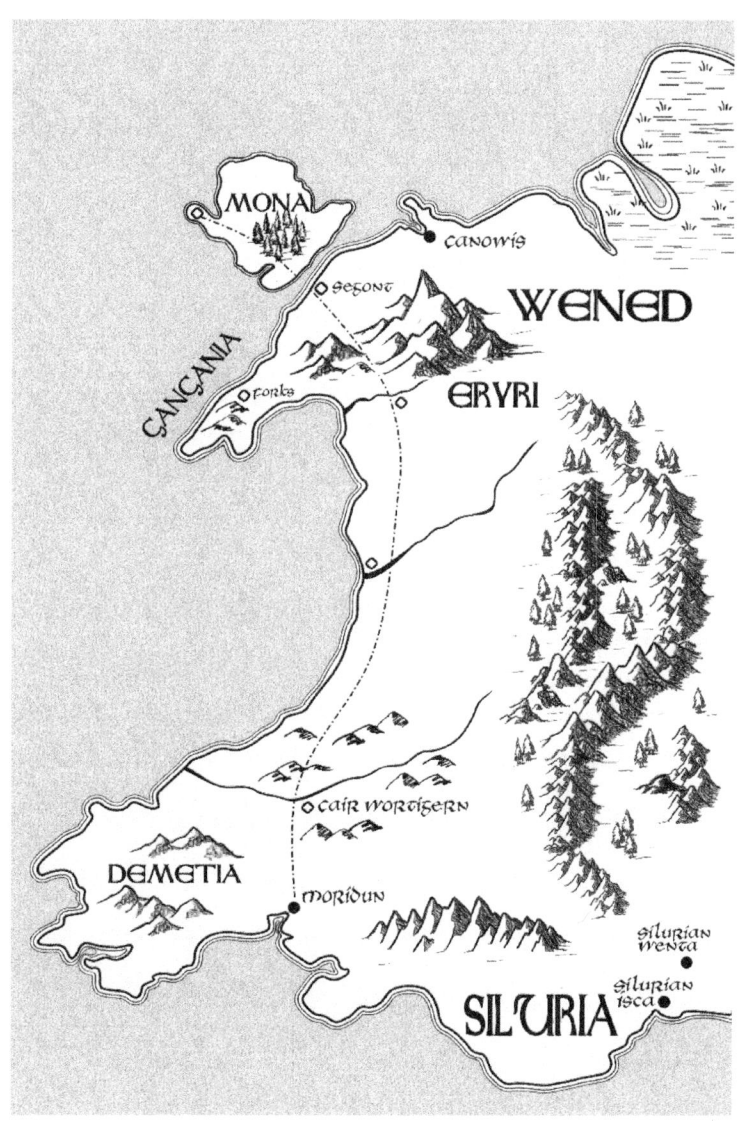

CAST OF CHARACTERS

Britannia Maxima

Aelle: *Rex* of the Saxons
Aeric I: *Rex* of the Iutes
Betula: *Gesith*, commander of King Aeric's household guards
Deora: a warrior in Haesta's band
Fastidius: Bishop of Londin, brother of King Aeric
Haesta: rebel chieftain of the Haestingas mercenaries

Octa: *aetheling* of Iutes, son of King Aeric
Ursula: daughter of Cantian nobles

Octa's riders:
    Seawine
    Acha
    Aecba
    Aerende
    Audulf
    Colswine
    Raegen
    Ubba

Armorica

Cado: surgeon in Marcus's detachment
Drustan: young officer in Marcus's detachment
Hleo & Haering: Iutish fishermen from Wecta

Marcus: *Decurion* of a cavalry detachment from Dumnonia
Mullo: former Legionnaire; Gaius Macrinus

Ahes: daughter of Graelon, *Comes* of Armorican Britons
Budic: Armorican Briton patrician
Graelon: *Comes* of Armorican Britons
Maegwind: Graelon's wife
Warus: Captain of the *Maegwind*, Graelon's flagship

Britannia Prima

Ambrosius: *Dux* of Britannia Prima
Cunedag: chieftain of the Wotadin settlers in Wened
Donwen: a *drui* of Mona
Eochu: chief of the Atecots
Felix: leader of Scillonian Christians
Fiann: an officer in Wortigern's army
Hrodha: chieftain of Saxon mercenaries
Myrtle, Madron: daughter of Wortimer and Rhedwyn, granddaughter of Wortigern
Ouein: chief elder *drui* of Mona
Niall: king of the Scots
Potentin: a local guide in Wened
Seleu: a *drui* of Mona
Silvia: a harbour wench in Dun Taiel
Sulien: leader of Scillonian pagans
Wortigern: former *Dux* of Britannia Maxima, now commander of Wened forts

GLOSSARY

Aetheling: member of the Iutish royal family
Avus: grandfather
Cair: hill fortress
Caldarium: hot room of the Roman bath
Ceol: narrow, ocean-going Saxon ship
Centuria: troop of (about) hundred infantry
Centurion: officer in Roman infantry
Chrismon: a monogram symbol of Christ
Comes, pl. Comites: administrator of a *pagus*, subordinate to the *Dux*
Decurion: officer in Roman cavalry
Domus: the main structure of a *villa*
Domna: Roman lady
Drui: druid, warrior and scholar of Mona
Dux: overall commander in war times; in peace time — administrator of a province
Equites: Roman cavalry
Fyrd: army made up of all warriors of the tribe
Gesith: companion of the *Drihten*, chief of the *Hiréd*
Hiréd: band of elite warriors of *Drihten*'s household
Hlaford, Hlaefdige: Lord and Lady in Saxon tongue.
Leh: slate stone
Liburna: Roman warship
Mansio: staging post
Pagus, pl. Pagi: administrative unit, smaller than a province
Plumbata: Roman throwing dart
Praefect: Roman military commander

Praetor: high administrative or military official
Praetorium: seat of the *Praetor*
Rex: king of a barbarian tribe
Seax: Saxon short sword
Scop: Saxon poet and bard
Sicera: cider
Spatha: Roman long sword
Torc: a metal neck ring
Villa: Roman agricultural property
Vigiles: town guards and firemen
Wealh, pl. *wealas*: "the others", Britons in Saxon tongue.

PLACE NAMES

Ake: Aachen, Germany
Andreda: Weald Forest
Arduenna: Ardennes
Arelate: Arles, France
Ariminum: Wallington, Surrey
Armorica: Brittany
Callew: Calleva Atrebatum, Silchester
Cantia: Kent
Demetia: Dyfed
Dorowern: Dorovernum, Canterbury, Kent
Dubris: Dover, France
Dumnonia: Cornwall and Devon
Dumnonian Isca: Isca Dumnoniorum, Exeter, Cornwall
Dun Taiel: Tintagel, Cornwall
Eobbasfleot: Ebbsfleet, Kent
Epatiac: Portus Aepatiacum, near Etaples, France
Gangania: Llyn Peninsula, Wales
Gesocribate: Douarnenez, Brittany
Icorig: Icorigium, Junkerath, Germany
Leman: Lympne, Kent
Londin: Londinium, London
Moridun: Moridunum, Carmarthen, Wales
Mona: Anglesey, Wales
Mosa: River Meuse
New Port: Novus Portus, Portslade, Sussex
Oriri: Eryri, Snowdonia, Wales
Redones: Rennes, Brittany
Rhenum: River Rhine
Robriwis: Dorobrivis, Rochester, Kent
Rotomag: Rotomagus, Rouen, France
Rutubi: Rutupiae, Richborough, Kent
Scillonia Isles of Scilly, Cornwall
Segont: Caernarfon, Wales

Sequana: River Seine
Silurian Isca: Isca Silurum, Caerleon, Wales
Tamesa: River Thames
Tanet: Isle of Thanet, Kent
Teibi: Afon Teifi, Wales
The Forks: Tre'r Ceiri, Gwynedd, Wales
Tolbiac: Zulpich, Germany
Tornac: Tornacum, Tournai, Belgium
Traiect: Maastricht, Netherlands
Trever: Trier, Germany
Uxant: Ushant, Brittany
Wened: Gwynedd, Wales
Worgium: Carhaix, Brittany

PART 1: ARMORICA, 458 AD

CHAPTER I
THE LAY OF DEORA

"There she is," whispers Seawine.

One of Haesta's men leads Ursula out of her tent. She seems unharmed, just tired – and famished. Her face is grey, smudged with grime and dust, her cheeks are sunken and sallow, her long, black hair has lost its lustre. Only her eyes still gleam with pride and subdued anger.

My heart starts to race, and my breath quickens. It's been three Sundays since I last saw her – our days counted only by the distant bells calling the faithful to the Holy Mass in the towns we passed by – and a couple more since we last spoke. In the four long years since we've become friends, I don't think we've ever been apart for longer than a couple of months... I'm surprised at how much I've missed her, and how wretched this forced separation makes me feel.

With her hands tied behind her back, she hobbles up to the campfire. One of the Haestingas hands her a bowl. Seeing her eat her meagre portion of a watery potage is enough to rouse my anger again. My fury is tempered when I notice everyone else in the camp is served the same miserable meal from the same cauldron. In their flight back to Britannia, Haesta's men had little time either for rest or for gathering provisions. Judging by how empty their saddle bags hang, this evening's potage may well be their last. Our bags are almost empty, too. Neither Haesta, nor we, counted on the pursuit to last this long.

The Wrath of the Iutes

Twice we got near to Ursula's captors, and twice the prey escaped us. The first was on the very day our chase had begun. I left Audulf in the care of the army surgeons at Icorig, and with the rest of my Iutes with me, I launched into a frantic dash to make up for lost time. Half a mile before Tolbiac, we saw Haesta's men before us. They were weary, slowed down by the wounds from Basina's arrows, desperate to get to the safety of the town's walls. Riding less than a javelin-throw behind the slowest of the Haestingas, I could see the defiance in Ursula's cold stare. Haesta shouted at me to stay away, threatened to slit her throat if I got too close, but I ignored him. I did not believe he had the ability to kill the girl in cold blood like that. Everything I knew about him told me he wasn't a murderer. Like us, he just wanted to go home safely. He didn't need to take Ursula hostage. It was all a misunderstanding. If only I could have reached through to him, if only we could talk, none of what followed would have happened.

But Fate wished otherwise. Haesta reached Tolbiac's walls just in time. The River Franks, who occupied the town, opened the gate for him, and shut it in our faces.

I did not yet then understand the respect Haesta commanded among the tribes living along the Rhenum River. The River Franks knew him only as The Hammer of Saxons, a fearless leader of a mercenary band that for a couple of years kept peace on the frontier – and they knew us as friends and allies of *Rex* Hildrik and the treacherous Salians, who mere weeks earlier attacked and slew their clan's chieftain. Haesta could have ordered them to hunt us back to Icorig, if he so wished, and they would have done so, gladly, even if it meant risking a battle with the fort's Roman garrison.

Several precious days passed before the River Franks, having plundered all there was to plunder, and grown bored of its cold stone walls, abandoned the scorched ruin of Tolbiac and we could, at last, renew our pursuit. By then, Haesta and his men, rested and healed of their most grievous injuries, were already far away…

The guard ties Ursula's legs and unties her hands. She slurps the thin gruel straight from the bowl, and picks with her fingers at the morsels of fat and boiled roots within it, with an expression as bland as the food itself. A rustle in the bushes makes both Ursula and the guard look up – him, in fright; her, with hope. But it's not any of us making the sound. A fat fowl flies out onto the glade. A few of Haesta's men rush out to catch it, but it's too swift and, after a few turns and leaps, it launches, heavily, into the sky, leaving the men with empty hands and stomachs.

We caught up to the Haestingas again at Traiect, a small town on the River Mosa, almost by accident. Beyond Traiect lay the land of the Salians, subjects of Hildrik and Queen Basina, our allies, and Haesta's enemies. It was there that we received the first report from the fast couriers Basina had sent out from Icorig where, like Audulf, she was still recuperating from the wounds she suffered at the Battle of Trever.

"We reached all the harbours on the western coast," the rider told us. "As far south as Epatiac. If Haesta wants to reach Britannia undisturbed, he'll have to cross Gaul."

The Wrath of the Iutes

"You haven't seen them on the Tornac road, then?" I asked.

"If he's in Frankia, he's hiding well. Maybe he's moving through the Charcoal Forest?"

But he wasn't in the Charcoal Forest; he was in the town's only remaining tavern, brooding over his misfortune, and trying to figure out his next move. One of my Iutes, Colswine, stumbled on his men as we were making ready to ride to Tornac; a fight broke out, at first just a tavern brawl, which soon grew to encompass the town's entire diverse population. Traiect is – or was, before the Huns marched through it – a border town, and its ruins were inhabited by Salians, River Franks, Latin-speaking Gauls, even a few Saxons. There were animosities there reaching back generations, made worse still by the recent wars. It didn't take much for this poisonous stew to boil over.

In the chaos and the panic of the brawl, as the ruins of Traiect burned around them, Haesta's men cut Colswine and fled across the Mosa Bridge. Once again, I was too late to stop him – all I glimpsed was fear and desperation in his eyes as he dragged Ursula to the other side of the river, into a land he knew was hostile to him. In Hildrik's kingdom, he was more than a fugitive – he was an enemy warchief, a commander of a mercenary band that chose the wrong side in the Battle of Trever. He knew he was running out of options, and I knew I could not risk confronting him in the open like that again.

"Queen Basina is said to be returning to her kingdom soon," the courier told us as we watched the Haestingas vanish in a cloud of road dust. *Rex* Hildrik himself was still campaigning in southern Gaul, fighting the Goths and the Burgundians by the Imperator's side, and in his absence, it was up to Basina and the Council of elders to govern his kingdom. "I'm sure she will grant you everything you need to hunt Haesta while he's within our borders."

"We can't wait that long," I told him. "I can't lose his trail – or I will never find him again."

"I pray that Naerth rewards your perseverance, Octa, son of Aeric," said the courier, invoking the name of a goddess of good fortune, and mounted his charger to take the news back to his queen.

Naerth, if she were indeed willing to reward us, took her time. Crossing the fields and forests, avoiding the main roads and settlements, sneaking through hill passes and traversing river valleys, Haesta travelled south-west for days, across an unfamiliar territory, presumably towards some harbour that only he knew about. I no longer had the faintest inkling of where in the world we were. A few times I'd decipher the name of the nearest town on a moss-grown milestone, but it would be just a meaningless collection of letters. Eventually, I realised that Haesta was our only guide through this inhospitable Gaulish countryside. We had to follow him not just to free Ursula – without him, we'd be lost in this empty land for good.

This isn't how I had imagined my return from Trever. By now, I should be in Cantia with my father, Aeric, *Rex* of the

The Wrath of the Iutes

Iutes, celebrating a hero's welcome. Betula is likely there already, with my father's household guards, the *Hiréd*, waiting for my arrival and telling everyone of our adventures in Frankia and Gaul, of fighting Odowakr and his Saxon army, destroying his siege engines, saving the city of Trever and, in doing so, likely changing the fate of Rome itself... But she must be growing worried now, too. We never reached Tornac, the Salian capital, where we were supposed to meet before going home. If anyone had set out to search for us, the last thing they'd learn from Basina's messengers would be that we disappeared, chasing some foe in the wild vastness of northern Gaul...

I wonder what my father must be thinking right now? Does he assume I am dead, and is he seeking another heir in my place? No, he wouldn't be so hasty... I've only been gone a month. Most likely, he's occupied with whatever new dangers threaten his kingdom. *Rex* Aelle's warriors will, by now, have returned from Gaul, and our Saxon neighbours might already be testing the Iutish defences. The sea raiders will, by now, have heard that the *Hiréd* have gone to the Continent, and renewed their attacks. Even the Britons might have grown restless behind their stone walls, emboldened by the chaos on the other side of the Narrow Sea... No, my father will be too busy to worry about me.

Ursula finishes her meal, scrubbing the bottom of the bowl with her fingernails. The guard takes the bowl away and grunts at her, but is cut short by Haesta. The Iute crouches down beside Ursula and says something too quiet for me to hear. She smiles, weakly, and nods, before returning to her tent.

I'm not sure why Haesta still thinks it necessary to drag the poor girl all this way. Does he even know we're still following him? I have tried to keep at a safe distance, until now. Maybe she's no longer needed as leverage to keep me at bay; maybe he's planning to use her in some other manner once he's back in Britannia... After all, she is more than just my friend – she comes from a noble family, a daughter of Dorowern's magistrates, and could be worth a decent ransom. Right now, Ursula might just be the only way for Haesta to return some profit on this unfortunate adventure in Gaul.

"We've seen enough," I tell Seawine. The two of us crawl backwards through the ferns, careful not to step on any twigs or snatch our clothes on the thorns. The guards at Haesta's camp are tense. I can't risk him moving the camp again – this might be our last chance before he reaches the coast.

We make our way back to the remainder of my little Iute detachment. After the fighting in Gaul, there's only eight of us left: myself and the seven Iutish warriors, who until a few months ago were serfs, sailors or servants... I know them all now as well as I would my own family. Their stories tell of the difficult lives of the Iutes dwelling in the open coasts of Cantia, still exposed to the raiders and bandits, despite my father's efforts. Aerende and Seawine, burly and muscle-bound crewmen on a merchant's ship plying the coastal waters between Robriwis and Port Adurn. Colswine, wounded at Traiect, narrow-faced and short-limbed, owner of a small herd of sheep near Leman; the Frankish slavers caught him when they raided the town's market. His wife and child likely believe him dead – unless the news Betula took

The Wrath of the Iutes

back with her has reached their farm already. Ubba and Aecba, sturdy, rugged fishermen from the northern coast, the only survivors of their hamlet, razed by a raiding party of Picts. Slim, sinewy Raegen, and the buxom, muscular Acha, who both hired themselves out as farmhands to a Briton nobleman, one of the brave few who still remained in Cantia, rather than move to Armorica like most of their kind; when the Frisians assaulted his seafront *villa*, the loyal servants rushed to its defence. Most were slain outright; others, like Raegen and Acha, taken to slavery.

All of them – all of *us* – are now war-tempered fighters, veterans of battles the likes of which few, if any, Iutes have ever experienced: Ake, of the hot spring, where we were baptised in the blood of a Saxon foraging party; Tolbiac, of the crossroad, where we first stood against Odowacr, and where Gille and Haeth fell; the long Siege of Trever, the greatest city in Gaul, where we lost four more, among them poor young Odilia…

I can only hope that all this hard-won practice will be enough to defeat the Haestingas, here in this nameless forest. Fittingly, there are as many of them left as us; like us, they are weary, hungry, injured. If possible, I would prefer to avoid a fight altogether – it would be a dangerous slog, the outcome of which would be left to Fate. I hope I can find a solution to this dilemma before Haesta moves out of our reach again…

We arrive at the damp nook in the slope of a beech-covered hill, where we set up our camp, when Seawine pushes me back into the ferns. Instinctively, I drop down, then look cautiously up to see what caused his alarm. He points to the mounts, tied to the fallen birch at the nook's edge. I count eight moor ponies – and next to them, a Thuringian warhorse.

"Weren't you supposed to go back to Britannia?" I ask.

"Weren't *you*?" Deora replies.

He glances nervously at the tips of five spears aimed at his throat, and swallows. He reaches to push the nearest one away, but Raegen only presses closer. I gesture at my men to step back, but keep vigilant.

It wasn't until he introduced himself that I recognised Deora. We only met once before, in the darkness, on the coast of Mosella. When I saw him last, he was riding off into the night after telling us everything we wanted to know about his chieftain and his comrades in arms' whereabouts. It was more than two months ago, and I was certain he was either dead or already back home.

"You know why we couldn't," I say. "What about you?"

"I was stuck in Traiect when Haesta found me." He shrugs.

"Does he know you betrayed him?"

"He does." Deora lifts the sleeve of his tunic to show a deep, jagged scar in the shape of the 'Hail' rune on his left forearm – the mark of a *hlafordswica*, a turncoat. That the scar is on his arm, where he can conceal it, rather than on his face,

The Wrath of the Iutes

as is more usual, tells me Haesta wasn't as angered by Deora's treachery as I'd hoped him to be.

"And still you stayed with him?"

"I had nowhere else to go. After the punishment, he forgave me and took me back into his band."

"And now he sent you here? Why?"

"I have a message."

"How did you find us?" asks Seawine.

Deora rolls his eyes. "You think we didn't know you were following us? You trample through these woods like a sow in heat." He rubs his neck. "Are we going to just stand here? I haven't eaten anything all day."

I order my men to stand down and invite Deora to the campfire. "Give him some bread," I say.

"You still have bread?" Deora asks, and I can see hunger breaking through his feigned disinterest.

"It's our last," I reply. "So it better be worth it. What does Haesta want?"

I wait for Deora to chew the piece of bread. He wipes a trickle of spit from the corner of his mouth before answering.

"Your woman, Ursula. We're ready to give her back, if you leave us alone."

"Give her back? Just like that? Why now?"

"Tomorrow we reach Rotomag. There's a ship waiting to take us to Britannia. We don't need the hostage anymore."

"Why didn't you bring her with you?"

"We still need you to stay out of our way for a day. You'll get her back tomorrow morning."

"How do I know you're telling the truth? How do I know Haesta's not going to take Ursula with him for ransom?"

Deora looks around and shrugs. "You can fight us for her – and risk defeat – or you could wait until morning and see for yourself. We have no more desire to lose men over the girl than you do. For what it's worth, I was told to stay here with you as assurance. I know –" He raises his hands. "– I'm not worth to Haesta as much as this girl is to you, but I'll have to make do."

I sit down. "Are you sure you're not here just to steal the last of our food?"

He offers his wrists. "You can tie me up if you wish. Look, I know how much you like subterfuge, but there is no ploy here. We are all tired, hungry and want to go home as soon as possible. You too can get a ship from Rotomag – it's a large harbour, I'm sure there will be someone sailing for Britannia soon."

I look to Seawine and the other Iutes, but the farmers and sailors around me can't give me any advice, beyond

The Wrath of the Iutes

expressing their doubts about Haesta's sincerity; not for the first time I feel the loneliness my father must feel when surrounded by his court, made up of the *witan* elders and the few high-ranking Iutes he trusts. He and I are the only ones of our tribe with extensive Roman education; he and I are the only ones fully aware of the greater world beyond our tiny kingdom's borders. Even Betula, the closest of his advisors, has little experience in politics and diplomacy, which means the king has to make most decisions regarding the tribe's fate by himself – just as I do, now.

"I find it hard to believe Haesta would just give her up like this," I say. "Ursula would fetch a good price on the Rotomag slave market. At least that way he wouldn't return empty-handed."

Deora looks to my arm, adorned with a silver armband – a parting gift from Arbogast, *Dux* of Trever – and grins. "You're right. We are going to need a *wergild* for her release."

I grin, too, though my stomach churns. "A *wergild* is fair, according to the custom." I take off the armband and throw it on the ground before Deora. "Treat this as an advance. I have no more on me, but I promise to pay the remainder as soon as we return to Cantia."

As he picks the armband up, Seawine takes me by the arm and asks me aside: "Do you believe him?"

"Haesta could've attacked this camp while the two of us were spying on him. Our men would stand no chance against an ambush." I glance to Deora. "Instead, he sends… him." I rub my forehead. "I don't know, Seawine. He's right. We *are* all weary."

"All the more prone to making mistakes."

"Maybe." I scratch the top of my nose. "Maybe it is one of those mistakes, but right now, I'm willing to take Haesta's word on this. What have we got to lose?"

"Ursula's freedom. Or worse."

I shake my head. "I don't believe Haesta would do something like that. I spoke to him long enough to get the measure of his character. He hates my father, and isn't fond of me, but Ursula never did him any harm outside of battle."

There is something else I don't mention to Seawine – the way Ursula smiled when she and Haesta spoke… If she suspected Haesta of any wrongdoing, would she be smiling like that?

"Just in case, send someone to keep an eye on his camp," I say.

"I'll send Aerende," Seawine replies. "He's the best at keeping quiet in the forest." He looks to the darkening sky. "It's going to be a long night, knowing they could attack us at any moment."

"I'll take the first watch myself," I say. "I doubt I'll get any sleep tonight anyway."

The Wrath of the Iutes

I never thought I'd ever pine for Cantia, but the low hill ridge upon which we stand, gazing onto the river valley below, looks so much like the southern slopes of the Downs, that I can't help but suffer a sharp pang of homesickness. The leaves in the beech trees back in Britannia must already be turning the colour of fire and copper. Here, further south, they're still bright green, tinged with gold only on the outer edges of the forest. The golden hue reminds me of how much time has passed since I stowed away on Legate Aegidius's ship. It was just after Easter then. An entire summer, gone. Looking back at myself, all I see is a reckless youth, caring only about himself and his feelings; bored with the uneventful, pampered life at the royal court; angry with my father — for what, I can no longer remember — playing a foolish prank on him and his noble guest. One rash decision led to another, until, at last, inexplicably, I found myself commanding a troop of Iutes, leading them into a bloody battle, and playing a part in a great war about which I hadn't even had the slightest inkling before leaving Britannia. I can only hope I've changed since then, grown into adulthood, just like my men have grown from serfs into warriors.

Somewhere up the river valley, according to Deora, is the city of Rotomag — hidden from sight by the morning haze and the river's high, twisting banks. We're still some way away from the coast, and if it wasn't for Deora's assurances, I would never have guessed that there was a harbour here from which we could sail all the way to Britannia.

"Are you sure this is the place?" I ask Deora.

He glances around, anxiously, then looks at the overcast sky. It's impossible to tell how much time has passed since we departed at dawn, heading towards the arranged meeting spot where Haesta's men were supposed to leave Ursula. She should be here already, waiting for us.

"I knew it," says Seawine. He draws the sword and aims it at Deora. "You lied to us. Your chief is now taking her to Rotomag while we sit here and wait."

"Wait, Seawine." I trot between the two of them. "Maybe something happened. Why hasn't Aerende returned yet?"

"I… don't know," admits Seawine. "Maybe they killed him, so he wouldn't tell us they're leaving."

"Or maybe they found him, and Haesta decided to change his plans." I turn to Deora. "How far are we from your camp?"

"An hour or so."

"Mount up," I order my men. "We're going to see Haesta in person."

"That wasn't the deal!" protests Deora.

"The deal was, Ursula would be freed in the morning. I don't see her anywhere, do you?"

We dismount and approach Haesta's glade quietly. Over the calming noises of the forest I can't hear any sounds of camp activity, even as we pass the clump of ferns through which

The Wrath of the Iutes

Seawine and I crawled the night before. I raise my hand and we halt. Seawine frowns.

"Aerende should be here…" he whispers.

I nod and put a finger to my lips. I draw the sword and part the bushes to reveal the glade on which Haesta and his men had set up their tents.

The tents are still there – trampled and flattened. The entire glade is trodden over with footprints and hoof prints. The ground and the canvas are splattered with bloodstains. Broken spear shafts and abandoned axes mark the spots where Haesta's men stood their ground.

One of them lies dead by the remains of the campfire, pinned to the ground by a javelin. Everyone else is gone.

There's a rustle in the ferns. I tense – my men draw swords, even Deora reaches for his knife, the only weapon we allowed him to carry while in our captivity. A man tumbles out of the bushes, bleeding, and crawls towards us. It's Aerende.

Seawine is the first to reach him. We help Aerende sit up against a tree. He's bleeding from two fresh wounds: one to his leg; the other to his shoulder, deep, wide at the surface and tapering into the flesh – an axe hack rather than a sword cut. If we were in a town, with access to a surgeon, and a bed to rest, he might just make it – but not here, in the middle of the forest, starving and exhausted after the long march. He knows it too; he pushes away Acha, trying to tend to his wounds, and gestures at me to come closer.

"They rode in… from the south…" he says, throwing his words out rapidly with every breath. "Thirty, maybe more… Small horses, like our farm ponies…" He gasps and winces. "Took – everyone. Barely a fight."

"Ursula?" I ask.

"Alive – and unharmed."

"Who were they? Barbarians? Saxons?"

He shakes his head and spits blood. "*Wealas*. Dressed like… peasants and townsfolk. Clubs and axes, no mail, no swords. Just… many."

"Some kind of tribal militia," I guess. "Did they have any markings? A leader?"

"Cloaks," says Aerende. "Cut in two. A mark on them – a sword or cross. Couldn't see. Their chief… Old, grey-haired… Many scars."

He winces again and asks us to lay him down on the grass. I realise that this is only the second time I'm about to see a man die like this, slowly, bleeding to death. The first one was Odilia, the faithful tracker girl, crushed by her own pony while saving me from Haesta's lance. All the other deaths I have seen in this war were quick – sword slashes to the thigh, spear stabs to the stomach, skull bashed in by an axe…

"*Aetheling…*" Aerende reaches out. A grimace of pain turns his face into a twisted mask. "End – please."

The Wrath of the Iutes

I put my left hand on his eyes, and with my right, I push the blade of my knife into his heart. "Wodan welcomes you, warrior," I whisper. He shudders and sighs one last time.

I stand up, wipe the blood from my hand and sweat from my brow.

"We go to Rotomag," I say. "If anyone knows who these men in half-cloaks were, we'll find them there."

For the first time, I notice hesitation in their eyes when I give the order.

"What is it?"

"*Aetheling...*" Seawine says, looking at his feet with unease. "We have followed Haesta for a month now – we've just lost Aerende, Colswine is wounded – and we're no closer to catching him now than we were at Tolbiac."

"You want me to abandon Ursula *now*?" I exclaim. "When she's in the hands of some local peasants?"

"We can't fight thirty men," adds Raegen. "We're out of food and water... And we're far away from home."

I don't know what to tell them. We crossed half of Gaul together, fought in countless battles, lost comrades, all without so much as a grunt or murmur... But now they've finally reached their limit, and I can't blame them.

"I can't leave her," I say, at last. "I will go after her alone, if I have to. Once we reach Rotomag, you can do what you want. Get a ship back home, or come with me, after you've rested and fed yourselves."

"I will go with you," says Deora, unexpectedly. He draws his knife and presents it on outstretched hands. "I offer you my blade, until we can find the men who did this –" he nods at the trampled glade "– and destroy them."

"Thank you, Deora." I take the knife and hand him back his sword. I can see the immediate impact his sudden action has on the others, put to shame by the man they regarded as a mere sword-for-hire. I hope the impression stays with them until we reach Rotomag. It would be difficult to seek out Ursula with just the six of them… It will be impossible for me to do it on my own.

"The *wealas* love to dwell in the swamps," remarks Seawine as we enter the town. "Why are all their cities so damp?"

Rotomag is nestled at the bottom of a deep valley, on the great elbow of a broadly spewing river. To the north, it is bound by some of those same hills that reminded me of the Downs so much. To the east and west spread mist-shrouded marshes, humming with blood-sucking insects.

"The river is a road and a wall at the same time," I explain. "The swamps are an impassable barrier to armies large and small. No roving band of raiders will threaten a city like this, unless maybe they come by boats – but I bet there is a fort further upstream to deal with those, or used to be. I don't suppose you know what the river is called?" I ask Deora.

The Wrath of the Iutes

"Haesta talked about us having to reach Sequana," he replies.

I have only heard this name once before; Hildrik mentioned it as the desired southern frontier of his father's would-be conquest of northern Gaul. The Sequana – if this is indeed the same river – spills in wide, meandering bends, barring all access to Rotomag from the south and west. The only entrance into the city is an old Roman highway thrown over the marshes on causeways and sandbanks. Rotomag itself is another place that reminds me of home. It's not much bigger than Dorowern, the Cantian capital. And just like Dorowern, it long ago shrank into its walls, leaving the outer suburbs, with the crumbling amphitheatre and the graveyards, to the encroaching marshes. There was a bridge thrown over the Sequana once, but only half of it remains, on the city's side. The seclusion and the absence of crossing meant Rotomag was spared by most of the wars and invasions that ravaged this part of Gaul. But it also meant it found itself cut off from most of what went on in the rest of the Empire – including trade. Impoverished, isolated and reduced in size and importance, in this, too, it resembles Britannia.

The guards at the eastern gate eye us suspiciously as we approach. We look haggard, wretched, our clothes and boots are in pieces – and we're all fair-hairs, barbarians, riding strange mounts and wielding all manner of foreign gear. The six of us must look like bandits ourselves.

"No troublemakers," the guard warns us. He looks at the sword at my side – a fine, ancient, Legionnaire's *spatha*, another gift from *Dux* Arbogast. A heathen like myself could only obtain a weapon like it through plunder or grave-robbing.

"Please," I say in Imperial Tongue, "we were attacked by some band of roughs in the woods. We're only looking for a place to rest."

"You, too?" He raises his eyebrow. "There's a guesthouse on the *Decumanus* and another by the Forum, but…" He stares at our grime-caked clothes. "You'll be better off going to Cassio's, by the pier." He points towards the river. "What were you doing in the woods?"

"We were hired as guard for a merchant's caravan, coming from Epatiac." It's the nearest town name I can recall.

"Not much of a guard, by the looks of it." His frown deepens. "Why would a merchant go from Epatiac by land, instead of by sea?"

"The sea!" Deora scoffs. "Don't you know what the Frankish pirates do to merchant ships in these waters?"

"I know what our Bacauds do to merchant caravans. And if you did, too, you'd have preferred to face the pirates." He sighs, and his face softens. "Fine, you can come in – but stick to the harbour. I'll have the *vigiles* keep an eye on you if you stray too near the Forum."

Cassio's is less an inn, more a collection of huts, built from various flotsam taken from the river, clustered around the

The Wrath of the Iutes

remains of a *mansio* that once served those crossing the old bridge on the Sequana. The original tavern's crumbled foundations mark out the borders of the new compound – but the building itself burnt down a long time ago. The old bridge's few surviving arches serve for a stable.

I still have most of the "salary" that my men and I were paid for our part in the Siege of Trever – there haven't been many opportunities to spend it in the pursuit; one of the silver coins, though clipped and defaced, is more than enough to pay for everyone's stay in one of the huts. Damp and cold from the river, it's only little better shelter than our tents, but it's got a roof that doesn't leak – and beddings of sheepskin and straw.

I leave Deora under guard – he still needs to earn my trust – and take Seawine with me to what counts for Cassio's hall: a span of tiled roof raised above the ancient L-shaped kitchen counter of veined stone, the only remainder of the old *mansio* still standing above ground. I notice most men here, both at the inn and in the harbour, walk about heavily armed and glance warily at each other, an unusual sight in a city so far removed from any war.

"Why is everyone so tense here?" I ask the innkeeper as I pick up the mugs of cheap wine from the counter.

"It's those damn Bacauds," she replies. "A large band of them was seen just off the east gate."

This is the second time I have heard that word today, but I'm none the wiser as to what it means – though it sounds vaguely familiar, as if coming from some old story I once heard.

"*Bacauds*?"

"You're new here, aren't you?"

I smile. "What gave it away?"

She shrugs. "Martinians." She sees my blank stare and adds, "Rebel serfs from Armorica."

"They wouldn't happen to be wearing army cloaks, cut in half?" asks Seawine.

"I just told you, they're Martinians," she scoffs and moves on to serve another customer.

"What does she mean by that?" Seawine asks me.

"Of course!" I shake my head. "I should have remembered. There was a Martinian monastery on Tanet once, after all." I turn to Seawine. "Martinus of Turonum was a famous Christian priest and soldier. There's a legend of him giving one half of his cloak to a beggar."

"Half a cloak?" Seawine looks at me dubiously. "Is it that easy to be renowned among Christians? Why not an entire cloak?"

"I don't know." I shrug. "Maybe it's symbolic of something – or maybe I'm misremembering the story."

The Wrath of the Iutes

"And these... *Bacauds*?"

"Followers of Martinus... They saw themselves as holy warriors, fought against the heathens and heretics throughout Gaul and Britannia, or anyone they saw as enemy of their God... I thought Aetius destroyed them all – I didn't know there were any left."

"Oh, there's plenty left, if you know where to look," says a man standing next to me, nursing a cup of ale. A short, deep scar on his brow, ending half an inch from his left eye, tells the story of some brutal knife fight. He's wearing military boots and a Legionnaire's belt. "Armorica is full of them. But they haven't come this far in a long time."

"The war made all the bandits and rogues bold again," says another patron. "The sooner it's over, the sooner whoever wins can go about bringing peace to the provinces."

"You have news of the war?" I ask.

The man, reeking of rotten fish and open sea, shrugs. "Only rumours I've heard in Burdigala," he replies. "The Goths sent all their warriors to defend Arelate... They say whoever wins that city, wins Gaul."

"What about Lugdunum? What about Burgundians?"

"Lugdunum?" The fisherman shrugs. "I haven't heard anything about no Lugdunum. How come *you* know so much about the war?"

Several nearby patrons turn to us with suspicious frowns. I laugh. "Like you, I'm just repeating rumours," I say. "But, never mind a distant war – we have a battle to fight much closer to home. We're looking for that band of Bacauds everyone's talking about – they caught some of our comrades… You wouldn't know where to find them?"

"Spend a night outside the walls, and they'll find *you*," says the innkeeper. I raise the wine mug off the counter to let her swipe it with a wet rag. "You're not the only ones they've recently attacked. Ask around."

She nods towards a man sitting on his own on a base of a shattered column, far away from the counter, his face shrouded in the shadow of the inn's roof. I sense his eyes on me. I approach him cautiously.

"I hear you've had some trouble with the Bacauds, too," I say.

"You've heard right. I was wondering how long it would take you to find me…" he replies and leans forward. His face comes into the light. "…*Aetheling*."

CHAPTER II
THE LAY OF MARCUS

Seawine reaches for his sword, before remembering we left our weapons in our hut.

"You've abandoned your men to the bandits," I say.

"I fought my way out," replies Haesta. He runs his finger down a fresh scar on his cheek. "To seek help."

"What help were you planning to find in this place?" I glance around.

"It's a harbour town. There are always men looking for employment. There's only one problem…"

I kick away a chicken, seeking worms in the cracks in the pavement, and sit down on a stone next to Haesta.

"The bandits took your silver. You have no money to hire swords. You were waiting for *us* to come help you."

He leans forward. "If you want the girl, you need my help. I know where those Martinians are going. I know how many of them there are, what weapons they have. Help me save my men and we will part in peace."

"I'm touched," I say. "I didn't know you cared for your men so much. After all, they don't care much for you."

"You know nothing about me and my men," he replies. "Deora came back to me, even though he knew I'd punish him for the betrayal."

"Or is it the silver that you care about," says Seawine. "Without it, you can't even afford to go back to Britannia."

"You can believe whatever you choose to believe." Haesta shrugs. "As long as you agree to help me."

I gulp down the wine and wince. It tastes like stale vinegar, but I gesture for the serving wench to pour me another – and bring us some bread and cheese.

"I don't need your help. I can find out everything myself, then hire these mercenaries you speak of…"

"And waste another day while the Martinians are well on their way. Waste your silver hiring drunks and tavern louts. Only I know how to separate real warriors from street brawlers. I know you're not that stupid, *aetheling*."

"Don't trust him, *Hlaford*," Seawine warns, but as always, that is all the advice he can give. We both know it would be prudent to accept Haesta's offer, despite everything he did in the past. I'm reminded of how my father allied with Aelle, long before either of them became leaders of their respective tribes. Just like Haesta's men killed my mother, so did Aelle slay Aeric's foster-father – worse still, my father witnessed the death, as a young boy. Still, Fate decreed that the two of them would become allies, many years later, against the common enemy. If my father could do it…

The Wrath of the Iutes

"Fine," I say. "I don't see any harm in you coming with us, in exchange for your information. What else do you need?"

He leans against the wall. "I lost my mount," he says. "And my sword."

"I lost a man to the Martinians. You can have his things." I nod at Seawine to go prepare Aerende's beast. He hesitates.

"*Aetheling*, I can't leave you –"

"Go, Seawine. I'm sure I can handle one unarmed, tired man."

I wait for Seawine to leave us before continuing.

"Without a horse, you couldn't have arrived here more than a couple of hours before us," I say. "How much, really, could you have learned about those *Bacauds*?"

He smiles wryly. "All the patrons in all the harbour taverns around the world are the same. You can find out anything you want in a place like this, if you know where to look."

"And what *did* you find out?"

"They're bad news."

"Worse than yourself?"

He chuckles. "I am a warrior. I kill men for gold or if they stand against me, but I treat every death with respect. Barbarians, *wealas*... I take no pleasure in those deaths. These bandits, these... *Christians*... They don't think of heathens as men. The only use they have for them..."

He pauses as the servant girl at last brings us the bread I requested. Haesta tears off great chunks of it and shoves it in his mouth. Within moments, it disappears. He asks for more.

"You haven't eaten anything since you were captured," I guess.

He shakes his head. "They don't care much about feeding their captives, as long as they can march. They only need them as slaves."

"They're taking them to a slave market."

He nods. "The nearest one where they can do trade is at Redones, in Armorica. That's a week's march from here, maybe more, plenty of time to catch up. They'll be slowed down by all the captives and plunder."

"And forage – a band that size..."

"I doubt they'll be stopping for forage. They're tough peasants, and their faith gives them strength – I'm sure they can march for days on nothing but water and prayer."

"Then we have no time to lose... Wait." I run through everything he said in my head. "You said they hate heathens,

[41]

The Wrath of the Iutes

but... Ursula is a Christian. A *wealh*. A captive of barbarians. What do they need *her* for? Why didn't they release her?"

He shrugs. "They're just dumb peasants. Who knows? They found her with us. Maybe they can't tell a Christian from a heathen."

"How many men do you think we'll need?"

"How many do you have left?"

"Six."

"There's me and Deora – and my six, once we free them." He scratches his nose and eats another chunk of bread. "We'll need ten decent fighters... Or five veterans."

"Can you find five veterans here?" I look around the tavern dubiously.

"I can, but it will cost you."

"I have a silver armband three-fingers wide," I say. "It was supposed to be a *wergild* for Ursula."

"That should do, just about." He nods with satisfaction, then glances towards the kitchen counter. "We can start by asking that man in army boots. Anyone who can survive a scar like that without going blind must be worth their price."

I don't know if the ancient Gauls ever built their hillforts the same way Britons did before Rome, but if they did, this would've been a good place for one. A low, flat-topped hill, hidden in a bend of some unnamed river, with a good view of the plain to the east and south, and protected by a steep chalk ridge from the north and west. A Roman noble must have once noticed the defensive properties of this place, in the days when this part of Gaul was still untamed, and chose it to build a small *villa*, fortified with a low earthen wall, to tend to fruit orchards and wheat fields spread throughout the river valley.

Neither the defensive position, nor the wall, helped to save the *villa* from some roaming warband, which many years ago passed through this valley, burning down all the buildings and turning the *domus* into a pile of ruins. I'm guessing it must have happened during one of the previous Bacaud uprisings – we're far away from any major highway, I doubt the Huns or Goths would have troubled themselves with coming all the way here for plunder.

Given the final fate of the *villa*, it might be foolish of us to put much hope in what remains of its defences to help us survive the night – but we have no choice. At least the ruined fortifications and the slope of the hill provide us with a semblance of safety, enough for us to catch some breath. The Bacauds chased us for miles over open terrain, before we reached the chalk ridge and, by some miracle, stumbled upon a river crossing and a path leading to the top of the hill.

"They're still there," Seawine says, nodding towards the other side of the river. "Stubborn bastards."

The Wrath of the Iutes

The bandits spread out along the shore, blocking our only way out. Some of them sit around a large campfire, preparing a meal, the others patrol the riverbank — or rather, stroll along it, from time to time throwing a curse or stone towards us, and kicking the body of one of our men, lying half-submerged in the shallow water as they pass it.

"What are they waiting for?" asks Seawine.

"Night," says Mullo grimly. He coughs into his fist and wipes his mouth. "They're like wolves. They prefer to fight at night. They only pursued us by daylight because we stirred their den."

Mullo, the man with the eye-scar, turned out to be a former Legionnaire — or so he claimed. He was a soldier in Aetius's army, and thirty years ago he fought the Bacauds here, in Armorica. He was our main source of information on the bandits during the pursuit — for all the good that did us.

"We can't wait until night for them to slaughter us," says Haesta. "Once we get some rest, we have to try fighting our way out."

"How?" I ask. I see no way other than straight through the Bacaud band. The *villa* is as much a fortress as it is a trap. "We'd have to wade through the river while they pick us out with their javelins, then climb up a high bank... I know they're just some peasants, but even so..."

Mullo turns sharply to me. "They're not just *some peasants*. They fight like animals. I once saw them destroy a *centuria* of

Legionnaires with nothing but clubs, knives and farming tools."

Inadvertently, I touch the flask at my belt: one portion of the henbane brew Betula left me when we parted. If it still works – I don't know how long it takes for the brew to go sour – it would impart me with the power to resist pain, wounds and fear… But there's only enough of it for myself, to use when all else is lost. Haesta notices my gesture, and his eyes meet mine, but he says nothing. He alone knows how to make more of it, but neither of us wants to mention the brew's existence before Mullo and his men. We may be enemies, but we're both Iutes, and henbane is a secret known only to chosen members of the tribe.

"We'll figure something out," says Mullo, not noticing our silent exchange. He points out a spot on the chalk ridge, beyond the river bend, to Haesta. "Do you see that line of trees? There should be a secluded ravine that some of the men could use to get at their rear."

"Then the rest of us would feign crossing to draw the Bacauds into the water," replies Haesta. A faint smile appears on his lips. "A pony charge from the south – we could conceal the riders among the trees in the orchard."

"We'll need to wait for the evening mist to shroud our movements," says Mullo, rubbing his chin. "It will leave a very short gap before then and nightfall."

They're ignoring me as they discuss the battle plan – and not for the first time. It's not entirely their fault. They are both far older, and far more experienced warriors than I am;

The Wrath of the Iutes

they know how to conduct this sort of mission so well, that they keep second-guessing each other. Naturally, they find it easier to talk to each other, without having to constantly explain their ideas to me.

But I need to remind them that it's me and my men who risk the most in the Bacaud pursuit. We form the greatest part of our small band, and we're its entire assault force, since we're the only ones with mounts; not forgetting the fact that it's my silver that paid for the five — now reduced to four — mercenaries we brought with us from Rotomag, including Mullo himself.

Besides, the last time I let the two of them plan an attack, it nearly ended in a disaster...

We reached the Bacauds on the fourth day of our pursuit, just as they entered a region of wooded, inhospitable rocky hills, penetrated only by a single Roman road. If there were any cohorts left in this area, they would have had no trouble stopping the band on its way to Armorica — but the small towns we passed didn't seem to have anyone to protect them other than the *vigiles*. It was the same everywhere in this part of Gaul; past Rotomag, I haven't seen as much as a watchtower manned by regular soldiers. *Rex* Meroweg was right to plan a Salian invasion here while the Empire fought its civil war in the distant South — it wouldn't take a great army to take these settlements one by one. If Hildrik and I hadn't stopped him, this entire province would have yielded to the Frankish *fyrd* within days.

We followed the warband for one more day, carefully. The hills would have been a good spot for an ambush, but the bandits were no fools, and they surrounded their camp with a heavy guard, so Mullo advised – or rather, decided – that we would wait until we were out in the open again, where they would feel safer.

Between them, Mullo and Haesta planned the details of the attack: a charge of my riders, as soon as we got onto the flat ground, followed by a flanking strike by the mercenaries. I wasn't convinced at first – it would've been difficult for the charging ponies to avoid hurting the captives in the brawl. At length, they persuaded me and Seawine, and I yielded to their experience.

"It will be just like our very first battle," I told my men. "Remember those Saxon foragers on the road from Tornac? We'll smash through those bandits just like then."

"There's less than half of us left since Tornac," remarked Raegen.

"And there are fewer than thirty of the bandits," I said. "With no shields, no spears. The only thing we have to watch out for is not to hurt the captives by accident. And yes, that includes Haesta's men. I gave him my word."

Not long after, Acha, returning from a lookout, reported that a mile ahead the Roman highway climbed a low incline, before descending towards a crossroad with another old track. We decided to strike there, hoping the Bacauds would spread in panic over the two roads, making it easier for us to pick them out. The incline concealed our approach. But it also

The Wrath of the Iutes

meant we didn't see what was happening beyond it – until it was too late.

We should have foreseen it. The crossroad, the haste with which the Bacauds marched... But I didn't know enough about these bandits to guess, and Mullo and Haesta were too certain of themselves to consider anything could go wrong.

The crossroad turned out to be a meeting point, where "our" Bacaud warband transferred its prisoners to another one, even larger, coming down from the distant hills. Altogether, there were at least fifty of the Martinians waiting for us beyond the slope.

"Stop the charge, *aetheling*!" cried Seawine.

"Too late – we have to save the mercenaries; they don't know what's waiting for them!"

We smashed at the warband in a thin wedge. They didn't even try to form a defence – they parted to let us through, wary of our sharp lances. To our left, Haesta and Mullo emerged on the Bacaud flank, but as soon as they realised what had happened, they pulled away. I turned us around for another charge, to draw the bandit attention away from the mercenaries, but this time, their ranks closed before us, bristling with long knives and axes, and I had to call off the attack.

As we rode past the captive train, I caught a glimpse of Ursula. She saw me, too. Her eyes gleamed defiance and hope, even as she saw us ride away. She knew, somehow, we would return for her and win her back. I wish I could share her confidence. As things stand, we can only keep running; the Bacaud warband split in two – one half took the captives back to the hill camp, while the other launched into pursuit, chasing after us until we reached the ruined *villa*.

"What if you're wrong again," I say, reminding Haesta and Mullo about their earlier mistake. "What if they're not waiting for the night, but for reinforcements? If the rest of that warband comes before the evening fog, we'll have no chance of a breakthrough, no matter what tactics we devise."

They turn to me in surprise, as if they've forgotten I am here. "And what would you have us do?"

"The same plan, but out in the open. If they see we're not hiding anything, they'll suspect we *are*. They'll think our movements are a ruse for something else – they'll get anxious, maybe even frightened. They're peasants – there are no strategists among them, no officers."

"Even serfs can count," Haesta grunts. "They'll know there isn't anyone else."

"No, the boy's right," says Mullo, rubbing his chin. I'm glad he agrees, though I'm not too pleased about him calling me "a boy". "They will think we're expecting reinforcements, just like they did on the crossroads. I'll have my men ready."

His men? I glance at Haesta – his eyes tell me he shares my concern. Mullo is just one of the random group of mercenaries we hired at Rotomag, but he behaves like a *centurion* in charge of his Legionnaires. Even in his army days, he was just a low-ranking recruit. But the men we hired all

The Wrath of the Iutes

know him and look up to him – they were all regulars at the tavern, where he must have regaled them with tales of his past in Aetius's Legions.

"Haesta?" Mullo prods. "Are you coming?"

"I'm riding with the Iutes," Haesta replies. "I prefer to fight mounted."

Pat – pat – pat – thud...

The earth trembles under the hooves of our ponies. The rumbling shears overripe apples from the boughs of the orchard we storm through. They splat into the mud, like strange drums accompanying our advance.

Against Haesta's protests, we set out too early, before Mullo's men were ready to join us. The Bacauds jumped up from their campfire as soon as they saw the mercenaries descend into the ravine. They all lined up along the riverbank, watching us perform the needlessly complex manoeuvres, setting up for a set-piece attack from two sides. I could sense their confusion. I was right – seeing us prepare for the attack in the open, they stepped away from the shore, unsure how to react.

But the confusion didn't last long. One of the warriors – the chief of the band, I guessed, since he matched the description given by Aerende – soon started rushing around, shouting, trying to bring a semblance of order to the bandit ranks. The Bacauds would soon form up into a defence line, and even without shields and spears there were enough of them to hold us back.

There was another reason for my hurry. I haven't told this to Haesta yet, but just before we descended from the hilltop, I'd spotted something on the horizon. A plume of dust, approaching from the north. It could only be another warband of Bacauds, coming to assist their brethren. Just as I feared, we had to break through before the two armies joined forces to annihilate us.

We splash into the river in a wide front. The objective is to get all riders to the other side as fast as possible – only then we can think of forming wedges to punch through the enemy horde. The ponies slip and slide down the tall muddy bank as we try to climb out. The mounts are tired, just as we are; we've been driving them to the limit of their strength for the entire day. A couple of the Bacauds get too close, trying to push us back into the water. I stab one of them in the shoulder; Seawine cuts the other across the chest. This makes the rest of the band break their line, retreat and form a loose half-crescent on the shore, waiting.

At last, I climb out onto the flat ground. I look to the ravine, but can't see Mullo's men yet. The Bacauds attack before the rest of my men can reach me. I tug on the reins; the pony rears defensively. I thrust the lance – another peasant falls, screaming, with his hands raised to his bleeding face. The rest of my men join me in the attack; we have our Iutish lances and *seaxes* against the peasant clubs and hatchets, but our situation seems hopeless. Surrounded tightly in the marshy ground, we can't make good use of our speed and manoeuvrability.

The Wrath of the Iutes

Everything Mullo told us was true. The Bacauds fight like savages. They don't care for wounds, for death – and they don't see me as human, except as a potential captive to sell to the slavers. They grab at me with bare hands. I kick, slash and thrust around me as the bandits reach out, trying to drag me off the pony. To my left, Colswine gets separated by the swarm of peasants and falls off, screaming. I turn my eyes away to not see him being clubbed to death.

I stab once more, and push forth, and suddenly I find myself out in the open again, with the entire warband behind me. I broke through. I turn about to assist my men, but the Bacaud circle closes after me, and I can't find an opening. To my right, on the riverbank, I spot Mullo and the mercenaries, climbing up to strike at the enemy flank – but the Bacauds spot them, too, and their commander, showing skill I did not expect him to have, splits his men in two unequal parts, sending the larger one towards the new threat. This is exactly what I would have done in his place; the mercenaries, scrambling up the shore on foot, are an easier enemy to destroy, even at the cost of letting the surviving Iutes go.

Using the confusion, Haesta and Seawine leap forward, but not far enough; all the riders are now split, surrounded, in danger of being overrun by the bandits. The mercenaries make a concerted push to get out of their encirclement, but their advance soon stalls, and before long, they're forced back to the shore.

We're losing. But we're not yet doomed.

"Come on, men!" I cry at the top of my lungs. "One more push! For *Rex* Aeric! *Hael* Donar!"

[52]

But my Iutes have no more strength left in them than I have. They, too, are being pushed slowly back to the river. I spur my pony to kick and bite; I throw the lance like a javelin, hitting a woman in the back. She screams and turns towards me. I draw the *spatha* and hack at her until, at last, she falls. I feel a sharp pain in my wrist, but it's not a wound – I only sprained it. I throw the sword to my left hand and slash again, but this time, I miss.

I hear a battle horn blowing. I turn to seek out the source of the sound; I can't see it at first, but I sense it in the trembling of the earth beneath my pony's hooves. The Bacaud reinforcements. We have taken too long to fight through – and now they're here; and judging by the noise, some of them are mounted. We have lost our chance to escape.

I reach for the henbane flask. At least I'll take as many of these damn Martinians to their God as I can before they subdue me. I'm not going to let them take me alive. I'm not going to let them sell me into slavery.

A wedge of warhorses smashes through the Bacauds in front of me, followed by half a dozen swordsmen. The first horse comes straight at me, its rider – in a Roman *eques*'s helmet, and wearing a tattered purple cloak – is too focused on the bandits before him to see me. I try to swerve aside, but I'm too slow; he notices me now, too, and tugs on the reins, but we're both too late. His mount crashes into mine. I grasp at the reins, but my twisted wrist fails to hold on, and as the pony under me whinnies and rears to avoid the collision, I fly from the saddle. I hit the ground; my head strikes something hard and sharp, and I sink into blood-red darkness.

The Wrath of the Iutes

The rider who crashed into me leans down and helps me up. With his helmet off, I can see he's got black, curly hair, speckled with red. His face is wide, angular, dominated by a broad, swollen nose, broken in some fight a long time ago.

I look around, rubbing the back of my head. I don't know how much time passed since I fainted, but it can't have been long – blood still oozes from the cut on my brow. The mysterious soldiers – I count a dozen of them altogether – made short work of the bandits. Their bodies lie scattered around the field, though these can't be all the enemies we faced; some must have escaped, judging by the trail of freshly trodden ground vanishing to the south. I don't see the chieftain's body among the fallen.

My men gather around me; to my relief, all are alive, even Colswine, though he's too weak to ride – Seawine carries him on his pony. I search for Mullo and his mercenaries, and find only three of them still standing. Mullo stares at me with a pained scowl; the mercenaries may have been just randomly chosen from among the tavern patrons, but over the few days of pursuit, he's grown to treat them as his soldiers, and now half of them lie dead at the riverside, hacked almost to pieces by the frenzied Martinians.

"You're fortunate my men didn't confuse you with these bandits," the rider says. He speaks Vulgar in a strong western Briton accent, the same as Councillor Riotham in Londin. "What made you enter their territory in such a small number?"

"They captured our companions a few days ago," I reply. "We pursued a smaller band at first, but they joined with another and together proved too much for us. Am I guessing right you're from Britannia?"

He salutes me with his fist to his chest. "I am *Decurion* Marcus of Dumnonia."

Dumnonia. I don't even know where that is, except that it must be somewhere in the West, in *Dux* Ambrosius's domain, the province of Britannia Prima of the old Imperial division. Only in that part of the island, where the banished Roman officials fled from Londin a generation ago, are the armies still organised in the old Legionnaire manner, an imitation, a memory of the Roman past.

"You're a long way from home," I say. "I am Octa, son of Aeric of the Iutes," I introduce myself. I can see in his eyes that he's as lost about my provenience as I am of his. "I hail from Cantiaca," I add hastily.

He laughs. "God is in a curious mood today!" he says. "Two warriors from opposite sides of Britannia meet on a field of battle in the furthest reaches of Gaul!" He scratches the back of his head. "You're one of Londin's heathen *foederati*, aren't you?"

"I... I suppose you could call us that. Well met, *Decurion*."

"Well met, indeed."

"What are you doing here, *Decurion*?" I ask.

The Wrath of the Iutes

He looks around. "We can talk about this later. You have casualties to take care of?"

"Only one wounded – but Mullo looks like he needs some help."

Mullo comes over to us and salutes him. "Gaius Macrinus, once of the Geminiacenses," he says. This is the first time I have heard his real name, and the name of his old Legion. "Nowadays, Mullo of the Rotomag tavern brawlers." He nods to his men. "We need to find a shelter for the wounded. Yours as well as ours."

"What's wrong with going back to the *villa*?" I ask.

"It's a death trap, if the Bacauds decide to return in greater numbers."

"We've set up a camp on the edge of a forest, a few miles north," says Marcus. "We should be safe there for the night."

"Lead on, *Decurion*," I say. "And tell us your story along the way."

"We can't stay here long," says Marcus as we approach the dark line of the trees. "The bandits have my men held up in the *cair*, and I want to free them before they're moved somewhere else, so we'll have to march out again before dawn."

"*Cair*?" I ask.

"An old hillfort. You haven't seen it? A great ruin to the south-east of here. It must have been the size of an entire city once. Now those bandits are using it to hold prisoners."

"We've been chasing our band since Rotomag. We haven't seen any forts, hill or otherwise."

"Rotomag!" Marcus exclaims. "I don't know Gaul well, but isn't that days away? I thought that was just some local band we stumbled upon!"

As the *Decurion* recounted, he and his cavalry wing landed in Gaul only a few days ago, in a small harbour of Abrincate; on their first night, they were attacked by a large band of unknown enemy. Marcus's men fought them back with some losses – but the bandits took off with half his horses and half a dozen captives.

"I knew things were bad in Gaul, but I had no idea there were such great roving bands still," he says.

"They are Bacauds," I tell him, glad to be able to provide him with some explanation. "Martinian rebels."

He shudders, visibly, and crosses himself. "That's an evil name from the dark past… Why did they attack *us*, though? We are all good Christians."

"These ones don't care," Mullo interjects. "They don't think anyone is Christian enough except those who join them. I saw them burn down churches and beat up priests who refused to condone their actions."

The Wrath of the Iutes

He's been silent most of the way. I can still sense his hostility – even though he'd agreed with me before the battle, changing the plan of the evening attack cost him two men, men who could've lived if we'd only waited a bit longer. We both know it's not fair of him to blame me for the loss – neither of us could have foreseen *Decurion* Marcus's timely arrival.

"What are they going to do with my men?" asks Marcus.

"They're taking them to a slave market in Armorica," I reply.

"Armorica." He grins. "How strange are the Fates. It's exactly where we ourselves were heading."

"We're not," I murmur. "All I want is to go back home to Britannia."

"I understand – you're even further away from home than we are. You must all be weary of marching and fighting." Marcus nods. "How many of your men did the Bacauds take?"

"One," I reply.

"Only one! And you've been pursuing them all this time?"

"Ursula is not just one of my warriors – she's my friend."

I glance to Haesta. He smirks, as I omit to mention that it was *him* we've been hunting for the past month, not the Bacauds.

"I see," says Marcus. "Don't worry, Octa of the Iutes. We will get our friends back tomorrow, and then we can all part ways in peace."

CHAPTER III
THE LAY OF COLSWINE

The cavalry camp is roughly fortified with fallen trees and tangled bramble. Half of Marcus's men are on watch at any time; if the Bacauds try anything, we'll be ready for them – though the *Decurion* assured us they had no trouble from the bandits after that first night, and don't expect to have any tonight.

We exchanged our stories on the way to the camp, though I talked more – it was my first chance to recount everything that had happened to me since leaving Britannia to someone, and I found words pouring out of my mouth in an unstoppable stream, until my mouth was parched and my breath ran short, though I only managed to tell him of our fighting in Frankia and around Trever before we reached the forest. Once we set up our lodgings for the night and had some rest and food – the Britons brought with them substantial provisions, including an entire boar haunch, and several bottles of fine Burdigalan wine, which mercifully survived the Bacaud attack – it was Marcus's turn to explain what he and his *equites* were doing in Armorica.

The Wrath of the Iutes

"Our troubles began two years ago," he says as he sharpens his *spatha* on a moss-grown outcrop of rock. "When a Roman ship landed at the Silurian Isca."

"The *liburna*?" I ask, remembering Aegidius's arrival in Londin in the spring.

"A *liburna*?" Marcus repeats, in surprise, then shakes his head. "No, just a small merchant galley, carrying a legate of the man who claimed to be the new Imperator of Rome. Imperator Avitus."

"The Usurper!" I exclaim.

"He wasn't a Usurper then. He was confirmed by the Senate, acclaimed by the troops… It was good enough for us. We accepted his legation graciously. We hadn't had an envoy from Rome in almost fifty years!" He raises the sword to the light and, satisfied with its sharpness, puts it back in the sheath. "The *Dux* agreed to all of their requests," he continues, and counts them off on his fingers: "Access for his warships to our ports; sending supplies for the troops in Gaul – tin and lead from our mines, leather from our cattle herds… In exchange, we'd receive exotic goods we haven't seen in decades. Newly minted gold coins. Glass. Wine! For a moment, it seemed as if we were part of the Empire again. Given a few more years of this, we hoped, we'd have fully returned to Rome. As soon as Avitus defeats all opposition, we told ourselves, and subdues the rest of Gaul…"

"He never got the chance. In the end, he proved a poor general."

Marcus nods. "We found out too late. We first gathered something was wrong when his legate requested soldiers. This, too, hadn't happened in fifty years – and for good reason."

"Have you sent any?"

He winces. "An *ala* of cavalry. Two hundred men, our best riders. You must understand," he adds quickly, seeing my disbelief, "*Dux* Ambrosius really believed it was our best chance of coming back into the Empire's fold." He falls silent. "None came back. We sent another ship, of spearmen and swordsmen. They perished, too. And then the legates stopped coming. Then the couriers. Then, the trade stopped. We got nothing for our tin and lead."

"When did all this happen?" asks Mullo.

"The last message we got from Gaul was in autumn, just before the storm season," Marcus replies.

"Whoever was sending you these messages, it wasn't Avitus," says Mullo. "He was already dead by then. Deposed by Maiorianus, he died when fleeing across Gaul. Fell off a horse, poisoned, strangled… There were so many rumours. Nobody truly knows what happened to him."

"So, you lost your chance to join the Empire," I say. I reach for the wine flask, pour myself a mug and drink it in several gulps. It's crisp and harsh, making the top of my mouth wrinkle; it fails to quench my thirst; instead it makes me yearn for dark meat. "That doesn't explain why you were sent to Armorica to seek help."

The Wrath of the Iutes

"I was just getting to that," says Marcus. He hands me a water-skin with a grin. "Old Burdigalan only makes one thirstier," he says. "Have some cheese; it goes well with this one," he adds, and one of his men throws me a piece of hard, barn-smelling cheese.

"We invested heavily in our friendship with Avitus," he continues. "Not only the soldiers, though that loss was the gravest and most costly. We sent provisions that we ourselves lacked. We spent the last of our silver building up harbours and coastal forts. We pulled men from the border fortresses to help with all the construction. All in the hope that once Rome took us in, all this would be repaid with interest. And now, we're left with nothing. We sent pleas to Rome and to Gaul... But Maiorianus refused to talk to us, labelling us rebels, and Avitus's Legions were by then already hunkered down in Lugdunum."

"All this must have weakened your defences significantly."

He nods. "We have many enemies, encroaching on our every frontier... And it didn't take long before they noticed our trouble. We fought back the Brigands and the Picts, with heavy losses, we subdued the rebellious Belgs, for a time... But when the Scots started an advance, not even Wortigern could hold them back –"

"Wait!" I almost choke on the water. "Did you say Wortigern? As in *Dux* Wortigern?"

"Nobody has called him a *Dux* in a long time..." Marcus muses. "But yes, Wortigern may be old, but he's the best general we've ever had. He's a *Legatus* now, holding our northern border with just a handful of warriors and local militias… Until now." He turns to me. "It was Wortigern who sent me to Armorica, to seek *Comes* Graelon. He's the only one we can still count on for help."

"Who's Graelon?"

"Chief of the Briton nobles who fled to Armorica. His court is supposed to be somewhere on the western coast. He's Wortigern's last surviving relative – a distant cousin – and he owns ships. A lot of ships. He was the commander of what was left of *Classis Britannica* in the West – and took almost the entire fleet with him."

"What do you need ships for?" asks Haesta.

"The Scots are coming from across the sea," explains Marcus. "If we want to defeat them once and for all, we need ships."

"Is there no one in Britannia who could provide you with ships?" I ask. "Even Iutes and Saxons have started building vessels to deal with the Frankish pirates. You could've come to us."

"And you could've come to me for men," grunts Haesta. "I would show those Scots the might of the Iute swords. For a decent price," he adds.

Marcus smiles. "If it was up to me, I would've preferred to go to Wortigern's old domain. He often told us of its beauty – the gentle rolling hills, the chalk-white cliffs, the

The Wrath of the Iutes

mysterious woods of Andreda… But my *Dux* prefers to deal with our own kin, and there are no closer kin than the Briton nobles of Armorica." He shakes his head. "Tomorrow, as soon as I get back all my men and horses, we're going west. You may join me if you wish – it will be safer to travel together, at least until we reach the coast."

"Thank you, I'll think about it," I say.

"I'll go with you," says Mullo. "There might be some mercenary work out in the West – and I don't want to be in Rotomag when the Salians come knocking at its gates. What do you think, Haesta?"

"I just want to go home," says Haesta grimly. "I've had enough of Gaul for a while."

Marcus was right – there must have been a great city here once, in some ancient past, before Rome, before Caesar conquered the Gaulish tribes. A great double wall surrounds a patch of high ground between two arms of a broad, fast-running river; the remains of the outer wall stretch for a mile out, enclosing what would have been a built-up area the size of a provincial capital. Little is left of it now, except traces of several grand avenues and what looks like a town square in the centre, overgrown now with clumps of trees and swathes of tall grass. The inner wall is in a better shape: a foundation of stone rubble rising up to six feet tall in places, with some of the outer cladding of mud and plaster still in place, despite centuries which must have passed since the wall was last used for its designed purpose. Beyond it, the earth rises to a flat-topped hill, strewn with debris from some forgotten buildings; I wonder what once stood on its summit – a temple to the ancient gods? A fortress, a citadel? A royal palace? Whatever it was, nothing remains of it but unrecognisable piles of broken stone.

I'm guessing there should be a palisade on top of the rubble, but the Bacauds took no further precautions to fortify their camp than setting it up beyond the ruined wall. They trust their numbers – and their faith. Marcus's lookouts counted at least fifty men in the warband.

"They're in a hurry to get out of here" says Drustan, a young, angel-faced *eques*, Marcus's second in command in the wing. "The supplies are running low, and the captives are becoming unruly."

"Did anyone get hurt?" I ask.

"A few got beaten up to keep them quiet, but other than that, they take good care of their merchandise."

"They know what they're doing," says Mullo. "This isn't the first time they've run slaves in these parts."

"Shouldn't we wait until they leave the fort?" I ask.

"That's exactly what they expect us to do," says Marcus.

"Because it's the only reasonable thing *to* do," snarls Haesta. "That wall may be old, but it's still solid. It would take a siege engine to break through."

The Wrath of the Iutes

He catches my eye, then turns away in anger; the mention of the siege engines brings a painful memory of the Battle of Trever, and his defeat at hands of the Salian army, in which I and my men played such a significant part.

"Not quite," says Marcus with a self-assured grin. "You're forgetting I have my men on the inside."

"You managed to contact them?" I ask.

"No need. I trained them well. They'll know what to do. Trust me."

He blows his horn; the sound reverberates throughout the enclosed space of the fort – the Bacauds and their captives must hear it, too. At this signal, the *equites* launch into a charge, with my Iute riders in tow, while the infantry – Mullo's surviving mercenaries, and those of Marcus's men who had their horses taken – line up at the entrance to the outer wall, to block the only escape route for the Bacauds. We ride up the slope, at the only opening in the inner wall, where a gatehouse would have once stood; the bandit guards spot us at once, and raise the alarm, but with no gate in place – not even as much as a tree trunk thrown over the entrance – they can do little to stop us.

Marcus's Briton warhorses would be no match for the Gaulish ones – they're too light, too small, their gait too ungainly; but they're good enough to break through the thin line of spearmen, hurriedly set up at the gate. The defences are weaker than Haesta and I feared, and as soon as I ride through the opening, I can see why: the Briton captives have risen and are fighting their captors to the best of their abilities, even though their hands are still tied, and they have no weapons.

I leave Seawine and the others to make their way through to the centre of the camp, where the fighting is the fiercest, and I ride down the eastern side of the inner wall, to where the other captives are held. There are more of them than I expected – not just Haesta's men, but a few others, fair-haired peasants who the Bacauds must have captured from surrounding villages. I search for Ursula – I spot her in the distance: she's holding a stick in her tied hands and leads a small group of captives in an attack on a cluster of bandit tents; but before I can get to her, a dozen Bacauds appear around me with knives and sickles. Alone, separated from the others, I'm an easier target than Marcus's riders. I cut down one of the bandits and pull away in haste.

There's just enough space within the inner wall for Marcus's horsemen to perform swift manoeuvres. They break off, draw a wide arc, split and strike at the Bacaud mass from two sides. Seawine and the Iutes try to follow them, but lacking their training, they get tangled in the fight with the bandits around what looks like their warchief's tent. The Bacauds know nothing of warfare – they're just a mob, but a mob that knows no fear; the only way to deal with them is to kill enough of them to break their resolve. Their strength is in numbers, and I can't tell what will run out sooner – the bandit bodies, thrown on the *equites'* lances, or the strength of Marcus's riders…

Bored with waiting for the fleeing bandits at the far entrance, Mullo and his men leave their post and join the fray; I look for an opening in the bandit mass that I could break

The Wrath of the Iutes

through and reach Ursula. At last, I spot it – a few feet of crumbled wall and an overthrown column of some ancient *portico* that disrupts a line of Bacaud spearmen as they try to cut off and surround several of the *equites*.

"Seawine!" I cry over the din of battle. He spots me. I point to the rubble. He nods and directs the rest of the Iutes towards it. We smash at the Bacaud spearmen from the rear and the front and send them flying; then turn to Ursula and her troop of prisoners. By now, they've been pushed back against the earthen wall; a few lie dead or wounded under the feet of the pressing bandits. I draw the lance. The shaft wobbles precariously. I expect this might be the last charge of the weapon – it has served me well since leaving Tornac with the Salian *fyrd*, but it's time to replace it, as soon as we win this battle…

"Arrow head!" I order the Iutes. It's not easy to gallop in this crowd, but we manage a semblance of formation. We press on, the crowd between me and Ursula thins out, but we're slow; too slow. More prisoners fall under the Bacaud blows. Ursula by now has freed herself from her shackles and exchanged her stick for a large woodcutter's hatchet. Its blade is already red with the blood of several of her victims.

The situation on the battlefield shifts. Some of the captured *equites* reach their horses and join the mounted battle. Others release the rest of the beasts; panicked, the riderless horses charge straight at the main host of the Bacauds, splitting it in two, trampling the men under their hooves; those fleeing before the beasts are easy pickings for Mullo's mercenaries, standing guard at the exit. The battle is as good as lost for the Bacauds – we're now at the gruesome task of finishing the frenzied mob off; still, I fear it's all taking too long for us to save all of the prisoners…

I grunt a swear word, and spur the pony to a blind charge towards Ursula's group. I break my lance in the chest of a tall, burly bandit; I draw my *spatha* again, and jump from one gap to another – with each leap getting closer by several feet. Again, and again, until only a few men separate me from her.

Ursula finally sees me, and smiles. The old Bacaud chieftain appears behind her, brandishing a short sword. I shout a warning, but my voice perishes in the noise of battle. I'm too far to do anything, too far even to throw the sword. She parries a club blow and skewers another bandit, when the man behind her leaps to a strike.

Like a sudden thunder, three horses storm into the side of the Bacaud line, with Marcus in front. They break through and trample all bandits in their way under their hooves. The Bacaud chief turns, distracted. Marcus throws a *plumbata* dart and hits him in the arm. The bandit misses his blow; instead of her head, his weapon strikes Ursula on the shoulder. It adds a deep, nasty gash to the wounds she's already suffered. Ursula swirls and digs her hatchet into the man's neck. Blood spurts in a bright fountain. She sways back. With one final slash of the sword, I finally break through the last of the bandits in my way and reach her.

I leap down and grasp Ursula as she drops to the ground. She's cut and bruised in many places; she's weakened by blood loss and exhausted – but none of the wounds seem fatal. She wraps her arms around my neck and smiles a weak smile. The familiar mischievous glint twinkles in her eyes.

The Wrath of the Iutes

"What took you so long, *aetheling*?" she whispers, and faints.

"What now?" I ask Haesta as we throw the last of the Bacaud bodies into the river. "Are you really going back to your mud huts in Cantia?"

We all agreed the hillfort was no place to bury the bandits – whoever lived here, no doubt regarded the summit as sacred; as we searched for survivors in the rubble of the ruined city, we found remains of a structure that Mullo – the only one of us native to this land – identified as an ancient Gaulish temple. And although none of us worshipped, or even knew, any gods of the Gauls, we felt it unwise to disturb their peace with a bandit burial.

"They aren't mud huts," Haesta grunts, then shrugs. "What else is there to do?"

"You could come with Marcus, to find this… *Comes* Graelon. Like Mullo says, there may be some mercenary work there – there's bound to be more of these Bacauds where they came from."

"I'm done fighting." He shakes his head. "For this season, at least." He remembers something and winces. "Aelle will be marching against your father soon."

"Are you sure?" I ask. I feel a cold shiver; I'm suddenly reminded of a world I thought I left far behind – the world of Iutes, Britons and Saxons and their petty rivalries, border skirmishes, quarrels over small farmsteads and tiny villages. I have just taken part in a war that would decide the fate of the Empire; I saw a city the size of Londin in flames; great siege machines spew fire and stone; hundreds perished in battle, mown down like wheat at harvest. I carried the Imperator's Seal. I helped to kill a king. Am I really ready to leave all that, to return to what my father called "the shrinking world", a world where a cluster of a dozen farms counted as large settlement, where battles were fought between a few scores of men rather than thousands, where marching distances were counted in hours, rather than weeks?

"He would've done it this year, if not for that adventure with Odowakr," says Haesta. "Most of the men he sent to the Continent survived, and gained the experience they needed – though no plunder to speak of. They'll be eager to fight again, against an easier enemy."

"Will you join him?"

"I told you. I'm done fighting." There's something about the way he says it that tells me it's not just because he's weary. Is this his way of showing gratitude for helping him free his men from the Bacaud thralldom?

"Thank you," I say. "I should go back and help him in the war."

He glances towards the Iutes resting in the shadow of the old temple wall. "With this handful of weary, injured men you've got left? I wouldn't bother if I were you."

"I should at least warn him."

The Wrath of the Iutes

"By now he probably knows more about Aelle's plans than I do." He looks at something over my shoulder. His gaze softens. "She's awake."

I rush to Ursula. I give her a long, careful hug, taking care not to disturb her left arm, hanging in a makeshift sling. Her forehead is wrapped in bandages, and the right leg of her trousers is soaked in blood.

"How do you feel?" I ask.

She takes a breath to reply. "…fine. I think."

She studies her left hand for a moment, then moves her right hand to test if it still works. She sweeps a clump of bloodied hair from her brow and looks around the fortress, blinking slowly.

"Where's Audulf?" she asks. "Don't tell me he didn't –"

"No, he's well," I reply. "At least, he was the last time I saw him. I left him recuperating in Icorig. He might be in Tornac by now – or maybe even back in Cantia."

"Icorig…" She narrows her eyes, remembering. "How long has it been?"

"More than a month. Are you sure you're alright? You've been in captivity for so long, I can't imagine…"

"I –" She breathes out. Her gaze turns misty for a second; she stares at something in a great distance. "I'm hungry," she says, at last, with what looks like a forced smile.

I call one of my Iutes to bring us some food and water. She devours it with the same eagerness I saw earlier in Haesta. I imagine the Bacauds fed their slaves just enough to keep them from starvation.

"I need to find the man who threw that dart," she says between bites. "Thank him for saving me."

"That would be *Decurion* Marcus."

I nod to the edge of the inner wall, where we laid bodies of the captives fallen in battle. A few of Marcus's men lie on the pile, and one of the Haestingas – the others are unnamed farmers and woodsmen the Bacauds captured along the way. *Decurion*'s soldiers are digging a pit for them just outside the enclosure. One of the local prisoners promised to bring a priest from a nearby town to bless the grave once we're all done.

Ursula stands up with a wobbly sway. I offer to lead her to Marcus, but she insists on doing it alone.

"You have lain with her," says Haesta, more stating the fact than asking, as we watch Ursula hobble away.

"I have," I reply. "Once."

"But she's not your woman."

"She's not anybody's woman."

"Yes, I can see how that would work…" He falls oddly silent. "You're fortunate to be able to call her a friend," he adds after a while. "I'll go check on Deora. He got stabbed with some nasty blade, a knife or a sickle. Dirty. It would be ill-fated if he came to such an end after everything he's gone through."

"You really *do* care about your men," I say, still somewhat surprised.

"Of course," he scoffs. "How else do you think I've been keeping them under my command all this time?"

"Not by winning any battles, that's for sure."

He glowers at me, then, to my surprise, laughs and shakes his head. "Not recently, no."

He walks away, and I remember that one of my men, too, needs looking after. I squat next to Colswine and study his injuries. Despite his already serious wounds from the fight at the *villa*, and my and Haesta's misgivings, he insisted on joining the attack on the hillfort. It's a miracle that he survived, due in no small measure to the skill of Marcus's surgeon. Colswine's limbs are wrapped in ointment-soaked cloths so tight he can barely move; his face is one big mass of lumps and fresh scars.

"You're in no shape to go with us anywhere," I say.

"I can't stay here."

"Haesta's leaving tomorrow. I'll ask him to take you with him."

He scowls. "Go with… that traitor?"

"He's proven he's worth our trust." I touch his shoulder gently. "It's time for you to go back to your family, Colswine."

"And what will you do, *Hlaford*? What shall I tell your father the king when he asks about you?"

I look up, to see Marcus and Ursula discussing something agitatedly and pointing towards me. The *Decurion* saved our lives – and helped us rescue Ursula from the Bacauds… We helped him in the attack, too, as much as we could, but was this enough to repay the debt of gratitude?

I imagine us all going down to Rotomag, boarding a merchant's ship, leaving Gaul for good, landing in Leman or Dubris after a few days… And I feel nothing. No joy, no relief. Perhaps I'm just too tired to feel anything yet…

As I ponder these emotions – or rather, their absence – Ursula and Marcus walk back towards me, having apparently just agreed on whatever it was they were discussing.

"We should go with the *equites* to Redones," she announces.

"Redones?" I scratch my head. "The slave market? Why?"

"To see if the Bacauds took any more of our kin there," she replies. "As the pirates did in Epatiac."

"It's… unlikely," I say. "We are far away from Cantia."

The Wrath of the Iutes

So at least Ursula would be willing to stay here for longer than is necessary... I look to my men, resting in the shadow of the wall, nursing their injuries. Can I really force them to march even deeper into Gaul at this slim pretext?

"How far is it?"

"Just a couple of days from here," says Marcus.

A couple of days... Surely, nobody could complain about us staying just a couple of days if it meant saving a few of our kindred from fate worse than death. We could rest and heal our wounds just as well in Redones as on a ship going to Britannia.

I turn back to Colswine.

"Tell my father I'll be back... as soon as I can."

Redones is a tiny town, considering it is still a capital of the entire surrounding *pagus*. Like other towns in this part of Gaul – and in most of Britannia – it has shrunk significantly compared to what its original wall once encompassed. Now it consists of only one main street, crossed by several narrow alleyways. The only stone buildings still standing are the church and a large tavern next to it, but as we've seen elsewhere, there is little trace of deliberate destruction. The tenements have been abandoned to the elements; fire, rain and frost reduced their walls to little more than nubs of stone peeking from the grass. If there was ever an amphitheatre here, there's nothing left of it.

The few pilgrims we meet in the town's tavern may have come to Redones to see its brand-new stone church, but most visitors must be merchants arriving at the great slave market, set up in the empty ground between the new and old walls. It is to this market that the Bacauds were driving their captives, and judging by the crowds, they weren't the only ones. The market is larger than the one at Epatiac, and so full of onlookers, merchants and merchandise, that I wonder if there aren't more people gathered on this flat rectangle of gravel and sand than live in all of Redones.

"This is a frontier town," Mullo explains, when I ask him about the market. "Beyond it, Rome's rule is only nominal. Briton nobles live on the coast, but the interior is ruled by warbands, clans of farmers, petty warlords… And Redones itself is ruled by no one. The bishop and his *vigiles* keep a semblance of calm within the walls," he adds, nodding towards a couple of guards in blue cloaks marked with crossed keys, keeping watch over the entrance to the market. "But other than that, it's a free city. There's no tax, no customs, no fees on trade – and no rules, other than the rule of profit. It's worth trudging all the way here for a good bargain."

"We don't get many Iutes around here," one of the slave merchants replies, scratching his head; just as I expected, then. "Too far south. We had a couple of fishermen last month, blown off course by a northerly wind, but most end up at Epatiac or Bononia. Now, if you want Saxons, we have a good selection – not as many as there were before *Rex* Aelle banned the trade, but I'm sure you'll find something interesting…"

The Wrath of the Iutes

I thank him and hurry back to the tavern by the church, where Marcus went to ask about the whereabouts of Graelon. Ursula is there, too, with Seawine and the rest of my men. The Iutes sit uneasy at the table; they believed we'd all be going back home by now, and are suspicious that our visit to Redones could be the beginning of some new adventure.

"How is it that you don't know where to find this Graelon, if he's Wortigern's relative?" I ask the *Decurion*.

"The Britons who moved to Armorica… don't want to look back. Most of the first generation fled the rebellions and the civil war. Those who followed moved out to get away from the encroaching barbarians. Graelon may be Wortigern's cousin, but there's no love lost between them. He crossed the Narrow Sea after we heard the news of the Iutes and Saxons defeating Wortigern's son in some battle…"

"The first one or the second one?" I ask.

He frowns. "The… first one, I think?"

"The Battle of Crei." I nod "Wortimer's first coup. He struck too fast back then, and it almost doomed him. If only Wortigern had banished him then, things would have gone so different…"

"How come you know so much of these matters?" asks Marcus.

"My father took part in all these events. He was a Councillor in Londin, and Wortigern's right hand at one point."

"Your father? Forgive me, I forgot the name –"

"*Rex* Aeric."

His frown deepens. "Wortigern told me many stories of his time in Londin, but I don't think he's ever mentioned an Aeric…"

"He would've known him better as *Ash*."

"Ash!" He almost jumps from the table. "*You're* the son of Ash of Ariminum? Lord's wounds! What good fortune it is that I found you! What divine providence!"

"Calm down, *Decurion*," I plead. A few of the tavern's patrons glance towards us. "It is no fortune – merely a coincidence. Look around you." I gesture around the table. "We're no stroke of divine providence. We are a few weary, wounded Iutes on their way home –"

"You don't understand," Marcus interrupts, lowering his voice. "I wasn't sent here just to seek Graelon. I was also told to keep an eye out for Ash's son and his band of Iutes."

"You – were looking for *me*? Why?"

"My lord Wortigern pays close attention to the events beyond his domain," Marcus says. "Closer than most other nobles serving under *Dux* Ambrosius. He heard the rumour that his old friend's son was fighting in Frankia and Gaul, but didn't return to Cantia with the other Iutes after the Siege of Trever; instead running off somewhere to the south… He probably heard the news even before it reached your father." He chuckles.

"Why didn't you tell me this before?"

"I had no reason to suspect who you were. Last we heard, Octa, son of Ash, was somewhere between Trever and Tornac. And we knew there were other Iutes in Gaul, not all of them trustworthy. I couldn't risk letting them know the king's son was somewhere nearby, unescorted."

"Those untrustworthy Iutes would be Haesta and his men," I say. "They fought with Odowakr at Trever. But don't hold it against them, they're just mercenaries – they would've fought for Rome, if they got paid enough for it."

Marcus nods thoughtfully. "His men were fine warriors – what was left of them."

"What were you supposed to do once you found us?" asks Ursula.

"Guard you, if I can. Help you go home, if you so wished. And let Wortigern know."

"And will you?"

"I'll send a missive to Rotomag. We have a trusted merchant there who should make sure the message reaches my lord." He bites his lower lip. "But this is no good. You should've sailed with your wounded man. It may be too late now."

"How come?"

"That may well have been among the last ships sailing from the North this year. The storm season is upon us. The seas will churn. The pirates will grow bold. It will be difficult to find a willing captain."

"You must have a plan to return home yourself?"

"Only if I can get one of Graelon's ships on time. Otherwise we'll have to wait until next year." He rubs his chin. "It'd be best if you were to come with us."

"Come with you – to Armorica? In search of some *wealh* nobleman?"

"Come with me to Britannia. The *Legatus* often said he could use Ash's help in holding the border. Bringing back his son would be the next best thing…"

"I'm not my father," I reply.

"No – you're more than him," says Ursula unexpectedly. She points at me. "And if Betula was here, she'd agree with me. Remember everything you did this year. No Iute achieved as much in such a short time. Not even *Rex* Aeric."

"What are you saying?"

"I'm saying he's right. We *should* go with him."

The Wrath of the Iutes

"You've said this before. And because I listened to you, we're here now… It's not too late to go back to Rotomag yet, if we hurry."

"*Decurion* Marcus helped you save me," she replies. "He saved my life."

"And we helped him rescue his men from the bandits," Seawine says. "I'd say we're even."

"Of course," Marcus says, raising his hands. "You do not owe me any favours."

I stare at Ursula as the question finally forms in my head.

"Why are you so keen on us not going back to Cantia?"

She laughs. "Because Cantia is *tedious*!"

"Aren't you weary of marching and fighting? We've been chasing you across half of Gaul, eating nothing but gruel. I would've thought you'd be the first to want to go home."

"I don't want to go home yet. There's too much world for me to see."

"We're young. Life is long."

She grows serious, and her gaze grows cold.

"We could die tomorrow," she says. "I could've died a dozen times since Trever. I could've died in any of the battles. Like Gille, like so many of our friends. Imagine if I died at that hillfort – I would have never seen Rotomag, or this town; I'd never see any town ever again. I've made my choice. I want to go see Armorica. And then I want to go see Ambrosius's Britannia."

I glance to Seawine. He listens to Ursula's words with growing annoyance and distaste. I may be vacillating, even leaning towards joining Marcus – Ursula does well to express, inadvertently, my own thoughts – but Seawine shares none of our enthusiasm for travel and distant lands. He's already protested our prolonged stay in Gaul once; if I press him again, he and the four Iutes might well *rebel*. *Aetheling* or not, here in Gaul I'm only a boy they choose to follow, and whom they might abandon if they so wished. Ursula notices my gaze and turns to Seawine.

"What will you do when you're back in Cantia?" she presses him. "Build a hut? Stay on a farm somewhere?"

"I was thinking of hiring myself as guard for some merchant," replies Seawine. "Or going back to being a mariner."

"So you would still travel. Still fight."

He shrugs. "I suppose so. But first, I would rest. I would buy a room in a tavern somewhere, with a view to the Narrow Sea. Spend the whole winter there. It's been so long since I slept in a bed. Or not on my own – if you know what I mean."

"I'm sure we can arrange you *that*," says Marcus. "This is a market town. A lawless town. It won't be hard to find –"

The Wrath of the Iutes

He stops to wave away a beggar who approaches the table. "I have no coin for you, poor man," he says. The beggar is dressed in a striped tunic, made of sewn-together scraps of various pieces of fabric – some of which I recognise as patterned and woven in the Iutish manner.

"Wait," I say. "What do you want?"

"Be you the one who was asking about the Iutes in the market?" the beggar asks – in broken Iutish.

"I might be. What's it to you?"

"Come with me, *Hlaford*. I show you something."

I look to the others. Seawine raises a doubtful eyebrow, but Ursula's eyes gleam. No doubt, she sees in the beggar's arrival another sign of divine providence – or at least, a seed of another adventure… I fear she may very well be right.

I feel myself standing on the crossroads. I could go back to Cantia, with Seawine and the other Iutes; I could follow Marcus to Armorica – or I could go with this strange beggar and discover a whole other destiny waiting for me in some dark corner of this small, nondescript town.

Which will it be?

"It might be a trap," says Seawine. I nod in agreement – though it doesn't affect my choice.

[84]

"No trap!" The beggar draws the sign of a cross on his chest and then, just to be sure, makes a Saxon sign warding off evil. "Come." He waves. "Come!"

Still hesitating, I rise from the table and test if my sword sits smooth in its sheath.

"We all come," I tell the beggar. "And if this does turn out to be a trap, you'll wish you'd never seen me."

"Of course, of course. Come all. No trap."

The Wrath of the Iutes

CHAPTER IV
THE LAY OF BUDIC

We follow the beggar down a narrow alleyway at the back of the cathedral. It's filled with waste of the ages: brick dust, seashells, fowl bones, pottery shards, dung and mud dried into an impenetrable, indescribable layer, upon which grow weeds, vines and even a few young birch trees. The rear wall of the cathedral throws a long shadow on the alley, shrouding its far end in almost complete darkness.

I spot a shelter in the shadow: a length of sail cloth thrown over some bricks, a hook in the wall on one side and a dead beech tree on the other. Underneath the cloth, two fair-haired men, wearing tattered cloaks, huddle over a clay oil lamp, giving them barely more than an illusion of warmth and light.

I notice the cloaks on the men are the half-cut cloaks of the Martinians, and step back with my hand on the sword's hilt; but the cloaks are torn, frayed at the edges, covered in muck and have obviously been taken from some refuse pile.

The men spot us and retreat further into the shadow. The beggar coaxes them out with the same sort of broken Iutish rambling he spoke to us at the tavern.

"You are Iutes?" I ask them in the language of our tribe.

The Wrath of the Iutes

The men nod vigorously. They're a curious pair – one is tall, lanky, narrow-eyed, the other short and squat, with a shed of unruly hair and a scraggly beard, dressed in the same sort of striped tunic as the beggar who brought us here.

"Who are you? What are you doing here?"

"I am Haering," replies the short one, "and this one is Hleo. We are fishermen – from Wecta. Our boat crashed on the coast here…"

"Wecta – you're the slaves the trader talked about! But – I thought he sold you to someone."

The men nod again. "The bastard sold us to a Briton noble… We fled a few days ago – but we only knew our way back here… We don't know how to get back to the coast."

A Briton noble… Of course. I sense sweat drip down my spine as I feel the cold grip of destiny reach for my soul. I'm afraid to ask the next question.

"Were there more of you in his thrall? More Iutes."

They nod. "We saw two, but there could be more."

"That Briton noble… Do you remember his name?"

Haering scratches his head. "Patrician… Budic."

I breathe out in relief. Not Graelon, then. For a moment, the hand of Fate recedes back into the shadows; but then, *Decurion* Marcus crouches down beside me.

"Did he say *Budic*?" he asks. Somehow he managed to catch the name among the Iutish words.

"What about it?"

"There's a Patrician Budic in Armorica who's an uncle of my *Comes*," he says. "If anyone would know where to find Graelon, it would be him."

I sigh.

"Would you…" I rub my eyes before posing the question to the fishermen. "Do you know how to go back to this Patrician Budic's house?"

The men look at each other, startled.

"We don't want to – we just got out –" stutters Haering.

"Who are you, anyway?" asks Hleo.

I straighten myself. "I am Octa, son of *Rex* Aeric and *Hlaefdige* Eadgith," I declare.

"*Aetheling*!" They drop to their knees and prostrate themselves before me.

I help them up. "If I ordered you to, could you take me to Budic?"

The fishermen tremble nervously. I look for traces of abuse on their bodies; I see whip marks under the cloaks and on their thighs, and some dark bruises on their faces. Nothing

The Wrath of the Iutes

serious on a slave, but I can imagine the terror the punishment must have wrought on the poor men who, until a few weeks ago, were quietly fishing off the beach of Wecta.

"I promise we would protect you, and make sure you get back home as soon as we found him," I assure them. I show them the hilt of my sword and nod to Seawine and the four Iute warriors.

I don't want to do it. I could refuse to do it. Forget about the other Iute slaves. I doubt I could do anything to free them, anyway. Leave Marcus on his own and take these two wretches back with me to Britannia. Eventually, someone else would guide the *Decurion* to Graelon.

As I glance back, I catch Ursula's eyes. She stares at me keenly. I know what she expects me to do.

"It's… It's not far," says Haering. "We had to run through fields, and hide in the woods, but by road it can't be more than a few days."

I turn to Seawine.

"A few more days," I say. "That is all I ask."

"You and I both know this is not going to end on that, *aetheling*." He shakes his head. "A few more days to find this Budic – then a few more days to Graelon – and then, what? Wait until spring for the storms to end? Sail to the West, to fight these… Scots for the rest of the year?"

"There will be time to rest, and heal wounds, before we go to any battle," says Ursula. "I hear these Armorican Britons have palaces and *villas* grander than anything we've seen outside Londin."

"It's true," adds Marcus, nodding. "The likes of Budic would have taken all their treasure with them here, taken over some abandoned *villa* and flourished as in the old days of the Empire. I've heard wondrous stories of these places – fields of golden wheat, mosaic floors, working hypocausts, fountains of crystal-clear water…"

His eyes gleam in awe as he speaks; I'm surprised at his enthusiasm. Everything he describes is what we were told to believe Britannia Prima looked like under the leadership of *Dux* Ambrosius. These are the kinds of things Councillor Riotham would boast about to other members of the Londin Council. My father was always doubtful about these claims – and it looks like he was right, judging by how impressed *Decurion* Marcus appears by the rumours of Armorica's wealth.

Marcus's wonder has an unexpected effect on me. I'm no longer interested in seeing the *villas* of the Armorican nobles – I don't believe the tall tales for a moment; instead, I want to see Ambrosius's domain with my own eyes. If the West is not as Riotham and his kin have been describing it to us, then what *is* it like?

"A few more days," I repeat my plea to Seawine. "Then we rest – then you're free to decide whatever it is you want to do."

The Wrath of the Iutes

If anything, Marcus's vision understated the reality of a Briton nobleman's life in Armorica. The old *villa* Patrician Budic took for his dwelling is enormous; the *domus* itself is one of the largest I've ever seen. It's more than a house – it's a small village under one roof. The whitewashed walls spread two hundred feet each way; the eastern wing rises, in staggered roofs, to three storeys, a pillared *portico* lines the western wall, leading to a full-size bath house attached to the northern wing. Judging by the state of disrepair – the crackling plaster, the crumbling walls, the roof full of holes – the southern wing, and the massive barn it leads to, have not been in use in generations, and the new host didn't consider it necessary to make any repairs to it, content with renovating the entrance porch and the baths. Steam rises in white wisps from the rear of the bath house, proving that it is, indeed, in working condition.

Despite its size, we'd never have found the *villa* without the help of our two runaway slaves. There are no straight, wide Roman roads in this part of Armorica, only narrow tracks, snaking their way through an odd landscape of long, low hills, twisting rivers and tall outcrops of limestone, hiding small farmsteads and fields of wheat and barley from our sight. For all we know, there might be more such *villas* secluded just behind another line of trees or a ridge of white rock.

Beyond the *domus*, the *villa*'s vast grounds are guarded only by a low drystone wall, with an ornate wooden gatehouse spanning the narrow road, carved deep with cart ruts. There are no guards at the gate.

"Strange," I note. "With all the roving bands of Bacauds around, you'd think this place will be more heavily guarded."

On closer inspection, I see fresh damage to the *domus* and the farm buildings. Black smoke still rises from a smouldering ruin of what would have been a granary or a barn. A few slaves are digging graves in the white soil next to the bath house. Others work on some construction along the side of the road, made up of many flat wooden boards. Here, at last, are some guards and soldiers, some helping to clean up the damage, others resting in the sun, letting their wounds heal.

Slowly and lazily, a group of these soldiers picks up their weapons and helmets, gathers in front of the *domus* and moves towards us, swords sheathed, spears slung over their shoulders.

"I will speak to them," says Marcus, moving ahead. I nod at Ursula, and we ride up to his sides. One of the soldiers steps forward and looks at us curiously. He's tall, lanky, curly haired under the old, dented Roman cavalry helmet, and wears a cloak that may have once been purple, but is now stained with dirt and grime beyond any recognition of colour. A large brown dog, of the sort popular among the *wealas* in Britannia, stands at his side, panting.

"*Ave*," Marcus greets him with the Roman salute.

The soldier looks beyond us, at the men gathered on the narrow road, and frowns. I can understand his apprehension. We are a large unit now: Marcus's *equites*, my five Iutes, Mullo, the two fishermen, clad in fresh, clean tunics instead of rags and armed with knives. More than twenty mounted warriors;

The Wrath of the Iutes

looking at the state of the soldiers gathered around us, if we wanted to, we could overrun the *villa* with ease.

"Who are you?" the rider asks.

"Marcus of Dumnonia. I come seeking Patrician Budic."

"What do you want with – hey!" He lowers his spear and points it towards our men. The other soldiers reach for their weapons. "You're the runaway slaves! We've been searching everywhere for you!"

"They are with me. I will reimburse their master for his loss," I say, though I know I don't have enough silver on me to pay for two slaves, even as poor as these ones. As I say this, I also wonder what need the master of an inland rural *villa* has for two fishermen.

His eyes narrow. "And you are?"

"Octa of the Iutes."

"Please," Marcus says. "We only want to ask your master a few questions. We will soon be on our way."

The soldier mulls over the proposition for a moment.

"You three can come with me. The rest of your men must stay outside the gate. I don't want your horses trampling all over my cabbages," he says, nodding to a vegetable patch sprawling along the drystone wall.

"*Your* cabbages?"

He hands his spear over to a man standing to his right and takes off his helmet. I see speckles of grey amid the black hair, and strands of wrinkles on his face; he's older than I guessed just by the youthful timbre of his voice.

"*I* am Budic," he announces. "The master of this house, and of this land. And you'd better have a good excuse to disturb my peace with memories of the past, Briton."

"If I wanted to stay in touch with my kin across the Narrow Sea, I would've just sent a letter," says Budic.

He moves one step to his right with a splash, to make a place for the naked female slave who pours a mixture of salt and aromatic oils into the bath. Such luxury I haven't seen even in Trever.

"It is a dire emergency, lord," replies Marcus. "And we only disturb you because we are looking for *Comes* Graelon."

"Graelon will not be any more content to see you than I am," Budic replies grumpily. "You realise, there's a reason why we cut ourselves from you in the first place, *Decurion*."

"What *is* the reason?" I ask. I scoop some water into my hands and raise it to my nose. It smells of roses and lavender. In the tepid chamber behind the wall, I hear Ursula talking to Helena, our host's wife; from the snippets of conversation that penetrate the bricks, it sounds like they're discussing the latest fashions in Cantia and Londin. I can imagine Ursula's squirming irritation; it is not a topic on which she would have

The Wrath of the Iutes

a lot to say, having always preferred to wear the simple clothes of a Iutish shieldmaiden.

Budic glares at me with a look that tells me that it is I, and the likes of me, that were the main reason the Briton nobles sailed for new shores. With a long sigh, he decides to indulge my curiosity.

"We fled a land torn by civil war, disrupted by serf rebellions, invaded by heathen barbarians," he says. "Roman Britannia was falling apart. Province against province, *pagus* against *pagus*. Maybe if we had a decent *Dux*, he could have stopped this calamity. But no – Londin chose that heathen-friend Wortigern. And he, at least, was a good general. We – we had Ambrosius." He spits on the mosaic floor. A slave rushes to clean it up.

"What's wrong with Ambrosius?"

"*Everything*. He's too weak, too soft, too…" He waves a hand in the air, looking for a word. "*Christian*."

"That's a curious way to insult a Roman *Dux*," I say.

"You of all people should know what I mean," he says. He clenches his hand into a fist, letting soapy water trickle between his fingers. "Over there, they're still trying to run things the 'civilised' way. The way they think Rome used to work in the old days. Deluded fools. How is that working out for you?" He turns to Marcus.

"Not great," the *Decurion* admits. "This is exactly why we've come –"

"I'm not surprised," Budic interrupts him. "I always knew Ambrosius's rule would end in disaster. You want to know how we survived – no, thrived – in this land, despite all the bandits and Bacauds roaming the countryside, despite being abandoned by the Legions, despite having to rely only on ourselves, not on the... *barbarian* levies?" He ends glaring at me again.

"I did wonder about that," I say. "We fought the Bacauds on the way here. They're as fierce as any enemy I saw in Gaul."

He chuckles and stands up. Despite his age, he's lean and muscle-bound; his body is as covered in scars as my father's. He reaches for the towel – his hand moves a bit too fast and the slave holding the towel flinches; I'm reminded of the whip scars on the backs of the runaway Iutes.

"Come with me outside," Budic says. "I'll show you something."

"The way I see it, the whole trouble in Britannia started with Pelagius," says Budic as we leave the bath house. He leads us back towards the road, where the slaves are putting finishing touches to the strange constructions. "You know about Pelagius, barbarian?" he asks me.

"I studied under Bishop Fastidius, in Londin," I reply proudly. "I know all about the heretic and his writings."

The Wrath of the Iutes

"Fastidius is the bishop now?" he scoffs. "I've heard of him. Another heretic and a pagan-lover. But well versed in the Church law," he admits. "Pelagius filled the heads of the Briton faithful with all this rotten talk of free will, of men being equal, of slaves deserving good treatment, of heathens having as much chance of getting to the Lord's kingdom as us." He laughs bitterly. "I'm telling you, if we believed in half of these teachings, we wouldn't have survived a month in this wilderness!"

A soldier runs up to us and salutes. "We are ready, Master Budic."

"Excellent. Proceed, *centurion*."

The soldier turns around and raises his hand. At this signal, the slaves start raising their constructions. Marcus gasps – he's the first to realise what they are. It takes me until they're raised to their full height to see it: *crosses*.

They line the road like trees, from the *portico* to the wooden gate. Men and women hang from the cross-bars, naked save the loincloths, whipped within an inch of death, bloodied, bruised. A few moan or cry in pain, others are too weak to do even that.

Marcus makes a sign of the cross and whispers a quiet prayer. Budic scoffs again, hearing him.

"They're just bandits," he says. "Bacauds we captured in a raid on their village a few days ago. Their friends tried to win them back yesterday – only added to the pile," he laughs and nods to the bodies being buried behind the bath house. "And a few runaway slaves," he adds. "A lesson to the others."

We are both speechless. I hear another gasp behind me – I turn to see Ursula emerge from the bath house. She turns pale at the sight.

"Trust me, it's the only way," says Budic. "When we came here, these *villas* lay in ruins, the fields lay fallow. Everyone fled in fear of the bandits. The runaway slaves ruled the woods, built whole villages for themselves. The pagans were busy rebuilding their shrines – the word of the Lord never penetrated deep into the forests. It was only with the sword and the whip that we brought order and peace." He shakes his fist. "We would have done the same in Britannia if we had the chance. It's a gruelling, slow work, and it will take generations, but by God, one day everyone here will be as Briton as if they were born on Tamesa's shores. Maybe more," he adds, glaring at me again.

"You're just the same as Wortimer…" I whisper inadvertently.

"Wortimer!" Budic claps his hands. "Now there was a man who knew how to deal with the heathens. A pity how he ended. It was a lesson to all of us: never put your cock inside a pagan wench, no matter how comely she may be… So, what is it that you need our help with? Saxons? Picts?"

"Scots," says Marcus hoarsely.

"Ah." Budic nods. "These ones we could never fully subdue. I can see why you'd be needing Graelon. And who

The Wrath of the Iutes

knows, you might even succeed on your quest. He lost his wife fighting in the North – but you probably knew that already."

"No –" Marcus stares in shock. "I did not know. Then, you will tell us where to find him?"

"Fine. If that's what it takes to get you out of my property."

"Nothing would make me as glad as getting out of here as soon as possible, Master Budic," I say to his satisfied chuckle.

Ursula insists that we examine the tortured slaves to see if there are any Iutes among them.

"It is why we came here, after all," she says.

It's a gruesome task. The slaves we pass are all still alive, but barely. We get more information from their handlers than from themselves. Most of them look local, as confirmed by the men resting in the grim shadow of the crosses after their hard work.

"The Masters brought few slaves with them," says one, biting on a piece of dark bread. "They had to get what they needed from the villages here."

"Villages? Then these are not all Bacaud captives?" asks Ursula.

The men laugh scornfully. "To Budic everyone here is a Bacaud. But the real Bacauds would rather die than get themselves turned into slaves. Mind you, for these poor bastards it no longer makes a difference."

He throws a ball of half-chewed bread at the moaning slave hanging above him. I notice Ursula's fists clench, and I pull her away, nodding at the armed guard standing nearby, looking at us suspiciously.

"I can't believe they call themselves Christians," Ursula hisses. "This is a mockery of our Lord's suffering."

"Bishop Fastidius would say there's more of your Lord in any of these poor souls than in Budic and his men."

"He'd be right." She looks at the crosses again, with pity, which turns into viciousness as soon as her eyes fall on the Briton guards.

"I never gave much thought to the fate of slaves," she says. "My family owns only a few, and we treat them like members of the household. I don't think I've ever seen anything like… this."

"Even in Cantia there are bad masters aplenty," I say. "Budic didn't turn into this heartless monster after crossing the Narrow Sea. If everyone treated their slaves like your mother, there would be no bandits in Andreda. When my father fought with Aelle, he counted several thousand Free Folk in the forest – slaves, serfs, city poor fleeing from debt…"

The Wrath of the Iutes

She shudders; not from the sight of the unfortunate tortured souls, but from something deeper inside. I wrap my arm around her.

"Were you frightened?" I ask, guessing it's a memory of her own captivity.

"At first," she says. "I didn't know what Haesta wanted from me. I didn't know if he'd abandon me in a ditch somewhere as soon as we got far enough, or sell me into slavery…" She falls silent for a moment. "Then it just got tedious, all the marching and running…"

"I'm sorry you had to go through all that."

"Gille and Audulf suffered worse than I did."

"They suffered in battle, as is a warrior's fate. Yours were injuries of the soul."

"I would've been more frightened if I had known what they did to slaves here." She glances at the last cross in the row, by the gates. "Look, that one is a fair-hair!"

We rush towards the slave. He's still conscious – he is, or was, before Budic's torturers got to him, a strong man, with muscular arms and barrel chest.

"You a Iute?" I ask him.

"Who wants to know?" he replies. Blood trickles from his mouth and oozes from the deep cuts on his arms and legs, but his stare remains clear.

"Octa, son of *Rex* Aeric," I say.

"Eadgith's boy?" He tries a chuckle, but only spits out more blood. "Did the bastards get you, too?"

Before I can react, I notice Hleo and Haering, the two fishermen, shuffling hurriedly our way.

"Seolh!" they exclaim at the sight of the slave. "You're here! What did they do to you?"

"You know him?" I ask.

"He's from Wecta. The best spear fisherman on the island. Went missing a couple of months ago."

"I've had enough of this," says Ursula. She draws her sword and starts hacking at the foot of the cross. "Help me, Octa! Get an axe!"

"Ursula, I don't think we should —"

"You're going to just let him die here?"

"I will talk to Budic. Wait here."

"No!" She cries. "He's dying — and he's one of your own people!"

I glance towards the *domus*; a group of guards runs towards us, spears in hand. Budic follows close behind them, tying up his robe.

The Wrath of the Iutes

"I think you should stop." I grasp Ursula's hand in the middle of another blow. Not that she managed to do much damage to the cross – the post is built of a solid oak beam. It would take a woodsman's hatchet to fell it.

"What are you doing to my slave?" Budic demands.

"I'm freeing him," I say. "Get him down from there."

"Careful, boy, or you'll take his place." He glowers. "I'm feeling generous enough to grant you these two bumbling fools," he says, nodding towards the fishermen, "but this barbarian slew one of my guards when trying to escape, and for that, there can be only one punishment."

He waves his hand, and the spearmen surround us.

"Leave me, *aetheling*," Seolh croaks. "I'm not worth your attention. I'm beyond saving –" He coughs. More blood spurts from his wounds and orifices.

"He's right, you know," says Budic with a foul grin. "My people know how to kill slowly, but inevitably. Even if I did get him down from there, he'd just bleed out inside."

Seolh groans in pain and tenses in the binds. Budic laughs.

"Not long now. But long enough."

"No more!" I cry. I wrestle a spear from one of Budic's men and stab Seolh in the heart. He thrashes three times, then lets out a long-drawn sigh and his entire body slackens.

"You'll pay for this." I point the bloodied weapon at Budic. The spearmen step forward – the tips of their blades touch our chests.

"What's going on here?"

It is now the turn of *Decurion* Marcus and his *equites* to join our growing gathering. Budic's guards look nervously at each other and at their master – they may have been eager to beat up just the two of us, but they're not so keen on fighting Marcus's trained soldiers.

"Right. I've had just enough of this," Budic snarls. "Get out of my land, all of you. Go bother Graelon, now that you know where to find him."

Marcus takes a quick glance around, and assesses the situation in an instant. "He's right. Come, Octa. We should leave."

"Not until I get this man's body," I say. "To give him a proper burial."

"Oh, fine, take him. He only gives the others hope of a quick death." Budic gestures to his men, and one of them rushes for a ladder. "But then, I don't want to see you anymore."

The spearmen and the *equites* disperse while Ursula and I wait for Seolh's body to be brought down from the cross. The only ones left are the two fishermen, uncertain what to do with themselves.

The Wrath of the Iutes

"You're free," I tell them. "You can go home."

"*Hlaford...*" Hleo starts. "We —"

"We would like to go with you, *aetheling*."

"Me? I'm sorry, but this is no leisure trip. We may end up going to war, and I don't have time to train you two. I don't even have ponies for you."

"Every army needs camp followers," says Haering. "You will need someone to take care of the ponies when you can't use them."

"And when would that be?"

He scratches his head in confusion.

"When we would have to storm a fortress," says Ursula. "Or sneak up on the enemy. We have to take them, Octa. If we leave them here, Budic will just capture them again — and they'll end up on one of those crosses."

"Fine. I can't forbid you to come with us. But I take no responsibility for you. You are *not* a part of my warband."

"Thank you, *Hlaford*." The two men bend in deep bows. "You will not regret it."

"I hope not. Your first task is to take poor Seolh and help me take him to that forest." I point to the line of trees in the distance. "We'll find a good oak grove to bury him in. One worthy of a true Iute warrior."

James Calbraith

CHAPTER V
THE LAY OF GRAELON

The town of Worgium grows suddenly out of the surrounding fields, first as a village lining the Roman highway from Redones, then as a grid of streets and low tenement blocks, culminating in a small Forum.

There is no city wall around Worgium, no gatehouse on the road – only the same sort of drystone barrier as around Budic's *villa*, separating fields and protecting them from wind and wild beasts. A single long line of brick arches extends towards the south-east, which I take for remains of a rampart at first, but then realise it is merely an aqueduct.

It's the first time I have seen a Roman town without any fortification, however feeble – and without any widespread destruction that would inevitably follow such recklessness. We are truly out of the way of any passing armies and warbands here; the main defence of the town is its seclusion. The only threat here would be the Bacauds and other bandits, but even they would first need to march through miles of dense forest and steep river gorges. From what I remember of the maps of Gaul, Armorica is on the furthest western edge of the Empire's road network, more remote even than Britannia – and judging by how far we have come down the road from Redones, Worgium is almost at its westernmost tip.

I slow down as we ride through the town. Many of the houses and farms along the road are abandoned, dilapidated. Others have only been occupied recently by new owners. Whoever lived here before the Briton lords took over, either disappeared, or were turned into slaves and serfs, serving the new masters. Only as we enter deeper into the centre, does the town show more signs of life, still less than a settlement this size should have. The Forum is almost empty, except for a single stall selling some woollen cloaks, and a baker's stand. I spot a small bath house, and a few other public buildings, but I can't find a church anywhere; the only other stone building is a *basilica*, bounding the Forum from the north. It's no bigger than a mead hall, and I assume it doubles as the *Praetor*'s hall, if such an official still rules here. It is here that we're supposed to find *Comes* Graelon, assuming he's not in one of the small *villas* that make up the town's southern suburb.

The townsfolk come out to see us, lining both sides of the road — an arrival of such a large band of warriors in the town must be a rare occasion. Looking at the faces we pass, I can't tell if they're Gauls or Britons — but most of them wear clothes that wouldn't be out of place in Dorowern or Londin.

"They're staring at you the most," notes Ursula.

"I guess they've never seen a fair-hair in Legionnaire's armour," I say.

"It's not wonder I see in their eyes," she replies, "but fear."

"They fled here before the likes of you and your Iutes," says Marcus. "They must think you're a vanguard of some invading force."

I halt before we enter the courtyard of the *basilica*.

The Wrath of the Iutes

"I'm not sure if I want to see this Graelon after all," I say. "If he's the same as Budic, he will only see me as another filthy pagan."

"We've come all this way," says Ursula.

"*They've* come all this way," I say, nodding to Marcus and his *equites*. "We've only been tagging along, and after what I saw in Armorica... I don't know if I want to continue. Why should I help these... *wealas*? They wouldn't help *us*."

"You wouldn't be helping them. You'd be helping Wortigern. You know he's different than the rest."

"It's Wortigern's own choice to defend that border."

"If he made that choice – if he persists in fighting the Scots – that means he believes Ambrosius is worth saving. Or at least his people."

"Or that he's an old warrior who prefers to spend his last days fighting instead of retiring at some summer *villa*."

While we talk, a delegation comes out of the *basilica* to greet us: several officials, in robes of the Magistrates, lined with purple and red, and plaid breeches. Leading them is a young girl, not much older than Ursula or myself. Despite her young age, there's a rugged, Northern beauty to her, as if a salty sea breeze swept her face. A thin silver diadem adorns her dark auburn hair, tied in a simple tail over her shoulder; her cheeks glow ruddy with excitement.

"We were hoping to meet *Comes* Graelon," says Marcus, after introducing himself. "Is he not well?"

"He's well," the girl replies. "But he's not here – he's at Gesocribate, inspecting the *garum* vats. I expect him to return in a few days."

"We are somewhat in a hurry," says Marcus. He looks over his shoulder at his riders and my Iutes, both equally weary after the long march across Armorica's wilds. "But, I'm sure we could all use a couple of days of rest – if you have enough space to accommodate my men. We have come a *long* way."

The girl smiles. "Warus will set you all up," she says, nodding to the official standing to her left. "There's space at the *villa* for the officers, and the warriors can be billeted in the houses of the townsfolk. The town's *mansio* closed down long before we came here – there are a few taverns, but they only serve food and drink… A long way, you say?" she asks. "How far?"

"Britannia," replies Marcus. "Dumnonia, me and my men – and the Iutes from Cantia, by way of Trever."

"Britannia!" she exclaims. "Trever! How exciting. You must tell me all about it. Come, come, we'll have ourselves a feast. Warus, send to the *villa* for my father's cooks."

"Your father?" I ask, raising an eyebrow.

The Wrath of the Iutes

"I am Ahes – *Comes* Graelon's daughter. And I will be more than glad to host you until his return. I can't wait to hear your tales of distant lands."

Ursula glances at me with a mocking smile. "So, *aetheling*. Do you still want us to go home, or are we staying here for a few more days after all?"

I scowl at her, then look back at Ahes. Rays of the setting sun gleam in her striking dark eyes, giving them a fiery hue, as if they were windows into a secret flame burning within her soul.

"A few days of rest can't hurt either way," I say. "And I'm always looking forward to a feast… Such as there can be in a place like this." I eye the town doubtfully.

"We may be a small and remote town," says Ahes, "but I'm sure we can prepare a few surprises, even for someone as worldly as yourself, Lord…"

"Octa," I reply with a bow. "Octa, son of Aeric."

"*Rex* Aeric," adds Ursula with a roguish grin. "King of the Iutes."

Staring at the painted ceiling above me, I realise I have never spent the night in a Briton nobleman's *villa* before, other than my father's old, empty house at Ariminum. We didn't get to stay at Budic's, either, after the quarrel over Seolh's body. Our hasty departure annoyed Seawine and the Iutes, who had already started preparing the camp at the drystone wall; it took Ursula's full powers of persuasion to convince them to accompany us further on, to Worgium – if only because, left on their own, they wouldn't know their way back the winding field roads to Redones. To placate them further, I asked Ahes to settle them in the free rooms of Graelon's *villa*, rather than houses of the townsfolk with Marcus's men.

"This was my father's life for his entire childhood and youth," I whisper. I can hear Seawine snoring behind the wall, in Graelon's study. "He would sleep in a room just like this. Eat in a dining room like the one where we ate supper. Play in a garden like the one outside. And then he ended up a barbarian king. Can you imagine what it must have been like?"

"Makes you wonder what will happen to us, in the end," says Ursula. "Though I can't imagine anything that would beat this year."

She sleeps on the bed while I lie on the sheepskins on the floor; if I remember father's stories correctly, this is how he used to sleep in Fastidius's room, when he was still a slave.

"Who's running your father's *villa* now?" she asks.

"Some acolyte in the bishop's name," I reply. "It's all Church property now. Not that there's much left of it."

"You've seen it, then?"

"After my mother's death, Father wasn't keen on ever returning there. Too many memories. But he would

The Wrath of the Iutes

sometimes go to dig up the gold coins from the hidden hoard, when we were in Robriwis, and sometimes he'd take me with him. It's the only place outside Cantia he ever took me to see, really, except Londin."

"And now you've seen more of the world than he's ever dreamed of," she says and chuckles. "Certainly enough of it to impress our beautiful host."

I spent most of the feast telling the wide-eyed Ahes of our adventures in Gaul; *Decurion* Marcus had no stories to tell, other than his skirmishes with the Scots and the fight with Bacauds – certainly nothing that would match taking part in the Siege of Trever, the battles of Tolbiac, or assassinating a Frankish king, an act to which I inadvertently admitted after drinking too much *sicera*, the heady local drink made from fermented crab apples: one of the "surprises" Ahes mentioned. The other was a bowl of fresh *garum*, the dark brown, thick sauce of fermented fish; I'd read about it, but I'd never tasted it, not even in Londin. The vats at Gesocribate still produce it, in small numbers for Graelon's table, though without having ever eaten it before I could not be sure if what we used to spice the food was truly the *garum* of the Ancients, or just a poor imitation. Either way, I did not care much for the taste.

"The way she looked at you…" Ursula continues.

"Stop it. Not every pretty girl we meet wants to get into my breeches. Besides, have you seen Marcus? He was smitten with her far more than I was. I wouldn't want to stay in his way."

"Come now. You're the Hero of Trever! Queen Basina didn't seem to mind –"

I raise myself on one elbow and stare at her in the dim light of the oil lamp. "Basina may have been a queen, but she was still a barbarian. This is different. Ahes is a *wealh*."

"*I'm* a *wealh*."

"You're practically a Iute." I chuckle, but I see she's serious – and wounded. "These people are different from you or your parents, you know that. They're all like Wortimer here. When I look at Ahes, I can see she's beautiful, but I can also see she would make an obedient daughter to someone like him."

"You shouldn't blame the poor girl for her father's sins," she says. "You don't know what she's really like. She seemed perfectly nice at the feast."

"Good for her, then – and good for Marcus, or whoever else would want to court her. But you can't believe that being raised in this… This hateful place, by these hateful men, would be good for anyone's soul." I lie back down. "Forget about Ahes. We always talk about me and the women I could lie with, but what about you?"

She lies silent for a while. "What about me?" she asks, at last. "You know what I think of men."

"Even Haesta?"

The Wrath of the Iutes

"Haesta?" she scoffs. "What are you talking about? He's old enough to be my father!"

"I saw how you smiled at him. How you looked after him, longingly, as he left for Rotomag."

She laughs a false laugh. "I was… I was just surprised how polite and charming he was."

"He *abducted* you. And dragged you across half of Gaul."

"I know. I thought he was a monster, at first. I know he killed your mother –"

"His men did," I correct her. "Believe me, if it was actually Haesta who had killed her, we wouldn't even be having this conversation."

"– and I know his history with your father… But he's not a bad person, when you get to know him…"

"Have I told you how he wanted to force my father to abdicate in exchange for my life?"

"And would that be any different to how your father forced Hengist to step down?" she asks. "Haesta told me how he was supposed to take over as *Drihten* before your father appeared."

"Oh, he would tell you that, wouldn't he? Hengist despised him. He knew Haesta would be a terrible leader for the tribe."

"That's just what King Aeric told you…" She shrugs. "It doesn't matter. Nothing happened between me and Haesta, so you don't need to be jealous."

"I'm not…" I pause. I can tell by the tone of her voice she's eager to change the subject — as am I.

"Have you noticed how few children there are in this place?" I ask.

"Yes — though I wouldn't have noted anything amiss had I not seen the villages of the Iutes and the Franks."

"How so?"

"Dorowern is just the same — and everywhere else in Britannia, as far as I know. My people… We don't seem to want to bring children into this world anymore. Especially in noble families. Nobody really knows why… My mother said it's because we feel our time is passing, and we have to make a place for your kind."

"You'd think things would be a bit different here. I thought these *wealas* wanted to come here to live as they did in the old days, without 'our kind' in their way."

"They've only just started coming here. Maybe more time must pass for things to begin to change. A generation. Maybe Ahes will bear dozens of children to whoever is fortunate to bed her," she adds with a soft chuckle.

The Wrath of the Iutes

We both fall silent. Seawine's snoring grows quieter; I can hear an owl hooting in the garden – then a rustle of bedding. Ursula climbs down from the bed and lies next to me.

"It's too soft up there," she whispers.

Her skin radiates warmth like a hypocaust furnace. I wrap my arm around her and nestle my head in the nape of her neck. I have missed this feeling; I have missed this scent. We haven't lain together like this in years. I wonder what really made her come down to me, but I'm afraid asking would break the spell.

"Have you decided yet what we're going to do next?" she asks.

"I haven't," I reply. "But I'm inclined to go back home now, rather than wait for Marcus. Graelon's harbour is just a day or so away – I'm sure they'll have a ship there than can take us to Cantia, or at least some larger port along the way."

"Seems a bit of a wasted journey if we just go home now."

"Not at all – I've learned what these Armorican Britons are really like. I've learned that they're not worth saving."

"You've only talked to two of them so far. And one of them turned out to be not so bad. I think you may be a bit too hasty in your judgement."

"This is why I haven't decided yet. I'm willing to wait until we meet *Comes* Graelon. Maybe Budic is just one rotten apple."

"Ugh. Don't talk to me about *apples*. Especially rotten ones. I don't think I'll ever eat one again." She groans and reaches out to extinguish the oil lamp. In the warm darkness, the house trembles with Seawine's renewed snoring.

They might as well be brothers.

All the Briton nobles we've met in Armorica, including the magistrate officials in Worgium, look somewhat alike, so much so that I'm having a difficult time telling them apart. From what Marcus told me, many of them are, indeed, related to each other – and to the noble families still remaining in Ambrosius's part of Britannia. But Graelon's resemblance to Budic goes further than just superficial physicality. He's got the same cold cunning in his eyes, the same half-sneer twists his lips. I can't fathom how a man like him spawned a fiery child like Ahes; she must have inherited almost all of her looks from her mother. The only thing Graelon has in common with his daughter is the glowing red on his cheeks when he's excited – or angry.

And he's been angry ever since he returned from the coast and learned of the purpose of our visit.

"I warned them," he booms. "I told them this would happen. The Scots, back again! What was the point of all my efforts?"

The Wrath of the Iutes

"What is he talking about?" I ask Ahes quietly. She sits by my side at the table which just a few days ago heaved under the food and drink of our welcome feast, but now is covered with scrolls, letters and maps brought by *Decurion* Marcus to explain the dire situation in the North.

"Father fought the Scots in his youth, when he commanded the fleet," she says. "It's how he met my mother."

"Ah, your mother was a Scot?"

She shakes her head. "She was the daughter of a Brigand chieftain. He and father beat the Scots back to Hibernia."

Graelon overhears her and leans over to me. "Yes, and I told Ambrosius they'd return again if he didn't keep watch of Mona."

"We are too short on men and ships to watch every coast," says Marcus.

"You've wasted your soldiers fighting Wortimer's battles for him," replies Graelon. He glares at me. He doesn't know who I am yet — but he can clearly see I'm a barbarian, and has little doubt on whose side I would've stood in Wortimer's War, were I old enough.

This is the first time I have heard of it as reason, or at least part of the reason, behind the Britons' recent trouble. Marcus didn't mention it before, perhaps wary of offending a possible ally. I had no idea the Westerners lost so many men fighting the Iutes. Ambrosius's main Legion did not arrive in the East until after Eobbasfleot, but his soldiers did bear the brunt of the fighting in the early stages of the war, helping Wortimer's militia against the best of the Iutish warriors.

"And you've wasted your gold building harbours and fortresses for Rome," the *Comes* continues. "Ambrosius commits mistake after mistake, and then he comes to us whimpering for help, like a hound that's taken on too big a wild boar by itself."

Marcus listens to this tirade in despondent silence. I feel sorry for him. As a loyal officer, he should be defending his *Dux* from this onslaught. That he says nothing means he agrees with at least some of Graelon's charges. A mere cavalry *Decurion*, Marcus would not have been privy to any strategic decisions made at Ambrosius's court in Corin. It was not up to him to question his superiors' orders, but to fulfil them, whether he agreed with them or not.

"None of this is a reason not to help our own kin," pleads Ahes. "If it's in our power. Think of what's going to happen to them otherwise!"

"Pah." Graelon waves his hand. "So Ambrosius will lose a few mountain valleys and some remote coast villages. The Scots will never threaten the heartland of his province. They don't know how to assail walled cities, how to fight against a Legion in open field."

"If they establish camps in the mountains, we'll never be able to push them back again. We won't be able to counter their raids on our farmsteads and *villas*," replies Marcus. "And

The Wrath of the Iutes

between Picts, Brigands and Saxons doing the same on every side, I don't see how we can survive for long…"

"Then come here!" Graelon spreads his arms invitingly. "We could use brave men like yourself in Armorica. And there's plenty of empty land for you to settle."

"And if it's not empty yet, you will make sure it is, right?" I say.

He stares at me for a long moment. "Lord willing, yes."

"So you'd rather fight fellow Christians, than help your kindred fight the heathens?" I ask. "Just because they're weaker; just because they're an easier prey."

"Are you calling me a coward, barbarian?" Instead of growing angry, Graelon smiles a wry sneer. He leans back in the chair.

"I know you fought bravely in the North," I say. "And I'm certain you would fight bravely in defence of your people here, if it came to it… I just wonder if, in your old age, you haven't grown liable to choosing the easy way over the hard…"

"You can't goad me, youngling." He wags his finger at me. "You may have fought at Trever, but I've seen more good men die than you've ever seen live. Easy way? You think clearing these woods of the Bacauds was easy? You think leaving a home of generations and moving my entire family across the sea was easy? I've had my share of fighting, of hardship. And I've had enough of it." He turns back to

Marcus. "I cannot give you what you ask for. I'm afraid you've wasted time coming here."

"Father – at least spare them some ships!" Ahes tugs on his sleeve.

"And what if Scots come raiding *our* coast?" scoffs Graelon. "I keep these ships for a reason. It's only a few days' sailing further here from Hibernia than to Britannia. And then there are Franks to our north, and Goths to our south. You would leave us defenceless?" He shakes his head.

"I am not cruel, you understand," he adds, after perusing the maps for a while. "But I do have my people to look after first, before I look to the needs of others. I can give you a ship that will take you back home – or, wherever it is you wish to go," he says, looking at me. "A fine ship. I will load its holds with grain. We've had a good harvest this year – the serfs can work hard if you motivate them properly." He sneers. "I would throw in some tin and copper, but Ambrosius's mines have always produced more metal than ours ever could… You *do* still hold the mines?"

"Most of them, yes. Though without slaves to work them…"

"You know the price of slaves on the Redones market." Graelon shrugs. "Return with enough silver, and I can sell you as many as you want."

"Father!" Ahes cries in despair. "They are our family!"

The Wrath of the Iutes

"And I would offer them a proper discount!" Graelon laughs.

Marcus grows red. "I am not a slave monger, and I did not come here to make petty trades. If you don't want to help us, fine, but I don't see why I should sit here and bear your insults."

Graelon lays a hand on his shoulder. "You're right, *Decurion*. My apologies. That was uncalled for. You are a brave soldier, to come here with just a handful of riders. And so are you, fair-hair, from what my daughter tells me," he says, turning back to me. "But then, that's to be expected of your kin. Fighting's about the only thing your lot are good for!" His belly shakes with an ugly laughter.

"Don't listen to him," whispers Ahes. "He often talks of how good warriors the barbarians are. Goths, Alans, Franks — we all know Rome wouldn't survive without your help."

She puts her hand on mine as she says this. I catch Marcus's eye; he blinks, turns red again and looks away. I pull my hand back. The *Decurion* clears his throat and starts rolling up the parchments and maps from the table.

Graelon holds his wrist. "Two ships," he says. "With crew. And you'll send them back in the spring, after the storms. I really can't spare any more than that."

"Thank you, *Comes*," says Marcus. "My *Dux* will greatly appreciate this gesture."

"Never mind your *Dux*." Graelon waves his hand. "I'm doing this for you, *Decurion*. You remind me of myself when I was young. Don't look so glum. How about some *sicera* to lighten the mood?" he asks, and before Marcus can respond, he nods at the slave. "Bring out the barrels, man! Let's see what the heads of Ambrosius's warriors are made of!"

As if to add to our misery, it has now started to rain. The Roman highway, already in increasing state of disrepair the deeper into Armorica we go, turns into little more than a swamp gravel path past Worgium, with the paving stones sinking into the mud and the rubble underlay spilling out into the roadsides. We pass no carts along the way, and I can't imagine how they would navigate this mire; all the traffic, such as it is, between Graelon's capital and the harbour at Gesocribate, is carried on the backs of mules – and slaves. Marcus's horses tread the road with their heads down, finding their way between the mud patches, while we forego the highway altogether – the peat-lined strips of grass and heath along the sides being a much more suitable surface for the hooves of our moor ponies.

As Graelon said, there's a lot of land to settle here, most of it dark and moist, good for wheat and rearing cattle; but it's remote and empty, gloomy and inhospitable, especially under the impenetrable shroud of the steel-grey clouds. We pass only one inhabited *villa*, not far from Worgium; beyond it, there are barely any signs of life. A few scattered farms here and there, and some abandoned fields, invaded slowly by the dark woods. Things get a little better when we approach the coast; as the road climbs the chalk hills, the thin line of

The Wrath of the Iutes

sea, as grey and immovable as the clouds, peeks from between the trees. The shrill cries of seagulls fills the sky.

Closing our miserable procession are a couple of Graelon's men on mules, sent with us to ensure we board the ships safely – and Mullo. To my surprise, he resolved to come with us and sail with Marcus to Britannia, rather than stay in the Armorican's employ.

"I'm a soldier, not a butcher," he explained his decision to me. "Fighting Bacauds and bandits is dirty work. I'd rather fight these Scots, or Brigands, or whoever it is that the Britons need fighting. They sound like honourable enemies."

"I doubt Wortigern has coin enough to spend on mercenaries. Not as much as Graelon."

He shrugged. "I just need a roof over my head and grain for potage. Anything beats retelling the same old war stories for the drunks at Rotomag in hope they buy me another mug of ale."

So at least Mullo knows what he wants to do; I'm still uncertain – or rather, I'm all but certain we're going home, unless something unexpected changes my mind. I just hope we can convince the crew of Graelon's ship to drop us off as near to Cantia as possible, somewhere on Britannia's southern coast. Ursula can see the resignation in my eyes; she rides at the back of the Iute pack, sulking.

The woods part, to reveal the coastal plain below, ending at a broad bay, lined with golden beaches. A small town rises at the far end of the Roman highway, focused around a neat harbour, and a low-lying island at the head of a river estuary, linked to the shore by a tidal causeway. Marcus halts. One of his men rides up from the rearguard.

"We're being followed," he reports.

The *Decurion* frowns. "How many?"

"Twenty, maybe more. A few horses."

"When did you notice?"

"An hour ago, when we stopped for rest. I… don't think they're hostile. They make no effort to hide themselves."

"Can't be too careful. Let's try to make it to that town before they reach us."

Marcus nods at me, and I call on my Iutes to pick up the pace as we start our descent towards the sea. It doesn't take long before the same rider returns again, with news that a couple of horsemen split from the group that follows us and are approaching fast along the middle of the highway, the only place where the ground is solid enough to gallop. The *Decurion* orders us to halt again, with a confused look.

"Come with me, *aetheling*," he says. "Let's see who these people are and why are they in such a hurry to meet us."

We ride back to the rear of our column, and wait for the two horses to reach us. As soon as they emerge from a dip in the road, I recognise one of them – by the dark auburn hair, flowing in the wind.

The Wrath of the Iutes

"Ahes?" Marcus exclaims. His face brightens, but his expression remains that of bewilderment. "What is she doing here?"

"Maybe we forgot something at the *villa*," I venture a jest.

We don't need to wait long for the solution to the mystery. Ahes and Warus – for it is the old man riding the other mare – reach us swiftly. Ahes breathes hard. I can see by the way she sits uncomfortably in her saddle that she's not used to riding such a long distance, and at speed – and Warus looks just as weary as a man his age would be after galloping for over a mile of uneven road.

"Take us with you," Ahes says after catching her breath.

"*Us?*" I ask.

"I have two dozen men with me, wanting to sail to Wortigern's help," she explains. "More will be here soon."

"Soldiers?" asks Marcus.

"Some of them. Some are sailors, who would go with you anyway – Warus is the captain of one of the ships my father promised you. But we're all warriors here, really – we have to be, to survive in this place. I myself killed a man," she boasts, "when the Bacauds attacked Worgium last summer."

The *Decurion* grimaces. "Does your father know about this?"

"He does not – and he doesn't need to. We're not his slaves. These men volunteered…"

Marcus bites his lower lip. "You must turn back and return to Worgium. I can't risk your father's anger, or he might retract what little he's offered."

"Before my father finds out about this, we'll be halfway to Scillonia!" says Ahes. "I don't care what he says. I want to help you fight the Scots. I want to see the land of my father – I want to see the world!" Her eyes gleam with sweat and excitement. "You've told me so much of what's outside Armorica – and I've never seen anything beyond Redones."

"We're going to a war, not to see the sights." Marcus shakes his head and tugs the rein to turn around. I grasp his wrist.

"Wait," I say. I recognise Ahes's lust for adventure; I feel responsible for igniting it with my stories. I know if I let her go back now, to her small, isolated town, to the cruel, gruelling life on her father's *villa*, among crucified Bacauds and whipped slaves, she will inevitably grow up to be just like all the other Armoricans around her: callous, narrow-minded, dull. We have a chance to change her life, just like Aegidius changed mine by taking me to Gaul. If I left her here, I would always feel guilty about it.

"What have we got to lose?" I say. "I'm sure Ahes and Warus can order the ships out to sea just as well as Graelon. Am I right?"

The Wrath of the Iutes

Warus nods. "She is the *Comes*'s daughter," he says. "Until Lord Graelon's orders say otherwise, the men will heed her every command as if his own."

We ride away a few steps, and I lean over to Marcus's ear. "Come now, Marcus," I whisper. "I know you want her to come with us."

His cheeks burn crimson. "I… It has nothing to do with what I want. I can't disobey the *Comes*."

"*You're* not disobeying him. *She* is. I'm sure we can work something out. You could always say that she misled you – that she told you her father sent her."

"I will not lie. Not like this."

"Fine, then don't. I doubt you'll ever need to worry about that. I bet you won't even see Graelon again. But you *will* see Ahes – every day, if you agree to take her on. And those two dozen men with her are not something to sneer at, either. Even if they're not soldiers, yet. I helped save Trever with half that number, and my men were farmers and fishermen when we started."

He looks over his shoulder. Ahes's little army appears on the hilltop. They're not marching in any sort of order – scattered all over the road, with a train of mules and slaves in tow. I doubt most of them would be good for anything other than spear fodder, and Marcus must know this, too; but it's better than nothing, which is what he would be returning to Britannia with otherwise.

"You would come with us, too?" he asks.

"I... I don't know," I say, surprised at the suddenness of the question.

"Two dozen untrained Armoricans is one thing. Ash's son and his band of lute heroes... That's something that would put a smile on Wortigern's face, at least. And *you'd* get to see Ahes every day, too," he adds with a grin.

Has he been talking to Ursula?

"I would need to ask my men," I tell him. "They are weary, and I promised to take them home before winter."

"Think of how you could change their mind," he says. "And I will think of how I can accommodate Ahes's request."

He trots back to the Armoricans. "You can come with us to the harbour," he says, looking somewhere above Ahes's head. "I will let you know my decision once we reach the ships."

The Wrath of the Iutes

PART 2 – DUMNONIA

CHAPTER VI
THE LAY OF SULIEN

Graelon's ships, some half a dozen of which are anchored in the Gesocribate harbour, are of the kind I haven't seen before. Smaller than Aegidius's *liburna*, they're about the size of a Roman merchant's galley, but longer and sleeker, as befits a warship. With only a dozen oars on each side for manoeuvring the ship in shallow waters, their main propulsion is two large square sails of bleached cloth, one in the middle, the other hanging off the bow. If anyone had any doubt that these are warships rather than unusual trading vessels, each one is armed with a bronze ram on the bow, and their sides are secured with raised rails upon which hang iron armour plates. Raised on a platform at the aft end of several of the ships are some large devices, shielded from rain with cloth. I'm guessing these are small versions of siege weapons, a *ballista* or a *catapult* of sorts.

Ahes selects the two ships Graelon agreed to give us: the *Maegwind*, captained by Warus, and the *Seahorse*; the *Maegwind* being the largest of all in the harbour, its mainsail decorated with the painting of a dark-haired woman in Briton robes. I embark on the *Maegwind* with Marcus, half of his soldiers, and Ahes, accompanied by her countrymen, while Ursula, the Iutes and the rest of the *equites* board the smaller *Seahorse*. As soon as we clear the harbour, the second, smaller sail unfurls in front, pulling us on the strong southerly wind – a device I've only seen on Aegidius's *liburna* before.

The Wrath of the Iutes

We reach our first stop long before twilight, and halt there, waiting for the winds to change to carry us further north. The small island, little more than a breeze-swept grey rock, is inhabited by a few fishermen and shepherds, speaking some garbled version of the Gaulish tongue that only our ship's captain seems to understand; but its harbour is surprisingly large, if long abandoned, and overlooked by what appear to be ruins of a substantial pagan temple, incorporating a still-functioning beacon tower.

"Uxant may be small, but it's marked on even the oldest of sea maps," Warus explains. "Back in the day, every tin ship would stop here for water and timber on the way to Iberia and Italia. But that is something only my grandfather remembers. Now if there are any merchants coming from Britannia – and they are few and far between – they prefer a safer harbour on the mainland, like our Gesocribate."

It takes longer to reach the next harbour. We set out with the morning tide, and by evening I still see no trace of land. This is by far the longest I've ever sailed, and the first time I lose sight of the shore. Whatever secret art our helmsmen use to navigate this empty, featureless expanse, must be verging on magic.

As the waves rise in the strong wind, so does the heaving and rolling of the deck beneath my feet. On wobbly legs, I stumble up to the rail, next to Ahes. She stares out into the horizon, unperturbed by the waves and the ice-cold spray splattering against our faces. I close my eyes and take a few deep breaths, until the churning in my stomach calms down.

"I've never been this far out to sea," I tell her. "What about you?"

"Only once, when we fled… *moved* to Armorica," she replies. "But I was only a child then."

"And have you sailed again since?"

"A few times along Armorica's coast… Once to Burdigala, with a wine transport."

"Then you've never been back to Britannia."

She turns to me. "My father never wanted to go back there. Bad memories."

"Your mother," I guess.

"She died giving birth to me – in the middle of a battle. Father was busy fighting off the enemy. Scots, Brigands or Picts… I can't remember." She shrugs. "They couldn't even say goodbye." She wipes her eyes with a quick motion. "This ship, *Maegwind*, is named after her," she adds.

"Is that her on the sail?"

"It's supposed to be, though whoever painted it hasn't seen her, and made her look more like the Virgin Mary." She laughs, then grows thoughtful again as she stares towards the horizon. I notice she's standing on tiptoes, holding tight to the rail, as if in that way she could see the distant shore sooner.

The Wrath of the Iutes

"I can't wait to see Britannia," she says. "Warus told me so much about it – the sandy beaches, the rolling hills, the broad valleys, the mist-shrouded mountains…"

"Mountains?" I frown. "There are no mountains where I'm from. Only the Downs and sea cliffs."

"There are true mountains in Britannia." *Decurion* Marcus joins us at the rail. He fares better on the deck than I do, but he, too, is struggling to stay upright, and his face is the colour of rotten cheese. "In the West and the North. Jagged towers of sheer, sharp rock. Eagles nest in their peaks. Their slopes give birth to clouds."

"I, too, would like to see those one day," I say.

"Then come with us," says Marcus. "It's not far from Wortigern's fortress in Gangania to the foothills of the nearest range. On a clear day, you can see the snow-covered peaks of the Oriri."

"You're leaving us?" asks Ahes with a tinge of regret.

"There's still some time." I smile weakly. I've been stalling the final decision, unable to make up my mind, though I already promised Seawine and the Iutes I'd send them home from the nearest harbour, even if I myself decide to go on. As for Ursula and myself… Now that I've rested and feasted in Graelon's *villa*, had a good night's sleep in a warm, dry room, I'm no longer the weary, famished, confused shell of a man I was at Redones. Suddenly, the prospect of seeing some new, exotic part of the world, even if it is only the other side of Britannia, sounds more appealing than simply going back to the mud huts at Rutubi.

And it's not just that. There's another reason why I'm not keen to go back. Something Ursula said in the tavern in Redones has been bothering me ever since. In Cantia, my father is the king, his word a command, his shadow long; but outside of it, I am my own man. And here, just like Ursula said, I am so much more than my father – I am a victorious commander, a world-weary traveller, a Hero of Trever, a leader of men. Am I really ready to throw all that away and go back to being just Octa, the son and the subject of *Rex* Aeric?

"When do we reach Britannia?" I ask Marcus.

"Patience. First, we have to make one more stop – at Scillonia. And we're almost there – look." He points, not to the horizon, but to the sky. The grey clouds part; a bright, late summer sun beams high in the blue sky; the wind turns into a gentle breeze, propelling us smoothly and steadily onwards, as the prow cuts the waves with none of the leaps and heaves we had to endure earlier.

"There's always good weather on Scillonia," says Marcus. "You'll both love it there, I'm sure. It's like an oasis in the desert, a green jewel. The people are a little rough around the edges, but they're honest and hard-working."

"It sounds like a paradise," I say.

"It might as well be. I was thinking of moving there myself in my old age." He turns to me. "And it might be of interest to you in particular, Octa. There are always ships

The Wrath of the Iutes

coming and going from Scillonia's harbour – it's a great crossroad of winds and currents. I'm sure you'll have no trouble finding someone willing to take you and your men to Cantia, should you make your mind up by then. Who knows, if you're fortunate, this might be the last day you and your men spend in our company."

"Not forever, I hope."

"I hope so, too," says Ahes with a sweet, sad smile.

"When was the last time you were here?"

The island itself indeed resembles the Garden of Eden Marcus described: a lush green jewel bound with a ring of beaches gleaming bright gold in the dazzling sun; but the harbour itself – a sheltered crescent of sand, nestled on the island's north-eastern coast – presents a vision of Hell.

There are no ships in port; the wharf lies empty, as does the large building overlooking the shore, which I'm guessing was built to accommodate the passing merchants and their goods. A few fishing boats are strung out onto the sand, abandoned. A large shipwreck, dark and crumpled by the tides, lies overturned on the rocks to the south of the bay's entrance. The only road from the harbour divides the village into two parts, before crossing the dunes, turning around a steep hill and disappearing further inland. The southern side of the village is razed almost to the ground, save for a few bits of stone wall and chimneys. Between them, rectangular patches of rubble mark the foundations; when the houses still stood, they must've resembled those in the Roman villages in Gaul and mainland Britannia. Some of the houses on the northern side, clusters of round huts in the old Briton style, have their low, whitewashed walls charred and their thatched roofs patched with hides, but for the most part, appear untouched by whatever disaster befell the other part.

Both sides are deadly quiet. No smoke rises from any of the roofs. A lonely goat bleats in some enclosure, hidden from view.

"Three years ago," says Marcus. His face is the same colour as the ash from the burnt huts. He stares, bewildered, at the destruction before us.

"What happened here?" asks Ahes. "Pirates?"

"The Scots don't come this far south," Marcus replies, shaking his head slowly. "And they wouldn't destroy just one half of the village…"

We wait for the *Seahorse* to moor beside us. Marcus and I take a few men each and tell the others to stay on the ship, ready to set sail at a moment's notice, while we ride out to investigate the mystery of the abandoned village.

Up close, the silence is even more eerie. Even the goat stops bleating, wary of our arrival. A cuckoo calls somewhere in the dunes to the east. A lizard flees from under my feet. Wind picks up sand from among the cobbles – it's a good road, in the village, but it turns into a dirt path as it winds higher up into the dunes. Weeds and ivy grow over the ruins south of the road; but on the northern side, the grass is

The Wrath of the Iutes

freshly grazed, and the vegetable patches are well kept. I send Seawine to check inside one of the larger huts.

"How long do you think it's been like this?" I ask Marcus. "Whatever *this* is…"

"Judging by how tall these weeds have grown, I'd say at least since late spring," he replies. "I just don't understand… This place was always so peaceful…"

Seawine hurries out of the hut. "The hearth is still warm," he says. "They can't have gone far."

I glance nervously to the ridge of the long, terraced hill rising over the village to the south. It's topped with a wood of dwarf trees, gnarled and twisted by the sea breeze, but packed densely enough to hide a small army.

"We should get back to the ships," I say, feeling suddenly cold despite the bright sun shining straight in my face.

We mount up, but before we can turn, the dwarf forest erupts with the shrieks and howls of a band of several dozen men, charging towards us. Uncertain whether to treat them as enemies, or just frightened locals, we let them surround us without drawing our weapons. They are armed with primitive spears, clubs and axes, but their leader wields a long *spatha* and wears a battered Legionnaire's helmet. Her skin is painted with swirls of blue and black pigment, her hair spiked with lime. I glance to Marcus and we both shake heads. We could cut our way back to the ships through this rabble, but not without heavy losses – and we still don't know if the men are truly hostile. It might all be a misunderstanding…

"Which one of you is the commander?" asks the woman with the sword, speaking Vulgar with the same melodic lilt as Marcus.

The *Decurion* raises his hand.

"First, tell the rest of your men to stay on those ships," the woman says. "If even one of them steps foot on the shore, we'll kill you all."

I nod at Seawine. "You heard her."

"I can't leave you like this, *Hlaford*…"

"We'll be fine. The *Decurion* knows these people; he knows they won't hurt us – right, Marcus?"

Marcus nods with an uneasy grimace.

"I think so," he says.

The spearmen part to open a narrow path for Seawine to ride back to the ships, then close it up again.

"Your weapons," the leader commands.

"Who are you to order us like this?" Marcus asks brusquely.

"My name is Sulien," she replies.

"Are you the chieftain of this place?"

The Wrath of the Iutes

Sulien laughs. "There are no chieftains on Scillonia. But I am someone who can order these men to skewer you with their spears, and that should suffice you for an answer."

Marcus unsheathes his *spatha* and throws it to the ground. Ursula and I follow, as do the two *equites* accompanying us.

"Now, get down from those mounts." Sulien waves at one of her men, who comes forth with a length of rope.

I dismount, but Ursula hesitates.

"What — what are you going to do to us?" she asks.

"Don't worry, girl," Sulien replies. "We're no slavers. We're just going to ask you a few questions — and if we like the answers, we'll send you all on your way. Except your *Decurion*."

They tie up our hands and lead us to the same large hut Seawine investigated earlier. Sulien bids us sit down by the hearth. A dark-haired woman, half her face painted with a blue pattern of spirals and flowers, gets to work on restarting the fire.

With the flames casting her shadow menacingly on the daub wall, Sulien towers above us, her hands on her hips.

"Who sent you?" she demands. "Dumnonians? Armoricans? Rome?"

"*Rome?*" Marcus guffaws incredulously. "Why would Rome want to come here?"

"Please – we're only weary travellers on our way to Britannia," I say. "We stopped here for the night."

"In two warships?" Sulien scoffs. "A likely story. I know all kinds of ships that ply these waters. These are no merchant galleys. You came here to fight."

"We are going to fight, yes," admits Marcus. "But not here – not you. We had no idea there was anyone *to* fight here. Scillonia was always a haven of peace…"

Sulien turns to him sharply. "You've been here before?"

"Several times. I'm a Dumnonian, from Isca."

"Then you *did* come from Dumnonia. I thought I recognised the accent." She rubs the tip of her nose. "Is Urbanus still your *Comes*?"

"That he is."

"These can't be Dumnonian vessels. Who else helped you?"

"Enough with the questions!" Marcus snaps. "You have no reason to treat us like this. We did you no wrong. We came here as guests, expecting a welcome. I don't know who you think we are, but you are mistaken. We have no quarrel with you or your people."

The Wrath of the Iutes

"Then… you did not come here to punish us?"

"*Punish* you?" asks Ursula. "Punish you for what?"

Sulien stares at her, as if it has dawned on her at last that we truly don't know what she's talking about.

"You don't need to know," she replies.

"She means what they did to the other half of the village," I say, looking straight into her eyes. "How long did you think you'd manage to keep this a secret? How many ships' crews have you destroyed since the massacre? I bet that wreck on the reefs didn't get there on its own…"

"We – we had to," she says. For a moment, the mask of a tough soldier drops, and I catch a glimpse of a frightened woman, in a situation beyond her experience and abilities. "To defend ourselves – to defend our faith…"

"Your faith?" Marcus asks. "What do you mean by that? And where's Tiberianus?"

The mention of the name brings a furious scowl to Sulien's face. "Enough." She kicks the *Decurion* to shut him up. "We'll keep you here until morning as I figure out what to do with you." She nods at the dark-haired woman, who brings us a jug of water and some dark, flat bread.

"You can't keep us here forever," says Marcus as Sulien turns to the door. "If we're not back by tomorrow, my men will assume you've killed us already, and come to avenge me."

"We'll be ready for them," Sulien replies, but then she turns back with a conflicted grimace. "You, come with me," she says, pointing at Ursula.

"Where are you taking her?" I protest.

"Calm down. I'm only taking her with me to the women's hut. You'll be spending all night here. It wouldn't be proper for you to all stay together."

"I don't mind," says Ursula. "I'm not going anywhere."

"Quiet, girl. Don't worry," Sulien tells me, "I will not touch a hair on her head. You have my word."

Ursula gives me a worried look. I glance at the armed men around us and lean back with a sigh. I nod. "Go, Ursula. I sense she's telling the truth. Besides, you know I'll always come for you if you're ever in danger."

They drag her out and leave us alone, still tied down, facing the dying fire. I take a sip of water from the jug, held for me by Marcus, and realise I badly need a piss – I'm glad now Ursula's not here as I crawl my way to the corner of the hut and fumble ungainly at my belt with bound fingers. Some of it gets on my breeches.

"Who's Tiberianus?" I ask after crawling back to the *Decurion*.

It's my turn to help him drink; one of his men wipes the crumbs of the dark bread from his mouth and chin.

The Wrath of the Iutes

"A priest. There was never a church in Scillonia, so he would preach from home to home, or out in the fields. Everyone here respected him. He was already very old when I was last here, so I wouldn't be surprised if he has died since then – but I'm certain that as long as he lived, he would never have allowed whatever happened here."

"Sulien and her men didn't strike me as particularly pious. Did you recognise any of them?"

He shakes his head. "No, but then I didn't spend much time outside the harbour."

"What were you doing here, anyway?"

"I was a merchant's guard before I became an *eques*," he replies. "Only for a few years. We'd stop here sometimes to wait for a change of winds, or for repairs if the storm caught us on the way."

An owl hooting outside tells us the dusk is drawing near. The flames crackle and hiss as they peter out. The inside of the hut grows cold. I yawn.

"We should try to get some sleep," Marcus decides. "No point wasting strength on idle talk. Tomorrow, hopefully, we'll know what they want to do with us. Besides, if my men decide to rescue us tonight, it's best if we are rested."

"Do you really think they'll come?"

"If I trained them well enough, they will," the *Decurion* says with a satisfied grin.

James Calbraith

Marcus shakes me awake.

"What…"

"Shush."

There's somebody on the roof. In the darkness, I hear them climb the rafters of the tall, conical roof, rustling the straw with their feet.

"I told you they'd come," Marcus whispers.

They stop in the far corner, over the spot where I took a piss earlier. I hear a blade cutting through the rafters, then someone tearing at the thatch with their bare hands. I glance nervously to the door; I know there are at least two guards outside, in a small courtyard bound with a low stone wall. I'm sure they must hear all this noise – but then I remember they're not soldiers, just some frightened villagers, and they must have both fallen asleep by now.

At last, a dim, blue light of the moon appears in the hole, bright enough for me to see the hands of the man on the other side, working fast on the opening with what looks like a sickle. At length, he digs out a hole large enough to squeeze through.

"Come, quick!" he whispers. I still can't see his face in the darkness.

"Who's there?" asks Marcus. "Gratian? Albanus?"

The Wrath of the Iutes

The man doesn't reply, only repeats his urgings. We scramble to our feet. With our hands still bound, our escape is a clumsy one. I let Marcus go first through the hole. He makes a dreadful din as he trips and falls out like a sack of wheat. This *had* to awaken the guards. I rush after the *Decurion*, but I get my tunic stuck on a broken rafter. The guards burst into the hut, one of them bearing a torch and a knife, the other a club. Somebody pulls on my hand, just as one of Marcus's men pushes me from behind. The tunic tears, the rafter breaks and I tumble out onto the dirt below.

"We'll hold them back," cries one of the *equites* – young Drustan, if I'm not mistaken. "Save yourself, *Decurion*!"

"Don't be fools," I shout back, but Marcus pushes me away from the hole in the roof.

"We'll come back for you, Drustan!" the *Decurion* calls, and pulls me away from the hut as it erupts in the noises of battle. "They're soldiers," he tells me. "They know what they're doing."

Our rescuers – I can see three men before me in the gloom – slash our binds and lead us out of the village, onto the high ground to the north.

"Wait, the ships are that way," I protest.

"They're too heavily guarded," one of the men says. "We'd never get through that way."

"Hold on!" Marcus grabs him and turns his face to the moonlight. "You're not my men. Who are you?"

"No time," the man replies. "We have to hurry."

"What about Ursula?" I say.

"Please – Sulien will follow us with her entire band," the man pleads. "We need to get to the marshes; we'll lose them there."

"The *marshes*?"

Torches light up, and shouts ring out between the huts and head our way in a great mass. We have no choice but to trust our unexpected saviours and follow them away from the harbour, over the dunes, past the rocky outcrops and the forest of dwarf, gnarled trees. I hear the pursuit close behind us. Our guides lead us in a winding path through the woods and hedges, over the drystone walls that divide the fields, until at last my feet splash into a pool of deep, sticky mud. I grab Marcus's sleeve to keep from falling into the dense reeds.

"Up here," our guide whispers.

We follow him through the reeds, onto a briny marsh, which soon turns into a current of sea water, knee-deep at first, but quickly rising with the tide. I glance over my shoulder – I can no longer see our pursuers, but I can still hear them, splashing and shouting in the distance.

"How… much… further?" I ask through chattering teeth. We now wade through water waist-high; already cold after the night on the floor of the hut, I'm now freezing.

"Almost there."

The Wrath of the Iutes

The ground under my feet begins to rise, until at long last we climb out, splashing, onto more mud, then dry land – a patch of soft rock and grass, rising further into a gentle slope. We cross some more of those drystone, weathered walls and emerge onto a vast, empty field, with a shadow of some steep, tall outcrop, overgrown with ferns, looming in the centre in the moonlight.

Our guides approach the outcrop – and disappear from sight. For a confused moment, I can't figure out what happened to them; then a hand holding a small oil lamp appears in a hole at our feet.

"Down here. Careful."

I kneel down and feel around first; I touch a step, carved in stone. Following the light of the oil lamp, I descend into a short, narrow, dark corridor, from which I emerge into a larger chamber, lit up with more oil lamps and some candles. On the walls of the chamber, made up of great boulders piled into a domed vault, I see symbols scratched with chalk: a *chrismon*, a cross and some roughly scribbled letters.

In the light of the lamps I can now take a good look at the three men who brought us here; they all wear tunics of green wool, lined with yellow ribbon. The one whose voice I heard in the darkness is the oldest, with speckles of grey in his long hair, bound with a thin silver wire; a broad-bladed knife hangs at his belt in a leather sheath, and a thick golden ring with a large, carved jewel adorns his left hand.

It's cramped in the chamber with all of us inside, but the man with the knife insists that we all must stay well away from the entrance.

"In an hour or so, the tide will rise too high for pursuit," he says. "In the meantime, it's best if we hide here."

"What is this place? Who are you?" asks Marcus.

"This… is a tomb of the Ancients," the man replies. "It was here long before any of us arrived in these islands. But it's a chapel now." He puts a hand to his chest. "I am Felix, these are Aesuc and Petiac."

"You must be survivors from that burnt side of the village," I guess. Felix nods.

"How many of you are there?" asks Marcus.

"Eleven," Felix says to our gasps. The village would have accommodated at least fifty people before the destruction. "You'll meet the rest in the morning."

"We don't have time," Marcus says. "We have to get back to our ships, and save our men."

The men look at each other nervously. "We… We were hoping you could help us."

"Of course, I understand. And as soon as I free my men, I will be able to provide you with any assistance you require. I take it you want to be taken from here? We should be able to fit eleven people on the ships without too much trouble."

The Wrath of the Iutes

"No, no, lord, you misunderstand," Felix protests hurriedly. "We do not wish to leave our island. The Lord granted it to us like a sliver of his own Garden of Eden, to own and cultivate. We could not possibly leave it to these heathens."

"*Heathens?*" I ask. "Then I was right – Sulien and her people are not Christians."

"Most folk on Scillonia aren't."

Marcus rubs his face wearily. "I understand your predicament, Felix, but I have neither men nor time to fight your war for you. I am urgently needed elsewhere. Perhaps after we get you to Dumnonia, my master Urbanus could send an expedition…"

"You misunderstand us again," says Felix. "We want not for war with Sulien, only for someone like yourself to facilitate a peace between us."

"I am not a priest. Nor a diplomat."

"But you are the first man of any power or standing to land here since… since Tiberianus died."

"And what does Tiberianus's death have anything to do with this?"

The three men look at each other again. "Perhaps we should tell the story from the beginning," proposes one of them.

"Perhaps you should," Marcus agrees. "If, as you say, we have to stay in this damp hole for another hour…"

"Seventy years ago, two men were brought to our shore on a Roman ship," Felix begins. In the far corner of the chamber, water drips through cracks in the vaulted roof, like a strumming string of a lute accompanying his words. "One, older, was Instantius, a bishop from Iberia, though we did not know yet what that meant at the time. The other, younger, was Tiberianus, his pupil."

"A bishop?" Marcus wonders. "What was a bishop doing here?"

"We thought he had been sent here to bring the word of the Lord to these heathen islands," Felix replies. "Much later, we learned they were both exiled here for following a man called Priscillian, whom the Church in Rome condemned for heresy."

"Another heresy spreading in Britannia." Marcus shakes his head. "Truly, this land must have been cursed for some past sins."

"We did not care about any of that," says Felix. He clutches a pendant under his tunic, a small wooden cross. "Instantius was a great and godly man, and Tiberianus even more so. Between the two of them, they taught and baptised many of us Scillonians, and we Faithful grew into a substantial community."

The Wrath of the Iutes

"Until you had to divide the harbour town between yourselves and the heathens," I say.

"For many years, the heathens treated us as little more than a curiosity," Felix replies. "We lived peacefully side by side – as long as there were few enough of us to not be seen as a threat to those worshipping the old gods."

"Then they started to fear you."

"Not without reason," Felix admits. "There were many, like myself, who were blind to what the others in our community did. Instantius and Tiberianus never preached to anyone who didn't go to them first. They knew they were only guests here. But when we grew stronger, some started talking about *forcing* the heathens to see the Light of the Lord."

"That never ends well," I note.

"As long as Tiberianus lived, those who preached this sort of aggression kept mostly to themselves…"

"I met Tiberianus three years ago," says Marcus. "He was frail, then, but still of sound mind."

"He would've died not long after you met him," says Felix. "Things quickly fell apart without his holy guidance. The impetuous men took over, and brought threat of violence to our communities, led by one called Clemens. He called himself the apostle, a bringer of light against the darkness… His followers would gather in large groups and march through the heathen villages with holy banners and trumpets... They'd interrupt the pagan rituals, throw mud at the idols and altars, desecrate the holy groves."

"As they should have," says Marcus. "It is the duty of every Christian to fight the demons."

"With respect, commander," Felix replies, his voice gentle but firm, "it is easy to preach this when you have the might of Roman arms behind you. Here, peaceful methods have always yielded better results. Violence brought not a single man to our Lord."

"So this is what Sulien meant when she said they had to defend their faith," I muse. "But, throwing mud, marching and shouting, none of this sounds like something warranting the destruction we saw at the harbour."

Felix nods and falls silent for a moment, as if he can't bring himself to tell the final part of the story. The pause allows me to reflect on what I've heard so far.

Here is yet another version of the same old tale that repeats itself from Cantia to Armorica. Men seeking refuge in a faraway land, among strangers, with different customs, faiths, language... Is it inevitable that their arrival breeds resentment and hostility? The Cants feared and despised the Iutes, even though the only crime my people were guilty of was not succumbing to the squalor of Tanet; instead thriving and growing stronger. The Britons arriving in Armorica entangled themselves in a bloody conflict with the natives from the moment their first ship landed on the distant shore... And even here, in tiny Scillonia, among a population that taken altogether can't be greater than that of a small

The Wrath of the Iutes

Briton town, the same sort of conflict has been simmering for more than a generation, before boiling over with disastrous consequences…

Surely, there must be another way. For a moment, it seemed, the two heretic priests here had found the solution to this conundrum; but the respect and patience they preached didn't last long beyond their passing. For every Instantius, trying to live in peace among his hosts, there was a Clemens, bringing fire and sword to the land he wanted to subdue; and after every Wortigern, welcoming the newcomers and appreciating the opportunities their arrival created, came a Wortimer, declaring the visitors 'invaders' and bringing his righteous wrath upon their hapless heads… A seemingly unending cycle of violence that will not end until this age of upheaval comes to a conclusion, and the tribes and nations stop their wanderings from land to land and settle down for good…

"It started just before the *Pascha*," Felix continues eventually. "First, the heathens gathered to celebrate the first sowing on their holy hill, south of the harbour. Ale and mead poured freely at the feast, and made their heads and hearts hot. When Clemens and his men came with their usual mocking and jeering, the heathen patience ran out. A great brawl broke out. Sulien emerged as a leader of the heathen band and routed the Christians… For a moment, there was peace."

"Often, the only way to bring peace is through war," says Marcus, nodding sagely.

"It did not last long," Felix says. "Not long after the brawl at the pagan feast, came the day of the *Pascha*. With no priest, we simply congregated to pray in our homes and in the fields, like Tiberianus taught us."

"I imagine Sulien and her men attacked these congregations," Marcus guesses.

"Not at all," Felix replies. "It was Clemens again. He promised to deal with the heathen menace once and for all. Many doubted him – we were outnumbered, and some of the heathens, like Sulien herself, had once served as mercenaries in Britannia; but Clemens claimed that the sword and the shield of the Lord were with him, and that was enough to convince a great number of us. Instead of praying for peace, he led his band marching through the heathen side of the town and put fire to the houses."

"That explains the scorch marks on the walls and roofs," I remark.

"This was too much for Sulien. She fought back fiercely; Clemens died, as did many of his followers. The rest, you've seen for yourself. The heathens, burning with vengeance, pursued all Christians throughout Scillonia, whether they were followers of Clemens or not. Those who survived, scattered to places like here, where the high tide cuts us off from the mainland twice a day, and waited for salvation…"

"How many altogether?" I ask. "There has to be more than just the eleven of you here…"

The Wrath of the Iutes

"I don't rightly know. We rarely dare to meet with the others. Fifty, maybe? Some sailed to the southern island; we haven't heard from them in months."

Marcus shakes his head and stands up, as tall as the vaulted chamber allows. He turns his back to Felix and sighs.

"We are not your salvation. We are just travellers on our way to Britannia."

"The Lord works in mysterious ways."

"Perhaps, but not this time. I don't know how to solve your troubles, other than take you from here to somewhere you can start your lives anew."

I stand up, too.

"I believe we should help them."

Marcus turns back to me, surprised.

"If there's anything I've learned from watching my father rule, it's that it's better to resolve conflicts with words than with swords," I say. "And he, himself, learned it from your master, *Dux* Wortigern. I am neither my father nor the *Dux*, but I have gained a little experience in Roman diplomacy, and I'm certain that between us, we can figure out how to bring peace to this beautiful island. Especially if it would mean saving your men and Ursula without a fight."

Felix's face beams. "You are a Roman official?" he asks.

"He's just a barbarian youth," says Marcus with barely hidden scorn. "I'm sorry, Octa, I've seen you and your men fight, but you've barely weaned yourself off your mother's teat. I don't think —"

"My mother died when I was fourteen," I say coolly. "Killed by a man called Haesta. The man I fought against at Trever, when he was on the Saxon side… And who helped us defeat the Bacauds at the hillfort in Gaul."

Marcus ponders my words for a moment. "Yes, I see what you're getting at. But what would you propose we do?"

"I don't know yet. But whatever we do, we need to do it quickly. In a few hours, our men on the ships will grow impatient with lack of news. I fear they might do something hasty if we don't go back before then."

"On that, we both agree." Marcus nods. "Whether to talk, or to fight, we have to get back to the harbour. Felix, how long before that tide recedes?"

"Four hours after dawn, lord."

"And there's no way to get back quicker?"

"What about the boat by the hermits' cells?" asks one of Felix's companions.

"The hermits?" I ask.

"A few followers of Tiberianus chose the path of asceticism, shutting themselves from the worldly temptations on the rocks just off the southern shore," explains Felix. "Sulien's people leave them alone, so we store provisions in their cells. We use a small boat to reach them at high tide."

Marcus tightens his sword belt and rubs the tip of his nose with a deep sigh.

"It will have to do."

CHAPTER VII
THE LAY OF SILVIA

Some twenty men, most of them Marcus's *equites*, press against a thin line of Scillonians, who try to bar them from leaving the wharf. There is no violence, yet – only a lot of shouting, pushing and waving fists in each other's faces. I notice Mullo and Ahes in front, shouting the loudest and pushing the strongest. Seawine and my Iutes stand in the back, watching this uproar with their arms crossed and their faces grim.

"We haven't heard from our commander and the officers since yesterday!" clamour the *equites*. "How do we even know they're still alive?"

"I can help you with that," says Sulien. She approaches the line and gestures at her men, who drag one of the two soldiers we left behind, barely conscious, his face and body black and blue in bruises. The Scillonians throw him in the sand before the raging *equites*.

"Your companions tried to escape last night," says Sulien. "We had to make an example of one of them. Don't worry, he'll live – but if you want the others to remain unharmed, you'll have to *stand back*!" She shouts the last word and stomps her foot, but the soldiers pay no heed to the threat.

"Show us Marcus," cries Ahes. "What do you want with him, anyway?"

"You'll see your precious commander as soon as I'm satisfied you are no threat to us," replies Sulien.

"And how are you going to do that – if I'm right here?" Marcus asks, emerging from our hiding place in a clump of bracken.

There was only enough space for the two of us on Felix's boat – more a raft, really, a wobbly construction of reed and hide; we arrived, paddling furiously against the receding tide, on the northern end of the harbour, just in time to witness the morning confrontation.

Seeing us alive and well, the *equites* finally break through the line of Scillonians. Ahes runs up to us with open arms; I step back to let Marcus be the first to welcome her embrace. Sulien's warriors, in danger of being overrun by *Decurion*'s soldiers, pull swiftly back, beyond the line of a barricade of tree trunks and boulders, which they must have thrown overnight across the road. She calls on a war horn, and the

The Wrath of the Iutes

rest of her men pour forth from the huts – dragging Ursula and Drustan with them.

"One more step, and these two die!" Sulien cries as her men put knives to the hostages' throats.

"Not this again," Ursula groans. She seems unharmed, only greatly annoyed. I'm relieved to see Sulien has kept her word.

Felix steps forward. "We are not here to fight you, Sulien," he announces, raising his hands.

"*You.*" Sulien seethes. "I knew *you* were behind all this. How did you manage to send a message to Britannia?"

"We had never seen this man before last night," I say. "What will it take for you to believe us?"

"They're telling the truth, my love," Felix pleads. "Please, these good men agreed to help us end this conflict…"

"Hold on –" I grab Felix's shoulder. "What do you mean *my love*?"

"You haven't even told them that?" Sulien says with a mocking smile.

"Told us what?"

"Sulien is –" Felix starts.

"– *was*," Sulien corrects him.

[164]

"In my heart and before the Lord you still are, and forever will be," says Felix.

"She's his wife," Ursula says. Sulien gives her an icy stare, which Ursula ignores as she pushes the rusty blade from her neck and steps away.

Marcus hides his face in his hands with a loud groan. "By Lord's wounds, this is much worse than some tribal strife – this is a lovers' quarrel!"

"Yes, I was once a follower of Tiberianus," admits Sulien. "Though not because I worshipped his desert God – because Tiberianus was a good and wise man."

"But you agreed to wed me before the Lord," says Felix.

"It was obviously important enough for you," says Sulien. "I saw no reason to deny you this small favour."

I wipe sweat from my brow. We sit in a blazing sun, on the bald top of the terraced hill overlooking the harbour, gathered around a stone altar inside a drystone wall circle. Remnants of thick oak pillars remember a roof they once supported. A ring of fern and bramble as thick as mail coat surrounds the summit. I rub my itching hands where the thorns scratched at my skin as we climbed up the narrow, overgrown path.

This is the very temple where the brawl between Clemens and Sulien turned the simmering conflict into an all-out war.

The Wrath of the Iutes

Felix agreed to this location for the talks as a sign of goodwill. Behind me and Marcus are some of Felix's fellow Christians, who waded across the low tide from the northern islet. Behind Sulien are her heathens, still insisting on holding Ursula and Drustan hostage, despite Marcus giving his word that his soldiers will keep peace in the harbour for the duration of the discussion – and despite Ursula clearly not being too worried for her safety in Scillonian hands.

I can see trepidation in Sulien's eyes. Now that all of our men have disembarked from the two ships, to wait for the outcome of our meeting on the beach and at the wharf, she finally must have realised what power she stood against. Never before has a warship carrying a troop of Roman cavalry landed on these shores – let alone two of them. She must know that holding two of our men hostage in no way guarantees her safety; and that were she to harm Ursula or the young officer, we would have no qualms about razing the town and slaughtering her people in revenge.

"And have you asked him to be wedded in the heathen rite, in exchange?" I ask.

"There was no need," she replies. Her gaze softens as she looks at Felix. "In my heart, I knew I loved him, so why involve the gods? It would only hurt him if I insisted on having our hands fastened at the Sulewi's altar, as was our custom before the priests came."

"Look at you both," says Marcus. "You loved each other so deeply once, and now you're ready to kill each other... And for what? You –" He turns to Felix. "You know Sulien had to defend her home and people from Clemens's aggression. And you –" He turns back to Sulien. "You know Felix and his followers had no part in those attacks. So why insist on continuing this senseless conflict?"

Neither of the two replies. Instead, they lower their heads and drop their gazes to the ground. I look around at the heathens and Christians gathered on both sides of the altar; I see no bloodthirst or vengeance burning in the eyes of anyone, only weariness and gloom. They all know that if the war continues like this, soon there will be no one left alive on Scillonia. The Christians are too scattered among the distant islands, too afraid to sail the shallow sea for fear of retribution – and the remaining heathens are too few to sustain the population, especially now that the ships from Britannia have become wary of stopping at the harbour. An empty, barren island, overgrown with weed and fern is their future if they don't come to an agreement.

"I'll tell you why," says Ursula. She pushes away the man holding her hostage; he lets her go without resistance. "It's shame. And guilt. You, Felix, are ashamed you didn't do enough to stop Clemens from escalating the conflict until it was too late. That much is clear. And you, Sulien – though you won't admit it, you feel guilty for unleashing your wrath on Christians. You let your people kill or banish those you once thought as neighbours, friends – lovers. You are both victims of what Clemens did to your island."

Silence from Sulien and Felix is enough to confirm the truth in Ursula's words.

The Wrath of the Iutes

"If you still had a priest here, this would have been easy to solve," Ursula continues. "He would have told you that God forgives you, and absolved you of your sins…"

"I don't believe in any of this," Sulien protests.

"Maybe not, but you have lived among the Christians long enough to start thinking like them," I say. "I should know – I am the same, a heathen, tutored by the bishop of Londin. I know all too well how heavy the burden of sin can be."

"No priest would agree to sail all this way," says Felix, despondent. "We tried to send for one once. He wouldn't dare to come to this den of heresy and heathenry."

"And we wouldn't allow one to land, anyway," says Sulien. "Now that we know how letting Christians into our midst ends."

"But you don't need a priest," I say. "You said it yourself, Sulien." I put my hand on Felix's shoulders. Ursula does the same with Sulien, on the other side of the altar. "The Lord – or the gods, if you prefer – knows what's in your heart, just like they knew of your love for Felix…"

"Just like they know you *still* love him," says Ursula quietly. She squeezes Sulien's arms and pushes her gently towards Felix.

"Is this true, Sulien?" Felix whispers.

Sulien turns her eyes away; her cheeks burn red.

[168]

"I have seen enough bloodshed this year," I say, "all over Gaul. Saxons fighting Romans. Armoricans slaughtering Bacauds. They fought for land, gold, glory, plunder, slaves… All those reasons make sense. But you – you fight because of what someone else did a long time ago. Neither of you is truly responsible for the deaths of Clemens and his followers. Only they are – and they're already dead."

"Their book of good and bad deeds has already been written, and they will be judged for it," says Ursula. "But you still have a chance to change what's written in yours. You can persist in continuing this petty circle of vengeance, or you can choose to break it."

"Less than ten years have passed since our people fought a bloody battle at Eobbasfleot," I add, nodding at Ursula. "Now, they are the closest of allies – and we are the closest of friends. So believe me when I tell you: this doesn't have to go on like this."

In the heavy silence that follows, I step away from the altar and take Marcus aside.

"It's your turn now," I tell him.

"Mine? What more can I do?"

"Ursula and I are just a couple of youths, but you are a Briton *Decurion*. In the eyes of these people, you represent the power and dignity of Rome. Your word could be decisive here."

The Wrath of the Iutes

Marcus takes a look around the hilltop, approaches the altar and clears his throat.

"If... If you agree to lay down your weapons, I will make a request to my *Comes*, Urbanus of Dumnonia, to help you rebuild the town."

"And send us a priest?" Felix asks in a hopeful voice.

"I'll ask, but I wouldn't put your hopes up."

"We don't need more Roman priests," says Sulien. "And we don't need anyone's help rebuilding our homes." She leans against the altar. "Just tell your merchants it's safe to stop here again."

"Then you would have peace?" I ask.

"I would." She nods. "You're right, Ursula. All those months I felt guilt gnawing on my guts like a rat. I can't take staring at the burnt-out ruins of my village anymore. I can't take the silence. The empty harbour. I want life and laughter to return to the island."

"So do I, my love," says Felix. He reaches out to touch Sulien's hands, but she pulls back.

"I still haven't forgiven *you*," she says. "There are things... Things this man did, things he wouldn't dare to tell you about," she tells me and Marcus. "But it doesn't matter anymore. There are still good men on this island, among your people and mine. If God won't forgive us our sins, we will have to do it ourselves."

She stands up and turns to the small group of Christians. "Come back, whenever you're ready. Together, we will rebuild our town more splendid than ever before. And you, wise travellers –" She bows before me and Ursula. "You have my gratitude. The gods do work in mysterious ways."

A splendid view spreads from the top of the hill, over all of Scillonia. Right now, at low tide, it's once again a single great island, with dunes and rocky outcrops rising tall over the salty marsh, bound by a halo of islets, skerries and reefs. The harbour town below fights an unequal battle against the encroaching ocean.

"It really is beautiful here," I say. "It's hard to believe this is where all this violence happened."

"Where man goes, violence follows," Ursula says philosophically.

We're the only ones who remained at the summit. The Scillonians returned to the harbour town to discuss in detail how to bring peace back to the islands – while Marcus and his men got back to the ships to, at long last, gather provisions and prepare for the last part of their journey to Britannia; though with the negotiations lasting long into the afternoon, it looks like we will have to stay here another night.

"I'm sorry you had to go through all of this again," I say. "I promised you'd never –"

The Wrath of the Iutes

"It's fine." Ursula shrugs. "I wasn't worried for a moment. I could tell Sulien was more afraid than angry." She chuckles. "I'm getting good at this."

"How did you know so much about her and Felix?"

"We talked all through the night. Or rather, she talked. She may claim to be a heathen, but she was in dire need of a confession. Words poured from her like wine from an *amphora*. I've learned more about this place than I'd ever care to know."

"I hope she and Felix will be together again."

"I wouldn't bet on that."

"You know what she meant at the end, don't you?"

"I do." She purses her lips. "But I'm not telling."

She rests her elbows on the drystone wall, stares into the northern horizon and sighs.

"There are no other ships," she says. "We'll all have to sail to Britannia Prima together, after all. Looks like Fate made your choice for you."

"Seawine won't be joyful about this. I saw him in the harbour – he couldn't care less about the Scillonians; he was just annoyed at the delay."

She turns to me. "And what about you?"

There's no point pretending further. She knows me too well not to sense the yearning that the unperturbed line of the blue horizon stirs within me, within my very loins; beyond it, the whole world spreads itself before me like a beautiful woman, eager to receive me. There is nothing back home that would ever match this thrill.

"One day, your father will saddle you with some official duty, and you'll *have* to stay in Cantia, whether you like it or not," she says, mistaking my silence for still more hesitation. "And then, when you become a *Rex*, you'll never go anywhere again. Like your father, you'll become a prisoner of the wandering court. Why hurry back now?"

"You're right," I say. "I… I don't think I'm ready to go home yet."

"Oh, good." She smiles, relieved. "I feared I would have to leave you."

"What do you mean?"

"I thought I would have to sail with Marcus on my own."

"You would do that?"

"If I had to. There's nothing waiting for me in Cantia – and I agree with Ahes: there's too much of the world to see to stay in one place forever."

"What about your home – your parents…?"

The Wrath of the Iutes

"I'm not a child anymore, Octa. I don't need to worry about what my parents think. I'm old enough to have my own children – and they're not senile enough yet to need taking care of. And… I already have a husband, Lord bless him." A melancholy smile lingers on her lips. "Even if only before the pagan gods."

"A husband?" I don't understand. "Who –"

"I mean you, you fool. Meroweg did fasten our hands. Just before we helped kill him."

I laugh nervously. "That was a false wedding."

"Not to Meroweg. Not to Wotan and Friga, if you believe in them."

"*You* don't. And I'm not sure I do, either."

"Does it matter?" she scoffs. "Have we not just spent a few hours trying to convince Sulien and Felix that what truly counts is in our hearts, not what we promised before the gods?"

I swallow. "What – what are you saying?" My voice comes out a hoarse whisper.

She turns her back to me. A lark sings in the silence between us.

"You know, you'd be surprised how much time to think one has when held hostage," she says, at last. "And Sulien's misfortune wasn't the only thing we talked about last night."

"So you talked about – us?"

"I told her of my misfortunes in Gaul, of your pursuit of Haesta… And then she asked me the question I never stopped to ponder before: if we really *were* wedded, you and I, before your gods or mine… What would be different between us?"

"I don't understand."

"Even Marcus was surprised you did what you did for me – he wouldn't have wasted so much time and effort chasing after only one of his men."

"We are friends. Best friends. I would do the same for Audulf," I say, and I regret it immediately, seeing the disappointment marring her face. She laughs bitterly.

"Is that all I am to you? Another Audulf, only one you'd like to lie with?" She turns away. "In that case, forget about everything I just said. All the more reason for me to sail with Marcus. Maybe I can find a *real* husband among Ambrosius's Christians."

I spot the lark now – it's close, perched on a thin branch of a low birch tree, on the edge of the enclosure. It falls quiet when it notices me watching.

I reach out and take her hand. "No, you're right," I say. "I left Audulf with his injuries to chase after you. I left Bana behind in Britannia. I would never leave you like them," I say.

The Wrath of the Iutes

She turns around abruptly – I don't step back fast enough, and she falls into my arms. She doesn't pull away. Awkwardly, I wrap my arms around her.

"But Marcus is coming back to a land of war," I say, breathing in the smell of her neck. "These Scots seem terrible enemies. What if something happens to you – what if you die, or worse?"

"Then don't leave me. Send Seawine back, if he keeps groaning, but stay with me in Britannia."

I slide my hands down her back and reach her behind.

"Very well," I say. "I will guard you as a husband should guard a wife, if that's what you want."

She takes my hands away and pulls back with a frown. "I'm a shieldmaiden, not some weak city girl who needs protection. I would prefer if we guarded each other – as friends," she says, and before I can find a reply, she storms off, leaving me confused and aroused.

There's a wharf here, of a kind, one hewn by nature rather than men: a stretch of flat rock, huddled to the side of a great promontory jutting out into the sea, high and long enough for *Maegwind* to moor, with the *Seahorse* tied to its side. There's space for a few storage huts, pillars of an unfinished pier, and even a winch for picking up crates from the decks of merchant ships; but I see no sign of a settlement that would justify the presence of a harbour this size. There's not even enough space here for any kind of village – we are anchored at the edge of a deep cove, hemmed in on both sides by tall cliffs of wet, grey rock, with only a narrow gravel beach at the far end, leading nowhere, and steep, slippery, winding steps, disappearing at the top of the cliff.

I know nothing of this place. From what I gathered from Marcus, the headland we traced for the best part of the day was called Belerion; now, at last, we're in the *Decurion*'s home, the land of the Kerns in the *pagus* of Dumnonia – as far in Britannia's west as Cantia is in its east. The landscape here looks like nothing I've ever seen anywhere on the island: all dark, jagged cliff sides, pillars of rock, giant boulders, small inlets, hidden coves and promontories. Before we could approach the harbour we had to wait for a local pilot boat to guide us through the reefs and whirlpools. We might as well be in Armorica; no wonder the Briton nobles from here found it so appealing.

"We'll be spending the night here," says Marcus. "My men are staying on the ships – you can remain with them, or come with me, if you like."

"Come – where?"

"Up there." He raises his eyes to the top of the cliff.

"And what's up there?"

"Dun Taiel," he says, providing no further explanation. "I need to send a message to my *Comes* Urbanus about what happened at Scillonia."

The Wrath of the Iutes

"Can we march home from here?" asks Seawine, joining us with Ursula from the *Seahorse*.

Marcus scratches his head. "The roads are poor and winding in this part of the world. The Roman engineers never quite reached this far. And the frontier with the Belgs is unsafe at the best of times. You'd be better off waiting until Moridun. It's only another day of sailing, and will save you a week of marching."

Seawine groans, nods and leaps over the ship's side, going back to his men. I turn back to Marcus and Ahes.

"Do they have a tavern up there?" I ask.

"Of a sort. There is space enough for a few visitors."

I invite Ursula to join us, and the four of us begin the long climb up the narrow stairs. I still can't see the reason for this harbour to be here – the promontory appears even more remote than Scillonia; the coast is treacherous and desolate, and we haven't seen any other ship passing us either way all day. At long last, we climb out onto the promontory's bald, round summit.

"I don't know what I expected," says Ursula. "But certainly not this."

The summit is full of workers – carpenters, stone masons, woodsmen, swarming around scaffolds, foundation holes, half-built walls. In any other place in Britannia, I'd say they were all dismantling some ancient Roman construction – a great bath house or an amphitheatre; but there are no Roman buildings here; no old structures at all. I don't think I have seen anything like this on the island before: a brand-new construction site.

"What are they building here?" I ask.

"It started as one of the new harbours for the Roman fleet I told you about. That idea was abandoned, but the location was too good to just leave. Now it's going to be a fortress. Or maybe a *Praetorium* for *Comes* Urbanus. I don't think it's been decided yet."

"A *Praetorium*, here?" I look around. "On this desolate coast? What's wrong with his old palace – wherever it was?"

"At Dumnonian Isca, the old capital of the *pagus* – but it's too exposed to raids from the Scots, and too far from Ambrosius's court. You can get to Corin in three days from here, and these days that's more important than having easy access to the route to Gaul."

"Did you say there was a tavern here?" asks Ahes.

Marcus points to a roofless rectangle of stone, at the end of the narrow neck of rock linking the headland with the mainland, surrounded by a cluster of simple huts.

"This will be a *mansio* for the *Comes*'s guests, when it's finished. For now, we have to stay in one of these huts."

"So, like the tavern in Rotomag, then," I note. "Nothing we're not used to."

The Wrath of the Iutes

The *mansio* may not have a roof yet, but the inside looks like that of any inn I've been to. Whoever built this, knew what they were doing – I'm guessing it must be a copy of a similar building in Dumnonia's current, soon-to-be former, capital. There's even a stone counter with holes for the *amphorae* and hot food stoves, though all are yet empty. Most surprisingly, the kitchen is already working, set up in one of the thatched huts at the back – and there are some patrons here, a few workmen and guards, making use of good weather to sit under the open sky, sipping some ale and slurping on a warm stew.

The roofless hall falls silent when Ursula, Ahes and I enter – Marcus having disappeared somewhere to arrange the courier for his *Comes*.

"I'm guessing they don't have many visitors here," I say.

"Not in a while," says a woman passing us by. She wears a leather apron, splattered with meat juices, and carries a jug; she must be the landlady of this unfinished establishment. "There were some Saxon tin merchants passing by some… two months ago?"

We sit down by a table made out of a barrel and a large piece of the flat stone that seems to be in abundance on this coast. I want to order an ale, but Ahes spots something on the counter, shrieks in delight and runs up to the landlady. Moments later, she returns with a large pitcher and three wooden mugs. She pours herself first, takes a sip and winces.

"It's not as good as the one in Armorica, but it will do."

The Dumnonian *sicera* is sweet and heady; it goes straight to our heads. Soon, Ahes's face is flushed deep red; she leans her head on her fist and, bobbing from side to side, she hums some broken melody. Ursula finds it difficult to focus her eyes on the mug. Eventually, she stands up, swaying, and announces she needs to search for a latrine.

Ahes moves closer to me, until her arm touches my arm.

"So, Ursula," she says.

"What about her?"

"Is she your woman?"

"She's…" I start, and then remember our conversation from Scillonia. "It's complicated."

"But you *have* lain with her, right?"

"Once, a long time ago."

She puts her chin on my shoulder.

"You have lain with many women?" she asks. Her breath tickles my ear.

"A few."

"What's it like?"

The Wrath of the Iutes

The question surprises me. "You haven't?"

"My father wants me to preserve myself for the man I'm destined for."

"And who would that be?"

"I don't know." She shrugs and belches. "I don't think I've met him yet."

I would never ask her a question this bold if it wasn't for the drink: "What about the *Decurion*?"

"Marcus?" She giggles and turns even redder. "He is a fine man, yes, and I would ride him like one of his stallions… But I don't know if he's the *one*."

I realise her hand has been on my thigh all this time – my senses are so numbed I haven't felt it until now. Though I have no interest in lying with her, my manhood rises of its own accord.

"I will thank you to not lay your hands on my husband."

Ursula looms over us. She shoves Ahes – she means to only push her away, but she's too drunk to control her own strength and the princess lands on the floor. Ursula rushes to apologise and help her up, but Ahes scrambles up without her assistance – though she sways and almost falls again, until she finds the support of my shoulder.

"Your… husband? I'm sorry – I didn't know." She notices she's leaning on me again and leaps away as if I was a hot stove. "My apologies," she repeats and bows – this makes her stagger again. This time Ursula holds her up. She calls for one of the tavern servants and tells him to take Ahes back to our hut – and keep her there.

"You haven't told her?" Ursula glowers accusingly. "What were you hoping for?"

"I – I wasn't hoping for anything." I take a gulp of the *sicera*, and I regret it immediately; it's one cup too many, and I can feel it coming back up. "I told you before, I'm not interested in Ahes." Encouraged by the drink, I grab her by the behind and pull in closer. "You, on the other hand… I was just telling the princess how long it's been since we were last together."

She pushes me away, though not as forcefully as she shoved Ahes. "You can barely stand."

"We don't need to stand for what I have in mind. If you insist on us being a husband and wife…"

"I'm going to sleep. And I advise you to do the same. This apple drink is turning us all into dumb beasts. If I take one more sip, I feel my head will burst."

She turns back and, struggling to stay in a straight line, walks away, leaving me alone and confused, with a good third of the *sicera* still in the jug.

"It would be a waste," I murmur to myself and pour another cup.

The Wrath of the Iutes

She enters the tavern just as I'm about to leave. The jug is all but finished, and I fear what ordering another one would do, both to my mind and my bowels. Once again, the hall falls silent, not with fear, but with awe. She swaggers towards the counter in a fur-lined cape thrown over a flowing robe, bound tight at the waist and cut along the leg, of cloth as fiery red as her long hair, tied in a tall bun, with a single curly lock falling down her brow. She seems to have arrived from another world, an angel or a demon sent to torture or bless the gathered guards and workmen with her presence.

She notices me and moves towards me – slides, rather than walks, floats with unseen feet, and sits down beside me just like Ahes did an hour ago, with her bare, warm arm next to my arm. She's wearing thick vermillion on her lips, charcoal on her eyelashes, green paint on her eyelids and a garish necklace of cheap brass, polished to resemble gold.

"You're new. Who might you be?" she asks in the singing western accent. Her voice flows like mead.

"Octa, son of Aeric… King of the Iutes," I reply, struggling to form the words in my numb mouth.

"I'm guessing you came with those two ships in the harbour."

"Yes… We're passing through on our way to uh… Moridun," I reply.

[184]

"A king's son, huh?" she says. "You must have come from far away – I've never heard of these 'Iutes'."

"Cantia," I reply. "The other side of Britannia. Near Londin."

"Londin?" She gasps, theatrically, putting her hand to her mouth. "I bet it was a long and lonely journey."

She throws her cloak off and presses her soft, round breasts against my side. Her robe is thin, cut low, tied with loose lace so it leaves nothing to imagination.

I lick my lips. "What do they call you?" I ask.

"I'm Silvia."

"Just Silvia?"

"I'm nobody's daughter, if that's what you're asking. Just... a local girl. I know how to relieve your... loneliness." She runs her finger against my cheek and neck, then brushes the tip of my cock. Already stiff from Ahes's caresses, it grows greater still, and painfully so. I remember I haven't lain with anyone since that night Queen Basina visited me for the last time, before her wedding with Hildrik.

"Which one's your hut?" she asks.

"It's..." I start, and then remember that I share my room with Marcus. Where is he, anyway? How long does it take to send out a messenger? I expected him to join us at the ale table a long time ago... It's too early for him to have gone straight to bed yet – is he off somewhere performing some official *Decurion*'s duties?

"It's the big one, by the northern wall."

"Perfect. Let's go."

"Wait – I have to pay for the ale…"

"You can do that in the morning. I have an… understanding with the landlady."

She leads me to the hut, to the accompaniment of sniggers and whoops from the tavern's patrons. The room is empty, but Marcus was here long enough to leave his cloak on one of the beds, to mark it as his. Silvia pushes me onto the other bed. With one swift move she undoes the laces of her robe and lets it fall to the floor.

She is well built, but in the faint light of the oil lamp, I can see traces of the ravages of time on her body; a mysterious scar runs up the side of her belly, and pock scars mark her thighs. I don't mind any of that as much as I mind something else I notice as I watch her nakedness.

"Your hair is not really red," I say.

"Of course not," she scoffs. "It's just a fashion. We all wear our hair like that in Corin. The customers like it."

"The *customers*…?"

I can only blame the drink for how long it has taken me to realise this. The painted face, the tight clothes, the sniggers as we left the tavern…

"You're a courtesan!"

She laughs. "I may have been a courtesan in Corin, boy. Here, I'm just a harbour whore."

She pulls off my breeches and sits down on me, taking my cock swiftly inside.

"What — uh — happened?" I ask as she begins to grind.

"Shh…" She puts her finger on my mouth. "You don't really care about that. You care about the colour of my hair. That really disappointed you for some reason." She leans down over me. "Who was the red hair? Your first lover? No, of course not." She rustles my hair, then leans down and lets me take her breast into my mouth. "It was your mother."

She rides me three times, each time taking a coin from my purse, until I'm all spent and sore.

"No more," I whisper as I slip out of her for the last time.

"Pity." She kisses me on the forehead. "I rather enjoyed that. The workers and soldiers here are not gentle lovers."

"Can't you stay?"

The Wrath of the Iutes

I reach out to hold her thigh. Our bodies are steaming in the cold night.

"You're a sweet boy, Octa, but my regular patrons would not like it if I cancelled their appointments without notice."

She reaches for the robe.

"Wait," I say. "I need to ask you about something."

She may be just a woman of the night, but she *is* a woman, and an experienced one at that, in life as much as she is in love. I may not have another chance to ask someone like her about my problems.

"*Ask* me?" She chuckles. "Nobody's asked me for advice in a long time." She sits back down on the bed. Her hands reach for my crotch. "Don't mind me," she says. "What do you need to know?"

I tell her briefly about my conversation with Ursula, of what our relationship looks like, and how I find it difficult to understand what it is that she truly wants from me. Silvia frowns.

"I think I see what's going on here," she says. "I knew women like her. Their husbands were my best customers… And sometimes, I would serve the wives, too." She chuckles. "I can't advise you on friendship – whores have no friends, except other whores… But I tell you this for free: there's more to love than what happens in the bedroom."

"Then you think she really does love me? Even if –"

"I'm sure of it – if what you told me is true. But it's not a simple love. And, whatever she may feel, if she truly wants to be your wife, you need to remind her of her responsibilities."

"Responsibilities?"

"A wife needs to provide her husband with a rightful heir. That's the only good reason I know for two people to get wedded – that, or an alliance between their families. Otherwise, you might as well just remain friends and lovers. Or, in your case, just friends."

"I don't want to force Ursula into anything."

"It was her idea in the first place. This is not a game. You're both too old to play house. Wedlock is a serious matter, especially for sons of kings."

"And what about… love?"

She laughs. "Trust me, boy – it's best to keep love and wedlock apart, if you want to stay together for a long time."

Her advice leaves me confused, but her handiwork makes me soon forget about the confusion. She looks down at the result – my cock, fondled back to attention – and grins.

"Get back on that bed, boy," she commands. "Looks like I may earn that fourth coin yet."

CHAPTER VIII: THE LAY OF WARUS

Marcus returns just before dawn. He thinks he's being stealthy, but he makes so much noise that he wakes me up.

"Where have you been?" I ask.

"I met some old army friends," he replies. His breath reeks of ale and *sicera*. "And then I… had an appointment with someone."

"In the middle of the night?" It dawns on me. "Was it Silvia?"

I can't see in the dark, but I imagine he turns red. "Please don't mention it to Princess Ahes."

"Your secret's safe with me."

My own secret, however, lasts only until breakfast. As we meet for the morning meal, Ursula gives me the mocking look I know so well.

"The walls are thin in these huts," she remarks. Ahes blushes and buries her face in the piece of bread.

"What do you mean?" I ask.

"Come now. I'd recognise that mewing anywhere. Who was it, some local whore? Or one of the kitchen girls? No, they wouldn't manage to ride you for so long."

"Ursula, please. You're embarrassing the princess."

"She can't be any more embarrassed than she was having to listen to your shrieks all night." Ursula shrugs. "I suppose it's none of my business."

"But I thought you were a husband and…" Ahes starts, then stops when Ursula stares her down.

"Indeed, my dear *wife*," I say. "Maybe next time my bed will not be so cold that I need to warm it with another's body."

Ahes and Marcus look at each other, both annoyed and ashamed by our exchange. The *Decurion* puts away a half-eaten piece of cheese and stands up.

"It's time for us to set sail," he declares. "Else we will miss the tide and will be forced to stay here for another night."

"And we certainly wouldn't want *that*, would we," says Ursula, wiping crumbs from her hands.

When we descend to the cove – the narrow stairs, hewn in rock, are still slippery with morning dew – we're met by Seawine and the rest of the Iutes, waiting for us before the ships, wearing travelling cloaks and carrying sacks packed and ready to go.

"What's this, Seawine?" I ask. "We've no time for… whatever it is you're planning – we're about to leave."

The Wrath of the Iutes

"So are we," says Seawine. "We're going home."

Through the still lingering headache, I'm slow to grasp the meaning of his words.

"I don't understand. You've heard Marcus – it will be faster to reach Cantia from Moridun, if that is what you decide."

"I spoke to the locals." He nods at the harbour workers, dozing off in the shadow of the winch. "They said all we need is to take the road to Dumnonian Isca and get a ship from there. Shouldn't take more than a couple of days."

I turn to Marcus. "Is this true?"

"It can be done, if the weather's good. But the mists that descend at this time of year…"

"I think we can handle a little fog," says Seawine dismissively. "We'd rather be on our way east, even if it takes longer, than keep going further away from Cantia on the vague promise of getting home one day."

I tell Marcus and Ursula to board the ship and leave me and Seawine alone. I take the Iute aside; there's not much space here in the cove, but the back of the stone parapet descends towards the shingle beach, and we climb down there, away from the listening ears of the others.

"You would go home without me?"

"We hoped to convince you to come with us, *aetheling*."

"That's not going to happen."

"Then we must bid farewell here."

I sigh. "Seawine... Listen to me. I'm going north, with you or without you. *Dux* Wortigern needs our help – and we owe him this help. *I* owe him."

"Owe him? What for? Why is this Wortigern person so important?"

Of course – Seawine, born a simple fisherman's son in the squalor of Tanet, would not be aware of the politics and intrigues my father was involved with in his youth, would not have listened to the songs the *scops* sang at the mead halls. To him, Wortigern is just a name; if he's heard it at all before, it would only be as the father to Wortimer, the bane of the Iutes.

"Without Wortigern's support, my father would never have gained the power and experience he needed to become the king," I tell him. "Without Wortigern's decision, the Iutes would still be stuck in the marshes of Tanet. There would be no settlement at Beaddingatun, no fort at Robriwis."

"All I know is that he spawned Wortimer," he says, confirming my fears.

"And he paid dearly for it. He was a *Dux*, the ruler of half of Britannia, and now he's stuck in some mountain fortress on a rain-drenched frontier, fighting raiders. And he needs our help."

The Wrath of the Iutes

Seawine looks at the waves crashing against the beach and rubs his chin.

"Will there be plunder?" he asks.

"I doubt it. We'd be defending a border. But we will be paid in silver, I'll make sure of that. And there will be glory uncounted. Wortigern is already a hero in the songs of my father's adventures. Think how famous we would become if we fought at his side in what may well be his last battle."

"If there is anyone left to tell our story."

I put my hand on his shoulder, in a gesture I saw my father do so often with his warriors when he needed their loyalty.

"We are Iute warriors, Seawine," I say. "Our souls belong to Wodan. The only thing we have to fear is to die of old age in our beds – and I guarantee you, this is what will happen if you take the road to Isca today. If you come with me, you will either die fighting, or win a great victory. Are you willing to give that up just to spend the rest of winter in some hut in Cantia?"

He nods slowly. "Yes, we are Iute warriors," he repeats, and his eyes brighten as he raises his face to the morning sun. "I'm no longer Seawine the sailor. I am Seawine the rider. The slayer of Saxons, the saviour of Trever." He strikes his chest with his fist. "I will go fight for this *Dux* Wortigern, to show these *wealas* what a Iute sword can do."

"It warms my heart to hear this. Will you convince the others to stay?"

"They will do what I tell them," he assures me, then lowers his voice. "But we're still going back as soon as we're done here, right?"

"You have my word."

"How far now?" asks Ahes, impatient since we left Dumnonia.

Marcus glances towards the helmsman, holding tight onto the steering oar, then at the sails, filled with wind, and the sun, beaming bright in the sky. "A couple of hours, I'd guess. This is the longest stretch of the journey, and we need to reach within sight of Demetia's shore before sundown."

"I wonder if *they're* going to make it," she says, nodding to our rear.

"They? Who's *they*?" I ask. I wipe the spray from my eyes and strain my gaze to see a dark spot, following us in a distance.

"Young eyes," says Marcus admiringly. "I haven't noticed them before."

"They've been following us for a while," says Ahes. "Maybe even since Dun Taiel."

The Wrath of the Iutes

Marcus frowns. He shouts to Warus and points towards the black dot. When the captain turns back, his face is grey. He starts crying orders to his crew. Soon, the ropes tighten, the sails grow taut in the breeze. The oarsmen, already working hard under the deck, pick up the pace.

"What's going on?" I ask.

"I'm not sure," says Marcus.

"Pirates?" There's more excitement than fear in Ahes's voice.

"The Scots shouldn't reach this far south," replies Marcus. "And they wouldn't dare attack a ship this size – unless…"

He stops, with a pointing hand hovering in the air. I look at the horizon again; there's another black dot, to the left of the first one.

"A whale pod," Marcus whispers. "A whale pod!" he cries to Warus.

"I see them," the captain cries back.

"Then these *are* the pirates!" Ahes claps her hand.

"Why? What's a whale pod?" I ask. "Just these two boats?"

"There will be more," says Ahes. "I've heard about this. They're coming from all the nearby harbours."

"Their lookouts must have spotted us when we sailed too close to the shore on that westerly gust earlier," says Marcus. "The Scots' boats are small, but fast. On their own, they're too weak to take on an entire galley. But when they gather together... Have you ever seen how the *orca* hunt?"

I admit to not knowing what an *orca* is.

"Big whales, black and white... Wolves of the sea. They hunt in packs. Lord knows how they gather together, but when they do, nothing can stand in their way."

"There's another," notes Ahes.

"How do *they* all know we're here?" I ask. "We're in the middle of the sea, sailing at full speed..."

"Hill beacons, runners..." Marcus shrugs. "Or maybe somebody told them we were sailing for Moridun." He gives me a knowing look, and I remember telling Silvia of our plans. Was she working with the pirates? It made sense – a harbour whore would know all about the comings and goings of the ships at Dun Taiel.

"It doesn't matter," he says quickly; I'm guessing he wasn't discreet with the woman, either. "If they're here, that means they have secret harbours somewhere on the coast of Dumnonia."

"As soon as we're done with whatever Wortigern needs us for, we'll help you with them," I say, before remembering the promise I made to Seawine.

The Wrath of the Iutes

Marcus laughs. "You really have changed your mind, *aetheling*!" he says. "But we have to survive this little skirmish first, if we are to be of any help to Wortigern or my *Comes*." He nods towards the south-eastern horizon. "There's a fourth boat coming. Now there will be more of them than us. But don't worry, Princess —" he adds, staring into Ahes's eyes and pushing his chest proudly. He's come to calling Graelon's daughter a "princess" recently, and I can see it's making the desired impression on the girl. "A bunch of filthy pagan pirates is no match for soldiers of Dumnonia. *Equites*!" he calls in the booming voice of a cavalry commander. "To me! Looks like we get to fight the Scots sooner than we expected!"

I crouch behind the iron-bound shields lining the ship's side, and peer through the gaps between them at the pirate boats. They're so small, compared to our vessel, that it's a wonder how the Scots dare to set sail in them across the open sea, much less to attack larger ships. They're built for speed: despite the small size, they sport two sails, just like the *Maegwind*: a large one in the middle and a smaller on the bow; their narrow, hide-bound, tar-black hulls cut through the waves like leaping salmon. There's barely enough space on deck for nine men — eight of them sitting on wooden benches at the oars, and the helmsman standing at the steering oar at the back. Alone, they would stand no chance against us; but by the time all the boats reach us, I count five of them, surrounding us on all sides. Warus orders all his men on deck, including the oarsmen — there's no point in them exerting themselves any further, once it becomes clear we stand no chance of outrunning the pirates.

Against the small boats, all the ship's weapons are useless. We can't ram them — they move too quickly, and turn too deftly. The *ballista* at the ship's bow manages to release only a couple of bolts before the boats get too close for aiming. Our grappling hooks are designed for larger vessels and would merely slide off the oiled hides of the boats. Warus commands a handful of archers to line the sides, but most of the arrows fly aimless and harmless in the strong wind, and those that do reach the target, bounce off the hide shields the Scots raise over their heads.

"It's a small pack," whispers Marcus encouragingly. "The others must have got lost in the sea."

He bids his men to hide in the shadow of the shields. It's unlikely that the pirates expect there to be trained soldiers on board; most ships our size passing through these waters would be packed to the brim with merchant goods, watched over by a handful of bodyguards. Ahes and her men hide on the other side. The girl holds onto her sword — a short *spatha* — with both hands; she refused to hide under the deck, despite our urgings. "I know how to defend myself," she claimed, defiantly, reminding us once again of the one bandit she once killed.

"Guard her for me, *aetheling*," Marcus requests, nodding at Ahes. "We would lose any chance of future pacts with Graelon if we let anything happen to her."

"We both know that's not why you want her protected," I say. "Don't worry. I'll make sure she comes out of this unharmed."

The Wrath of the Iutes

The Scots shower the deck with a rain of feathered javelins, more for show and to keep us down, than for effect. One of our oarsmen falls down with a groan, clutching the shaft sticking out of his chest. Next come the grappling hooks, clunking against the railings. The ship's crew rushes to unhook them, but they're too many, and coming too fast. Another, well-aimed salvo of javelins hits the deck, this time reaping a bloody harvest among the defenders.

"Shouldn't we help them now?" I ask.

"Not yet," says Marcus. "The Scots are as deadly with those *clettini* darts as my men are with *plumbatas*. I don't want to lose a man to a stray missile."

I hear the pirates leap from their boats and climb up the sides of the ship. Marcus nods at his men; they all draw their swords. The warhorses whinny in the hold, trained to sense danger.

"Hooold," Marcus calls, even as the first of the Scots scramble over the railings. The *equites* are eager to charge into battle; at last, they can face their old enemies again, rather than bandits or some frightened villagers. "Hooold!" Another pirate appears. Only when the third one hits the deck, does the *Decurion* give a signal for the attack.

As the *equites* rush into the brawl, I run past them, to Ahes's side. Just in time; a burly, red-bearded Scot jumps over the side, holding a great, crude, two-handed sword. Judging by the number of precious metal bands on his bulging arms and neck, he must be a battle-hardened hero, maybe even a clan chieftain. He lunges at Ahes, thinking her easy prey, but to his surprise, she manages to parry his first blow; I can tell, though, by the way her right arm trembles, that the next blow will surely fell her.

The ship heaves from side to side, sending me sliding straight at the chieftain. He blocks my strike with little effort; his weapon may seem heavy and unwieldy, but he swings it as if it was a birch wand. I've seen enough men fight to tell that this randomly met pirate from a cold, distant island might just be one of the toughest opponents I've ever faced; indeed, he might well prove to be the one to best me…

He growls at me and shakes his beard before raising the sword in two hands over his head. I try to stab at his torso, seeing an opening, but he's too fast and I have to leap back to avoid the falling blade. I glance to Ahes; she's safe for now, surrounded by her own men. I parry another blow, letting the chieftain's sword slide along my blade. The ship heaves again. The pirate's thrust throws him forward, but I wobble too, and our blades miss each other by a good foot. I step up, trying to shorten the distance. If I can get within his blade length… But the chieftain notices my attempt; he throws the sword into his left hand and punches me with his right fist so hard, black spots dance before my eyes. As I fall forward, I grapple him at the waist. He hits me in the back with the pommel. I endure; at close distance, his great sword is of little use. But I can't last like this forever – sooner or later, his blows will crush my spine.

With the oarsmen busy fighting, and the sails hanging freely, the ship is rolling and leaping in the waves like a leaf in a swollen stream. With another dip, we both slip on the deck slick with surf and blood, and tumble down, dropping our

The Wrath of the Iutes

weapons. I scramble up first, but I can't reach my sword, kicked away by some other fighter. I see the chieftain grasp for his blade. I reach for the knife in my boot and throw it – it digs deep into his thigh but doesn't cut through the thick muscle. He rips it out with a growl. While he's distracted, a crewman charges at him with a rope-cutting hatchet. He manages to glance the pirate on the arm before the great sword severs his head clean off his shoulders.

I find another sword – a short, leaf-shaped blade dropped by one of the pirates. I hesitate; the chieftain is no longer a threat to Ahes, safe for now behind her kindred. I could die here fighting him – one misstep, one more slip, and that great sword would slice right through me – or I could leave him for others to deal with and find myself an easier enemy… But the chieftain makes my choice for me. With a roar, he rushes forth. He whirls the sword over his head and brings it down on me. I duck and lunge under the blade. I cut his calf; more blood spurts from the wound, but there's no stopping him. I turn around and slash across his back. The blade barely cuts through muscle and scrapes on the bone. He spins; the tip of his sword draws a bloody line across my chest. I fall back, but then the ship rolls again and throws me back up, right past the chieftain's sword. At the last moment, I grab my weapon with two hands and hold it out in front of me as I slide on my knees. The leaf-shaped blade goes smoothly into the enemy's stomach, just over his left hip.

His fist crushes into my face again and sends me flying. For a moment, I'm blinded in one eye; I feel blood gushing from my nose. The chieftain staggers back, wheezing. Even this wound is not enough to stop him, but it seems he's lost the will to fight. He looks around. His men are losing the battle. Though many of the ship's crewmen lie dead, so do many of the pirates; Marcus's soldiers split them into two groups and are pushing them apart towards aft and bow. Worse still, the *Seahorse*, noticing something's wrong, has now turned around and is heading towards us, though slowly, working against the wind and current. The chieftain grunts, reaches for a long, twisted bronze horn hanging at his belt, with a sculpted boar's head at the mouth, and blasts a desperate call.

At the signal, the surviving pirates break away from the fight and, one by one, leap overboard. Within seconds, the deck is empty of enemies — except the hacked bodies, strewn everywhere. I turn to the chieftain — he cuts down a hapless crewman standing in his way, and before anyone can stop him, plunges into the depths.

"Grab those javelins!" cries Marcus. "Get them before they sail away!"

"Aren't we done?" I ask, wiping blood and sweat from my face. My back aches, and a stinging pain in my side tells me I haven't quite managed to avoid the chieftain's great blade.

"The more we kill here, the less we'll have to deal with later," the *Decurion* replies. He throws me a couple of feathered darts. The blade of one of them, torn out of the deck board, is bent and useless, but I take the other one and lean over the edge, looking for a target. I spot one of the pirates still in the water, just a few strokes away from the nearest black boat. Most of the other boats are already full, and sailing away at full speed on the fresh breeze. I aim

The Wrath of the Iutes

carefully; the dart is unwieldy, sporting a loop of metal at one end that I'm guessing would make the throwing easier in some way, if only I had any idea how to use it.

I toss — and miss by several feet; but at the exact same moment, another dart hits my target straight in the back. I turn to seek out the man who threw the missile with such skill, only to see Ahes, leaning over the ship's side and beaming back at me.

"That's my second one!" she announces, holding two fingers in the air.

"Heave — ho!"

With every pull, I wince as my wounds burn and spurt a little blood through the wrappings. This isn't rowing the small fishing boat across the Tanet channel, though it helps that thanks to our races I'm not completely unfamiliar with working the oars. The oar of Graelon's ship is a massive plank of heavy timber, more than twelve feet in length; it rests on an iron spur and hangs on a leather strap before going through a port in the ship's side.

The tattered, straw-filled cushion under my arse belonged to one of the unfortunate oarsmen who perished in the fight with the pirates. The crew lost so many men, it seemed we'd have to sail back to the nearest harbour, rather than our destination on Demetia's coast — until Marcus proposed his men could replace the oarsmen, relieving the mariners to more urgent duties.

"It takes years to train an oarsman," says Marcus. I can hear the strain in his voice with every heave; he sits behind me, on another bloodied cushion, with the rest of his soldiers across the aisle, along the port side. The casualties among the *equites* were slight; the pirates, surprised to face trained soldiers on deck, put up only a little fight. "I can see why. This is a slave's work."

"The men whose place we took weren't slaves," I remind him. "They were free, and they died free because you wouldn't risk your soldiers' lives. They wouldn't even be in these seas if they hadn't agreed to take you home."

"I'm well aware," Marcus replies. "But they knew they were sailing into a war. Sooner or later, they'd have encountered the Scots while in Wortigern's service."

I pause to catch a breath before another heave. Under the deck, the rolling of the ship is much more noticeable than above, and if I wasn't so weary and focused on the rowing, I'd no doubt be retching onto my boots by now.

When I can eventually speak again, I ask a question that's been on my mind ever since the battle started. "The ship wasn't of much use against the pirates," I note. "Neither was its crew. What was the point of your journey to Armorica?"

I wait until the *Decurion* gathers strength to reply. "I hoped for an entire fleet, not mere two ships," he says. "But even these two are of benefit when we crew them with Wortigern's men. We're not going to use them to hunt the Scots in the open ocean – it would be as pointless as trying to kill a fly with a sword. We need ships to strike at their hidden

The Wrath of the Iutes

harbours, which can only be accessed from the sea — and to take the war over the channel, to Hibernia. Wortigern hopes if we can inflict enough damage to their homes, the Scots may leave us alone — for a time, at least."

"And do you share this hope?"

I can almost hear him shrug. "We kill the Scots by the dozen. You saw how they fight — with the exception of great warriors like that chieftain, they come in great mass, easy to outmanoeuvre, easy to cut down. But there seems to be no end to them — and they're spreading all over the coast and the mountains. The Romans never managed to conquer Hibernia — what chance do we have?"

"Then it is only duty that makes you fight for Wortigern."

"There is always hope — and I will defend my land and people for as long as I can hold a sword and ride a horse. Who knows — maybe if we hurt the Scots enough, they'll get bored and go bother someone else? I hear the North is weak these days," he chuckles.

I know most Iutes or Saxons would be surprised at his jest. To them, the *wealas* are all kindred, united in their fear and hatred of the barbarians. But I know the relations between the tribes and clans of the Britons are as complex and often hostile as those between the tribes and clans of the fair-hairs. The "North" Marcus speaks of is controlled neither by the Council in Londin, nor by *Dux* Ambrosius's court in Corin. Though it was once part of Roman Britannia, it is now another country altogether, inhabited by tribes with exotic-sounding names like Brigants, Parisii, Wotadins, Wortriu…

Some of those names I've only heard of in stories told by merchants; others, I met as captives my father's warriors freed from the sea raiders. Their *Comites* and *Duces* were as likely to attack their *wealas* brethren in the South, like King Drust once did, as help them in the fight against barbarians.

The helmsman's "heaves" and "ho's" begin to slow down. A handful of crewmen descend under the deck.

"Get out of here, boy," one of them tells me. "Let the real men take over."

"What's going on?" I ask, relieved of the change. I wipe my sweaty hands on my tunic. I can sense the blisters forming on my palms; I need an ointment, or I won't be able to hold a sword for days. How do the oarsmen *do* that?

"We're coming to port," the crewman replies. "Wouldn't want you whitebait to crash us into a pier."

With an aching back, sore arse, blistering hands and chafing thighs, I climb out onto the deck, shielding my eyes from the evening sun, and take my first glimpse of Demetia's coast... in seven years.

I've been here before, I realise. Not this particular stretch, but I recognise the landscape; it's all coming back to me now, through a haze of the years. Somewhere along this shore stands a hermitage to which Ambrosius's men took me and many other Iute children after abducting us from our homes during the war. It was the only thing the *Dux* could do to save us from Wortimer's wrath, though I did not understand it at the time. During the two years I spent here, learning to

The Wrath of the Iutes

read, pray and write, I had little time or inclination to see the sights, but I remember enough of it to be certain now that we're not far from the place of my captivity.

We pass through a narrow entrance and, with the sails rolled and fastened, enter a river estuary, bound with a ribbon of golden sands and grass-covered dunes. The tide is ebbing, making the job of the oarsmen all the harder; as the sea recedes, only a narrow channel remains leading towards the harbour. The *Seahorse* is already there, with an ant-like crowd of mariners and labourers working to moor it to a timber wharf at the tip of a peninsula created by a confluence of two rivers. The settlement, which I'm guessing to be Moridun, is a typical old Roman town, rising a short distance from the harbour and linked to it by a stretch of a broad, paved road. Ruins of a bath house and a small *basilica* loom over the striped wall, and a hillock of a crumbling amphitheatre gleams dusty white further upstream.

I have seen too many towns like this in my life, even before I left Cantia, to be interested in finding out what this one has to offer. All we need is somewhere to stay the night and leave our wounded in the care of the local priest – or a surgeon, if there is one in town. Of more interest to me is the chain of several hillforts and watchtowers that I spot on the summits on both sides of the river valley, once guarding the entrance and testifying to its ancient importance. Not all of them seem abandoned – it seems the threat of the pirates has brought these ancient ramparts back to life.

Ahes stands beside me. She was relieved of the rowing duty, but she offered to help the crewmen with whatever work needed doing on deck during the passage, and seems just as tired and aching as I am. Still, she stares at the landscape around us with gleaming eyes and wide-open mouth.

"It doesn't look that different from Cantia or northern Gaul," I say with the air of a bored explorer.

"It's different enough for me." She takes a deep sniff. "Even the sea smells different here than in Armorica."

"That'll be the seaweed," laughs Marcus, emerging from under the deck with bloodied cloth tied around his palms. He points to the thick, dark stripe marking the tideline halfway along the beach. "There's so much of the stuff here, we had to learn how to *cook* it."

CHAPTER IX
THE LAY OF EOCHU

The arrival of two warships, filled with so many soldiers and warriors from distant lands, causes no small amount of confusion and consternation. It seems like the entire town has rushed out to welcome us. A troop of *vigiles* arrives to form a line separating the harbour from the crowd of curious onlookers. By the time Marcus and I disembark, a balding, corpulent official, wearing a white robe with crimson lining, rides up in a carriage, accompanied by a retinue of armed guards.

The Wrath of the Iutes

"*Ave, Decurion!*" he announces, seeing Marcus approach. He eyes the bodies of dead soldiers being brought down from the deck, to be buried at the town's cemetery. "Trouble?" he asks.

"*Ave, Comes,*" Marcus replies, pressing his fist to his chest. "The Scots struck us just a few hours ago. You haven't had trouble from them here?"

"Lord forbid." The *Comes* makes a sign of the cross. "The *Cairs* still protect the estuary," he says, glancing towards the twin hillforts looming over each riverbank.

"Not for long, if the Scots can sail this close to Demetia," Marcus remarks.

"Now that you're back, we should have even less reason to fear them, *Decurion*." Scowling, he studies the troops descending from the *Seahorse* – the Iutes and the Armoricans, shambling past without armour and carrying all sorts of gear and weaponry, appear like some random band of barbarians picked up along the way compared to the orderly detachment of Marcus's cavalry. "I'm guessing this is only a vanguard of some greater force you've arranged for our relief?"

"You guess wrongly, *Comes*," Marcus replies. "But these are fierce warriors, especially the Iutes – the household guard of Prince Octa," he adds quickly, patting me on the shoulder.

"*Iutes.*" The *Comes* sneers. "More barbarians for Wortigern to play with. How are we supposed to defeat the Scots with just two ships and a handful of heathens?"

"Is the *Legatus* here, then? I was hoping to speak to him as soon as possible."

The wince is barely noticeable, a mere twitch of a lip.

"You know he prefers to spend as little time here as necessary, *Decurion*. He's in his *Cair* on the Teibi." He looks around again, then glances at the sky, reddening with sunset. "You'll be wanting to stay the night in town, I presume?"

"If there's enough places at the inn, yes."

This time, the wince is fully visible. "There's always enough, as you're well aware. I'll have the rooms at the *Principia* prepared for yourself and…" His eyes fall on Ahes and gleam lustfully. "…our noble guest."

"Princess Ahes, Graelon's daughter," Marcus introduces her.

"I can see the family resemblance. I knew your father, child." The *Comes* takes Ahes's hand and slobbers over it. She endures it with a slight grimace.

"If I had to guess, I'd say the *Comes* and Wortigern are no great friends," I note when the official finally climbs into his carriage and rides back to Moridun.

"You'd guess rightly," Marcus replies curtly. He turns to his troops. "Hurry up, men," he calls. "We need to sort ourselves out before nightfall. Drustan, get those horses on the grass! Cado, bring the worst injured out – I know a good

The Wrath of the Iutes

surgeon in Moridun. I want him to take a look at them first thing in the morning!"

"This isn't how I imagined Britannia Prima," says Ursula.

"How so?"

"We were always told it was the last place on the island where the ancient glory of Rome still remained. But it looks just as old and crumbling as any town in Cantia."

I look over my shoulder at the striped walls and the square towers of the gatehouse. There is one feature that makes Moridun different from most similar towns I've seen: only one Roman highway leads into it, from the north-east. All the other routes are just dirt roads and field paths, splitting away from the main road past its only gate. It means the town and its handful of public buildings were the final outpost of Rome in this part of the world; the last fort, guarding the last harbour. Beyond the perimeter of *villas* protected by the town's garrison, beyond the ring of hills and dunes, lay a wild, untamed land of beasts and barbarians, untouched by the civilising hand of the Empire.

"We are on the far edge of Ambrosius's domain," I say. "Among the last vestiges of civilisation. Maybe things look better nearer Corin."

It's starting to rain — a miserly, cold drizzle, reminding us that Britannia is already deep into autumn — when we pass the overgrown ruins of another *villa* and begin our descent into the valley of the Teibi River. Thankfully, it's a shorter distance from Moridun than I feared – we only rode for a few hours; any longer in this rain and I would start to worry about my Iutes wanting to go home again. It's damp and freezing here in the hills; the evening dew rises from the slopes, shrouding the peaks in billows of grey mist. Once every few miles, I see the jagged teeth of a hillfort rampart on top of a bald hillock. I've seen a few of these structures in the east, on the Downs and in Andreda – sometimes used as fortified camps by forest bandits – but never so many in one place and preserved in such good condition.

"This must have been a place of constant war," I note to Marcus. "Before the Romans came."

He shrugs.

"I wouldn't know. There are no stories from that time. The Demets wanted to forget about their uncivilised past – they wanted to be more Roman than Romans. And Rome rewarded their eagerness for as long as they could afford."

"The amphitheatre," I guess.

"The amphitheatre, the baths, the *basilica*…" He chuckles. "These hill folk had no idea what to do with any of it once the Legions were gone. They turned the bath house into a fish farm, and the *basilica* into a grain store. If it wasn't for Wortigern and us, they'd all have turned into Atecots a long time ago."

"*Atecots?*" asks Ursula.

The Wrath of the Iutes

"Ah, here we are," Marcus says, instead of answering. The Teibi valley opens before us. A smattering of farmsteads lines the river's winding shores: roundhouses in the old Briton manner, with heavy thatch overhanging the walls of sticks and mud. Up ahead, the river twists around a tall hill, gentle and bald from the west, precipitous and wooded from the east, with a good view of the river ford and an old road wending its way into the northern hills beyond; a memory of our battle with the Bacauds flashes in my mind – the landscape here is too similar; only instead of a *villa*, the peak is occupied by a fortress, built on the foundations of yet another hillfort, not round like the ones I'm familiar with from eastern Britannia, but angular, five-sided. A new wooden rampart stands on top of the tallest of three earthen banks surrounding the summit, with a timber gate tower guarding the south-western entrance through an outer wall of earth and rock rubble. In the distance, a few miles upstream, I spot another hill, topped with what looks like another rampart and a watchtower.

"And what exactly is 'here'?" I ask.

"*Cair* Wortigern," the *Decurion* replies. "Of all the hillforts the *Dux* rebuilt in his name, this one's the oldest, and the largest."

"Graelon sent us his daughter?" Wortigern announces with wonder. He clasps the girl on the shoulders before turning to inspect the men she brought with her.

"Not… not exactly," says Ahes. "My father doesn't know I'm here."

"I'm sure he's realised by now," notes Marcus. "But yes, all that Graelon offered us were the two ships that brought us here. I'll explain the rest later."

"You'd better." Wortigern laughs and, as he looks past the Armoricans, his eyes fall, at last, on me. "And who are you, young man? You look… familiar."

I stare at him in silence. I can't muster the courage to speak. The man before me is a myth, a legend; Wortigern, the *Dux* of Londin for more than thirty years, the last man to keep the peace in the entire east of the island – his son's brief rule was an unending struggle, not just with the barbarians, but with the leaders of the Briton tribes supposedly under his control, and after his demise, no other man was ever deemed worthy of the *Dux*'s seat.

He looms large, not just in Britannia's past, but that of the Iutes, and of my family. It was Wortigern who commanded the Briton *Comites* to invite the barbarians to their defence; it was Wortigern who agreed that the Iutes would move out of their island of refuge and settle in the lands belonging to his supporters around Londin – like the grounds of Ariminum, the *villa* where my father grew up. My father, who was Wortigern's Councillor and, briefly, before the disaster that engulfed the province and ended the *Dux*'s rule, his right hand and prospective heir.

And it was Wortigern's evil spawn, Wortimer, who destroyed my home village, waged war on the Iutes and killed

The Wrath of the Iutes

my foster-father – though, I remind myself, one shouldn't blame fathers for the sins of their sons…

He was already an old man when I last saw him, six years ago, when he took me from the hermitage on the western coast and brought me back to Cantia, to meet my real father. He's grown older still since then. He still has a full head of hair – but it's white like dove's feathers; underneath it is a face made up of wrinkles, folds and sorrow. His arms are still muscular, but the skin on his hands is thin like papyrus sheet; his right eye is still sharp, gleaming, but his left is shrouded in white. Old age bent his back and twisted his fingers; death lurks over his shoulder; he looks like someone knowing he's not long for this world but decided to go down fighting.

"Who are you, boy?" he repeats the question.

"I am Octa, my lord," I reply, at last. "Son of Ash. *Aetheling* of the Iutes."

His eyes narrow, then widen. He bursts into a laugh that turns into a cough. "I sent you to Armorica to bring me Britons, *Decurion*, and you bring me a Iute from Cantia? However have you managed that?"

His hands grip my shoulders with the strength of a bear. He raises me up like a child, though I'm taller than him. "Octa. Little Octa. What gods brought you here, to see me in my twilight hour?"

"It's another long story to tell, if you have the time," I reply, rubbing my bruised shoulder.

"I'll always find the time for Ash's son. We'll talk at the *cena*. For now, settle yourself somewhere. There's not much space here – it's only an old *cair*, after all – but should be enough for everyone."

"I know you expected me to bring an army and a fleet, *Legatus*," says Marcus apologetically. "Not a couple of ships filled with town guards and a handful of barbarians…"

"You did what you could." Wortigern waves his hand. "I knew Graelon would be a tough nut to crack. Those Armoricans would rather forget they ever had anything to do with those of us who stayed behind. They're blaming us for all their misfortunes – and who knows, maybe they're right." He waves at one of the servants. "Show the soldiers where they can set up their tents. Don't get *too* comfortable here, *Decurion*," he adds. "Soon, you'll be marching off to war again."

This isn't one of those warrior feasts at which I would regale the guests with tales of my adventures and glories. This is a solemn, military *cena*, where officers discuss strategies while their soldiers exchange bawdy jests and memories of recent battles outside. We're lounging, Roman style, around a horseshoe-shaped table set up in the main hall of a large stone building, the only one topped with tile instead of thatch, that serves as the combination of the fort's main administrative buildings, the *Praetorium* and the *Principia*. There is something perverse in the way this meal is prepared, in the old Imperial manner, as if we were in some rich nobleman's *villa* in Gaul, not on top of an ancient, mist-

The Wrath of the Iutes

shrouded hill in the most remote part of Britannia. The food, at least, reminds us of where we are. There's only one flask of wine to go round for all of us, and it has an odd, harsh taste to it.

Dux Wortigern is at first only interested in the part of my story which explains how I met Marcus and came to find myself in his fortress.

"There will be time to talk of the past when we have dealt with the present," he says. "I've heard of Trever and of the war in Gaul – I'm sure Marcus explained we're not completely cut off here – but it is far away, and bears little significance on the events in Britannia."

His indifference surprises me; as the *Dux* in Londin, it was one of his duties to deal with foreign affairs, to keep track of the events on the Continent, as much as anyone could at the time. Now, he's only interested in what affects his little corner of the world, his remote frontier. He wants to hear only the news that could help or hinder his campaign against the Scots, delay or hasten the demise of his enemies. Is this just the weariness of old age?

It is to this campaign that the attention of everyone at the table turns once all the introductions and explanations are over.

"So, what happened while we were gone that was so important?" asks Marcus. "Have you lost another battle?"

"Not yet," replies Wortigern. "But if we don't hurry, we might lose the entire war. A new warband landed at Mona a few weeks ago, greater than any before, if the reports are to be believed. I expect they'll be crossing the Narrows as we speak, somewhere between Segont and the Whirlpools. Utir holds the eastern flank as far as Canowis, but is too weakened after last year's raids to come to our aid."

"What of Cunedag?"

"He's holed up at the Forks, in Gangania, with most of his warband, waiting for my orders."

"The Forks!" exclaims Marcus. "Is young *Domna* Madron safe?"

"If I thought she wasn't safe there, I'd have brought her here," Wortigern replies brusquely. "No, the Scots are not interested in Gangania – they'll be coming here, to the south coast, where the plunder and glory are. And it will be their downfall. We will march to meet them, and in the narrow mountain passes that only our men know, we will trap and destroy them so thoroughly, their wives and children will never hear from them again!"

He slams the table, raising a plume of dust and food scraps. "Now, we can talk of past glories. Eochu, bring us some of that heather wine I know you've been hiding in your hut!"

By day, the land around *Cair* Wortigern is a grim, desolate, grey region, shrouded in mist in the evening, or swept by the howling wind, racing down the narrow river valley. But the

The Wrath of the Iutes

night sky, with the clouds cleared, more than makes up for it. Above me spreads a clear carpet of stars, a sea of twinkling jewels, with the broad, bright strip cutting straight through, a heavenly highway the Romans call *Via Lactea*, and the Saxon sailors know as the Winter Road. The moon's thin crescent serves only as another ornament to this scattered treasure, a silver brooch pinned onto the woad-blue cloth.

"We never saw stars like these in Londin," muses Wortigern.

"Do you not miss the city?" I ask.

We stand alone on the top of the wooden tower of the eastern gatehouse. The *Dux* requested a private conversation after the *cena* ended and everyone went back to their tents and huts – some to continue the drinking with members of the local garrison, others to rest after the long march.

"Not a day passes that I wouldn't think about it," he replies. "Especially on a cold, autumn day like today, after a feast – or what counts as feast in these hills…"

"It would barely count as breakfast at The Bull's Head."

He chuckles, then sighs. "I yearn for the taste of good Gaulish cheese and wine. This is what I envy you most of your recent adventure. Have you had a chance to taste the Mosellan white?"

"More than I could ever wish for," I reply. "In Trever, it flowed like water."

"And here we have to content ourselves with whatever the Atecots concoct from the local herbs and weeds. Mind you, they're not half terrible with the heather…"

"There's that word again – the Atecots," I note. "Marcus mentioned them also. I thought this was the land of the Demets?"

Wortigern turns his back to the river and leans against the breastwork. He picks up the jug of the heather wine and pours it into a beaten silver goblet, marked with the Imperial Eagle crest.

"When I came here eight years ago, I didn't know what to do with my life," he says between sips. Wind tears at the tufts of silver hair peeking from under his woollen hat. I tighten my cloak. It's a cold night, and the wine is the only thing that keeps us warm. "Ambrosius and his nobles showered me with gifts and respect as befitted a former *Dux*, even one who was overthrown by his own son. But they remembered their defeat in the civil war, and did not want me anywhere near the court at Corin. My dear late wife Sevira had some lands here in the West – it is her *villa* that you passed at the entrance to the valley – so I moved here, thinking of retiring in peace."

"And you found only more war."

"What I found here was a situation that was all too familiar. A frontier on fire, crumbling defences, a court too busy with its own intrigues to stop the invaders, and a tribe of newcomers, refugees from another land, eager to fight for their homes if only anyone would let them."

The Wrath of the Iutes

"The Atecots?"

The *Dux* leans down over the fort's yard and shouts at a passing soldier. "Eochu! Come up here. We're talking about your people."

As the short, stocky man with dark, curly hair and a sharp nose climbs up to the top of the tower, Wortigern introduces him as the *Praetor* of the fortress, and the warchief of the Atecots.

"Tell us your tribe's story, *Praetor*," the *Dux* invites, handing Eochu his cup.

"What is there to tell?" Eochu shrugs. "A long time ago, we came to this land from Hibernia, like the Scots. Only instead of raiding Britannia's shores, we preferred to settle here in peace. We are Christians, for which we are forever exiled from our homeland. Some of us have even served in the Legions. My great uncle is buried somewhere in Illyricum," he adds proudly. "But," his voice turns melancholy, "Ambrosius's courtiers and generals never trusted us with protecting their frontier. They thought us barbarians, and always suspected us of secretly allying with the Picts and the Scots. Until *Legatus* Wortigern's arrival, we weren't even allowed to enter the walls of this fortress."

"You were able to do for the Atecots what you were never allowed to do for us," I say to Wortigern.

"Not everything was the same here," he replies. "The land here is sparsely populated and not as desirable as in Cantia, so few minded when I gave some of it to Eochu's people, in exchange for their services. And it helped that they were already Christians – though not as much as I'd hoped."

"Even so, we have achieved some great things together," says Eochu. "Remember the siege of *Dun Ambrosius*? Three times we burned the place down before we got rid of those bandits for good!"

They both nod and chuckle at the memory. I see a youthful glint in Wortigern's eye, and I remember how close he was once with my father, when 'Ash' was still a courtier in Londin.

"The *Comes* at Moridun didn't seem impressed with your achievements," I note.

The *Dux* scowls. "Pah. He's as much of a fool as anyone in Londin. The Britons had no trouble wasting men to try to keep my son in power, or please a fallen Imperator, but still they'd rather see the Atecots go back to Hibernia or, at best, to their mud huts in the hills, rather than employ them to protect their borders. They claim to be like Rome, but their idea of Rome is outdated by centuries. Even the Imperators have learned the worth of barbarian allies. Not that I think your people are barbarians," he tells Eochu.

"Will men like them ever see the value of friendship between those who dwelled on their land for generations, and those who arrive from abroad?" I ask. I share with Wortigern my thoughts from Scillonia, and the two men nod approvingly as I speak.

The Wrath of the Iutes

"Only if they learn how not to fear them," the *Dux* replies. "I was never afraid of those who came to Britannia seeking peace. Raiders and invaders are one thing; those need to be repelled at all cost. But your Iutes, your Saxons, your Atecots… All of you deserved to be given a chance to prove your worth, to become a part of us, and we would have been all the better for it."

"What are they all afraid of?"

"They fear because they know their time is done. They fear being supplanted, replaced, by a more vibrant, youthful breed, of becoming a mere memory, only a mention in the chronicles – or maybe forgotten completely, like the nameless people who built the stone circles and the rock-hewn tombs that dot this land…"

"Are they not right to be afraid? The Franks and the Goths rule half of Gaul between them. The Vandals conquered Hispania and sacked Rome. And even here, in Britannia, Aelle's Saxons have already taken over the rule of their land from the Regins."

"Perhaps they're right. But then, so what?" To my surprise, Wortigern shrugs. "It is only natural for the stronger to push out the weak. Rome conquered the Britons once and moulded them in its image. If it is now time for the Iutes and the Saxons to do the same, so be it. It is foolish to resist the passage of time."

"A wise man in Coln told me the same thing once," I muse.

"Wise men have been saying this since the dawn of mankind. The Hellenes taught us that everything flows like a great river. A man can no more stem the current of change than he can stop a river from flowing."

"A man can build a dam," notes Eochu. "Or an aqueduct."

"With great effort and resources, yes," Wortigern agrees. "But Britannia has neither. My son tried to build such a dam with nothing but sticks and mud. And when it finally burst, it brought a disaster greater than any flood he could have hoped to prevent."

"You don't think such a disaster could happen here?" I ask.

"Not while I'm alive," the *Dux* replies. "After that, who knows… I hope Eochu's people will have proven their worth enough by then – though it's just as likely that there won't be anyone left in Britannia to throw them out."

"You're being gloomy again, *Legatus*," says Eochu.

"I'm being old." Wortigern chuckles. "This may well be my last campaign. And if I'm gone, who will hold this frontier against the Scots and the Picts? Cunedag is eager, and his people will follow him into Hell's fires, but I fear he lacks the talent. Utir is too embroiled in the intrigues at the court…"

"We're boring our guest," Eochu notes. "I assure you, we can hold our own against the Scots with your guidance as well

The Wrath of the Iutes

as without it. We will keep Demetia safe after you've gone – and Lord willing, it won't be for a long time yet."

"I'll drink to that," I say, raising my cup, filled to the brim with Eochu's potent heather wine.

More tired than I thought, I sleep long into the morning, past breakfast; what wakes me up at last is the commotion in the *cair*'s yard. I dress unhurriedly, wincing and rubbing my eyes – the heather wine pummels at my brows – and walk out of the hut I share with Seawine and Ursula to see what's going on. The two of them are already outside, in the small crowd that gathered around a weary, ragged horseman, wearing the crimson cloak of an *eques*.

"Philippus!" Wortigern rushes out of the *Praetorium*. "What news? You look haggard. Bring him water, somebody!"

"I rode… all through the night," the rider replies, gasping for breath. Some men help him dismount and lead him into the shadow of a nearby hut. "Segont has fallen," he says at last. "The Scots crossed the Narrows."

"Cado," Wortigern commands, "take this brave man and make him well enough to talk. Marcus, Octa, meet me in the *Principia* as soon as you're ready. If what Philippus said is true, we may have to change all our plans."

It takes an hour for the surgeon to restore some of Philippus's strength and bring him into the *Principia*'s hall. As breakfast is brought for us into the hall, he is laid on one of the dining couches, on a bedding of straw and furs; pale, gaunt and swaddled in warm wrappings, he looks unnervingly like a corpse on a bier, until he begins to speak.

"This is no mere warband," he says. He picks up a piece of stewed pigeon and chews it slowly. "It's an army, and it's led by one man – he calls himself *ri*, or *Rex*, and goes by the name of Niall."

"King Niall…" Wortigern scratches the tip of his chin. "Have you heard of him, Eochu?"

"A cow thief and a common bandit, if it's the same man," the Atecot *Praetor* replies with a scowl. "But of noble blood. His father banished many of us from Hibernia. I know nothing about his skill as a leader."

"He must be quite a warchief to have captured Segont so quickly. Did he bring siege machines with him?"

"They flooded the walls with a great number of men," replies Philippus. "No machines other than ropes and ladders, from what I heard – but it was enough."

"I *told* them the garrison at Segont needed strengthening!" Wortigern slams the table with his fist. "Cunedag's men could only have done so much on their own." He rubs sleep from his eye. "Right. A new plan, then. No point marching head-on against an army that size. Marcus, I will need one of your men to ride to Utir with new orders."

"Of course, *Legatus*."

The Wrath of the Iutes

"And then prepare to march back to Moridun. I want you back on those ships by tomorrow morning. There's no use for cavalry here."

"Gangania?"

Wortigern smiles. "I knew I could count on you. Octa, I think your riders will be of more use in the North, as well, if you're still willing to help us."

"Gangania…" I repeat, uncertain. "I'm sorry, but – do you have a map of your country?" I ask. "It would be easier for me to follow the situation…"

The *Decurion* laughs. "Young Octa gained a reputation of something of a *strategos* in Gaul," he says, patting me on the shoulder. "But even the best *strategos* can't devise war plans without knowing the lay of the land."

"Like father, like son," Wortigern chuckles, amused. "No, I don't have a map, *aetheling* – we have little use for such fancies here. Not that anyone ever managed to map the twisting valleys and mountain passes of Wened – not even the great Roman generals who campaigned here. We have to depend on guides and on officers who were born here and know every road and river of their homeland."

"Still," says Marcus, "we can explain at least the general situation to our guests."

He picks up the bits of bone and gristle from his plate and forms them on the table into a gruesome design, in the shape somewhat resembling a reversed letter 'C'.

"This is where we are, in Demetia," he says, pointing to the lower arch of the 'C'. "Cunedag and his troops are here, in the north, with their main fortress on the Ganganian peninsula," he says, pointing to the upper arm. He pauses to pick a tiny speck of grain from a bowl and puts it above the upper arch's tip. "This is the Isle of Mona. We don't go there," he adds with a mysterious frown. "*Cair* Segont is just below, guarding the passage through the strait. Everything between the two arms is Wened: a land of mountains, valleys and mists, where an entire army could hide for weeks before we'd even notice it."

I study the 'map' for a moment. The strategic situation reminds me of something I'd seen a few months before, when *Dux* Arbogast told me of the Imperator's plans against the Goth and Saxon armies. It's not difficult to grasp what Wortigern has in mind – the land itself dictates only one possible course of action.

"A pincer movement," I say. "If you can muster enough men."

Wortigern chuckles lightly. "Let me worry about the men. The Atecot warriors number more than a cohort. They're no more eager to fall under this Niall's rule than the rest of us."

"*Atecots* – Marcus mentioned that name before," Ursula whispers. "Some local tribe?"

"They're Hibernians, too," I reply, and explain what I learned last night from Eochu.

"Are they as reliable as the Iutes?" she asks.

The Wrath of the Iutes

"Nobody is as reliable as the Iutes," Wortigern replies, nodding towards my men. "If I had a hundred Iute warriors at my command, I would have destroyed those damn Scots a long time ago. But the Atecots can hold their own in a fight – and that's all I need them for in this campaign."

"They are the anvil," I guess. "And the forces you send to Gangania will be the hammer."

"I couldn't have said it better myself." Wortigern nods.

"What distances are we talking about?" I ask. "How do you plan to coordinate the attack?"

"We've done this sort of thing before," says Marcus, wiping the crumbs and bits of meat off the table. "Though never on such a scale. There are few roads an army can take in these mountains, and we have eyes on all of them. The Scots will be slowed down by many small forts along the way – long enough for us to execute the attack, I hope."

"This is why I trust you with this mission, *Decurion*," says Wortigern. "I'm certain you'll know what to do."

"And this Cunedag – do you trust him as well?"

"More than I'd trust my own son," the *Dux* replies. He looks at me with a glint in his eye.

"That's not saying much," I murmur to Ursula, quiet enough for Marcus not to hear.

"We'll find out soon enough," Ursula replies and reaches for the mug of ale. She sips it and winces. "I hope these Westerners fight better than they brew. This is vile."

"They did lose the civil war," I remind her. "But that was when Wortigern fought on the other side."

PART 3 – WENED

CHAPTER X
THE LAY OF POTENTIN

This, at last, is something new.

A great mountain, its summit split into three peaks, rises in swollen inclines straight from the sea; gorse and heather covers its slopes at the bottom; from about halfway up, patches of bare grey rock and fields of stone rubble peer through the undergrowth, coming together to form greater swathes, until the three peaks rise bald and jagged in the mist.

More such bare hills rise to the east, and in the distance, a chain of even greater mountains looms over the horizon, like saw teeth. The entire coastline is elevated into an inaccessible plateau, except for one narrow beach, formed at the mouth of a small, wooded creek. There is no harbour here, only a few fishing huts and a short timber quay with a long, sleek boat, painted black, with a hound's head on the sail; our two ships halt at anchor in the shallows while we wait for the ferry boat to take first us, then our mounts and supplies, onto the sandy shore. The entire operation takes up the better part of the day, and by the time it's finished, Marcus declares it's too late to go further today.

"The fort is on the top of that hill," he says, pointing to the southernmost of the three peaks.

The Wrath of the Iutes

"It doesn't look more than a couple of miles away," I say doubtfully.

"How good a climber are you?" he asks.

"I don't know – I never climbed anything greater than the Downs."

"I thought as much. It would be close if we could all sprout wings and fly – but the only way up there is a twisting, narrow path and the higher it goes, the more twisting and narrower it gets. We'll have to start at dawn if we are to reach the summit before night."

I watch the first of my men reluctantly board the wobbly ferry boat, and I remember what Wortigern told me before we departed his fortress; I was still reluctant to embark on Graelon's ships and sail even further north, without at least finding out how my father and my people were faring. I'd hoped that once we landed in Britannia, I'd have time enough to send a messenger to the east, who would bring us some news from Cantia – news that might calm down my men, eager to learn the fate of their kin in their absence.

"I have *some* news from Londin, if it helps," Wortigern said, but what he told me did little to ease my anxiety.

Just as Haesta had predicted, when Aelle's warriors returned from Gaul, he launched attacks all along the border. Stopping short of an all-out war, the bands he sent harassed the village folk, razed the farms and abducted livestock; at first, he did it in his usual way, one that allowed him to still pretend these were just forest bandits, but when Wortigern last heard, an army of Saxons was marching north along the Medu, to face my father's *fyrd* in open battle.

"You will do what you wish, of course," Wortigern told me. "But by the time you reach the east, that battle will be over, one way or another, and the campaign will likely wind down for the winter; here, the war's only beginning, and it's one that might well decide the fate of this part of the world. You and your men will be of much more use to me than you could be to your father."

I was forced to admit his words made sense; I could force-march my Iutes back to Cantia, but it might take weeks, most of it through land as unfamiliar and hostile as Gaul or Germania. By sea, it would take almost as long, if we could even find a captain willing to take us all the way this near the season of storms. With the hostilities open between Iutes and Saxons, landing at New Port was out of the question – we'd have to sail all the way to Leman, or maybe even Rutubi. It was just as Wortigern said: there was no point in us going back to Cantia just yet.

I doubted my men would understand this reasoning. For now, I had to hide the truth from them if I wanted them to follow me to the cold north. I managed to convince Seawine to come with me to Moridun only by describing Cantia as a land of tedious peace, where no glory could be found; if he knew that it, too, was now threatened by war, he would no doubt insist on rushing to my father's aid, no matter how much I tried to convince him otherwise.

I still think Marcus was exaggerating the distance, even as we finally march out from the beach in the grey light and

The Wrath of the Iutes

soup-thick haze of an early autumn morning. I soon realise that, if anything, he understated the effort required to climb to the top of the Forks. It takes us half an hour just to climb out of the valley, up a snaking ox track. By the time we stop for a midday meal, we're not even halfway up. From there, the passage grows even tighter, the path disappearing in places under thick gorse, forcing us to use hatchets and even swords to cut a way through. At long last, weary, saddle-sore and covered in cuts and scratches, we reach the gate of the hilltop fortress – just as the sun sets beyond the sea.

The fort is enormous – the largest I've yet seen in Britannia, and almost as great as the place in Gaul where we defeated the Bacauds. The first ring of walls encloses terraced fields and sheep pastures and some scattered farmsteads; only a few of them appear still inhabited – and only one belching a thin wisp of smoke from the roof hole as some shepherd family prepares an evening meal.

The inner wall rises to over twelve feet of densely packed drystone and encloses the entire summit in an elongated loop, a thousand feet long from end to end, in shape resembling the sole of a soldier's sandal. Within it stands an entire town – or rather, the remains of one; dozens of foundations of round stone huts and, among them, newer, more primitive shelters built of gnarled wood and gorse thatch, some larger roundhouses of an odd design and, around the raised mound at the far end, dozens of army tents, surrounded by a simple palisade.

"There are children here," notes Ursula. A gaggle of dark-haired younglings runs after us as we ride the stone road linking the outer gate with the palisade. They're dressed in drab rags, or naked, but they don't seem miserable – I can tell they're as well fed as any Iutish children.

"This is a living village," says Marcus. "Not just a war camp. Cunedag brought entire families with him from the North – they've been settling all over Gangania."

"The North?" I ask. "He's a Brigant?"

Marcus smiles. "He'll tell you himself."

There are even more children *beyond* the palisade, running among the tents, campfires and stacks of weapons. The lack of discipline makes Marcus wince. He draws the horn and blows a brisk alert. The soldiers rush out of the tents and huts at the sound and, seeing the *Decurion*, begin to form unruly lines on the empty field in the middle of the camp.

A man walks out of the largest tent, tall, lanky, wearing a bright red tunic and a thick golden ring around his neck. He tussles his black hair, yawns and stretches himself before coming up to greet us. A servant woman emerges behind him, leading a little girl, no more than seven years old, staring at us – me and my Iutes in particular – with inquisitive dark eyes. Her hair is the colour of fresh golden straw and tied in a long braid down her back.

The tall man watches in silence as the column of riders passes through the palisade gate and lines up on the muster field.

"Is this all you brought, Marcus?" he asks, disappointed.

The Wrath of the Iutes

"And two ships, with crew," the *Decurion* replies. "We'll have to manage with what we have, Cunedag."

Cunedag comes up to me and looks me over. "And who is that? You picked up a Saxon band along the way?"

I introduce myself formally.

"*Aeric?*" Cunedag frowns. "Somehow, I always imagined Councillor Ash would end up leading the Iutes…"

"That's him," says Ursula. "Aeric was Councillor Ash when he lived in Londin."

Cunedag steps back; he's more than surprised – he's shocked. "You're *Ash*'s son?"

"Yes – why does that surprise you so?" I raise my eyebrow and look at Marcus. "Did everyone here know my father in his youth?"

Cunedag laughs. "I've only met him once. We were both little more than boys back then. Wortigern told me stories about him when he brought me here."

"We need to rest," Marcus reminds him. "We've been climbing all day. We can tell old stories later."

"Of course – just one more thing," says Cunedag. "The introductions are not quite over yet."

He nods at the servant woman to bring the little girl forward.

"I was just about to ask," I say. "She's not from around here, is she? She looks more like one of us."

"As well she should," says Cunedag. "This is young *Domna* Madron – though you knew her as Myrtle, I think. Daughter of Rhedwyn, princess of Iutes – and Wortimer, *Dux* of the Britons."

In the morning, Cunedag invites Ahes, Ursula and myself to a breakfast in an unusual setting – the northern rampart of the fortress, overlooking the plain below. The sky is clear, but the freezing wind tears at our clothes and makes us shout to each other. As the servants set up a table on the stone parapet, and spread a windbreak made of tent cloth along the wall, Cunedag leans over the battlement with a wondrous stare.

"I've never been this high up," Ahes shouts over the breeze.

"Me neither," I reply. "I don't think. There were tall hills in the Arduenne, but everywhere you looked, there were just more hills and woods. Nothing like this."

The view from the top is breathtaking. A broad, flat plain stretches for miles to the south and east; the sea, steel-grey and pocked white with billows, heaves to the west. To the north, the valley soon rises again, into more hills and, eventually, true mountains – the jagged, saw-toothed line of peaks I saw from the ship is now a blue-black mass of ridges and clouds.

The Wrath of the Iutes

"I'm glad I came here, after all," I say. "I've never seen anything like this."

"This would be just a small hillock in the North," says Cunedag. "My home was in the highlands like these." He points to the northern horizon. "Only our mountains are even greater and spread out forever, a never-ending wall of stone and forest, separating us from the lowlands. Beautiful and majestic – but cold and barren."

"Is this why you came here?" I ask. "To seek warm weather and fertile soil?"

He chuckles. The windbreak is now bound to the supporting pole firmly, so we move into its shadow. I welcome the quiet.

"When I was a boy, I travelled south with the Picts, under King Drust," Cunedag says.

"My father fought in that war. Is that when you met him?"

He nods. "I was captured by the Iutes. Ash brought me to Londin for interrogation – it's where I first saw Wortigern, too. I stayed – as a captive, at first, but after Wortimer's first coup, I was released. Eventually, the *Dux* grew fond of me, in the same way he'd grown fond of your father. I think he was always looking for a better son than Wortimer. One that would replace his eldest, who died too soon."

"How long have you lived in Londin?"

[242]

"A few years, on and off… I was Wortigern's envoy to the North. When the Sorbiodun Council came, he sent me with the invitation to the Bishop of Ebrauc. I stayed there waiting for the results of the Council – which is how I survived Wortimer's second coup. He would've got rid of me with all the other loyalists."

"So how did you find yourself here?" asks Ursula. "With an entire tribe of followers?"

"And who are these people?" I add. "Brigants?" I tear a chunk of black bread and cut a wedge of goat cheese. It is a simple breakfast, more suited to a shepherd's table – but the surroundings make it one worth a king.

"They're *my* people," Cunedag laughs. "The Wotadin. After King Drust's death, there was a war in the North. We were losing – Bremenium fell to the Brigants, Coria to the Damnonians… It was at that time that I discovered Wortigern was still alive, here, in Ambrosius's land, fighting the Scots. I asked if he needed help – turned out, he was desperate. So I gathered my clan and a few others, and we crossed the great moors until we reached the Lugwall, and sailed here on a few hide-bound ships… Just in time to save Wortigern from being besieged by a band of pirates here in this very fort," he ends, knocking on the stone of the rampart. "I've been helping him hold the frontier ever since."

"That's… quite a story," says Ahes, though I can see by the confused expression in her eyes that she found following Cunedag's tale difficult, unfamiliar with any of the names or events he mentioned – as was I; the North beyond Wortigern's former frontier was a land of mist and legend,

The Wrath of the Iutes

with only a few cities and tribes known to us in the South. "I would like to hear more of it one day."

"Once we deal with Niall and his army, there will be plenty of time for old tales, I'm sure," says Cunedag.

"And how does Wortimer's daughter fit into all that?" I ask. "Why is she here, instead of some safer place?"

As I ask, I can't help but wonder: how much does my father know about any of this? We never spoke much of what went on in the West, but I'm sure he must have kept abreast of the news during his visits to Londin, where he'd meet with men like Riotham, Ambrosius's representative. How much did he know about the whereabouts of the little girl – Myrtle, as her mother called her, or Madron as she was later baptised? The last time I saw Rhedwyn's child, she was an infant, brought, like me, by Wortigern to the battlefield at Eobbasfleot as hostage, to facilitate the peace talks. I guessed she was being kept in some monastery or hermitage on the southern coast, like I once had been, not in a fortress on the burning frontline.

"It's as safe as it gets," Cunedag replies. "This isn't Segont. The Scots would need to bring siege machines to invade this fortress – and there's nothing here that would be worth the bother, except stones and heather. This will be the last place to fall if we lose the war."

"Still, shouldn't she be somewhere like Ambrosius's court, in Corin?"

"That's the last place she should be!" Cunedag laughs. "The only surviving heir to *Dux* Wortigern's crown? The factions in Corin would tear themselves apart to gain access to her hand."

"Isn't she too young?"

"She's old enough to be betrothed to some ambitious family's son, if not now, then in a year or so," says Cunedag. He shakes his head. "No, she's much better off here, in this remote, windswept wilderness."

I shift the windbreak aside and take a look at the landscape below. There's a road running along the bottom of the valley, from inland to the coast, and further on, towards the distant mountains, not straight enough to be a Roman highway, but broad enough for an army to march at speed. If an enemy decided to strike at the fort, after all, this is the road they would take, and I can't see anything that would stop them in their path – not even a watchtower or a road block. I can't share Cunedag's belief in the impregnability of the fortress; its walls are impressive for a provincial hillfort, but I have witnessed Odowakr's barbarian army besiege a great Roman city and know that a place like this wouldn't even slow them down.

"What kind of army does this Niall command?" I ask. "How many men? Horses?"

Cunedag smiles and raises a mug of warm, but quickly cooling in the icy wind, ale to his lips. "We don't have much to go on," he replies after quenching his thirst. "They move so fast, our patrols can barely keep up. We do know it is the

The Wrath of the Iutes

greatest warband we've ever faced. The Scots never dared to invade Segont before, much less capture it, even with its garrison as weak as it's been in recent years." For a moment, I think I sense some odd tone in his voice when he reports on the Scots' progress, but it might just be his northern accent. "Finding out the disposition of Niall's troops will be the first task for Marcus and his *equites* – and you're welcome to join them, if you want to."

"We came here to fight," replies Ursula. "Not admire the views. When do you need us?"

"The first patrols are leaving in a couple of hours," he says, looking at the grey sky. A lonely eagle circles above our heads. "It's brightening up in the east," he adds. "Should be good riding weather."

"I haven't seen you this merry in weeks," I say to Seawine. The Iute bobs in the saddle beside me, looking around with a broad grin. "I take it you no longer wish you'd gone back to Cantia?"

"We're out fighting again," he replies. "Not marching, not sitting around in inns, not chasing bandits across Gaul. A proper war patrol, before a proper battle… I feel like a warrior again." He slams his chest with his fist.

"But you're fighting for the *wealas*," says Ursula. "You have no quarrel with the Scots."

"We're fighting to keep Princess Myrtle safe," he replies.

The Iutes behind us raise a cheer, even the two fishermen we picked up in Armorica. Until yesterday, none of them even knew Rhedwyn's daughter existed. Not that my father made an effort to conceal her from his subjects – it just wasn't something an average Iute farmer or sailor would have had a chance to find out about. I can see the revelation changed them, invigorated them. They no longer talk of going home, or of having to rest. All these men remember Rhedwyn from their youth: when the Iutes all lived in the squalor of Tanet, she walked among them every day, the bright-eyed princess, the ray of light on which the entire tribe pinned their hopes and dreams for a better life. Now that they've met her daughter, it's like Rhedwyn is born again; it doesn't matter that *Domna* Madron was spawned by that hateful monster, Wortimer – they know he forced himself on Rhedwyn. As far as they're concerned, she's *their* little princess – and they are ready to die for her.

It's more than what happened to them after Tolbiac. Back then, they changed from a gathering of commoners into a band of warriors. Now they're even more than that. They think themselves a household guard – the princess's very own little *Hiréd*. I don't understand this transformation, myself. When I look at Madron, all I see is just another little girl – she doesn't wear a circlet on her head, or a band on her arm; she has no power, no title. I didn't know Rhedwyn, but I knew Wortimer, or rather, I knew what he did to my people – and I couldn't help but see him in the girl's dark, Briton eyes.

I tighten my coat to shelter from a sea breeze. The coastal plain narrows, hemmed in between the mountains, rising steep to our left, and the wide ocean sprawling to our right. It's hard to believe the Romans reached even here, but the

The Wrath of the Iutes

road beneath the hooves of our mounts is undoubtedly their creation, though it hasn't been used by their armies in generations. The place we camped at last night was surrounded by a rounded rectangle of an earthen wall, an unmistakable hallmark of a Roman fort. Back when Roman generals, who must have ordered these forts and the roads linking them built, ventured to subdue this part of Britannia, the Legions would still have been recruited from the sunny South, the land of eternal summer. What must have the soldiers settled here thought about this place, the cold, grey mountains, the cold, grey sea, so far away from home?

"Is that the river we're supposed to reach?" Ursula asks.

"Yes," replies our guide, a short, dark-skinned and dark-haired man, with thick black eyebrows over round black eyes. All I know about him is his name: Potentin.

Before us spreads a broad estuary of sand and swamp. The road turns inland – the river is too wide to cross for many miles; there's another Roman fort guarding the crossing, according to our guide.

"I feel exposed here," I say. There is no shelter anywhere on the coast plain, except some dunes along the shore. Our ten-man mounted patrol must be visible for miles, especially to someone watching us from one of the lofty peaks surrounding us. The bulk of Niall's army passed through here several days ago; the mud along the highway's sides has been trampled and churned by hundreds of feet, a testament to the size of the invading force. An army this large, crossing a hostile land, must have left some troops guarding its rear. I expect us to meet our first enemy soon.

We heard nothing from the garrison at Segont. Everyone there must have been either slaughtered or enslaved after the fortress's capture. There wasn't anyone in the fort we passed last night, either, though I saw no sign of battle, and it's possible it was abandoned long before the coming of the enemy. In the morning, Marcus and his *equites* separated from us and rode east, following another, less trodden branch of the Roman road through the burnt-out fortress at Dun Ambrosius, in an effort to bypass the bulk of the slow-moving Scots army and take a good look at his forward guard. Our task, for now, is to investigate what defences Niall has put up in his rear – and how he's keeping himself supplied.

"At least we're not going to be ambushed," notes Ursula.

"We can't *stage* an ambush, either," says Mullo. Until the last moment, he wasn't sure whether to stay at *Cair* Wortigern with Warus and his Armoricans, or sail with us to Gangania. He's not a cavalryman – he sits awkwardly in the saddle of a pony we borrowed from Cunedag; and his military experience is in infantry work – defence of fortified positions, sieges, pitched battles. But waiting for an unknown enemy in a remote fortress, cut off with no hope of reinforcement, didn't lie well with him. "It reminds me too much of waiting for the Huns, seven years ago," he told me. "I'd much rather take the fight to the enemy than wait for death on this windswept hill."

"We're following a river into the mountains," I say. "And if I know anything about rivers and mountains, that means we're heading into a steep valley. Am I right, Potentin?"

The Wrath of the Iutes

The guide nods. "I would not lead you into an ambush, commander. My kin lives in these forests. They'd warn me if we were heading for any danger."

"And who are your kin?" asks Ursula.

"We're Laigin. Hibernians, too, like those who settled on the southern coast. Many of us arrived here after the Britons abandoned the valley farms and pastures and moved to their cities of stone. My clan lived here long enough for us to know every nook, ditch and peak as well as any Briton."

"Potentin sounds like a Roman name," Ursula notes.

"It's a Christian name," the guide announces proudly. He reaches in his tunic and takes out a small brass cross. "My birth name was Cormac. I was baptised by Bishop Palladius himself, before he sailed to Hibernia to preach to those of us who remained there."

"There are still Christians on your home island?"

"A few, hiding from the heathens like Niall, waiting for the light of True Faith to illuminate the cold, dark hearts of our kings and chieftains."

"But you don't mind fighting alongside us?" I ask. "Most of us are heathens."

"I was taught to seek Christ in everyone, if they show inner goodness," he says, making me wonder if Pelagius's teachings reached even Hibernia. It certainly sounds like something a heretic preacher would have said. "Except Niall and his dogs." He spits. "They can all burn in Hell for all I care."

"You know this Niall, then?"

"I know his kind. They are Laigin, too. *Sons of Cearba, Sons of Liathan, Sons of Fidgen,*" he lists the clan names as if reciting a part of a poem. "It was their fathers who banished us here – and now they're coming to enslave us again. Not while I and my family are alive, they won't!" He raises a fist to the sky.

"Hush," Seawine quietens him. "Look. Someone's coming."

I see it, too, as we reach over the summit of a low hill. A cloud of dust hangs over the road, a mile or so ahead, just where the river disappears into the steep, wooded valley Potentin warned us about. At first, like Seawine, I take it for a plume raised by approaching horses; but as we come nearer, I realise the dust cloud doesn't move.

"These are no riders," I say. "This is a fight. Someone's in trouble."

We pass an overthrown oxcart first. The oxen stand by the side of the road, chewing the cud in stoic silence. A dead, bloodied body of a half-naked man lies thrown over the cart's edge. Another body lies on the road a little further on – a tall warrior, his hair spiked with lime, in a thickly woven plaid tunic, still holding a long knife in his dead hand. In the ditch on the south edge, a cluster of bodies, four of them lying on

[251]

The Wrath of the Iutes

top of each other; more dead are scattered along the highway, some armed and died fighting, others killed while fleeing, stabbed in their backs. It was a brutal brawl, shattered spear shafts, abandoned hatchets and knives spread everywhere – and arrows, long, thick ones, scattered over the road and stuck in the dead bodies.

I take quick note of all these grisly details as we rush past them. We reach the edge of the forest in time to see what looks like the last stage of the battle; three warriors in long, hooded, plaid cloaks, wearing bronze helmets of ancient design and wielding large, straight-bladed swords, are pinned to a broad oak, defending themselves from seven mail-clad spearmen.

"What's going on here?" I ask our guide as we get near. "Do you recognise any of these people? Who do we help?"

"I don't know who these three in plaid cloaks are," he replies, breathless. He's finding it difficult to keep up with our charge on his little Hibernian pony. "But the spearmen are Scots, no doubt about it."

"That's good enough for me. Men!" I point to the attackers. "These are the enemy!"

I don't need to give them any further orders. We've been fighting together long enough for all of us to know exactly what to do. We form into three wedges and strike from the centre and both flanks. Most of the Scots don't even have time to react before we smash into them; I skewer one with a lance through the shoulder. The weapon, wrought for me by Wortigern's smiths to replace the one I lost in Gaul, carves

[252]

the meat smoothly like a butcher's knife. Seawine slashes another's chest with his sword. Ursula misses her enemy – he dodges her lance, just to find himself pierced by Raegen, coming after her in the second wedge.

For a few moments, all I hear around me are slashes, swishes, bloody gurgles and the dull thuds of bodies hitting the paving stones. I finish off another Scot with a flourish of a whirling lance to his neck, then jump off the pony to stop Seawine from delivering a final blow to the last of the enemies.

"Stop. We'll need this one for interrogation."

Seawine picks the man up and breaks his nose with a punch while I approach the three cloaked figures, sheathing my sword and raising my hands in greeting.

One of the warriors steps forward, with her sword still raised warily. She drops her hood and takes off her helmet to reveal neatly trimmed dark hair and bright green eyes over a straight, aquiline nose. Her two companions look similar, though the one on the left is much older, bald, with tufts of grey over his ears; the one on the right is short and fit, with the fire of youth still burning in his eyes. All bear thick golden rings on their necks, like the one Cunedag wore, with wolf head carvings at the ends. Half of the woman's face is painted with blue patterns, reminding me of those worn by Sulien and her people on Scillonia.

"It's fine," I say calmly, in Vulgar. "We're not going to hurt you."

The Wrath of the Iutes

"You are not with Niall?" she asks. I can't place her accent, and I can tell she struggles with the Vulgar tongue.

"No, we're not. We're with Cunedag."

"The Northerner in Gangania?"

"Yes. We're tracking the Scots army."

"You're not from… here."

"Neither are you, by the sound of it."

She laughs and translates my words to the other two in her own tongue, who join her in the laughter. Hearing them talk, Ursula stands beside me and asks them a question in what sounds like the same language. The woman replies, surprised. There are words in the strange tongue that I can almost understand; it sounds like one of the ingredients of the stew that, when combined with Latin, Saxon and countless other tongues of passing merchants and settled Legionnaires, made up the Vulgar tongue spoken in Britannia's east; but they speak too fast for me to make out the meaning of whole sentences.

"What's going on?" I ask Ursula. "What language is this?"

"The old language of this island," she replies. "Before the Romans came, and before the fair-hairs landed, this is how we Britons spoke. It was forgotten by all but the noble families – we speak it to each other when we don't want the serfs to understand us."

"Who are you?" I turn to the woman. "You carry yourselves like warriors – I didn't know there was another army here."

"We are of Mona," the woman replies. Our guide gasps and takes a few staggered steps back, making the sign of a cross.

"The island?" I ask, remembering the map of crumbs Marcus made. *We don't go there.* "I thought the Scots held Mona."

"They thought so, too," she replies with a wry smile. "As did the city-dwellers and the Romans before them. Nobody ever holds Mona for long."

"You're not on Mona now," I note, still puzzled as to who she and her two companions are. "What were you doing here?"

"We…" She pauses and speaks in her tongue to Ursula.

"They came to free their kindred, captured by the invaders," Ursula translates. "Or, failing that, uh…" She pauses. "She said, 'set them on the path to the next life'."

"She must mean killing them."

Ursula listens to the woman speak again.

"They ask us to let them take care of their fallen."

The Wrath of the Iutes

"Of course." I order my men to step aside and make way. The woman nods at her companions – they move to pick their dead up from the road.

"The *druis* of Mona thank you for your help, fair-hair," she says, pressing a fist to her chest and bowing.

The *druis!* I feel a chill; for a moment, I feel I'm not talking to real human beings, but to spirits from ancient past. Weren't they supposed to be all wiped out by the Legions? I suppose it's yet another of Tacitus's mistakes – Bishop Fastidius was always keen to point them out when I read his Histories...

"Wait," I say as she walks past me to help her companions with the gruesome task. "We haven't been introduced properly. I am Octa, son of Aeric, *aetheling* of the Iutes."

She tilts her head and raises an eyebrow.

"I am Donwen, seeress of Red Stone Island," she says. She takes a few steps, then pauses and turns back. "You... you are not like the others." She nods towards my men. "You're neither Britons, nor Romans."

"No, my people came from the North, across the Narrow Sea."

She asks Ursula another question. Ursula looks at me, hesitantly, before answering.

"What is it?" I ask.

"She asked what gods you worship. I told her the Iutes have their own gods – that you're not Christians."

Judging by Donwen's smile, it is the correct answer.

"You go to see the old Roman *cair* across the river?" she asks.

"That was our plan, yes."

"Many guards on this road," she says. "There's a better way. I show you."

CHAPTER XI
THE LAY OF DONWEN

Donwen makes good on her promise; she leads us down the secret passes, hidden ravines, forest paths and ridges that even Potentin has no idea about. This shortens our journey by half, and before long, we reach the river crossing – not the decrepit Roman bridge on the old military highway, but a secluded ford further up the stream, used only by shepherds to gather their flock from the mountains.

"Why did you think we were with Niall?" I ask the *drui* as we wade across. "We can't look like any of his Scots."

"He's been gathering – what's the word – *locmilwir*..."

"Mercenaries," helps Ursula.

"Yes, mercenaries, from many places. Some look like you."

"Saxons?"

She shrugs. "I don't ask. I just kill."

After a couple of miles, we emerge onto a wooded spur of a hill, overlooking a damp valley, a peat moor, criss-crossed by a myriad of streams and man-made ditches. The entire spur is taken over by the remains of a Roman fortress;

judging by the foundations of several large stone buildings still rising from among the tufts of the tall, rust-coloured grass, this was once a small town, at least the size of Icorig and other similar places I've seen in my travels in Gaul; it would have once been the only outpost of civilisation for days, a lonely station guarding a lonely road leading nowhere, built and maintained only to keep the unruly mountain clans in their place. Judging by the state of its crumbled walls, the fort must have been abandoned centuries ago. Was it because the local tribes had finally been subdued, or because Rome decided it no longer cared about this part of Britannia, generations before it departed from the rest of the island?

From our vantage point, I can see great swathes of the grass and heather around the fort recently trampled, burned and otherwise disturbed. A large army made camp here and remained here for a few days; all that is left now is a handful of tents, some thirty men, keeping watch of the meagre traffic on the Roman road and of any enemy that might be marching down it from the north.

"What were they doing here all this time?" asks Ursula.

"Foraging," I guess. "Gathering supplies for the march south."

"But there's nothing here," she says, gazing around the wild, empty moor. "Shouldn't they have brought supplies with them?"

"This isn't just another raiding party," says Donwen. "It's an army. You can't feed an army from boats."

The Wrath of the Iutes

Something about this place, and about our presence here, is bothering me. I lean over to our guide. "Where is that road coming from?" I ask quietly.

"Mona," Potentin replies. He glances at the *drui* nervously. I can see he's terrified of her and her two companions; to him, too, they must feel like wraiths, ghosts, emerging out of a distant legend. "The Romans did not build this road just to control the mountains. They planned to conquer Hibernia, too. They built a fort and harbour on Mona, at the road's end. Niall must be using it to transport his troops and provisions from his home island."

I turn to Donwen. "Did Niall try to conquer Mona first, before coming here?"

She looks up, surprised. "How do you know?"

"You said the sea route alone is not enough. And judging by the size of his army, I'd agree. Where else would he be getting the supplies from? Besides, there had to be a reason why your kin were captured. Niall's chief quarrel is with Wortigern, not with you."

Donwen nods slowly.

"Our home is not like here," Ursula translates her answer as Donwen gestures at the grey, windswept moor. "It is green. Flat. Fields heaving with wheat and barley. Apple groves buzzing with bees. Cattle growing fat on juicy grass."

"She's right," says Potentin. "Everyone here knows Mona is like a Garden of Eden compared to the rest of this country. It can sustain a great host of men."

"So this is how Niall was able to bring his entire army to Wened," I realise. "He could never mount an attack like this just by feeding his men on mountain goats and heather wine."

"He controls only a narrow strip along the old road," says Donwen. "And the Roman mines in the north. If he tries to strike deeper, the entire island will rise against him."

"But you're not at war with him now," I say. "If his men hadn't captured your kindred, you'd never have bothered to fight back."

She shrugs and reverts to the Vulgar tongue. "Many come to Mona, and many go from Mona. We survive."

"By hiding in the woods?"

"We survive," she repeats through clenched teeth.

I notice a movement on the road to our north. I order the others to fall silent. Before long, a caravan rides down from the hills: four oxcarts filled with sacks, crates and barrels, escorted by a dozen men. The guards at the fort welcome the arrivals and guide them to an empty courtyard beside the ruined *mansio*, where other soldiers begin to unpack the load.

With help from Donwen and her companions, I reckon we'd be able to capture the fort from the Scots – there aren't that many more of them than us; but we'd suffer losses, and

The Wrath of the Iutes

the victory here would be short-lived before Niall sent a force to recapture the place. It would be far more effective to interrupt the transports at the source.

"There are wounded men on that last cart," notes Seawine. The Scots guards help the injured off and carry two bodies away somewhere — I can't tell from a distance if they're dead or too wounded to walk.

"Is this your kin's doing?" I ask Donwen.

She grins and shakes her bow — a stout weapon made of wych elm wood, longer and tougher than the bows of Iute hunters or Roman *auxilia*: a weapon capable of launching the arrows we saw on the road, almost the size of javelins.

"I thought you weren't at war with the Scots."

"They take our cattle — we take their lives."

"Do you know how often a transport like this leaves Mona?"

"Daily," she replies. "Sometimes twice a day, if the tide is right."

"Imagine if we could stop them altogether…" I muse to Ursula and Seawine. "Niall could be forced to retreat before he even reached Moridun."

"We could seize one or two transports," says Seawine. "But after that, we'd have the whole Scots army on our backs."

"Not just the transports — halt the entire route. Raze that Roman harbour Potentin mentioned, destroy the boats, burn the piers. It would be better use of Cunedag's forces than chasing after Niall in these mountains."

"Wouldn't Wortigern have already thought of that?" asks Ursula. "I know you like making these mad plans of yours, and they have mostly served us well so far, but this is the *Dux* we're talking about."

"Did *Dux* Wortigern ever try to contact you?" I ask Donwen. "Or Cunedag?"

"We do not speak with Romans," she replies. A dark, vengeful gleam in her eyes reminds me of the ancient stories; of the Legions slaughtering women and children in the *druis* villages, burning down the sacred groves. Donwen's hatred for Rome is as strong as mine for Wortimer and his men — only Wortimer's War happened in my lifetime, while Rome's conquest of Mona is ancient past.

"The Romans are gone," I say. "Only Britons are left."

"They speak the Roman tongue," she spits. "They worship the Roman God. They dwell in the Roman cities. The Legions may be gone, but the men in the stone *cairs* are not true Britons. They're no better than the Scots."

As I ponder her words, Ursula's eyes meet mine. "Don't you dare —" she whispers.

"Would your people speak to me?" I ask the *drui*.

The Wrath of the Iutes

She looks up. "You?"

"I'm no Roman. Or a Christian. The Britons hurt my family, too."

"But you fight for them."

"I fight for peace in Britannia," I say. "Tell her about *Domna* Madron," I ask Ursula. "Tell her it's a family matter."

Though I can't understand most of the words, I hear reluctance in Ursula's voice.

"I wish to meet with your elders," I say when she's finished. "Maybe I can convince them to help us."

Mullo, overhearing our conversation, sneaks over. "What are you talking about? We have orders to pursue Niall, not to wander around Mona."

"We are not here as mercenaries, Mullo," I remind him. "I'm an *aetheling* of the Iutes, and I don't take orders from anyone. Not even a *Dux*."

Donwen looks to the fort. The carts have already been unloaded, and Niall's soldiers are preparing for the night.

"We need no allies," she replies. "We can handle ourselves."

"I have no doubt," I say. "But *we* need help from your kind. And maybe we could work something out – if only I could talk to your elders."

She scratches her nose. "Help me find the rest of my band, and I will consider your request."

"What happened to them?"

"We got separated in the attack on the caravan. The Scots pursued them into the woods around Festiniac. I expected to find them here, as captives, but they must still be out there somewhere."

"Very well. We will help. Maybe we can even kill a few Scots along the way."

In response, Donwen grins and shakes her bow again.

Stealth and surprise are impossible here. The entire slope is built out of the odd, crumbling stone called *leh* by Donwen, weathered into thin, silvery tiles, shattering further under our feet. We slip and slide on it, every step rings out like a million tiny bells. It's as if we are walking on the floor of a mosaic layer's workshop.

"How can we track anyone with all this noise?" I ask.

"*Leh* always moves," says Donwen. "Wind, animals, its own weight… Scots can't listen, always. Watch."

She moves in a shifting, dragging pace, without rhythm, making the movement of the stone sound like a natural

The Wrath of the Iutes

phenomenon. Step... drag... drag... step... step... wait... drag... step...

We leave the ponies with Hleo and Haering at the bottom of the mountain and follow after Donwen, doing our best to imitate her shifting manner. Unfamiliar with these sharp, lofty, mist-shrouded mountains, we can only hope the *druis* know where they're taking us. Donwen claims to be following some track up the slope – we have to take her word for it, as all the rocks look the same to us. She's certain her men are up there; we checked a few other hiding places in the woods below and found only remains of a night camp in one of them. The one we're heading for now, she tells us, is the last possible location her missing men could be sheltering from the pursuing Scots.

She halts, abruptly, and motions us to fall down behind an outcrop of black rock. The cold, sharp tiles poke me through the tunic cloth; there's moisture in the air, piercing my nostrils painfully – dew, or mist, or maybe clouds? I don't know how high we've climbed; with the jagged, grey hills rising all around us it's impossible to tell, but once in a while I catch a glimpse of the bottom of the valley we left behind, far below, as if I was looking through a window to another world, emerald green and sunlit, while we shuffle ever upwards into the dusty gloom.

I peek over the black rock to see a group of some ten men, gathered at the entrance of a dark cave. They're warriors – Scots, judging by their weapons and short tunics; a man I guess to be their chief sits on a boulder, sharpening his long knife in thought. He's the only one wearing a shirt of mail, and he has a round shield slung over his back. A long sword hangs at his belt, similar in shape and size to the one carried by Donwen.

"Is this the place we're looking for?" I ask in a whisper.

Donwen nods.

"Why aren't they going in?"

"Afraid," she replies with a cold grin. She points to a body I haven't noticed before – a Scot in a grey tunic, lying on his back on the threshold of the cave. "The first to go in gets an arrow through neck."

Seawine taps me on the shoulder and nods towards the western slope; another group of Scots climbs up from the forest below, dragging leafy boughs and lugging bundles of firewood on their backs.

"They're going to smoke them out," says Ursula.

"How many men are there in that cave, do you think?" I ask.

"Four, maybe five," replies Donwen.

"That means there's more of those Scots than all of us put together," says Mullo. "If we could ambush them maybe we could stand a chance, but how do you ambush someone on this damn jangling stone?"

His foot slips, releasing another trickle of shards. I glance quickly at the Scots, but they don't seem to notice; it's just as

The Wrath of the Iutes

Donwen said, they don't pay attention to every little noise, too certain of the strength of their numbers.

"We need to get to higher ground," I say. "Somehow."

I look around, seeking a way out of the stalemate; there's another outcrop of the black rock a few dozen feet up the slope, but to reach it we'd have to cross open ground. Then I notice it: a small, flat boulder overhanging the cave's entrance, barely hanging on to the pile of rocky debris it's embedded in, its base weathered by winds and rains into a thin, layered, crumbling wedge. I point it out to Donwen.

"Can you hit it with your arrow?"

She narrows her eyes and studies the rock, before nodding. "I understand."

We wait for the Scots to set up the firewood around the cave's entrance and start a fire under it. The noise they make allows my men to carefully shuffle towards the other outcrop. I watch with satisfaction as Mullo obeys me; without men to command, he's no longer equal to me in the band – he's just another of my soldiers, even if he's the most experienced in combat out of all of us.

At my signal, Donwen draws her bow and aims carefully, biting her lower lip. She waits for the wind to turn before releasing. The arrow strikes the boulder just right; dislodged by the impact, it flies from its nest of pebbles and rolls down in a small, tinkling avalanche. This, at last, is loud enough to draw the Scots' attention. They turn towards the rumble with weapons drawn. By the time they realise no enemy is coming their way from that direction, my men are already on the slope above them, ready to pounce.

Ursula, the *druis* and I leap from around the outcrop. Donwen shoots another arrow, before throwing her bow aside and drawing her straight-bladed sword and a short, leather-bound knife. The Scots commander, with an impatient grimace, orders half of his men to move against us; they don't seem worried or surprised – I'm guessing they expected a few missing *druis* to try to rescue their brethren. But just when the ten Scots are about to overwhelm the five of us, Mullo, Seawine and the rest of the Iutes launch from their hideout, yelling and waving their weapons over their heads.

This, finally, makes the Scots chieftain leap from his boulder. For a moment, he's too confused to give orders. The ten warriors facing us make their own decision; we're an easier target – and we're in their way if they need to flee. Donwen parries an axe with her sword and cuts an enemy warrior through the stomach with the knife. She then jumps back, puts her hands to her mouth and lets out a shrill cry. At that signal, the men hiding in the cave storm out, joining the brawl at the entrance.

The Scots chieftain yells at the rest of his men to pull back from the Iutes and focus on the five of us instead. Within moments, I'm surrounded on three sides by Scots warriors, trying not to trip on the slippery rocks. The tallest of the enemies, holding a great two-handed axe, pushes me back to the outcrop. Sparks fly when the axe meets the rock, too close to my head for comfort; I stab the enemy to my right under the arm and lunge to my left to avoid a falling

The Wrath of the Iutes

club. I shove the second Scot; he slips and falls on his bottom. I draw a bloody line across his chest. The axeman grabs me by the collar and throws me against the outcrop; my head hits the stone and for a split second I see only a flashing light. When I open my eyes again, the axeman lies dead, his neck sliced halfway through by Donwen's sword.

She gives me a strange smile – I can't tell if it's a mocking or approving one – before launching herself into a whirlwind of blades, the sword and the knife drawing blood with every stab, slash and slice. She fells two more men before the Scots chieftain decides to join the battle himself. He shouts a challenge in his harsh tongue and slams his sword against his shield. Donwen stands against him, sword raised over her head, the knife in front. The Scots commander is as tall as her and more muscular under his mail shirt.

As I scythe my way through enemies, in the haze of the grey smoke from the burning wood, I catch only glimpses of the fight around me. We are winning, of that I'm certain – surprise and, with the men from the cave finally joining us, the numbers are on our side; but the battle is tough. One of Donwen's companions falls, pierced by a short spear. Aecba is bleeding from a wound to the left arm. I can't see Ursula anywhere, but I spot Mullo with a broken knife stuck in his shoulder blade, fending off two enemies at once. He falls to one knee, takes an axe blow on the buckler and thrusts his sword forward; then I lose him from sight again.

When I next see Donwen, the enemy chieftain grabs his shield in both hands and bashes her down. They both fall and wrestle in the grey dust, until the chieftain overpowers her, pins her to the ground and rises above her with his long knife in both hands.

Just then, Ursula flies out of nowhere; she tumbles down onto the chieftain and tries to throw him off of the *drui*. He punches her in the face; as she falls back, she drags him with her, the knife in her hand leaving a bloody line across his cheek. He cries out in pain and hits her again. By then, I have finally shoved aside the last of the Scots standing between me and Ursula. I stand over the chieftain and whirl the *spatha* above my head.

"Aside!" I cry.

Ursula rolls away; I drop my blade with full force. The Scot swerves to avoid it, but misjudges the direction, and instead of dodging, he moves straight under the falling blade. My sword hacks right through his neck. Blood bursts in a fountain and into my eyes, blinding me for a moment. The enemy's head rolls down the slope. Donwen leaps after it, picks it up by the lime-spiked hair and raises it high with a triumphant roar.

The remaining Scots, seeing the demise of their chief, launch into flight; they stand little chance against the *druis'* bows. Within seconds, all lie dead, save one, who stumbles and rolls down, turning left and right to avoid the missiles.

"He's going to warn the others!" cries Donwen, but the wily Scot dodges behind a rock and reaches the line of the trees before she can release another arrow. She starts after him, but I grab her and pull her back.

[271]

The Wrath of the Iutes

"Wait."

A moment later, two figures emerge from the forest, dragging a limp body: Hleo and Haering; I can't see their faces from this distance, but I'm certain they're beaming, proud of their first kill. They throw the last surviving Scot to the ground and raise their knives over their heads; the blades gleam blood-red in the grim sun.

We leave the bodies of the fallen enemy to the crows and the wolves, except their commander; the *druis* bury him together with the one man they lost in the battle, under a cairn of jangling stone shards.

"Is this enough?" I ask Donwen.

"This is how we honour all those who fall in battle," she says with a shrug. "You can stay to dig a hole or build a pyre, if you like – but we'd much rather focus on helping the living."

We descend into the woods and reach a heather glade on the banks of a shimmering stream, where Donwen decides to set up camp for the night. Her men help us tend to our wounds with the herbs and ointments they produce from their satchels. Aecba winces when one of the *druis* tightens the wrappings around his arm, but I can tell he's going to be fine after some rest. Worse off is Mullo; the knife in the shoulder is only one of the many injuries he sustained in the charge.

"I have to return to the fort," he says, between groans, as Donwen replaces a blood-soaked patch of ointment on his shoulder blade. "I can't fight anymore, not until these wounds heal."

I know he speaks from experience – with his tunic off, I can see his body covered in old scars, some far deeper and longer than the wounds he received today.

"And I need to get to Mona," I tell him. "I don't know if I can spare men to take you back."

"We'll go with him," says Donwen. "He fought well."

"I thought you were taking me to the island?"

"I speak with your guide," she replies, nodding towards Potentin, who was hiding in the forest all this time with Hleo and Haering; "He knows the way."

"But how will I get your elders to talk to me? I will be just another stranger to them. They'll think we're Niall's mercenaries."

She doesn't reply. Instead, she moves to tend to the wounds of one of her companions, the most injured of all her men. I notice her demeanour soften as she rubs the ointment into the gash on his stomach.

"Friend?" I ask, pointing at the man.

"Brother," she replies after a pause.

The Wrath of the Iutes

"Oh."

He's younger than her; I'd say he's even younger than me, little more than a child; he's unconscious, moaning in pain when Donwen touches his wounds.

"Is the rest of your family… safe?"

"No more family," she says. "No more clan. Niall kill all."

"You fought Niall?"

"When he…" She scowls as she struggles to remember the words of the Vulgar tongue. I call for Ursula to help us with the translation.

"She says Niall attacked her clan's village three years ago, when he was still a pirate chieftain," Ursula explains.

"Then it's not just some stolen cows that made you chase after him."

"Our elders… They think they can keep peace. But they don't know Niall."

"You saw him, then? You know what he looks like?"

Donwen nods. "If I see him again… He's dead."

She kisses her brother on the forehead and orders her men to carry him to the tent. She goes to the stream to wash her hands and face, then returns to the campfire. Her expression changes again; her face brightens, as if with the blood of the wounded she washed off the pain and weariness of the battle.

"How many of you *druis* are there still on Mona?" I ask.

She chuckles. "Not all *druis*," she replies. "Only the elders and warriors."

"What do I call the others, then?"

She shrugs. "You can call us *druis*. Everyone else does. But we are Briton. True Briton. Not like your Romans."

"I am one of these Romans," Ursula reminds her.

"I didn't know Roman women fought so well," Donwen replies with a soft smile. Only now I notice the glint in her eyes when she looks at Ursula; it's similar to the one with which Marcus looked at Ahes.

"I always said she's more a Iute than a *wealh*," I say.

Donwen studies us with a curious look, then asks Ursula a question in her language. Ursula looks at me and laughs.

"What is it?"

"She… asked if we are together."

"What did you tell her?"

"That we're friends."

The Wrath of the Iutes

"That's not what you told me on Scillonia. That's not what you told Ahes."

"Is this not true? Are we not friends?"

"No, that's not what —" I frown, confused; before I can gather my thoughts, Donwen asks Ursula another question. Ursula shakes her head and turns red.

"What did she say now?"

"Nothing," Ursula replies curtly. "It's getting cold," she adds. "I'm going to the tent."

The cold wakes me up. In the haze of shattered sleep, for a moment I can't remember where I am, and why. Then I realise Ursula's not with me. We share the tent for warmth, back to back — it's her absence that froze me out of slumber. She must have gone to relieve herself in the woods. I try to fall back to sleep, but she's not coming back, and eventually I, too, need to take a piss.

It's freezing outside. My breath forms an icy cloud, twinkling in the faint moonlight. I tie up my cloak. I spot Ubba, holding watch at the edge of the glade, and wave to him, then go the other way, towards the clump of low birch trees where my men dug a shallow latrine.

As I pass the tents, I hear a quiet, passionate moaning coming from one of them. I chuckle to myself, thinking it must be Acha and Raegen, the two farmhands, finally consuming their growing friendship. Then I realise both voices are female – and one of them sounds like Ursula. I stand before the tent for a while, eavesdropping, until I grow embarrassed of my manhood, bursting from my breeches at the sounds of Ursula's culmination; I go into the birch trees to relieve myself, though in a different manner than I planned when leaving the tent.

I confront her in the morning, just before we depart for Mona. I try to sound playful about what I heard, but I surprise myself at how bitter my question sounds.

"A woman has her urges," she replies as she ties her blanket to the saddle.

"You don't. Not usually."

She shrugs. "I didn't mind. Donwen knew what she was doing. It must be that *druis* magic I heard so much about…"

"Then perhaps you would prefer to be betrothed to *her* instead."

Ursula stares at me with burning eyes. "At least I didn't have to pay for it."

"I only had to pay for it because the girl who claims to be my *wife* is a cold –"

I stop as I notice the *drui* approach us, rested and bright-eyed. She touches Ursula's cheek with the back of her fingers, and they both smile. Donwen then reaches to the golden ring at her neck. She takes it off and hands it to Ursula.

[277]

The Wrath of the Iutes

"What is it?" I ask, suspicious.

"This shows I sent you," she says. "For the elders. As you asked."

"Are you sure?" asks Ursula. "It must be worth a fortune."

"Then don't lose it," says Donwen. "I will want it back."

"Is this it?" I ask. "It doesn't look much wider than Mosella."

I look down from a low cliff onto the narrow channel that separates Mona from the mainland. These are, according to Potentin, the dreaded Narrows, the supposedly impassable barrier that would have once so stumped the Roman invaders, until they hired Batavians, skilled in swimming in armour.

We marched for half a day along its southern shore, avoiding Scots patrols and the vicinity of Segont. At Segont, the crossing is the easiest – this is where the Roman road ends with a ferry quay, once used to transport Legionnaires to the island and back. Niall left a sizeable force to guard the fortress, and so we were forced to find another place to swim across.

"Remember what Donwen said," warns Ursula. "The currents are swift and treacherous. Even boats can get lost here."

I don't like how vexed Donwen's name on Ursula's lips is making me feel.

"She got here somehow," I say.

I look around. The shore below us is a narrow strip of gravel, bound by a dense wood of low pines. The tide is ebbing fast, revealing mounds of mussels and oysters under the surface, and stone reefs scattered in the middle of the current.

"I wonder how far the water can recede," I say.

"Not far enough," replies Potentin. He points to a dark line of tide in the gravel bank opposite. "It still looks like a good half a mile."

I sense suspicion in his voice. Even after spending a few days in the company of Donwen and her men, the old superstitious fear of the *druis* still darkens his thoughts.

"You don't have to come with us all the way," I say. "As soon as you get us near enough to the elders, you're free to go. Will you be able to make your way back to the Forks on your own?"

He nods with palpable relief.

"Right, then." I turn to my Iutes when we climb down to the water line. "Ursula and I have done this before. The ponies will carry you, if you let them. They're better swimmers than any of us. Hold on to the reins, and float, if you can. Whatever happens, don't panic – if you lose your

The Wrath of the Iutes

grip, go with the flow. The currents will throw you out onto the shallows eventually."

"Is it even possible to swim across?" asks Seawine, eyeing the eddies in the middle of the stream.

"An entire Batavian warband once swam here, if the Ancients are to be believed," I say.

"And how many of them were lost to the tides?"

"This, the chronicles do not say…" I admit.

"We will have to write our own chronicles, then. You heard him, men," Seawine calls on the Iutes. "We can't do worse than some ancient Batavians – whoever they were. We are Iutes. We sailed the whale road. We fought at Trever. We're not going to be thwarted by some muddy old stream!"

There is no trace left of old Seawine, the sailor. Already a figure of authority when I made him a commander of the pony riders at Tornac, the past few months have transformed him the most out of all my Iutes: he is a warchief now, rousing his men with speeches worthy of a Roman general. Where did this come from? My father and my uncle taught and trained me for years to lead men, and still I found it difficult to inspire them at times. But for someone like Seawine, it all came so naturally, even though he's only a fisherman's son.

I can see him as my Gesith *one day. If we both live long enough.*

James Calbraith

I take my pony's reins and lead it into the sea. Even with water reaching just to my knees, I can already feel the strong current tugging at my feet. I look at Ursula; she's biting her lip, her eyes focused on the other shore. I have Hleo holding on to the other side of my pony, and Haering is riding with Ursula; I'm hoping the two fishermen, at least, will know how to conduct themselves in the churning waters. Behind the four of us, Potentin is the next to enter the water, clinging desperately to his mount's mane.

As I plunge into the waves, I hear Ursula start a loud, frantic prayer.

I drop to my hands and knees, gasping and wheezing. I cough and splutter, almost retch from exhaustion. Dark spots fly before my eyes. My heart is pounding in my ears. My limbs are numb; I can't feel my legs, and my hands are twitching from holding on to the reins.

I shake my head, rise and turn back. Seawine is the second to emerge from the churning currents, in not much better shape than me. I help him up and, together with Hleo, we wade back into the water to drag out Ursula and Haering, both struggling in the viscous mud of the low tide. Acha and Raegen are next – the waves cast Acha out onto the gravel shore a hundred feet to our south, and we find Raegen clinging to a tree branch overhanging the water while his pony stands calmly on the beach, staring bored at our rescue efforts. The last to appear on the shore is Ubba; he took his time getting across, but thanks to his slow pace, he's the least tired of us all.

The Wrath of the Iutes

"Is Aecba with you?" he asks.

"He's not here yet," I say. "Neither is Potentin."

"I don't know about the guide, but I saw Aecba drift past me halfway across the strait."

We search the entire length of the shore for the two missing men, from the tall cliffs to the east to the marshes in the west, until at last we find Aecba's pony on the high ground where the forest meets the beach – spooked, but otherwise unharmed.

"You don't think…" Ursula starts.

"Aecba is strong," says Seawine. "He lived by the Medu – he knows how to swim, even with the injuries. I'm sure we'll find him somewhere."

"Keep looking," I order. "The tide must have taken them further west, towards that spur of rock."

"No sign of even Potentin's pony," says Ursula. "What if it cast him back to the other side?"

"We search until dusk," I say. "Then we must move inland, no matter what, or we risk stumbling on Niall's patrols."

"Without Potentin, we don't know where to go."

"Too bad you were too busy meeting your urgent needs to ask Donwen about the way."

We wade further westwards along the gravel shore, until the tide begins to turn – in rivulets, at first, then waves. It's a violent one, thrashing against the current from the opposite direction, spawning even more whirlpools and eddies.

"The water will soon cover all tracks," I note. "We need to hurry."

"Over here!" cries Raegen. He's the youngest of us and has the keenest eyes. We rush to where he's standing – on an outcrop of grey rock, washed over by the waves of the coming tide. He points to a set of shuffling tracks leading from the water – first eastwards, in the direction we came from, but then suddenly veering inland, into the forest.

"We need light to go into these woods," I say.

"My bags are all soaked," says Ursula.

"As are mine," adds Seawine.

I rummage through the saddle bags, until I find a fire striker and some tinder, stored safely in a tightly bound leather purse. By a miracle, both are dry. I search in the gravel at my feet and find a nice, sharp flint stone. I wipe it on my tunic, climb away from the sea and after a few frustrating minutes, I manage a small, miserable flame while my men scrape woodchips from a nearby birch.

"I have oil," says Haering. "But my lamp is shattered to pieces."

The Wrath of the Iutes

"Oil is enough," I say. "Tear your undergarments, soak them in oil."

The primitive torch can't last long, but I'm hoping it'll be enough to at least see in which direction the tracks lead. We tie the ponies to a fallen tree, making sure they're away from the high tide line, and enter the wood. We follow Aecba's trail for a while; before long, I notice he wasn't alone. The forest floor and the brambles are trampled by at least two other men, none of them Potentin, judging by how long their strides were. I nod at Seawine. Quietly, he draws the sword.

We reach a wall of thorns, broken through by the recent passing of Aecba's captors. Carefully, I part the boughs to reveal a glade. It's empty, but there's a trace of a campfire in the middle.

"Look out," I whisper. "They may still be around here."

We enter the glade to seek Aecba's track, but the mud around the campfire is too trampled. Just as I decide to give up the search – the torch fizzles out, and the sun is all but gone beyond the trees – the bushes rustle all around us.

Five men step into the glade, all wearing the plaid hooded cloaks and blue plaid breeches of the *druis*. Four of them hold bows as long as Donwen's, aimed straight at us. The fifth one grips Aecba by the tunic, pressing a leaf-shape blade to his neck. The Iute is not hurt – no more than he already was – but he's so exhausted he can barely stand. All five men stare at us in grim silence.

I throw my sword in the mud and wait for the rest of my men to do the same. I nod at Ursula. She raises her hands to her neck and pulls down the collar of her tunic, to reveal Donwen's golden neck ring.

"We want to speak to your elders," I say in the old Briton tongue – the one sentence Ursula taught me before we crossed the Narrows. "We were sent by Donwen of the Red Stone."

The man holding Aecba grunts an order. The *drui* standing closest to him lowers the bow, reaches for something in his satchel and approaches us, holding long straps of cloth in his hand.

"What's going on?" I ask Ursula.

"He's going to blindfold us," she explains.

"Ask him about Potentin."

Ursula repeats my words, and the *drui* scoffs.

"He says… don't worry about the Hibernian. Worry about yourselves."

The man with the blindfold steps up and wraps it around my eyes. The cloth is drenched in fragrant oils. The darkness smells of oak leaves and juniper berries.

The Wrath of the Iutes

CHAPTER XII
THE LAY OF OUEIN

We set out in the morning, across a gloomy, mist-shrouded plain. I'm thankful that we have only been blindfolded until our departure from the night camp, for I would be loath to miss out on the landscape that surrounds us. Like the *druis* themselves, their land is one born out of myth and mist of ages past. Before long, we pass the first strange stone, standing upright in the field. Then another – and a stone gate, leading nowhere, in the middle of a heath. I have seen a few stones like it in Cantia, and a few more in Scillonia; not even the Briton scholars knew who set them up, or why.

Our captors remain silent; they won't even tell us whether they know anything of Potentin's fate and, not having seen either him or his pony, I fear the worst. Whether it's because they don't know our language, or are simply not interested in what we have to say, I can't tell. Maybe it's both. I can see they're not bad people by the way they treat our ponies, brought from the beach at my prompting – fed with fresh oats and groomed, the beasts seem in better shape than they've been in weeks. But the men are clearly confused by our presence, and uncertain whether to treat us as prisoners of war, or guests. They took our swords, but left us our knives – and the lances are still in the holsters by the pony saddles.

We reach a tall earthen mound, its base bound with great flat stones. I glance at Ursula – she nods, confirming it

The Wrath of the Iutes

reminds her, too, of the mound where we helped slay King Meroweg – and had our hands fastened before the Frankish gods. We walk around it and turn deeper into the marshes.

"We must be getting close," I say as we enter a maze of narrow causeways and hidden paths. "This looks like a good place to hide a secret camp."

We reach a small river and follow it until we reach another clump of woodland. The *druis* suddenly stop and drop to the ground.

"What's going on?" I whisper. Ursula repeats my question. The chief *druis* winces.

"*Quiet,*" he hisses. "Get down."

I spot the source of his concern: a patrol of four mounted warriors, moving slowly and carefully along the edge of the woods. They seem to be searching for something – a way in, I'm guessing, onto the secret path we've been following.

"Hibernians," whispers the *druis* chief.

I notice one of the *druis* reaching for the bow on his back. He looks to his chief – the commander nods. The *drui*, still lying on his stomach, draws and aims the bow. His companions reach for the long knives. I glance over my shoulder – the warrior closing the rear pulls our ponies back behind a low hillock.

I draw the knife, though I'm not sure what good it will do; the riders are a good two hundred feet away. The archer rises slightly on elbow and releases the arrow. Even from this awkward position, the missile flies true and hits one of the riders on the shoulder. The other three stare at their companion in silence for a moment, before turning towards us and spurring their mounts to a charge – though they can't yet tell where the attack is coming from.

The archer nocks another arrow while the other *druis* scatter from the road into the marsh, leaving us to fend for ourselves. The archer stands up and shoots, just as the riders approach within sword range. This close, the missile hits a rider in the chest and throws him off the saddle.

I notice two of the "Hibernians" are fair-hairs, armed with *seaxes* and small round shields. I spring up from the ground with my arms spread wide and a loud shout: "*Stoppa!*" I cry in Saxon. The horse before me startles and rears; the rider stares at me in confusion. Before he realises what's happening, Ursula ducks under the hooves and leaps to drag him down. Seawine and the Iutes surround the remaining foe; he tries to fight them off with his *seax*, but he's no cavalryman, and soon Aecba tears the weapon from his hands while Raegen stabs him in the leg. Still, the rider manages to break through and turn around, whipping the horse furiously. I throw my knife after him, and miss.

"After them!" I call. I run back to the ponies. There's nobody here – the *druis* have all disappeared. Seawine and Ursula join me in the pursuit. We ride across the moor – the ponies have no trouble finding their way through a land that's so similar to their home – and soon cut short in front of the two enemies. The Saxon dashes to the right to ride around us, but Ursula bars his way; he swerves again, his horse stumbles

The Wrath of the Iutes

in the marsh and throws him off. The last one – a Scot, the one with an arrow in his shoulder – tries to pass by me. I thrust my lance in his side. He slashes wildly and rides away with my weapon still in his body. A few steps later, his horse slows down, and he slumps from the saddle with a groan of pain.

Moments later, the *druis* appear on the road in the same out-of-nowhere fashion as they disappeared earlier. Before I can dismount, they rush to the fallen Scots and finish them off, slashing their throats. As they throw the bodies into the marsh, I stride over to their commander.

"What was that all about?" I ask, fuming. "You left us alone to defend ourselves against them, with nothing but knives!"

The *drui* smiles wryly. "You did well," he says.

"I don't appreciate being tested this way. My word should be enough."

"This –" He points to a raised causeway, running straight across the marsh, about half a mile away. "– a Roman road. Hibernians and their hired spears come here every day to seek the elders' village."

"That's not an explanation."

"You look like one of them." He points to the dead Saxon. "We had to be sure. The village is too close."

"The village of your elders is next to a Roman road?" I laugh. "Have you thought about hiding it somewhere less conspicuous?"

"The darkest shadow is nearest the campfire. Now, come." He pats my shoulder. "Chief Ouein awaits."

The village of the *druis* elders, a cluster of large, thickly thatched roundhouses, is nestled within a spilled meander of a lazy-flowing river, bound by the thick oak wood on three sides and an impassable moor on the fourth; in its centre rises another of those low burial mounds that dot the island surrounded by a circle of great bluish-grey stones, all but one of them fallen over and half-buried in the mud.

Our captors lead Ursula and me to the largest of the houses, raised on pillars in the middle of the river, linked to the shore with a narrow causeway. The roof beams and the door frame are carved into snakes and wild boars. Two tall, fierce-looking spearmen guard the causeway. The inside is damp and stuffy, full of smoke, brightened only by a simple hearth with an iron cauldron hung over it from the eaves. There are no benches or stools, except a strange, tall and broad seat of moulded bronze opposite the entrance, on which sits an old man, supporting himself on a curved staff, topped with a golden carving of a wolf's head. He's flanked by two, equally old, women, sitting on animal hides on the floor. The fantastical designs embroidered in the elders' white robes in green, blue and golden thread – dragons, wolves, oak leaves, flowery swirls – are reflected in the patterns painted

The Wrath of the Iutes

onto their hands and faces. The smoke belching from the hearth is thick and dark and smells of wet leaves.

I press my fist to my chest, bow deeply and look around for somewhere to sit. The man with the staff points to a boar skin in front of him.

"The *torc*," he says, reaching out his hand.

"I don't…"

He points to his neck, adorned with the thick golden ring, then to Ursula.

"Oh, of course."

Ursula struggles a moment before removing the neck ring and handing it to the man. He studies it in silence.

"It is Donwen's," he says with a nod, before handing it to the others for inspection. He turns back to me. "She is well?"

"Last we saw her."

"Toranis guards her. Why did she send you here?"

"She did not – I came of my own accord."

"Why?"

"To ask for your help."

The three elders murmur among each other.

"Help?"

"I fight the Scots — the ones you call Hibernians. You fight the Scots. We could work together."

The elder smooths his snow-white moustache in thought.

"Donwen misled you," he says. "We do not fight the Scots. She alone takes war to Niall — for her own reasons."

"That's not what I saw before coming here. The Scots are seeking a way to this place. They're looking to destroy you, and to take this island for themselves."

"I've heard of these riders… But they come in small numbers, and we don't know if it's Niall who's sending them. These might just be the mercenaries from the northern fort."

"What's the difference? Either way, they're a threat to you, and I could help you get rid of them."

He looks at me studiously, then at Ursula. "Why do *you* want to fight Scots? You're not from Wened yourself. Are you another mercenary?"

"I am bound to this war by threads of friendship, loyalty and old alliances. My father is an old friend of the Briton *Dux*, Wortigern. The princess of my people lives under his care. I have many reasons to wish to see Niall's army brought down."

The Wrath of the Iutes

The elder speaks good Vulgar, but this, Ursula needs to translate, as it's too much for him to grasp all at once. The elder nods when she finishes.

"Old alliances, we understand," he says. "Loyalty, we understand. But do you understand old enemies?"

"I know your history. I read about it in ancient chronicles. I know what the Romans did to you. But we are not Romans. I am a Iute from across the Great Sea. I never had any quarrel with your kin."

"Yet you would have us help them. You would have us fight for the city-dwellers, and risk our destruction – and for what?"

"Not for nothing, certainly," I say. "*Dux* Wortigern knows how to show his gratitude, and I offer you myself and my men to do with as you please. If there is anything you require; if there is anything that would make you consider my proposal…"

The elder raises his hand to silence me.

"I am Ouein of the Wolf, chieftain of the Cefni Clan. What do they call you, warrior?"

"Octa, son of Aeric."

He stands up and stamps the staff. The flames of the hearth burst brighter, and in their light I see that his seat is made out of a bronze-bound platform of an ancient, battered chariot. Centuries ago, some Mona chieftain must have ridden this vehicle into war, maybe even against the Legions.

"I sense you're an honest man, Octa, son of Aeric," says Ouein. "But you must understand – we want no fight with Niall. If he wants to take the South, and the city-dwellers are too weak to stop him, I say let him have it."

I bite my tongue. It takes a great effort for me to not accuse him of cowardice; I know that would end any chance of convincing him to my cause.

"If Niall takes the South, there will be no one to stop him from coming back here to finish you off," I say. "You must see this. You're not as strong now as you were when you fought the Legions. And Hibernia is closer than Rome. A *lot* closer. No matter how valiantly you fight, you will succumb eventually."

The three elders murmur with each other again, for far longer this time.

"Go rest now, Octa, son of Aeric," the woman on the left says at last. "We will let you know our decision."

"If I could only…"

"Go rest," the elder presses. A *druis* guard stands before me, glowering, spear in hand. I stand up and bow with my arm pressed to my chest.

"We Iutes are newcomers to this island," I say quickly. "You are its eldest people. There are uncounted ages between

The Wrath of the Iutes

us. Centuries I cannot fathom. Yet I sense – I *hope* – we have more in common with each other than either of us has with those... city-dwellers."

As the guard pushes me out of the hut, I think I notice a glimpse of a smile under Ouein's white moustache.

"City-dwellers." Ursula chuckles. "Is that what you think we Britons are?"

At long last, we're given food – we haven't eaten anything since we set out to cross the Narrows. An old woman brings us some potage with bits of meat, a stodgy dark bread and a strange dish smelling of sea and salt which I identify with some surprise as boiled seaweed. Marcus was right – they really do eat it...

"Not Britons – Romans. Isn't this what Donwen called you? And in this, she's right. You are the only ones who *like* to live behind walls, not just when there is a war. Here, and in Gaul... Remember Weldelf and his River Franks? Even when they conquered a city, they wouldn't want to settle in stone houses."

"Do you think the Iutes will ever move to the cities?"

"I don't know. We will use walls for defence, like in Robriwis, but I can't imagine an entire *city* inhabited by the Iutes. We are farmers and fishermen. As are the Saxons. For generations, we lived only in villages and farmsteads. All we need is an assembly ground and a mead hall. What use would we have for streets, for bath houses, for theatres?"

"I fear you may be right," says Ursula. "Even the Briton nobles prefer their countryside *villas* to cities these days." She sighs. "Who knows, one day, even Londin may stand empty, with only wind blowing dust across its empty avenues, its people faded away into nothingness…"

I force a laugh. "I can't imagine *that* could ever happen. Londin will stand forever."

But I remember what Wortigern told me about the Britons fearing that their time is passing, fearing the fading away she mentions – and I remember Ursula, however much she prefers to dress in the Iutish manner and fight alongside my warriors, is one of those very Britons, raised to inherit all of their doubts and worries.

A guard enters the hut and tells us the elders have made their decision. He waits until we finish eating before taking us back to the house on the water.

"What would you be prepared to do to secure this alliance?" asks Ouein when we enter.

"Anything, Elder," I reply with conviction which surprises myself. "You need only name your price."

Ouein invites us to sit down. This time, there are two wooden stools waiting for us beside the hearth – and the cauldron is bubbling with hot mead.

The Wrath of the Iutes

"You say you've read about our wars with the Romans in the writings of your Ancients."

"Yes, Elder," I reply.

"And did these Ancients write about the king called Caratacos, and the queen called Cartismandua?"

It takes me a moment to remember. It's been years since I read this chapter of Tacitus.

"I… am familiar with those names."

"Caratacos was the last chieftain fighting against the Roman conquest," Ouein explains. "When he lost the final battle, in the mountains of the Ordows, he fled to Cartismandua, Queen of the Brigants…"

"She gave him up to the Romans, if I remember correctly."

Ouein's face brightens in a smile. "You *do* know the old tales!"

"This all happened countless generations ago – how do *you* still remember it so well?"

"We are not barbarians, son. We have our ways of keeping our history alive just as well as your Romans – if not better. What these Ancients wouldn't know is that before fleeing north, Caratacos sent his *torc* and his sword to us, for safe-keeping."

"His *torc*... The neck ring?"

Ouein nods. "We kept it in our *cair* on the north coast... The last to fall to the Romans. They built their fortress and harbour there, and kept Caratacos's treasure in their vault, out of our reach for centuries."

"But the Romans left a generation ago," says Ursula.

Ouein winces, as if reminded of some shame. "We... feared their return for too long. Soon after, the Hibernians arrived. This was their first fortress in our land. We missed our chance. Now, we have no way to breach its walls – the Romans knew how to build well..." he admits grudgingly. "We tried subterfuge, but the Scots have become too wary."

"You want me to sneak inside," I guess. "But why should I succeed where you have failed?"

"There are men like yourself among Niall's band," he says. "You've seen them."

"Mercenaries."

Ouein nods.

"Do the Scots know about this... treasure?"

"If they did, they'd have already tried to bargain with us for it," says Ouein. "They have no need for such trinkets, while to us it is worth more than a chest of gold."

The Wrath of the Iutes

"How do you even know it's still there?" asks Ursula. "After so many centuries?"

"Twenty years ago, we sent a band to try to capture the fort from the Hibernians… A few reached the vault and lived to tell us they saw Caratacos's sword there. We believe the *torc* must be there, too."

I look to Ursula. "What do you think?"

"It's no madder idea than anything we've done in the past," she replies.

"I know. Sounds almost exciting." I turn back to Ouein. "If I bring you the *torc*, what aid will you offer in exchange?"

"I have warriors of four clans waiting for my word," he says. "A hundred men, altogether, scattered all over the island. They would all be at your disposal."

"If they're all as good fighters as Donwen and her men, it should be enough to upset Niall's entire provisions trail."

"For a time." Ouein nods. "Your… *Dux* Wortigern would need to do the rest."

"I understand. You would risk destruction if you angered Niall and we failed to destroy his army in the South."

He sighs and straightens his back. "I would not agree to this if I feared defeat," he says, then leans closer. "Four centuries have passed since Caratacos's defeat. If the gods see it fit to ruin us now, so be it. We survived long enough." He stands up and stomps his staff on the floor twice. The servant boys rush to fill our mugs with the hot mead.

"Now, ask," Ouein declares. "You will receive all you need for the mission."

I sip the mead, gathering my thoughts. There isn't much to think about – Ouein pretty much devised the plan for me. Only small details remain.

"I need one of your men. Not too weak, not too strong. And a boat."

"Only one boat? That will not be enough for all of you."

"One is enough."

"Very well. Seleu will go with you to the mouth of the River Frau. The Otter Clan has a dwelling there. They will provide you with the boat. Anything else?"

"If I think of anything before dawn, I'll let you know."

Ouein comes up to me and studies my face for a long while by the light of a torch.

"I heard you fair-hairs were – what do the Romans call us – heathens? You have your own gods?"

"Most of us do. What of it?"

The Wrath of the Iutes

"I would pray for the success of your mission. I would offer sacrifices to our gods and yours, if you so wished. Why have you not asked for it?"

He must still suspect me of being a Christian, then, rather than a heathen, like himself. How can I explain to him, the chieftain of what amounts to an army of priests and bards, that I am neither?

I decide only boldness and honesty will work here.

"Forgive me, elder, but your gods… have not served you well in the past. I would rather depend on the favours of my own deities."

The other two elders gasp. Ouein opens his eyes wide in surprise – then laughs.

"Well said!" He slaps my shoulder. "Nevertheless, I will perform the rite of the oak and bull tonight. Just in case. You're welcome to take part in it, if you wish – or not, if you feel our gods' favour would only hinder your efforts," he adds with another chuckle.

It is strange to think that, many years ago, hundreds of miles to the east from here, I watched an ancient priest perform a ceremony so similar to the one Elder Ouein conducts before me. The two old men had nothing in common; one, a Iute, himself come to this island across untold miles of the Whale Road a mere generation ago – the other, a *drui*, descendant of countless sons of *druis* like him, native not just to Britannia, but to this particular speck of land. And yet, I believe if they could have ever met, they would've found more in common with each other than either of them would with the Latin-speaking city-dwellers that call Britannia their home.

The main difference between the two rites that I can see is that the beast being led to the slaughter is not a horse, the sacred animal of the Iutes, but a young white bullock. It looks wretched and famished, barely standing on its thin legs – it must have been kept especially for this sort of event, rather than fed for meat and milk with the village's other cattle. This is not a sacrifice with which any Iutish god would be content.

Ouein, wearing a crown of oak leaves and mistletoe twigs, approaches the stone altar, carved in the same shapes and figures as are painted on his robe. A small flame burns on its flat top – it should be a great bonfire, but it would betray the village's position to the Scots patrols. The elder throws a handful of wet herbs and leaves on the fire, a gesture I've seen so many priests do so many times before, my father among them; a single puff of thick black smoke bursts from the altar and disperses in the wind.

One of the two elder women approaches Ouein with a jug and pours a thick, dark red liquid into an oak wood bowl he's holding. Once it's filled, Ouein takes a sip, then offers a sip each to every *drui* gathered around the altar. At the end, he approaches me and Ursula – and throws it in our faces. The liquid smells of blood, earth, rotten wheat and mushrooms. While I still splutter and wipe the dirt from my eyes, Ouein grabs my face, opens it forcefully and pours some more of the strange water into my mouth. I push him away,

[303]

The Wrath of the Iutes

coughing and spitting, but not before a great portion of the bowl's contents ends up, burning, in my throat.

I look at Ursula — she takes the bowl from the elder's hands and drinks the red water herself with barely a wince. I don't know why she decided to take part in the rite; as a Christian, she must be treating it all as the work of demons. I've never seen her at any of our Iutish rituals. Does she see it as a test of her faith — or is she truly curious of what the Briton gods can tell us about the future?

As the burning sensation spreads through my body, my legs buckle under me. I fall to the ground; I feel like retching, but nothing is coming up. I see everyone around us kneel down as the poison takes control of their limbs. Ursula falls on all fours, groaning and spitting bile. The insides of my arms and legs are on fire.

Ouein remains the last one standing. He approaches the bullock, draws a golden sickle and with one swift move slashes its throat. Blood spews in a waterfall; the beast lets out an agonising bellow and staggers. Ouein gives it a shove and it falls on its side, thrashing its legs.

"I've seen this before," I whisper to no one in particular. But how could I have seen it? There are no *druis* left anywhere in Wortigern's domain. No heathen priests of any kind, except those of the Iutes, Saxons and Angles in the North. So why does this seem so familiar?

It's not that I've seen it — I've *heard* of it described in one of the *scop* songs about my father's life. The betrayal at Sorbiodun — and the ritual performed over my father by the mysterious priest. But that was all pretend — a fake *drui* Wortigern brought in to prove to the gathered bishops the healing power of the pagan gods, where the Roman God failed. This one is real — or at least, these *druis* believe it to be; whatever vision the combination of the poisonous drink, the smoke and the blood in the air will provoke in them, they will take it for reality.

"I'm flying," says Ursula.

I look at her — she remains firmly on the ground, but her body appears to me strangely elongated, bulbous, her eyes change size and colour. It's not just her — the entire world is flashing all colours of the rainbow, vibrating and undulating in the rhythm of some unheard music. I stare at my own hands and legs, and I understand now what Ursula means — I myself appear to be suspended by some unseen force a few inches above the ground…

A blood-red mist flows from the gash cut by Ouein's sickle in the bullock's steaming carcass and cloaks us all. I hear Ursula's voice through the fog:

"Octa, I'm scared. What's going on?"

"It's alright," I tell her. My voice is once booming, once a whisper. "Look around. Everyone else is the same."

The others writhe in the sand, moaning and tearing at their faces. I reach out to her. She extends her hand — or what I believe to be her hand; our fingers meet, and the red fog explodes in all-enveloping light.

The Wrath of the Iutes

All is dark now – except for the great funeral pyre blazing at a short distance. At length, people appear out of the darkness all around me, a great crowd, Iutes, Saxons and Britons gathered together.

"Whose pyre is this?" I ask the man standing close to me. He stares at me in disbelief.

"*Rex* Aeric's, of course. The king of Britannia."

"Don't you mean, 'the king of the Iutes'?"

"He is that, too, yes – but who are you to come here and not know King Aeric? A spy of the Franks?"

He steps forward, his hand reaching for the sword at his waist. I step back and fall backwards into the red mist.

I come back to a spacious room, with stone walls and a large window, overlooking the roaring sea. Ursula sits in a chair by the window, holding a bundle of cloth. She appears just like she is in reality, wearing the same clothes as in the *druis* village. She turns to me and smiles.

"Look, Octa. A son. Our son."

I step closer. I can't see a child inside the cloth, but the bundle lets out a gurgling laugh.

"How do you know he's ours?" I ask.

"Who else's should it be? Look, he's got your hair."

She points to a piece of cloth where a head should be, fiery red, with streaks of gold.

"Have you brought me a gift?" she asks.

"A gift?"

"From your travels."

A box appears in my hands, a small ivory casket, sculpted in flowers, vines, and the bee-shapes I remember from the Frankish king's palace in Tornac.

"Ah, Hildrik's bees." She smiles sadly. "What's Frankia like these days? I haven't seen it since the Siege of Trever."

"Why didn't you come with me?"

"It is a wife's duty to take care of the heir," she says, echoing Silvia's words. "And for that, I must stay here, in your father's fortress, forever – and admire the world through the gifts you bring me."

She reaches out for the casket. When she touches it, the ivory flashes the same bright light as the red fog before; the stone walls disappear, as does the entire fortress and the hill upon which it stood. All that remains is the sea, raging, devastating, ravaging the shore, tearing out great chunks of the beach, the cliff, the fields beyond it. I see a great swarm of men, building sea defences, raising banks of earth, digging canals to control the flow, all to no avail; the sea swallows

The Wrath of the Iutes

them all, their stone fortresses, their marble *villas*, their walled cities, their amphitheatres and bath houses; when it retreats, all that is left are little hamlets of thatched huts, small farms, a few wooden mead halls and a smattering of burial mounds. What remains of the walled cities are empty husks of ruined houses, avenues devoid of all life, wind rising dust on the squares overgrown with grass and weeds; wild beasts roam where once traders had their stalls; mud and silt covers the harbours; bones whiten, unburied, under the sun.

"This is what I see in my dreams," says Ursula, standing beside me. The child is no more; she wears the mourning robes. "This is what I fear. This is what we *all* fear."

"I know."

I take her by the hand. I spot something gleaming in the sand at my feet. I stoop to pick it up – it's a cloak pin, the same I once left in the mud of Beormund's Isle, when my father came to take me to Cantia. The ancient spiral brooch I found back then lies beside it, too.

I unclasp the pin that holds Ursula's cloak around her neck. It is a simple brooch, with a disc of bronze enamelled in blue and white swirls.

"I promise, whatever happens, I will never let us be forgotten," I say and put her brooch with the other two in the mud.

The earth rips apart. A great hand appears through the mud and reaches for me. Ursula cries out and disappears. The hand grabs my nose, forces my mouth open and, once again, some unknown, bitter liquid is poured down my throat.

The bitterness forces the contents of my stomach out. I kneel down, retch out my insides, and with every retch, the vision recedes and the reality returns, until I'm back in the *druis* village, staring at the pool of bloody vomit before me.

"Welcome back, Octa, son of Aeric," says Ouein, helping me up. "The rite is over. You have seen all there was to be seen."

"What have you done to us?" I rush at the elder, but the others grab my hands and hold me back. "What kind of poison have you fed to us?"

"It has many names," Ouein replies softly. "Wheat fire. Horned rye. The black grain. Don't worry, it is harmless, once you rid yourself of it. If you are fortunate, it should tear open the cloth of heaven for you. If not – it just makes your stomach burn."

"I saw… things."

"Then you have been blessed. What about you, child?" He lays his hand on Ursula's shoulder. "You are shaking. What wonders have you witnessed?"

"Nothing," she replies. I can see in her eyes that she's lying. "Your demons have no power over me."

The Wrath of the Iutes

Ouein chuckles. "It matters not if you believe or not. I have seen the black grain work even on your Roman priests, a long time ago, in the previous life."

"What do you mean, *previous life*?" I ask, but the elder only smiles and shakes his head.

"We have to keep *some* secrets."

"And what have *you* seen, elder?" I ask. "Did your gods bless our mission?"

He shrugs. "Does it matter? You didn't ask for their favour. Would you not go if I told you they didn't?"

"I would be more careful, perhaps."

"It is always prudent to be careful, young Octa."

He leaves us with that as one of the women approaches us with a bowl of cold water and cloth to wipe our faces. I reach out to Ursula. She seems still shaken with what happened; her hands are trembling. The white-and-blue brooch still pins her cloak on the shoulder. Somehow, it makes me feel relieved to see it there.

"I know you saw *something*," I say.

"I don't want to talk about it. It's just pagan sorcery. Father Albinus warned me about these rites…"

"Then why did you come here? What did you want to see?"

"I... I don't know. I haven't been to a mass in so long – I think I hoped God would come to me even through this demonic haze..."

I take her hands in mine and wipe a tear from her eye with my thumb.

"Was it our child?" I ask. "Have you seen our son?"

"It was just a phantasm," she replies. She doesn't seem surprised by my knowing what the wheat fire showed her. "A dream."

I move closer. "It doesn't have to be."

She pulls away. "At a moment like this, you'd –"

"No, wait – that's not what I mean..."

Her face contorts in what I take at first for the scowl of fury, but soon realise it's a grimace of pain.

"Oh, Lord's wounds. Step back. I can feel it all coming back again."

I'm too slow to react. She bends in half and spews out a pool of bile and vomit, straight at my boots.

CHAPTER XIII
THE LAY OF SELEU

"Someone's coming," says Seawine.

"Now, Seleu!" I order.

The young *drui* rushes out of the reeds, with Seawine chasing after him. They climb up the dune slope to the top of the Roman causeway and stage a mock fight for a few blows, before I run out and help Seawine pin Seleu to the ground – just as the Scots patrol emerges from behind the bend.

The Scots shout something in their language and run towards us, weapons drawn. I pick Seleu up, holding him by the tunic and pressing my knife to his throat.

One of the Scots approaches carefully, pointing his spear at us. He looks at me, then at the *drui* warrior in my grasp, then at Seawine and the other Iutes, now climbing towards us from the beach. Ursula is not with us; she's hiding in a nearby hazel grove with Hleo and Haering. It would be difficult to explain a Briton's presence among us to the Scots, and somebody has to take care of our ponies, which are our only way of escape should things go wrong.

"What —" he starts, but that seems to be the extent of his knowledge of the Vulgar tongue. "Who?"

"Niall sent us," I say slowly. "Our boat crashed." I point towards the beach with the knife. The Scot's eyes follow – from the top of the dune, he can see the boat I borrowed from the Otter Clan, beached and hacked to pieces. "These men attacked us," I add, shaking Seleu. "We captured this one; the others got away."

"Niall?" the Scot repeats the only word he understood from my speech.

"Yes, your chief, Niall," I say with an exasperated sigh. "We're Saxon mercenaries. *Gall óclach?*" I add, pointing to myself and Seawine.

His eyes brighten, and he nods vigorously. Ouein taught me this and a few other useful words – they fought with and lived alongside the Hibernians long enough to have learned a little of their language.

The Scots make a clumsy, hesitant effort at surrounding us in a circle of spears – there are as many of them as us, and they must see we could destroy them if we wanted to.

"Come," their chief says, waving his spear in the direction of the fort.

"You don't need to point this thing at me, I know the way," I say, pushing the spear blade away.

An odd feeling comes over me as we march up the road to Niall's coastal fortress as it climbs up a rocky hill in a broad arc. This is the last Roman road; the end of the Empire. Even more so than Moridun – there, at least, there was land

The Wrath of the Iutes

further on, *villas* and farmsteads inhabited by the citizens of the Empire. Here, there's nothing but the sea. No Roman soldier, as far as I know, ever marched further – no commander attempted to conquer Hibernia. As far as Rome was concerned, this here was the end of the world.

Somehow, this feels right. It's a barbarian land; windswept, rugged, empty, dotted with ancient remains of some unknown people. The Romans only felt safe here within their stone walls – they built no *villas* here, no farms, no roads other than the one we march on now, with fortified *mansios* strewn along it as the only other sign of civilisation. No wonder the *druis* managed to survive so long here even after they were supposedly "destroyed" by the Roman soldiers. I can imagine the Legionnaires, huddled in the forts and watchtowers, peering cautiously over the battlements into the wilderness beyond in fear of the wild-haired warriors and their mad priests, clad in nothing but plaid cloaks and body paint. What was Rome doing here, anyway, at this end of the world? What was here that was worth conquering, worth slaughtering women and children, worth destroying the sacred groves and overturning the ancient stones?

I find no answer to this question as we reach the gate of the fort – and, judging by its size, neither did the Romans. This place is hardly worth being called a "fortress". In Gaul, it would count as a mere walled outpost. It's half the size of the Saxon Shore forts I'm familiar with from Cantia, like Rutubi or Robriwis: a walled-off rectangle no more than two hundred feet across, with a round tower in each corner. There are hardly any buildings, or their remains, visible from outside; a triple-vaulted bath house, attached to the outside of the western wall, is about the only facility offered to the

Legionnaires to sweeten their stay in this inhospitable garrison. Its roof is now fallen in, and the Scots did not bother to patch it up; I doubt they're even aware of the empty building's purpose.

A small village had once grown along the road south of the fort's only gate, protected by a low earthen wall and ditch, but little is left of it now, replaced by a cluster of poorly built round huts of daub and straw and some tents made of stitched leathers.

"Wait," the Scot tells us and goes inside, leaving us under more guard – the sentries from the gate join their comrades. The Saxon mercenaries in Niall's army must be feared, judging by how concerned the guards appear with our unexpected arrival.

"This is the great fortress the *druis* were unable to conquer?" Seawine whispers, eyeing the wall. It's in surprisingly good shape but can't be more than fifteen feet high and just a little over five feet thick – again, merely half the size of those at Rutubi. The round towers are more substantial, but after our experiences in Gaul, it's difficult to imagine how a fort this size could have proven impregnable to even the smallest band of warriors, provided they were determined enough.

"I know, right?" I reply. "How many men would have been stationed here? A couple of hundred at most…"

"I don't see any vaults here, either," Seawine notes. "Are you sure we've been sent to the right place?"

The Wrath of the Iutes

"No matter how small a fort, there must have been a *Praetorium* or a *Principia* inside. Maybe it's still there – let's wait until they let us in."

The gate opens again. An aged, stocky Saxon, with long, scraggly beard and clumped-up hair bound with a silver diadem strides towards us, accompanied by two Saxon guards.

"Who in *Hel* are you?" he asks suspiciously.

"Who are *you*?" I ask him back.

He huffs. "I am Hrodha, commander of this fort. I know each and every Saxon in Niall's army. I don't know *you*."

Hrodha… Why does this name sound familiar?

"That's because we're no Saxons," I reply. "We're Haestingas. I am Deora, son of Aec, this is Seawine, my second in command."

"Haesta's men?" he scoffs. "Niall is really scraping the bottom of the stew pot." He spits at my feet. "What are you doing here?"

"Niall sent us to help you with the caravans," I reply. "He's worried about the *druis* attacks."

Hrodha scratches his cheek. "It's true we've lost some men recently on Niall's wild chase. I told him we should've left the *druis* in peace…" He eyes our weapons and our muscles. "These are some good swords," he notes. "Got them in Gaul?"

"You've heard?"

"We may be in Erce's arsehole here, but we're not wholly cut off from what goes on in the wide world," he says, and I'm reminded that some of *Rex* Aelle's men also took part in Odowakr's campaign. "Come with me." He waves. "You're fortunate – we're almost ready to send out the next transport. It's just the four of you?"

"Just four left," I reply grimly. "The seas were rough."

"Should've come down the Roman road. Or were you too afraid of the *druis*?"

We enter the fort, and I can see that it has no wall to the east – instead, it opens onto a small harbour, with a pier raised on stone foundations, where the leather-bound black boats deliver their loads after the long, perilous journey from Hibernia. A column of oxcarts awaits in what was once a muster yard, to be burdened with these supplies and embark on another arduous trek in search of Niall's main army.

"The Briton patrols are out in force," I say. "Some new riders arrived from the South."

He chuckles. "Oh, I know all about it. You have nothing to worry from them."

What does he mean by that?

I glance around the fort, looking for what Ouein could have interpreted as the "vaul". Only two structures are left standing from the Roman occupation – a granary, now taken

The Wrath of the Iutes

up as command post by Hrodha's men, and half of a *Praetorium* – just one room, really, in which I presume Hrodha himself lives. The garrison is made up half of Saxons, half of Scots; I'm surprised Niall puts so much trust in the Saxon mercenaries, and express this surprise to Hrodha.

"They say Niall is himself half-Saxon," he replies quietly. "Though you wouldn't guess that by looking at him, right?"

"Right," I reply with a forced chuckle.

"You can set yourselves up in that corner." He points with his sword. "Ask Nath for some tent cloth. He's in the hut by the old bath. He speaks a bit of our tongue."

He nods at the two guards. They step up to Seleu. I pull him back.

"He's ours," I say.

"And what were you planning to do with him?"

"None of your business."

"Look, I don't care whether you cut his head off or hump him." Hrodha shrugs. "As long as you make sure he doesn't run away and bring more of his filthy kin."

"What do *you* do with your prisoners?"

"I don't take prisoners." Hrodha grins. "But if I did, I'd slam them over there." He nods towards the half-ruined *Praetorium*.

"Isn't this where you live?"

"There's a small cellar underneath. It's full of rats and dung. If you put your captive there, I swear my men won't touch him – unless you tell them to."

"Fine. Take him." I shove Seleu forward. "No need to be gentle."

"The caravan leaves in the morning," Hrodha says as the guards march Seleu away to the granary. "Make sure you're ready. We're already late and Niall's growing impatient. He doesn't like his men going hungry."

"We'll be ready."

"I'm having some song and stew in my quarters later. You're welcome to join me, Deora, son of Aec."

"Gladly. It's been a while since I've had some civilised food."

"I knew your name sounded familiar!" I declare. "You fought Haesta a few years ago, didn't you? At Port Adurn, was it?"

I slurp the stew – it's watery soup of kid goat and carrot, with some odd leaves and grains; a Hibernian recipe, Hrodha tells me. The ale is Saxon, and well brewed.

There are just the two of us at the small table; this would've been the *Praetor*'s personal office and bedroom,

The Wrath of the Iutes

built to a Roman standard, same as in any other fort – Icorig or Robriwis, except, like everything here, only half the usual size. Hrodha's bedding occupies a third of the floor, by the fire; next to it stands an iron-bound chest, covered by red cloth embroidered in patterns strangely similar to those on Ouein's robe.

Hrodha… The brave Saxon warchief who stood with my father against Haesta's warband at the Battle of Seal Isles. Fortunately, he never met me – I was still living in Londin then – or our ruse wouldn't survive our first meeting. I wish I could tell him how grateful my father was for his help that day, and how much we both admired him for disobeying *Rex* Aelle's orders. If not for him, my father would've likely been slain, along with his entire *Hiréd*. There would be no *Rex* in Cantia, no kingdom of Iutes – and I would be fully orphaned.

"And a fat lot of good it did me." Hrodha runs his fingers through his beard. "*Rex* Aelle blamed *me* for the war with the Iutes. He took my fortress from me and forced me and my men to seek work for hire. Now he's waging a war on Aeric himself, and won't even let me guard his camp. This is how I found myself in this forsaken place, a harbour guard for the Scots."

"When Niall conquers this land, I'm sure he'll reward you greatly for your service," I say, struggling to feign disinterest in Aelle's war in the east.

"I don't care for rewards." He waves his hand and coughs. "I am an old man, Deora. I was old when I fought your *Hlaford*. I expect to die here. When I do, my men will be relieved from duty – I wouldn't be surprised if they came back with you to join Haesta, especially after everything we've heard from you."

Urged by Hrodha, I told his men the tale of Haesta's campaign in Gaul, as much of it as I knew – and made up the rest; it's unlikely that they'd ever find out the real story. The warriors murmured in grim satisfaction as I described the final, bloody battle at Trever. My listeners did not care much for the fate of Odowakr and his army. Blood, guts and glory was all they wanted to hear about.

I finish the stew and glance nervously at the trap door under my feet.

"Don't worry," Hrodha says. "Your *drui* will be just fine. If you want to sell him, the Scots over on Hibernia pay good price for men like him. Nath could arrange the transaction for you."

"I'll think about it." I nod. "I was just going to whip him slowly to death, but slavery sounds good, too…"

Poor Seleu. He hadn't volunteered to join our mission – Elder Ouein ordered him to. I only needed him as a ruse to get into the fort, and I didn't give much thought to getting him out again. Then again, I hadn't exactly formed a plan for getting *ourselves* out of Hrodha's fortress, once we find Caratacos's treasure… *If* we find it.

If the "vault" is to be found anywhere, it's under the *Praetorium*. I checked the ruined bath house when we visited Nath for supplies – there didn't seem to be anything hidden there. And if Seleu has enough wit to do anything in his

The Wrath of the Iutes

captivity other than defend himself from hungry rats, he might be the one who discovers the *torc*'s whereabouts. Unless…

I lean over to Hrodha.

"Tell me, chieftain…" I whisper. "Is there any truth to the rumours some of Niall's men have been spreading about this place?"

"Rumours? What rumours?"

"The *druis* treasure."

He smiles mysteriously. "I fear you're too late, Iute. We found a few chests in the cellar, but sold it all off long ago."

"Was there gold?" I ask.

"Not much. Silver and copper, mostly. A few trinkets, some old coins. Weapons."

"Weapons?"

He waves his hand. "All rotted and rusted through. Although…" He takes a gulp of ale and glances around. "I did find a curious sword. It was wrapped in embroidered cloth, and the hilt was studded with jewels… Not worth selling – I guessed it must have belonged to some warchief, so I kept it for myself." He nods towards the iron-bound chest.

"Maybe the *druis* would pay you for it?"

"Maybe I'll ask them when this war is over." He nods. "If there are any left by then."

We both laugh. A guard approaches the table and leans down to whisper something in Hrodha's ear.

"Ah." The chieftain taps the table.

"Problems?" I ask.

"Not at all. It merely looks like today is the day for unexpected visitors. Forgive me, Deora. I must go down to the harbour."

"I understand. I'll go check on my men."

We exit the granary together, before parting our ways. There is, indeed, a new vessel approaching the shore. It's hard to see the details in the quickly descending gloom, but the shape, carved out of the dusk by the lanterns on prow and bow, is unmistakable. It's long, sleek, painted black – and when the evening gust fills out the sail, the white hound's head gleams in the light of the lanterns.

I rush back to the tent my men set up in the far corner of the fort.

"Hide yourselves," I order them. "Don't come out until I tell you."

"What's going on?" asks Seawine. "Are we under attack?"

The Wrath of the Iutes

"Worse," I say. "For some reason, Cunedag's ship just arrived into the harbour."

"What now?" asks Seawine after we watch Cunedag enter the *Praetorium* with Hrodha. It's already dark out; most of the fort is shrouded in shadow, with only a few braziers burning on the ramparts and campfires scattered throughout. The *Praetorium*, lit brightly from outside, is a gleaming jewel of flame in the darkness.

"Change of plan," I say.

"There was a plan?" Seawine chuckles.

"I was hoping we'd have more time to prepare." We were supposed to leave with the caravan and flee with the loot once we were safely away, but Cunedag's arrival changed everything. I can't let him recognise any of my Iutes, and we can't possibly hide from him in daylight, or it would raise Hrodha's suspicions…

"Make ready for tonight, before dawn," I tell Seawine. "But wait for my signal. First, I need to find out what Cunedag's doing here…"

"Be careful, *aetheling*."

I nod and slip away into the night. It's not easy to reach the *Praetorium* without being spotted; the campfires and braziers turn the fort into a labyrinth of light and darkness. I sneak along the wall first, then past the granary, casting a long shadow onto the courtyard. I wait for a couple of drunken

Saxons to pass, then crawl the last few feet in the long grass growing to the north of the *Praetorium*.

A few years ago, my father, in one of his better moods, taught me how to eavesdrop through the wall of a Roman building. "It's the most useful skill. It saved me a lot of trouble in my youth," he said, "and would've saved me even more if I knew how to do it earlier." Still, the Romans built their forts solidly, and if all of the *Praetorium* was still there, it would've been difficult for me to find a good listening spot. But with an entire southern wing dismantled, and most of the northern crumbled into dust, there are enough holes and cracks, some as big as my fist, through which I can clearly hear everything that's going on inside.

"…twenty of your shieldsmen."

I only met Cunedag briefly, and his voice is distorted through the crack, but there's no mistaking his hard, Northern accent.

"That's almost half of my entire band," replies Hrodha. "What do you need so many for? Isn't your fortress mighty enough?"

"Those *equites* Wortigern sent… They may be a problem. I need to set up an ambush, and for that I need a shield wall. My warriors don't have the skill."

There's a pause, broken only by the sounds of slurping; it seems Hrodha welcomed Cunedag with the same thin stew he served me.

The Wrath of the Iutes

"I don't want my men to die needlessly," says Hrodha eventually. "Can't you get them from Niall?"

"Niall's army is too far away now to make a difference. Yours is the only force in the region. I shouldn't worry too much about your men – it will be a short battle, if all goes well."

"And if it doesn't, I will have no one left to defend this fort with. The *druis* will have my head on top of one of those leaf spears of theirs." I hear the sound of fingernails scratching a hairy chest.

"You're afraid of a bunch of peasants in woollen blankets?"

"You haven't fought them, so you don't know how dangerous they can be when roused. Besides, what if Wortigern sends more men? I'm in a very vulnerable position here, Northerner, in case you haven't noticed."

"I wouldn't worry about the *Dux*," Cunedag replies with a soft chuckle. "*I* don't. I have a way to ensure he's not going to be our problem."

"You put this much faith in this hostage of yours?"

"She is worth more to Wortigern than his life," Cunedag replies.

Fingers tap on the edge of a cup.

"I can give you a dozen," Hrodha says, at last. "It should be more than enough. There's no road in these mountains that a dozen men wouldn't be able to hold."

"A dozen it is, then," Cunedag says with an eagerness that tells me this is the number he wanted all along. The goblets clink, and the two men toast their deal.

I stay to listen some more, but their talk turns to local gossip and tales of old battles, from which I can gather that the two men are much more familiar with each other than I'd ever have guessed. Where could a Saxon warchief and a Northerner from beyond the Wall have possibly met before they both found themselves in this armpit of the world?

I stifle a sneeze; the evening dew crawls up my breeches. Just when I decide to go back to the tent, I hear Cunedag raise one last toast.

"*Ad Victoriam!*" he calls in Latin.

"*Aet sige!*" Hrodha joins him in celebration of this strange alliance.

Then again, who am I to ponder what is strange and what isn't? A few months ago, I was a Iute, allied with Franks against Saxons to help the Romans in Gaul. Now, I'm assisting Britons in a war against Hibernians and Saxons, with help from other Hibernians – and some *druis*…

Someone yawns – I'm guessing it's Cunedag, for he announces he's tired and goes back to his ship. I sneak away, and traversing the labyrinth of lights again, return to Seawine.

The Wrath of the Iutes

"Is everything ready?" I ask.

"It wasn't easy – the dew made everything damp," replies Seawine. "But we managed."

"Then it's time. Gather everyone."

We wait until the lights go out in the *Praetorium*, and the campfires die down, one by one, until only the torches at the wall remain. I send Seawine and the Iutes away, while I go back to Hrodha's house. Once I'm safely in the shadow of the old Roman gable, I put my hands to my mouth and call out in imitation of an owl's hoot, twice.

It takes a while for the flames to spread enough for any of the guards to notice. As Seawine said, the hay bales gathered under the south-western corner of the fort's wall are soaked in dew and sea spray. When finally the fire penetrates deep enough, the densely packed hay, mixed with oil and dried peat, explodes, spreading sticky, burning debris everywhere.

The guards are too stunned at first to raise the alarm – only when a gurgling, agonising cry breaks through the noise of the flames, do they start to call out. The guard at the gatehouse rings the bronze cauldron used in place of a bell. Within moments, warriors run out of their tents in sluggish confusion. At last, the door to the *Praetorium* opens. Hrodha bursts out, fastening the sword belt around his waist.

"What in Hela's hairy cunt is going on?" he bellows.

"We don't know, *Hlaford*," a guard replies. "The southern wall is on fire."

"I can see that – what was that shout?"

"It's Seofon!" cries another warrior from the burning corner. "A *druis* arrow in his throat!"

The arrow is ours – we brought a few for this occasion, hidden under our cloaks. One of the Iutes would've stuck it in unfortunate Seofon's neck – after slitting his throat in the dark.

"They're coming!" Hrodha calls. "Get everyone to the ramparts. How did they get through the outer wall?"

"I don't know, *Hlaford* – maybe…"

Just then, another, smaller fire bursts out – this time on one of the provision carts, standing in the harbour, adding to the chaos.

"Water!" Hrodha cries. The Saxons and the Scots, with no clear enemy to fight, are running around aimlessly, from one fire to the other, while their chieftain tries to bring a semblance of control and order. "And man those ramparts! Somebody check on the outer wall! Do I have to do everything myself?"

He runs off towards the gate house – and suddenly, everything around me falls silent: all the warriors and sentries have rushed away in various directions, leaving me alone in front of the dark, empty shell of the *Praetorium*. It's time.

The Wrath of the Iutes

The flames raging outside illuminate the interior just enough for me to find my way around Hrodha's small room. I tap with my foot to find the trap door. I unlock the latch and heave the door open; a musty odour hits my nostrils – stench of rotten flesh, dust and rust.

"Seleu," I call into the hole quietly. "Are you there?"

A painful groan is the only response.

"If you can, try to climb out," I say.

I hear Seleu scramble up the ladder, then fall, then scramble up again.

"Wait," I tell him.

I climb carefully down, until my feet touch the dirt floor. The cellar is not deep – I can reach the trap door with my fingers. A rat squeaks from under my feet. I sense around and touch Seleu's arm.

"Hold tight," I say as I help him up.

Grunting and puffing, we clamber out. I put the *drui* down in the corner of the room, by the door. In the light, I see his hands and face are covered in a myriad tiny scratches and bites. His eyes are wild and bloodshot.

I hurry over to the iron-bound chest. It's shut with a simple bronze padlock. I draw my sword and smash at it; first, a few times with the pommel and, when that doesn't work, with the blade. At last, it shatters. I fling the chest open.

James Calbraith

There's the usual treasure one would expect to find in a Saxon warchief's chest: armbands of bronze, silver and gold, to distribute to his retainers; trinkets and trophies collected in various campaigns; a few bags of coins. The more unusual find is a thick book, bound in leather and silver. With my fingers, I sense a metal *chrismon* emblem on the cover.

Scripture? Is Hrodha secretly a Christian? Is this why he found it so easy to ally himself with Cunedag's Northerners?

I have no time to ponder this new revelation. I rustle deeper through the chest, until my hand wraps around the hilt of a sword. I pull it out – the blade is short, narrow in the middle, tapering to a long point. It's like no weapon I've seen; this must be the sword I seek. The hilt was once studded with two large jewels, of which only sockets remain – Hrodha, or someone before him, must've sold these on.

As I drag the sword out, the blade gets tangled in something. I pull harder; with a loud jangle, a thick, golden neck ring hits the floor. The *torc* – Hrodha kept this, too!

I grab both treasures and turn towards the door.

"I knew there was something suspicious about you, Deora, son of Aec."

The Saxon chieftain stands in the doorway, his sword drawn.

"Or should I say, Octa, son of Ash?"

"When did you guess?"

The Wrath of the Iutes

"Cunedag just told me of his new visitors – five Iutes, led by a young boy, a son of my old acquaintance… A bit too much of a coincidence, I thought, but I couldn't be sure – until now."

"Please, Hrodha – for my father's sake, get out of my way."

"So you *are* Ash's son! Tell me, did the *druis* send you here to settle the old scores, or are you just a common thief?"

He steps forward. I stand between him and his shield and mail shirt, but I don't fancy my chances in this fight. I am burdened with loot; in the tight confines of the room, his short *seax* is a better weapon than my long *spatha* – and he's a warchief with decades of experience. Still, he doesn't leave me a choice.

"There's no need to fight," I start. "I only need this sword, and then I'm –"

I lunge forward mid-word. Hrodha parries at the last moment, and thrusts; his blade tears at my shoulder. He draws upwards, I step back, the point flies inches from my throat. I slash again; the blades clash, throwing a shower of sparks. He pushes forth with all his strength. I struggle to keep upright. The chest is right behind me; if I make another step back, I will trip over it and fall.

With a roar, Seleu throws himself forward and wraps his arms around Hrodha. The Saxon punches back and tries to wrestle himself out, but the *druí*'s grasp has the strength of desperation. At length, Hrodha manages to free his sword hand and cuts Seleu across the face. The *drui* flies back with a terrible cry, holding his face in his hands, blood seeping through his fingers; Hrodha swiftly turns back to face me – only to find the blade of my *spatha* in his chest.

"I'm sorry, chieftain," I whisper as he drops to his knees. "This isn't how I wanted to meet the man who saved my father's life."

"You two…" He gurgles and chokes. "…bastards… are worth … each other…"

The Wrath of the Iutes

CHAPTER XIV
THE LAY OF MULLO

Only one man in the entire camp sees us as we board the boat – first Aecba and Ubba, helping Seleu into the vessel, then Seawine and I, clambering after them to take the oars, while Acha and Raegen push us away from the beach.

Only one man remains calm in the chaos that engulfs the fortress once the guards discover Hrodha's body: Cunedag, standing on the deck of his black ship and staring at us from above. He knows there's nothing he can do to stop us: the small, sleek, hide-bound Scots boat slides into the waves like a knife, and by the time his large ship would be able to set sail in pursuit, we'd be long gone. In the noise of the camp, his calls of alarm would soon get lost, and so he just stands there, observing in silence as we struggle with the oars and the coming tide.

It won't take long before Hrodha's warriors realise we're missing; the Hibernians in his command know the local coast better than us, and certainly know better how to take advantage of their boats' speed and agility: we struggle to keep her going straight in the current, and every wave hitting us from the side threatens to capsize us. We would stand little chance evading the pursuit by sea – if my plan was to escape this way.

As soon as the lights of the fort disappear in the night behind us, I turn the boat landward and crash it into the reefs.

"Hack the stern off," I order the Iutes. "Send the rest of it to the bottom of the sea."

The hide-bound vessel yields with ease to our swords, and soon all that remains of it afloat is a few boards of the frame, and the stern, torn at by waves and wind. We leave it on the rocks and, Seleu in tow, still dazed and bleeding, follow the moonlight towards the hazel grove where, I hope, Ursula and the two fishermen are waiting for us with the ponies.

She's asleep when we find her, wrapped tight in blankets and boar skin – the night is cold, and the two Iutes, left to their own devices, didn't want to start a fire for fear of the Scots discovering them in the thicket. I shake her awake.

"What..." she groans groggily.

"It's us."

She shakes her head and rubs her eyes. "It's dark. You were supposed to come at dawn."

"Change of plan."

"Do you have what we came for?"

"Yes. Get on that pony, and hurry."

She starts to pick up her blankets, but I tell her to drop them.

"But what if they find..." she says, still a bit hazy.

The Wrath of the Iutes

"No time. We no longer need to just get to Ouein — we have to ride back to the Forks as fast as possible."

"The Forks?" This wakes her up. "Whatever for?"

"I'll explain along the way. Hleo, Haering, help me with that poor *drui*!"

"He's wounded, *aetheling*!" cries Hleo.

"I know. It's nothing serious — I hope."

We tie Seleu to my saddle. I shove Caratacos's sword into the saddle bag and put the *torc* around my left shoulder as if it was an arm band. We ride slowly through the hazel — it's dark, and the trees grow dense here. As soon as we reach the Roman road, however, we launch into a mad gallop. When we reach the summit of the hill I glance over my shoulder. At first I see nothing but pitch darkness, with the sea to the east carved from the night by the shimmer of moonlight; then I spot it — tiny, bright dots, leaping in a line. Men with torches — on horseback, judging by the speed with which they spill out from the fort's gate.

"They're coming," I say and kick the pony's sides.

We reach Ouein's village some two hours later, at the first light of dawn. His warriors rush out to help Seleu down, and take him to the healer's hut. Ouein himself emerges from his house on the water and walks up to me, slowly, leaning heavily on his staff.

I give him the *torc* and reach for the sword. He stops me.

"Keep the blade," he says.

"You don't need it? But we fought so hard to bring it to you."

As the rays of the rising sun peer through the oak leaves and shine on his face, I can see he looks weary, grey, as if he's grown older in the few days we were away.

"What happened, elder?" I ask.

"I too saw something in the bull's blood," he replies.

"You didn't want to tell me back then."

"It wasn't a message for you. But you might as well know now. I saw our demise. For four hundred years we survived one invasion after another – but at long last, our time has passed."

I don't have time for this – we should keep riding onwards, back to Cunedag's fortress, not stay to listen to the prophecies of some old priest; but I'm intrigued enough to hear him out – and the ponies could use a bit of rest after the race from Hrodha's fort.

"How can you be so sure?" I ask.

"It is because you brought me this sword that I am certain of the vision's truth."

The Wrath of the Iutes

"What's so special about this weapon?"

He smiles. "You wouldn't understand. Neither the Christians nor the fair-hair heathens know the truth of the world."

"I am neither," I tell him. "I found neither the desert God of the Romans nor Wodan and Donar could answer my prayers. Perhaps your truth will convince me?"

"A challenge." He chuckles. "Very well. Come with me to the water."

We climb down to the river, and Ouein invites me to sit down beside him on the muddy shore. He takes off his sandals and immerses his feet in the current.

"The Romans and the fair-hairs all believe a man has only one chance to prove himself in this life, do they not?" he starts.

"It's true," I reply. "One way or another, our deeds in life are weighted after death, and we are rewarded or punished accordingly. Whether it's Heaven or Wodan's Mead Hall, we all get only one life to reach it."

"Does that seem fair to you? The oldest of men live less than a century. Most of us perish in half that time. And what of children? Younglings?"

I shrug. "It is what it is," I say. "The world is not fair while we live, why should it be fair in our death?"

"And yet, you yourself seek another truth."

"I am not a *philosophos*." I look up at him. We speak in Vulgar, and Ouein is surprisingly fluent, much more so than he seemed when we first met, but we are discussing matters which strain even my knowledge of the tongue. "Do you understand that word – '*philosophos*'?"

He laughs. "Yes, I understand it. Some of those *philosophos* of yours came closest to finding out the truth."

"Which is?"

He reaches into the river and scoops water into his cupped right hand.

"The soul is like this water," he tells me. "It flows unending, from source to the sea… But sometimes, briefly it fills a vessel."

"A human being," I guess.

Ouein nods. He then pours the water from his right hand to his left, then back into the river.

"Did you see what I did there?"

It takes me a moment. "I read about something like this," I say. "In Augustine's writings. A soul passing from one mortal vessel to another."

"You are well read for a heathen." Ouein chuckles again.

The Wrath of the Iutes

"Is this why you don't bury your fallen?" I ask, remembering the meagre cairn Donwen raised for her comrades.

"Those who led great lives, who died in battle or helping others, will want to move on swiftly to their next birth. Why burden the living with the care of their empty corpses? We do what's necessary to prevent spreading disease or attracting vermin, but we leave the rest to nature."

"Makes sense, I suppose," I say. "And what does it all have to do with the sword?"

"It's *my* sword," Ouein says. "Returned to me after all those centuries."

"Your sword… You believe yourself Caratacos?"

"You think I'm a fool to believe this."

"It is no more foolish faith than believing in the great Mead Hall in the sky," I say with a shrug. "And you think my getting back this sword means…"

"What else could it mean?" he says. "It must be a sign from the gods. A portent of doom – if another one was needed, after the wheat fire's vision." He sighs sadly. "They will crush us, just like Rome crushed my army all those centuries ago – and there is nothing we can do about it, other than fall bravely."

A breathless messenger runs up to us, looks at me confused, and bows before Ouein.

"Speak, boy," the elder commands.

"A troop of riders approaches from the north," the messenger says. "They're coming straight here."

Ouein looks at me knowingly. "You've been followed," he tells me.

"But I made sure we didn't leave any tracks…"

"It doesn't matter," he says sadly. "The gods have made their choice. They will come here."

"You will prevail." I look around the fortified village. "There must be enough warriors here to win over one small Saxon pursuit party."

"We will this time, yes." He nods. "But this will be only the beginning." He gazes forlornly at the *torc* in his hand. "Don't worry, fair-hair. We will keep our word, though it will destroy us."

"As soon as Wortigern beats Niall back, we'll come help you."

"Your Wortigern…" Ouein's hand rises, then falls back down. "But I already said too much. There is always hope, even in prophecy. Perhaps you're right to doubt me, young Octa. Maybe I've been looking into the mists of time for too long. Now, go. I can see you're in a hurry."

"The sword –"

The Wrath of the Iutes

"It fulfilled its purpose. Maybe you will find a better use for it." He takes my hand and puts something in my palm. "If nothing else, it will be something for the world to remember us for."

We climb back to the village and stumble on Seawine. He gives us a puzzled glance, sensing something odd just happened between us; but he, too, has no time for the *druis* mysteries.

"I checked the ponies," he says. "They're good to ride, but they won't make it across the strait. Not without proper rest."

"We can't afford to rest." I look to the elder. "Can you help us?"

Ouein scratches his beard. "You want to reach the Forks swiftly?"

"Yes – do you know another way?"

"The Otter Clan."

"The sea, again?" I groan.

"It is the only way," says Ouein. "In a few hours, the news of your attack will reach Segont. The entire shore of the Narrows will be brimming with patrols. If you stay to rest, you will never leave the island again. If you don't – your ponies will drown in the crossing."

I know he's right, but I'm hesitant about the idea. I remember the village of the Otter *druis*; though they live on the coast, they are no seafarers: their fishing boats were good enough to carry us along Mona's shore, but I doubt they'd take us and our ponies all the way to Cunedag's fortress – a journey that requires crossing at least ten miles of open ocean.

"Don't underestimate us, fair-hair," Ouein says with a chuckle. "We know the seas around Mona better than anyone. The Otters will take you wherever you need."

"I hope you're right. Perishing in these waters is not how I want my life's tale to end."

"I hope so too, young Octa." He raises his eyes. The sky is clear and quiet, with barely a cloud. "The gods of the sea rarely hear the prayers of us, dwellers of marsh and forest," he says, which does little to calm me, "but I have a good feeling about today. Toranis is asleep. Go, son. I have seen your death in my vision, and it is yet far off – it is not your destiny to die in Wened."

"I'm glad to hear it," I reply. "Come, Seawine. Get the others, if they're ready. We're off to the sea once more. I *swear* this is the last time."

I drop to my knees and retch Hrodha's Hibernian stew onto the sand. The two hours we spent on the Otters' boat proved two hours too long for my stomach. Around me, the Iutes do the same; only Ursula and Seawine still stand upright. Seawine

The Wrath of the Iutes

has the constituency of a seaman, but I can't guess how Ursula manages to hold her food in.

The dash across the rolling ocean was worth it; Cunedag's ship is not yet here, and we haven't seen any trace of pursuit on our way south. The *druis* fishermen proved as skilful as Ouein promised, though they showed little concern for our well-being along the way. As they make ready to sail back to their village, one of the sailors hands me a water-skin. I drink half of it and pour the rest over my head, to sober up. The day's not over yet – and we're still in a hurry.

"Don't mount up yet," I tell the others. "The ponies need rest – lead them on for a while."

"I need rest, too," groans Ubba, massaging his shoulder, sore from holding the boat's ropes. I look at the other Iutes; they're in no shape to climb to the top of the fort's mountain. I'm not sure I will make it myself – and I *know* what's at stake.

"You know what, you're right," I say, to his deep relief. "I don't need you all going with me. Ursula and Seawine will be enough. The rest of you get to the ferry and board the *Seahorse*. Tell them to prepare to set sail as soon as we return."

"And when will you return?" asks Ubba.

"Soon," I reply. "I promise we won't dawdle any longer than is necessary. But if we're not here by nightfall, set sail anyway. Go back to Moridun, ride to Wortigern. And… if Cunedag's ship arrives, try to stay out of sight."

"What do we tell Wortigern when he asks us why we returned?"

"Just... Tell him to prepare for the worst."

I look up to the summit of the Forks and sigh. My legs and arms ache; my arse is on fire. I haven't eaten since last night, and what I had eaten is now spread on the sand before me.

"Why do we need to get there in such a hurry, Octa?" Ursula asks, eyeing the peak with weary eyes. "Shouldn't we be sailing to Wortigern with the others?"

"There's one more thing I need to do," I reply. "Come on. We can make it."

"Octa! What are you –?"

Ahes stares at my bloodied, tattered, soiled clothes, at my pony, foaming at the mouth, then at Ursula and Seawine behind me.

"What happened? Where's everyone else? Are they –?"

"They're fine, Ahes..." I say. "Everyone's fine – for now." I lean on her arm to stop myself from falling. I cough and splutter. My heart is in my throat; drums boom in my ears; fire burns in my calves and thighs.

"What do you mean, for now? Octa, what's going on?"

The Wrath of the Iutes

"*Water*," I croak.

She sends a guard to fetch us the drink. Until the man returns, I'm too weak to speak. Seawine sits under the wall, breathing heavily. Ursula simply lies down on the ground, groaning with exhaustion.

Instead of the guard, it's Mullo who returns — and Potentin, each carrying a bucket of cold water, freshly drawn from the fort's well. Mullo pours his over my head while Potentin draws a mugful from his and hands it to me.

"Potentin!" I cry in joy. "You've made it back! How?"

"The *druis*," he replies. I notice his left arm hangs limp, torn out of its socket, and a bloody hoof print marks his sunken cheek. "I don't remember much. They left me by the side of the Roman road. My pony and my bags were gone."

"We owe more and more to these people," I note.

"I take it you've met the elders of Mona," says Mullo quietly. "Any news?"

"Plenty, and none of it good," I say once I quench my thirst and hand the mug over to Ursula. "Marcus's men — have any of them returned yet?"

"No — they're still out on patrol. They're not due back until tomorrow. Why? What happened on Mona?"

I close my eyes, wipe my face and take a deep breath. "Where's *Domna* Madron?"

[346]

"The little girl?" asks Ahes. "In her house, napping." She points to one of the roundhouses by the mound on the northern edge of the fort.

"Ursula, come with me, please."

I help Ursula up. She groans again. "What do you need me for?"

"I need someone to help me talk to the child."

"Just because I'm a woman, you think…" she scoffs.

"It's not that. I'm –"

"I'll go," says Ahes. "The girl and I grew close over these past few days. What do you need to tell her?"

I nod at her to follow me to the roundhouse. The guard at the door bars my way with a spear, but steps back when he notices Ahes. The inside is dark and smells of milk. A nursemaid wakes up, startled, when we enter. Ahes smiles at her and asks to leave us alone with the girl. She's sleeping, tucked warmly in a roll of blankets and furs. I kneel down and caress her golden hair.

"Octa, what happened out there?" the princess whispers. "Are the Scots coming to attack us? Cunedag left yesterday, not telling anyone where he's going…"

"I know. I saw him."

"Saw him – where?"

The Wrath of the Iutes

I raise a finger to my lips. I shake the little girl gently. She opens her eyes slowly.

"I don't want to eat yet…" she says in Imperial Latin.

"Wake up, Princess," I say. "We have to go."

"*Go?*"

She sits up abruptly. "You're that Iute."

"Yes – I need to take you away from here."

"No!" she cries, now fully awake. She pulls up the blanket to her chin and retreats into the corner. I step away, surprised at her reaction.

Ahes crouches beside her and tries to coax her out of the bed with kind words and caresses, but it has no effect.

"Cunedag warned me about you!" the girl says. "He said you'd want to take me away."

"Cunedag is a bad man," I say. "He's not to be trusted."

"What?" Ahes turns back to me. "What are you talking about?"

"I saw Cunedag in one of Niall's forts," I explain. "He's working with the enemy. And, he knows I saw him. He'll be here soon… Listen, Myrtle –"

"My name's Madron," she protests.

"Of course – *Domna* Madron." I kneel again. "Cunedag has allied with the Scots against your grandfather. You have to believe me."

"I don't believe you. I don't even know you!"

"But I know you. All Iutes do. You're the daughter of our princess. My father is the king of all Iutes – and he was your mother's friend. And your grandfather's."

"Your father is… Ash?"

"Yes, yes he is."

Ahes takes my hand and pulls me aside. "Is all of this true? What were you doing in Niall's fort?"

"It's a long story. But I swear, I saw Cunedag betray us. And he's planning to kill Marcus and his riders, too."

"Marcus!" she exclaims, putting her hand to her mouth. She turns back to the girl. "Dear, you must go with Octa. He'll take you back to your grandfather. You'll be safe with him."

The girl still hesitates, but she lowers the blanket slowly.

"I don't like the sea," she says.

"Our ship is big," I assure her. "Not like the one Cunedag uses. You'll barely notice you're not on dry land. And it's fast. We'll be back in Moridun in no time."

The Wrath of the Iutes

"He's right, dear," Ahes says. "You'll be fine."

"Are you coming with us?"

"No," I reply in Ahes's place. "Ahes must stay here."

"I do?" Ahes asks, surprised.

"Someone needs to find Marcus and warn him about Cunedag's trap," I tell her. "Someone he can trust."

"How would I even find him?"

"Potentin – the guide. Take him with you. Marcus's patrol is at *Dun Ambrosius*, in the east. Can you do it?"

She swallows and nods with a determined glint in her eyes.

"I can – I *will* do it."

She helps the girl dress and pack a small bag of few belongings. I leave the hut first – Ahes and Madron follow a few minutes later, to avoid the guard's suspicion. We meet everyone at the gate, by the ponies.

"As soon as we're out of sight of the guards, we start riding as fast as we can," I tell Ursula and Seawine. "Mullo, are you fit enough to ride with us?"

"Not gladly, but I'll manage."

"Have you ever ridden a horse?" I ask the girl. She nods. "Good." I raise her onto Ursula's saddle. "Hold on tight. Both of you."

"Wait —" Ahes grabs my pony's reins just as we're about to move. She stands on her tiptoes and pulls me down. Her lips meet mine for a brief, shy moment.

"I will pray for your journey," she says quietly.

"Right now, your mission is more dangerous than ours," I reply. "Keep your prayers for your own good fortune, Princess. May we all soon meet in Wortigern's fortress!"

"Octa, look!" Ursula cries out. She raises her finger north, towards the sea. I strain to see what she's pointing at, but then I spot it — a large black dot on the horizon, heading to shore on the same strong southerly wind that brought us from Mona.

"We're too late," says Seawine grimly.

"No," I say. "We can still make it. But it'll be tight."

We reach the sand just as Cunedag's ship reaches the pier. The tide is on our side — it makes the *Hound*'s mooring difficult, and brings our own ships closer to the beach. But we still need to get to them — and that means getting on the wobbly ferry boat and rowing there and back again — twice, since the boat is too small to take all of us and our ponies in one go.

The Wrath of the Iutes

An arrow flies past us and lands harmless on a dune. At this range, in this wind, even a *druï*'s bow would have no chance of hurting us, but it means Cunedag's men saw us, and are making ready to fight us as soon as they can disembark.

"Take the girl," I order Ursula. "You and Seawine go first."

"Octa – you're the *aetheling*!"

"This protects me. Cunedag will want me for ransom. Mullo and I will go in the second boat."

"Cunedag doesn't strike me as someone who cares about ransoms."

"Please!" I shout at her. "Just take her!" My outburst startles Madron; her lip begins to wobble. Ursula leans to calm her down.

"Come, child," she says. "We have to get to that big ship."

The girl pulls away. "The waves are too big!"

"It only looks like that. Once we get to the ship, you won't feel a thing. Come on."

Another arrow lands – this time near Madron. The girl shrieks in panic. I step forward and cover her with my shield. "Hurry!"

James Calbraith

Ursula grabs the girl, despite her protests, and packs her onto the boat, then she and Seawine follow, along with their ponies. The ferryman looks at me in confusion.

"Take them, or I will kill you and row the boat myself," I snarl at him and kick his boat. He grabs the pole and pushes the ferry away from the beach, just as more arrows land around us.

A dozen men leap from Cunedag's ship onto the pier, not waiting for it to finish mooring. I can't tell if Cunedag's leading the warriors – they're all wearing hooded rain cloaks, torn at by the wind. I nod at Mullo. We draw our lances and start into a trot. Our foes halt fifty feet from us and scatter into a half-circle. Steel flashes from under the cloaks. Cunedag throws down his hood.

"You're not getting out of here alive, Octa," he calls. "Give up."

"You're too late, Cunedag. My men are on the ship, waiting to set sail, with *Domna* Madron and news of your betrayal. And you can't do anything to stop them."

"I will chase after them. I will sink that ship. After I deal with you."

The sureness with which he says it shakes my confidence. I don't know what his black ship is capable of – or how many of his allies, the Scots pirates, he can gather at short notice. I glance to the sea – the ferry is halfway back to the beach; but Cunedag's men now separate us from its landing site, and we would have to fight our way through…

The Wrath of the Iutes

A loud whistle cuts the air – and a *ballista* bolt strikes the sand, then bounces, hitting one of Cunedag's warriors. It only glances his thigh, but it's powerful enough to sever his leg off. As the bloodied chunk of limb flies through the air, the other men leap back and look around in confusion. A moment later, another bolt hits Cunedag's ship, tearing through the black sail.

Two bolts shot in such short succession… No *ballista* can shoot this quickly. Somehow, my men succeeded in convincing *both* of Graelon's crews to join the fight on our side. I don't know how long it takes the crews to reload and aim – but neither does Cunedag, and he doesn't even know how many *ballistae* there are on board. At any moment, another salvo could kill one of his men, or damage his ship for good this time.

I can see in Cunedag's frown the pain his dilemma must be causing him. He knows if both of the ships sail for Moridun, he will only be able to catch up to one of them. Killing me and Mullo would give him a grisly satisfaction, but wouldn't solve his problem… And if he stays to fight Graelon's crews, the *ballistae* might tear his black ship to shreds.

"Get him," he orders at last, pointing at Mullo. The warriors rush the Legionnaire's pony, but he launches into a charge.

"Save yourself, Octa!" he cries as he smashes into Cunedag's men. His lance flashes back and forth; each cut ends with a red fountain and one of the enemies falling back with a cry.

I ride through the gap he cut through the enemy's line and splash into the sea. I reach the ferry before it grinds onto the beach. I glance back – Cunedag's men overpower Mullo and throw him off his mount. Cunedag calls for them to chase after me. They wade into the sea and start swimming towards me.

The water's too deep for my pony to climb onto the ferry without capsizing it. I have no choice. I whisper a farewell in the beast's ear. He was with us from the very beginning, riding with us through Frankia and Gaul, first as Huda's mount, then, after Trever, my own. Somehow, I feel worse for leaving him here than I would for any of my men. They, at least, followed me of their own will…

"Go, man, go!" I cry at the ferryman and grab at the spare oars to help him against the rising tide.

"Octa!" Cunedag booms over the howling wind. I turn to see him holding Mullo up, his face beaten to a bloody pulp.

Cunedag cries again, his words torn away by the wind, but it's enough for me to get what he's saying:

"…you shoot… dies…!"

He needn't worry. I don't intend to waste time fighting his black ship. Mullo must fend for himself – that Cunedag is willing to use him as hostage is enough of a good sign for me. Mullo will live, or he'd already be dead.

The Wrath of the Iutes

The last thing I see as I turn the boat away towards the *Seahorse* is my poor, faithful pony, standing silent and proud as the billows of the coming tide crash around him.

PART 4 – DEMETIA

CHAPTER XV
THE LAY OF WORTIGERN

Wortigern holds his head in his hands for what feels like an hour. I can count every wrinkle, every blue vein showing through his translucent skin, every white hair on his knuckles. The person sitting before me is not the famous, battle-hardened warlord of Londin's legends, but an old, weary man, shattered by the news I brought him.

"He was just a boy when I first saw him in the cell in the old bath house in Londin," he says, at last. "Frightened, but pretending to be brave. I could tell he was of noble blood by the way he carried himself, the language he used, even if at first I could barely understand his distant northern accent."

He sighs and leans back. He reaches for a reed stylus and plays with it for a while.

"His grandfather was a *Praetor* on the Aelian Wall," he continues. "Though his people struggled in the grim, cold North, sometimes with barely a bowl of oats between two men, his father taught him Latin and Roman custom… and the art of war, though back then he, a lowly recruit in King Drust's army, had no way of making use of that knowledge…"

The Wrath of the Iutes

"He sounds like my father," I say. "You were always looking for a son to replace Catigern. When it didn't work with Ash, you turned to Cunedag."

"I trusted him." The reed breaks in his fingers. "I helped him bring his entire clan here. Families, with children. I would never have held the frontier for this long without his help. Once, I saw him slay seven men in one battle against a Brigant band."

"Niall must have offered him more than you ever could."

"No," Wortigern says firmly. "He wouldn't betray me for a reward, or titles, or land at someone's mercy. He's too proud for that, and too clever. Remember, he's no mere mercenary captain — he's a clan warchief now. He must've seen a chance to carve a kingdom for himself in the chaos of the war."

"Is that something you couldn't have given him?"

"I am not the lord of this land, Octa," Wortigern reminds me. "I'm not the *Dux* anymore. I can settle him on my domain as an ally, but I can't make him a *Rex*, or even a *Comes*. Only Ambrosius could do that, and he never would've agreed."

"Does it matter *why* he betrayed you?" asks Ursula. "We have to fight him now, that's all."

Wortigern looks at her sharply. "You have no stake in this fight, girl."

Something changed in Ursula after we left the Forks beach. She's grown stern, grim, determined. I haven't seen her smile since the *Seahorse* set sail, except when she was talking to Madron. It was she who convinced the two crews to join the battle at the beach; it didn't take much persuading, as she told me later. The Armoricans had no love for Cunedag's Northerners – to them, they were little better than barbarians from across the Narrow Sea. Less than a generation ago, they fought against the Picts and Brigants just like him, defending the Aelian Wall and the western coasts from their incursions. They had been reluctant to trust their new allies – and they were proven right. After we set off, she took over the duties of commanding the Iutes and the crew from me, for which I was grateful, too weary to give orders to anyone anymore; she found herself surprisingly capable in this new role, and seemed reluctant to give it back once we landed in Moridun.

"He threatened the little girl," Ursula seethes. "He wanted to use her as hostage. I will never forgive him for it."

"It's a pity," Wortigern says. "I was hoping to send you away with her."

"Send away?" asks Ursula. "Where?"

"Further east. To Isca, then to Corin. Somebody needs to take Myrtle to Ambrosius."

"You don't believe this place will hold?" I ask.

"The Ancients built this fort to guard shepherds from bandits and their livestock from wolves, not to stand against a

The Wrath of the Iutes

besieging army. Certainly not one the size of Niall's warband. Cunedag's pincer was our only hope of winning this battle."

"Maybe not the only one," I say.

"What do you mean?"

I tell him about my deal with the *druis*. "Right now, a hundred trained warriors are wreaking destruction on Niall's provisions train all over Mona and Wened," I say. "Soon, he will run out of food, grease, firewood… He can't find any of it in this cold, barren wilderness. If we hold out long enough, he'll be forced to retreat."

Wortigern scratches his chin, covered in a thick, white stubble.

"This is exactly what I needed Graelon's fleet for," he says. "You are Ash's son, alright – I sent you to help with patrols, and you recruit a new allied army I haven't even heard of before…" He shakes his head. "But it's not enough. Between Cunedag's men and Niall's rearguard, those *druis* won't last long, no matter how valiant they are. It will buy us only a few days at best."

"A few days might be enough," says Ursula. I notice her fists are clenched. "We saved Trever in less than that."

"What about Marcus and his *equites*?" I ask. "If Ahes found them, they should be here any day now."

"No, we need something more, if we are to even stand a chance." Wortigern stands up and walks up to the door.

"Graelon's ships," he asks, looking out onto the courtyard where the Atecot troops practice muster. "Are they in good shape to sail again?"

"We suffered no damage on the way here," I say. "The crews may be weary…"

"Too weary to sail back to Gangania?"

"They will if I tell them to," Ursula replies before I manage to open my mouth. "But why would you want to send anyone there now?"

"I'm not going to send anyone. I'm going there myself."

"What?" I stand up. "Are you mad? This is exactly what Cunedag wants!"

"I hope so."

"And what exactly are you hoping to achieve by doing this?" asks Ursula. "Alone?"

"Not alone. I will take my Atecots – just enough of them to seem a threat. He knows me – he knows I don't need a great army to be a danger to him and his plans."

"You want to draw him out," I guess. "Keep him away from Mona."

Wortigern nods. "There's little time. I'll start preparing."

The Wrath of the Iutes

"Wait." Ursula stops him at the door. She's counting something on her fingers. "To go there and back again… You'll never make it in time for the battle here."

"No, I won't." He turns to me. "Octa, you and Eochu will lead the defence."

"Me?" I press my hand to my chest. "Don't you have officers to do that sort of thing for you?"

"I trust none of them enough," he says. "If even Cunedag could betray me… You're Ash's son; I know you will manage. You've broken a siege once – maybe you'll achieve the same miracle again. And if we're fortunate, Marcus will soon be here to help you."

Ursula helps Madron onto the single-axle cart, ready to take a handful of women and children for Moridun. The girl whimpers quietly; she's tired and sleepy. "But we just got here," she whines. "I don't want to go."

"We're going to a big city," I hear Ursula say quietly. "You'll have a nice bed there, and a bath…"

"I don't want to leave *Avus*," she says, using an Imperial word for grandfather.

"He'll come join us as soon as he's finished with his duties here."

"Thank you, Octa," Wortigern says, putting his hand on my shoulder. The hand twitches, and there's an emotion in his voice which I haven't heard before. I turn to him.

"For what?"

"For bringing Myrtle back. If Cunedag had used her for leverage, I… I don't know what I would've done."

"You'd give him the fort in exchange for the girl?"

"I'd give him *all* the forts. I'd open the gates for him all the way to Corin."

The confession shakes me. I'm certain my father would never do anything to put his tribe in jeopardy for my sake; and Myrtle isn't even Wortigern's *daughter*.

"You really care for her," I say.

"She's the only family I have left. And, in a way, she's your family, too."

"What do you mean by that?"

He opens and closes his mouth, then scratches the back of his head. "That's not…" He stutters. I look at him in confusion. "I mean, your father was supposed to marry Rhedwyn, instead of Wortimer. She would've been your sister, then, Octa."

"But not your granddaughter."

The Wrath of the Iutes

"If everything went as planned, I would've adopted your father," he reveals, then chuckles lightly and shakes his head. "We'd all be one content family."

"Your son was responsible for ruining many such content families," I note. "Including mine."

"I know." He nods sadly. "I have been taking care of Myrtle all those years, as penance for bringing *him* to this world. I made sure she was properly baptised – I chose the new name for her, the name of an ancient goddess worshipped from Italia to Britannia, hoping she'd protect the girl if the Christian God fails… And now it's somebody else's turn."

He nods towards the cart; Ursula finally sits Madron on the seat next to the driver and moves to prepare her pony for the road. Wortigern's eyes turn dark and sombre.

"You don't expect to come back from Gangania," I guess.

We approach the carts. I smile at Madron, but she stares back at me angrily, crossing her arms and pouting. I turn to Ursula.

"Take care of yourself," I say as I stroke the back of her pony.

"Make sure the girl gets to Isca safely," Wortigern tells Ursula. "Then, you can do whatever you want."

"I'll come right back here as soon as I can," she replies.

"Please, don't," I say. "There won't be time. If we win the battle, we'll all meet at Moridun, anyway. And if we lose…"

"I'll be back," Ursula repeats firmly. For a moment, her expression softens. She leans down and kisses me on the forehead. "Don't you *dare* be getting killed before me. I don't want to become a widow so young."

"I'll do my best."

"What about you, *Dux*?" she asks. "Aren't you supposed to come with us to the harbour, to sail north?"

"I need to gather my soldiers first. I'll join you in the morning. Make ready to set sail as soon as I'm there. Tell Graelon's crewmen if they come with us, they'll have more Northerners and Scots to kill than they ever wished for."

Ursula nods.

"They'll be ready."

"Come," Wortigern says once the last of the carts passes through the fort's gate. He invites me back inside the hut. "I'll show you something."

He takes me to an iron-bound chest in his room, similar to the one Hrodha owned; I'm guessing it was once standard military issue for *Praetors* of frontier fortresses. He reaches inside and takes out a bundle of cloth the size and shape of a

[367]

The Wrath of the Iutes

small helmet. He unwraps it to reveal a thick band of gold, carved into leaves and studded with jewels.

I've never seen it before, but I've heard it described enough times – in the corridors of Londin, whispered about by nervous Councillors, reminiscing of the old days, discussing transition of power, wondering if one day someone could take over the rule of the city and the surrounding province from the unruly Council and bring back a semblance of ancient order and glory…

"The *Dux*'s diadem," I whisper, licking my lips. "You kept it here, all this time."

"Did Ash ever tell you what would happen if this was returned to Londin?" Wortigern asks, raising the diadem to the light. It looks sturdy, and must have been heavy and uncomfortable to wear – from what my father told me, Wortigern wore it only on rare occasions, and I can see why.

"Chaos," I reply. "Division. Factions fighting for power. I never understood it – it's only a golden hat. Surely if Ambrosius or Riotham or whoever wanted to wear the diadem, they could have just forged one of their own."

"We Britons have always depended on symbols and old rules too much," says Wortigern. "It's easier for everyone to pretend there can never be a *Dux* in the East again with this damn thing out of their way." He turns the diadem in his hand. There are a few scratches on its surface. One of the jewels must have been recently replaced, its socket more polished than the others.

"Why are you showing me this? Why not just send it with Myrtle and Ursula to Ambrosius?"

"Ambrosius fears it. They all do in Corin – and those who don't are fools. It would only make their position more difficult, embroil them in the old conflicts they have neither time nor strength to fight."

"Then just throw it away. Melt it down. Sell the jewels."

He presses the diadem to my chest. "You can do it yourself when you're back home."

"Me?"

"Why not?" He shrugs. "You *are* the closest I have to an heir. Had things gone differently, your father would have inherited it according to Londin's laws – and eventually, if I lived long enough to keep the Council in check, it would've belonged to you anyway. As much as I don't let providence guide my actions, I have to admit that finding you, here, now, strikes me as more than just a coincidence."

"All of this is in the past. My father is no longer a Briton Councillor. He's a Iute now – and he already wears a *Rex*'s circlet. A man's head can only hold one of these at a time."

"You'd be surprised how capacious men's heads can be."

He waits until I take the diadem from his hands before continuing.

The Wrath of the Iutes

"Do you know how many people – great, powerful people – asked me for this trinket? Even Cunedag wanted it – and who knows, maybe I'd have given it to him if he was patient enough. But you're the first one who told me to just throw it away. You may be the only one on this whole island who doesn't care about it."

"I… I already have one ancient relic to take care of," I say. I show him Caratacos's sword at my side and explain what it is. He waves his hand.

"This is nothing," he says. "A curiosity. A collector's item. Only the *druis* care about such things, and they faded away a long time ago. This –" He pokes the diadem with his finger. "– is real *power*. At least as long as there's a court in Corin and a Council in Londin."

The diadem feels suddenly even heavier in my hands.

"What if I don't make it out of here alive?"

"Then Niall will have a fine addition to his chest of spoils."

"Fine." I wrap the jewel back in its cloth and shrug. "I'll take care of it."

"Good." He smiles and pats me on the back. Just then, Eochu enters the *Praetorium*. He stands to attention and salutes us.

"The men are ready, *Legatus*. I chose them myself."

"They are aware of what the mission entails?"

"Yes, *Legatus*. Their families have already begun to mourn them."

A trumpet sounds at the northern rampart; the gate opens. The first to ride through is Marcus, followed by his men — and, closing the rear, Ahes, dishevelled and exhausted, her mount's flanks and chest covered in lather.

"At last! Thank the gods," I exclaim, relieved. "They're here!"

Marcus takes a long glance at the warriors gathered at the courtyard, before noticing me and Eochu, both wearing officers' helmets and cloaks, standing before him.

"Where's the *Legatus*?" he asks.

It's been four days since Wortigern set sail from Moridun with a *centuria* of Atecots and a handful of his personal guard, made up of Briton soldiers who came with him from Londin to this exile. It would've been an insignificant force if led by anyone other than Wortigern — and even with him at the helm, it will be little more than a distraction.

"He went north to fight Cunedag," I say. "We haven't heard anything from him since."

"Then who's left to lead the troops?"

The Wrath of the Iutes

"We are," says Eochu. "And now you've joined us."

Marcus dismounts and lets a servant take his horse away. "That explains why Niall slowed down his progress. Finding out you have the greatest Briton general threatening your rear would make anyone think twice about pushing blindly forward."

"And where is Niall now?" asks Eochu.

"He crossed the Black Stream. Razed the *mansio* at the old bridge. He's less than two days away – haven't you sent out patrols?"

"None have returned."

"Then the woman was right," says Ahes.

"What woman?" I ask.

"I was attacked by the Scots when trying to reach Marcus. Potentin didn't make it… A woman saved me, an archer in a plaid cloak –"

"Short red hair? Painted face?"

"That's the one. You've met her?"

"What did she want with you?"

"She said Niall's men hold all approaches south," says Marcus, "and she showed us a way around them, through the mountains. We'd never have got here if it wasn't for her."

"Did she say anything else? Did she have any news from Mona?"

"Mona?" Marcus gives me a confused look. "No, she didn't mention Mona. She said she was going to hunt for Niall, or die trying. How do you know her? What is this about Mona?"

"I'll explain later – you look like you need rest." I turn to Eochu. "Were there any provisions stored at that Black Stream *mansio*?"

"Some, but not enough for an army the size of Niall's."

"Then we have even less time to prepare. He'll be in a hurry to get here – the stomachs of his men will have already started rumbling."

The campfires of Niall's army twinkle at the foot of the hill like a sea of stars. The enemy camp spreads to the east of the *cair*, south of the river bend. There aren't enough of them to surround us on all sides, and there's no need for it – they know nobody's coming to save us.

"A thousand men," I muse. "Not even two full *cohorts*. At Trever this would've been a mere detachment."

"We're not at Trever," says Marcus.

The Wrath of the Iutes

"No, we're not," I admit. "There were thousands of Legionnaires at Trever. Walls as tall as mountains. Impervious gates."

"Every siege is the same. Whether it's a *centuria* assaulted by a *cohort*, or a *cohort* defending from ten Legions."

As we watch, one of the campfires at the edge goes out. I wait for it to light up again, but the spot remains dark.

"They're running out of firewood," says Marcus.

"How long do you think they have left?"

"Two days, at most, before the hunger stirs unrest."

When Niall first reached the fortress, he sent his vanguard to try to simply overrun us, as he did with so many forts along the way, without even pausing to rest or break camp. It was a mistake – his first in the campaign. The ramparts, reinforced by Wortigern, held fast; under Eochu's lead, the garrison – most of them personally trained by the *Dux* – inflicted heavy casualties on the attackers. We even managed to capture some weapons and a few prisoners, though they proved useless to our interrogators. There was nothing we could find out from them about Niall's forces that we couldn't see with our own eyes just by looking down from the walls.

The one valuable piece of information we did get out of them, however, was not what they said, but how ravenously they attacked the bowls of honey-sweetened barley potage we served them, or the rashers of bacon we offered. These men haven't eaten anything nourishing in days.

Wortigern left his *cair* well supplied. We have enough food for a week, and plenty of fresh water from the well dug in the middle of the courtyard. The siege itself was never a threat to us; only through a direct assault can the Scots break our defences.

"Why aren't they attacking?" asks Ahes. "What are they waiting for?"

She's wearing her auburn hair short now, cropped neatly under the helmet. I can't see it now in the dark, but her face is still bruised black and blue from a fall she suffered when chasing after the *Decurion*. Led by Donwen down the narrow mountain paths, she intercepted the *equites* as they were returning from their patrol, just a few miles from the ambush prepared by Cunedag's and Hrodha's men in a desolate mountain gorge. The warriors saw her ride past, but were too surprised and confused by her sudden appearance to stop her — to their doom; Marcus, forewarned, struck Hrodha's shieldsmen from the flank, and shattered his line, losing only one of his men. Facing the Saxons was enough to convince him of the truth of Ahes's words and head straight for Wortigern's hillfort.

Not all of his horses survived the long, difficult ride south unscathed; three had to be put down, two have gone lame and joined the other animals destined for slaughter should we run out of food. Not that it matters now. There's not much use for horsemen in the siege. As Marcus noted, we're not at Trever anymore, in more ways than one; there are no hidden

The Wrath of the Iutes

sally gates, and not enough space on the plain below to stage a mounted charge. The mounts of the *equites*, as well as the ponies of my Iutes, are merely taking up space in the fort's stables – and fodder.

"We bruised them badly in that first assault," says Marcus, rubbing a fresh scar on his left cheek. "Maybe they're just being careful."

"Or they're waiting for something," I guess. "The outcome of the fight in the North, perhaps?"

"We'll soon find out, one way or another," I say. "It won't be long before…"

A whistle of alarm rings out from the fort's southern gate. The gatehouse there is manned by the Armorican volunteers, under Ahes's command. Seeing how their sailor kin found themselves in the midst of war time and time again, they, too, are eager to prove their worth in battle, but so far, they have had little opportunity to do so. They're shouting something in their rough accents, but the breeze carries the words away. By the time Ahes and I reach the gate, the guards decide to open the postern and let inside whoever is causing the commotion.

A single rider trots into the courtyard on a tired moor pony. She throws down the rain-sodden hood of her cloak. I catch her as she slides off the saddle.

"I told you I'd be back," Ursula says feebly.

The sleeve of her woollen tunic is soaked in blood. An arrow from a Scot's bow, broken in half, juts out of her shoulder.

"That stirred them up," Marcus says, nodding towards the river.

Flickering dots of lights scatter throughout the enemy camp, leaping from campfire to campfire, scurrying between the tents and gathering into squares in the empty spaces. Shouts of alarm and ringing of bronze bells reaches us on the ramparts.

"Shouldn't we prepare, too?" I ask.

"They won't attack before dawn. We're as ready as we can be. Let's see her now."

We climb down and go to visit the fort's surgeon. The smell of ointments and aromatic smokes fills the hut. Ursula lies asleep in the corner, her shoulder wrapped tight.

"How is she?" I ask the surgeon.

"Tired," he replies. "I took the arrow out – just one more scar added to many, from what I've seen."

"Can she fight?" the *Decurion* asks.

"Marcus, she just got here –!" I protest.

The Wrath of the Iutes

"She knew what she was coming back for."

"If she's right-handed, she can," the surgeon replies. "But she won't be able to hold the shield for a while yet."

I squat beside Ursula and shake her gently awake. She opens her eyes and stares at the ceiling for a while, blinking, remembering.

"The fort," she says.

"Yes, you made it."

"I thought I'd slip past them unnoticed… Stumbled on a patrol on the ridge, a mile south."

"We were fortunate that you did," says Marcus. "It provoked the enemy to a hasty attack."

Ursula rises fast from the bedding. She winces and sways.

"Careful," the surgeon warns her.

"I'm fine. Give me my sword."

"They won't charge for a few hours yet," says Marcus. "Until then, rest."

"I don't need to –" She sways again and falls on her back. She closes her eyes and takes a few deep breaths.

"How's Madron?" I ask when she calms down.

"On a boat to Silurian Isca," she replies, rubbing her brows with a pained grimace. "With everyone else."

"Is that a safe place?" I ask Marcus.

"It's safe from Niall," he replies. "It's our largest fort on the south coast. But… it's close to Corin."

"I understand."

"I don't," says Ursula. "What does it mean? Is she in danger?"

"Remember, Wortigern wanted to keep her away from the intrigues at Ambrosius's court for as long as he could," I explain. "But I suppose it's no longer possible."

"No harm will come to her there, I can assure you," Marcus says. "But her life is going to change in ways I cannot predict."

"Not least because her grandfather will no longer be with her to protect her," I say.

"Then I should have gone with her," says Ursula. She raises herself on one elbow.

"No," I say. "That is not our fight. We did what we could there. Now we must do what we can *here*."

The Wrath of the Iutes

If this was a *cohort* of Legionnaires, or even auxiliaries under a Roman-trained commander, they'd assault us from all sides at once. It would mean our doom; there aren't enough of us to man the whole length of the ramparts. But these are not Legionnaires. This is a band of a thousand Scots raiders, pirates, marauders and clan warriors, gathered from all corners of Hibernia by Niall – not to assault Ambrosius's kingdom, for there were always too few of them to achieve that, but to conquer Wened, overrun the frontier forts, defeat the combined might of the Britons and their Atecot allies and gather the greatest plunder their poor, distant island had ever seen. And we're the last fort that stands in their way before the real prize: the city of Moridun and the wealthy farms and *villas* of the fertile river valley around it.

They come from the south at first, where the wall is the lowest, but bound with a ditch and a line of sharpened poles and stones. A howling, shrieking wave of young warriors, most eager, least skilled, fastest to die and thus the most dangerous. They bring no ladders, no siege hooks, no ropes – there's no need when the rampart is made of jagged, crumbling drystone and only seven foot tall, too low to even have a breastwork.

Marcus raises his hand, and the Atecot soldiers pick up flaming torches from the stands before them. The *Decurion* waits until the Scots youths descend into the ditch, and waves. The torches fly down, striking the pool of tar at the bottom of the ditch. Along the entire length of the southern wall, the tar erupts in a bright flame and black smoke. Cries of terror and pain fill the air; for a while, we see nothing through the smoke. When it clears, we see the young warriors flee in panic – those that can. A sickening odour of burnt flesh reaches my nostrils. I dare not look down — I still hear the moans and groans of men dying a terrible, fiery death.

"They won't fall for that again," says Eochu.

"But they'll be wary," replies Marcus.

"North!" cries a lookout on the other side of the courtyard. We leave the southern rampart to the Armoricans and cross the yard to reinforce the defenders on the opposite side. The second wave is better prepared; there might be Niall's veterans among them; a few carry simple ladders and climbing poles, forcing me and my Iutes to run from spot to spot, pushing and kicking the ladders away. The wall here is nine feet tall, and the ditch behind it is deeper, but we had no time to fill this one with tar.

"Have you ever used these?" Marcus asks, nodding at the basket of *plumbata* darts, razor-sharp and weighted with lead, at my feet.

"I've *seen* them used…"

"It's easy when the enemy is this close."

He peeks over the rampart, grabs a dart and lobs it with full force over the wall. A squelchy thud and a cry of pain tells us the missile has met its target. All along the wall, the Briton soldiers launch salvo after salvo; within seconds, we're out of darts — and the enemy's first wave is out of men, the ditch filled with groaning and writhing Scots. A *plumbata* doesn't kill, unless it hits a vital spot — but the barbed tip can't

The Wrath of the Iutes

be taken out safely without a field surgeon's help, and woe to the inexperienced warrior who tries to tear it out.

It takes us the better part of an hour to repel the onslaught on the northern wall, just in time for us to turn our attention again to the south and east. I look back as we cross the courtyard; our casualties are slight compared to the slaughter we inflicted on the Scots, but we can ill afford any losses in face of the enemy's overwhelming numbers.

On the eastern rampart, the fighting turns into a desperate, chaotic brawl. Once Niall's men broke through the line of sharpened stakes and iron spikes with which we reinforced that side, they started throwing themselves on the exposed parapet with little regard for pain or injury, as if they'd taken henbane. I move to the right flank, where the attack is the fiercest. I hack, slash and thrust until my sword arm goes numb and my tunic is soaked with the enemy's blood. Once in a while, one of the Scots manages to push through and runs out into the courtyard, only to be pierced by a spear or battered by clubs held by one of our reserve detachment – a random assortment of camp servants, cooks, sick and wounded who wouldn't leave the fort with the refugees. Ursula is among them, trying to command those who know how to follow orders; as I glance over my shoulder, I can only tell where she is by the flashes of her sword, as she's the only one in the detachment wielding such a weapon.

I glimpse a falling axe in the corner of my eye and take it on the shield. I thrust underneath it; I hit an armpit – blood spurts from the wound into my eyes. I shove the enemy back, and he disappears over the battlement with a cry and a thud. I look around for another foe to fight, but I find none. I glimpse over the rampart and see the Scots fall back from the wall. I lean against the stone and take a deep breath, knowing I will have little time to rest.

"Arrows!" a shout spreads along the wall. Without looking, I raise the shield over my head. Thwack, thwack, thwack – three arrows hit the shield, piercing the leather and the wood by less than an inch. Judging by the cries of pain and agony around me, not everyone is so fortunate or quick to react. Most of the cries come from the yard; the archers overshot the wall, which means they must be near, shooting up the slope. But their error turns into our disaster. The men in the reserve detachment carried no shields or helmets, nothing with which to lessen the damage from the deadly missiles.

"Ursula!" I shout and rush to seek her out in the crowd of wounded men.

"I'm here," she cries. I find her huddled in the corner, in the shadow of the granary wall, together with Hleo and Haering who cover her, and themselves, with a plank of wood they found somewhere. As I reach her, she tears out an arrow from her shoulder. The missile leaves a shallow wound in her flesh.

"Twice in the same place," she says and wipes a tear of pain from her eye. "Can you believe it? It's a good thing these barbarians don't know how to shoot."

"You have to get out of here."

The Wrath of the Iutes

"I'll be fine – but they won't." She nods at the "detachment". She pushes me away and runs towards them, waving her hands. "Hide!" She shouts. "Run! Before they reload!"

The men scatter just as another round of arrows falls from the sky. I pull her down and cover our heads with my shield while all around us ring out cries of pain and fear.

"We're pinned down!" Marcus yells at me from the eastern wall. "You have to help at the southern gate!"

"We have to do something about those archers," says Ursula. "They may be poor shots, but we're a big enough target."

"There's nothing we *can* do…"

"We're cavalry, aren't we?" She grins.

"Trapped behind a wall."

"We don't have to be."

She points to the stack of thick wooden planks lying in the corner by the *Praetorium*, where Hleo and Haering found their "shield"; they're supposed to be used to reinforce the ramparts in case of a breach.

"They'll never hold," I say.

"They just might."

[384]

James Calbraith

"It's a mad idea."

"Just the way you like it, then. Go get the others, I'll be at the stables."

Dodging arrows, I reach the southern gate and pull my lutes from the rampart. The battle there is fierce, and they're covered in blood and guts, but as yet they're unharmed. Battle rush runs boiling in their veins and gleams bright in their eyes.

"Get to the ponies," I tell them.

"We're sallying?" Raegen exclaims. "At last!"

"We'll try."

The unseen archers quieten down in preparation for another assault on the eastern wall; the attack seems weaker this time, as if Niall's men have finally grown weary after what must be a third hour of the battle. The soldiers of the garrison are tired, too, but they fight with the desperation of men knowing death or slavery awaits them in defeat – while the Scots fight only for the spoils and glory.

"I thought Marcus would join us," says Seawine. "Is it really just the seven of us?"

"It's enough," says Ursula. "There can't be more than twenty of those archers. I counted the arrows in the last barrage."

The Wrath of the Iutes

"We'll count them when they're dead," I say. I look at the mount Ursula prepared for me in place of my moor pony. "Wait, isn't that –?"

"Marcus's horse," she says, beaming. "He's not going to need it. You want me to find something else? There are some mules, waiting for slaughter…"

"It's fine." I grab the horse's reins. The beast stares at me defiantly and splutters, but lets me mount it without protest. "Let's see if those Briton warhorses are half as good as our ponies."

CHAPTER XVI
THE LAY OF NIALL

With the two gates barred shut, there's only one way for us to get across the wall: up the stack of crates and barrels piled up next to Wortigern's house, then onto the planks we laid on its roof – the only one in the fort covered with strong Roman tiles, instead of thatch – and a perilous jump over the western battlements. There are no attackers on that side: a dense, nigh impenetrable forest, shrouded permanently in dense fog, grows on the western slope of the hill, stretching far into the river plain below. I'm hoping it will cover our sally from the Scots assaulting the southern wall.

"There's no ditch over on this side," I tell my men, "but the trees are close by, so be careful not to leap too far!"

I go first, despite Ursula's protests – she pushes her way to follow right after me. My mount neighs uneasily as we climb the roof; the tiles slip from under its hooves; the rafters creak under our combined weight. I would pray for the roof to hold, if I knew which deities or martyrs were responsible for soundness of wooden planks. When we reach the wall, the horse stumbles and hesitates.

"I know you can do it," I whisper. "You're a trained warhorse. You know no fear. My pony would do this – surely you can do no worse?"

The Wrath of the Iutes

I jab my heels into its sides and let out a war cry to give myself and the horse courage as we leap into the milk-white mist beyond. For a moment, it feels like we're flying; I am weightless, suspended in the air, in the emptiness. Then the horse hits the ground, and I barely manage to hold in the saddle. I feel the impact deep in my loins; blood trickles from my lip — I must have bitten it as I fell.

"Out of my way!" I hear Ursula cry, and I tug at the reins at the last second. She lands right beside me; her landing is softer than mine — the pony is lighter and surer on its hooves. One by one, the other Iutes join us, but when Acha, the last one, launches into her leap, the planks finally give way and the entire roof caves in behind her with a loud crash. Acha's pony trips when it hits the dirt. I grab her reins to stop her from falling.

"Alright?" I ask.

She pats the pony's front legs. The beast limps for a few steps, but then recovers its pace.

"Alright," Acha replies.

We ride in silence through the wood and emerge in the rear of the force attacking the southern wall. From the outside, the fort's situation appears even worse; the enemy swarm the ramparts like ants crawling over a dead rat. We pass unnoticed — nobody cares about a few pony riders trotting at the rear; those who see us must take us for couriers or a returning patrol.

"How are we getting back?" asks Seawine.

"I'll think of something," I reply. I have given no thought yet to our return – I hope an opportunity provides itself once we disrupt the Scots' attack; for now, I focus my attention on the success of our attack – and our survival.

The archers prove easy to find. Just like Ursula predicted, there are maybe twenty of them, gathered in one spot, on a stretch of heath across a small stream at the bottom of the eastern slope, the fog around them brightened by a few sentries with torches. Up close, they don't appear to be Scots – they wear their hair differently and don knee-length tunics instead of the short Hibernian ones. Like Hrodha's men, they must be mercenaries Niall picked up somewhere to fill out his ranks for the campaign.

"Wedge," I order. "Ursula, to my –"

I look at her and realise she's holding on to the reins with her one healthy hand, the other still wrapped up and hanging limp at her side.

"You can't fight like this," I say.

"Watch me."

She lets go of the reins and draws the lance. Her thighs tighten around the pony's flanks as she moves to her position to my right in the wedge.

"Let's do this," she says, lowering the lance.

The Wrath of the Iutes

We smash into the archers at full speed. I feel the difference of charging a warhorse instead of a pony instantly; two of the archers disappear, trampled under my mount's hooves. I can barely feel their deaths. I strike the third one across the head. To my left and right, the Iutes charge onwards, each downing one foe as we burst through to the other side of the heath. "Back!" I call; we draw a tight turn, before the enemy even realises what's happening, and strike again. What follows, for a few moments, is a bloody slaughter. Without the protection of spearmen or shieldsmen, the archers have nowhere to hide from our blades. Their blood splatters the heath. My horse's training and battle instincts kick in; it knows better than me how to flank the fleeing archers, how to lead me to the best position for a strike. My lance shaft breaks on the head of what must be my fifth or sixth victim. I draw the sword and look around. We've destroyed at least half of the archer detachment, if not more. None of my Iutes is so much as scratched. Beyond the light of the torches, abandoned in the grass by the fleeing sentries, I notice groups of Hibernians, with spears and axes, running towards us from the east and the north – and, much worse than that, a small wing of riders, heading our way from the camp. I didn't expect the Scots to have any cavalry at all – and I haven't prepared for that eventuality.

I put two fingers to my lips and whistle. We've done enough. "Back!" I call. "Turn back!"

We ride back the same way we came, around the rear of Niall's southern flank, towards the western slope, but this time, with what looks like half of his army in hot pursuit. I still don't know how we'll get back to the fort; I'm hoping to come up with something in the safety of the forest – if we can reach it in time…

I glance over my shoulder. A few iron-tipped darts land harmlessly behind our backs: wasted missiles, since we're too far even for the skills of Hibernian javelin men. But the enemy is still too close, and the damp soil, trampled into quagmire by besieging troops, slows our ponies down. I look to Ursula: she clings to her mount's mane, her teeth clenched, her face white. I notice she begins to slip to the left. I ride up to her and help her straighten up. She nods in silent gratitude.

We reach the line of the trees. "Each to their own," I order. "We'll meet by the river." The Iutes scatter: Acha and Raegen to the south, the other three to the north; only Ursula stays with me as we trot deeper west. I hear the Scots rush into the wood close behind us – too close. We have no terrain advantage here. We're as alien in this land as they are, and in the misty gloom we have to be careful not to stumble onto windthrow or fall into a ditch. Already I spot three riders following us between the trees – and another to our left, trying to outflank us; this one proves too reckless and disappears from sight in an instant when his horse hits some unseen obstacle. But soon, two more take his place. Niall – or whoever else is in command of the southern side of the siege – isn't sparing his men in this pursuit. One more leaps out in front to our right. We swerve to avoid him. The two on our left move to cut us off while the three behind us pick up the pace, heedless of the danger of holes and branches.

"Go left," I cry to Ursula. "I'll hold them off."

"I'm not leaving you!"

The Wrath of the Iutes

"You're too weak!" I tell her. "You're of no help to me like this!"

She purses her lips and tugs at the reins, stopping the pony in place. She draws the sword and turns to face the enemy.

"Ursula! What in *Hel* are you doing?"

"Being helpful."

I glance to our sides – I can't see either of the two riders; they must have shot out far to the front, failing yet to notice our halt. But the three horsemen before us raise their short lances and hunker down to a charge. I draw the *spatha* and ride out in front of Ursula, shielding her with my buckler.

"We'll die here, you know," I say. I see more Scots in the distance: footmen, approaching cautiously through the undergrowth. There must be at least a dozen of them in that first line; more will be coming after them.

"Then we'll die together."

The first of the three riders comes within lance range. I duck to avoid his strike – and when I look up, he's gone. So are the other two. Only the horses remain, riderless, still riding past us. For a brief moment, I can't tell what has happened, until I see their bodies in the brambles, each pierced with a great *druis* arrow through the chest.

I turn back. Three familiar figures stand in the middle of the path, in plaid cloaks, lowering their bows.

James Calbraith

"Donwen!" Ursula cries in joyful recognition.

"Over here," the *drui* says, pointing to a clearing in the bushes I haven't noticed before. "Hurry."

She bids us to dismount and guides us down a narrow ravine, along a creek overgrown with hazel and willow so thick it conceals us from view completely.

"Leave the ponies here," Donwen commands when we reach a dip in the landscape, surrounded by ancient yews. We do as she says; I have no idea what she's doing here or how she found us, but she seems to know how to disappear in these woods, and that's good enough for me.

"Get down."

We all drop into a damp ditch and wait for a group of Scots to run past.

"Have you seen my other men?" I whisper.

"They're safe, for now," she replies. "Now quickly, after me. We're almost there."

"Where?"

She leaps up and runs along the creek; we follow for a few hundred feet, until we emerge onto a sandy patch of the shore of the Teibi, where the river forks in two. Raegen and Acha are already there, with the fourth *drui* guarding them and their mounts. The other three join us not long after.

[393]

The Wrath of the Iutes

"There aren't many safe hiding spots around here," says Donwen, "but this one will have to do for now. We'll wait until dusk, and then we'll try to get you back to the fort."

"How did you –?"

"We've been watching the siege since yesterday. I saw your entire attack unfold."

"Why are you here?" asks Ursula.

"Why do you think?" Donwen smiles bitterly. "To finally kill Niall."

"It's all over," says Donwen. "Just like Elder Ouein foresaw. The *druis* of Mona are no more."

She wades into the river and scoops water into her mouth.

"What happened?" I ask.

She takes off her tunic to wash it from the grime and blood. I glance at Ursula; she turns red, but doesn't look away from the *drui*'s taut, muscular body.

"I wasn't there when it happened – I only heard about it from the few who survived," Donwen replies. "First, the Otters raided the watchtowers along the Roman road to draw the Saxons out. Then Ouein stormed Hrodha's fortress. With their warchief dead, and most of the warriors chasing our shadows all over Mona, Ouein's band overran the ramparts with ease and burned the whole place to the ground, along with all the provision carts and boats in the harbour."

"And then…?"

She wrings her tunic.

"Then, the Saxons came back. With the Northerners. Ouein and his men fought valiantly in the charred ruins. Twice the enemy charged the walls, and twice they were pushed back. Of Hrodha's men, few lived to see the morning. But when the Northerners arrived by boat and struck at us from the sea, the *druis* could hold out no longer."

She pauses to run her fingers along a fresh, deep scar running down her face; it looks like an axe wound, and it ends half an inch from her left eye.

"Ouein sent six men away at nightfall," she continues. "When it was clear we had lost. He wanted them to carry the tale of the *druis* last stand. That's the last…" Her voice breaks for a moment. "…the last I heard of any of my people."

"And where are these six men now?" I ask.

"I found them last night in the forest, by the Caurasian Stone. They were ambushed by Niall's foragers. Only one was still alive – long enough to tell me the story."

We all fall silent out of respect for the fallen folk of Mona. In the silence, I slowly realise something that, in the rush of things, I haven't noticed until now.

The Wrath of the Iutes

"You speak Vulgar," I say. "Better even than Elder Ouein."

She looks up, startled. "Yes," she replies. "It… it all started coming back to me after we met."

"Coming back? You – you're not from Mona?"

"I was… I *am* the daughter of Antonius, once *Comes* of Demetia."

"You're from here? No wonder you know these woods so well. How did you find yourself among the *druis*?"

"I don't remember much of my childhood," Donwen explains. "When I was… five or six, the Scots pirates attacked our ship and abducted me and my brother. When they were sailing back to Hibernia, a storm caught us off the coast of Mona and shipwrecked us off Red Stone Island. The *druis* raised me as one of theirs, but I remembered… I remembered I once had a different life." She shakes her head. "All of it is gone now. Demetia, Mona… Only one thing remains. To bury my arrow in Niall's heart."

She puts her tunic back on and picks up her bow.

"And you will help me put it there, Octa, son of Aeric."

"Me? How?"

"I don't yet know – but this was Ouein's last message to me. Six men died to bring me his words. I swear before all the gods, their deaths will not be in vain."

"I really thought we were gone back there," I say to Ursula as we approach the edge of the forest at nightfall.

"Were you afraid?" she asks.

"Of course," I scoff. "Weren't you?"

"There are worse things that can happen than death in battle."

"You mean slavery?"

She falls silent. A moment later, Donwen halts us.

"This is as close as we can get to the walls without being spotted," she says. I can see the torches on the rampart gleaming through the trees. "I must bid you farewell."

"Is there anything we can do to thank you?" asks Ursula.

"I will get Niall on my own, if I have to," the *drui* replies. "But if you can think of a way to help me get close to him –"

"I understand," I said. "I'll try my best. We all will."

She nods and vanishes into the darkness like a wraith. We sneak up to the line of the trees and hide in the tall grass, watching the siege unfold above us.

"So, what is it that you fear the most?" I whisper.

The Wrath of the Iutes

"What I saw in the vision on Mona," Ursula replies.

"What was it that was so terrifying?"

"I saw myself living the same life as my parents do. A *normal* life. Raising children, running a household, dealing with petty trade and small town politics…"

I stifle a laugh – only because I fear giving out our position to the enemy. "*That* is what scares you the most?"

She reaches out and holds my hand.

"Promise me our life will never be like that, Octa," she says; she never sounded more serious.

Her words remind me of my own vision induced by Ouein's wheat fire; the forlorn, longing smile with which she accepted her fate as my heir's mother; the sadness in her eyes when she reached for the ivory casket I brought from my travels…

"I am the king's son, Ursula," I tell her. "Whatever my life will be, I doubt it will ever be *normal*."

The mourning calls of war horns echo throughout the battlefield, from north to south. All along the wall, the Scots fall back, leaving behind dozens of bodies scattered in the ditch. Now is our chance.

"To the gate!" I call. We mount up and charge out of the forest and up the slope, past the retreating warriors. I reach for my own horn and hope its clear sound can break through the noise of the flight.

"It's Octa!" I hear a familiar voice cry from the top of the southern gatehouse. Ahes, standing on the rampart with one last unused *plumbata* in her hand, calls down to her men: "Open the gate, hurry!"

There's an agonising pause before the leaves of the gate creak slowly open. We storm through the narrow gap in single file; I ride last.

"Shut it!" I cry as I pass the stunned guards.

"Octa – where did you – *how* did you –?" Ahes runs up to us. Judging by the fresh scars on her arms and face, and the tattered, red-soaked tunic, she threw herself into the fiercest fighting at the southern wall. "We thought you were all dead!"

"Later – now, water…" I croak, and slide off the saddle onto the blood-spattered sand.

"How are we doing?" I ask Marcus.

I sit against the wall of Wortigern's *Praetorium* in the rubble of the crumbled gable. A young Atecot girl pours ice-cold water on my head from a clay pitcher, then proceeds to rub my sore shoulders.

The Wrath of the Iutes

"We lost a third," the *Decurion* replies. "Some of our best men were in that third. And we would've lost many more if not for you."

"I didn't think killing a few archers would make such a difference," says Ursula. She winces as Cado the surgeon tightens the binding on her shoulder.

"You did more than just kill the archers," Marcus replies. "They didn't see you ride out of the fort. It made them think you were the vanguard of a relief force." He glances at the fallen roof. "I wish I'd thought of making that sally. I never would've guessed this roof can hold a horse."

"It almost didn't," I say.

"Wortigern won't like what we've done to his house," notes Ahes.

"Wortigern won't…" I stop myself. I touch the bulging satchel at my side, heavy with the jewel-studded diadem. Nobody here knows I have it – not even Ursula.

The *Decurion* looks at the quickly darkening sky. "In the morning, when the mounted patrols return and Niall realises nobody's coming to our help," he says, "he'll send all his men for the final push."

"Are we going to make it?" I ask.

"I don't know. Losing the archers will force him to come up with some other strategy – as much as he's capable of making strategies."

"Give him some credit. He's come this far," I say.

"He's just a filthy barbarian," Marcus says, spitting a globule of pink spittle. "Numbers are on his side, that's all. Any decent commander would've overrun us already."

"I'm a filthy barbarian, too," I remind him. "As are all my men."

"That's different," he says. "You speak Latin; you read. You're practically a Briton."

"Don't let my men hear you say that. They might take offence at being compared to you *wealas*, considering what your kin did to us."

He hangs his head and takes a few deep breaths.

"I apologise," he says. "This battle is taking a strain on my nerves. You are valuable allies, and if we survive this, I hope our friendship will only grow stronger."

I laugh. "Don't worry. I've been called worse. And you're more right than you know – I *am* a Briton, as well as a Iute," I say, reaching to my hair.

"I was wondering about that," says Ahes. "That red hair…"

"My mother –" I start, but the sound of trumpet from the northern gatehouse interrupts us. "– that is a story for another time," I finish. "Looks like those patrols returned sooner than we hoped."

The Wrath of the Iutes

This is the first time any of us sees Niall. I'm surprised at how old he is — or maybe it's just the long, grey beard, reaching his belly in great clumps, that makes him appear so ancient. He's of average height, no taller than me, but he is a knot of muscles and scars under the thigh-length tunic of white linen. His hair, too, is long and grey, bound by a diadem of bronze. A golden *torc* as thick as a thumb adorns his neck, and seven bands of gold wrap around his right shoulder.

He rides up to the northern gate on a slender black mount, not dissimilar from our moor ponies, with the banner of truce in his hand. He's flanked by two men clad in plaid, hooded cloaks and white robes, each holding a staff of raw wood, topped with a blazing torch. They look like the *druis* of Mona, except the patterns on their robes and faces are drawn in different hues. They stare at our ramparts in grim silence.

At a bow shot's length behind these three, what looks like Niall's entire remaining army stands spread out in a broad crescent at the foot of the hill, to our north and east. Every tenth of them holds a lit torch menacingly before their face. In the scarcely illuminated darkness, their numbers prove even more intimidating than they appeared in the midst of the dawn battle. It's as if we've barely made a dent in Niall's ranks.

Marcus, myself and Eochu ride out to meet them. Up close, I notice Niall's eyes are bright blue; it seems rumours of Saxon blood in his veins might be true after all. I see decades of strife, both in war and politics, in these eyes. I know exactly what kind of man stands before me. He is a

Wortigern of the Scots, he is Hibernia's Meroweg – a man who's spent his life uniting the unruly tribes of his cold, distant island. This campaign must be a crowning achievement of a lifetime; he will not suffer to see it fail because of some tiny, damp mountain fortress standing in his way.

We exchange greetings; to my surprise, Niall speaks neither Imperial nor Vulgar tongue – or he refuses to. Our words are translated by one of the *druis*.

"What is it that you want, chieftain?" asks Marcus.

"Isn't it obvious?" Niall waves towards his army. "I don't want to turn this battle into a slaughter. And it will be a slaughter if we continue like this. My men are as tired as yours, and hungry, and will not take kindly to your opposing them for much longer."

"You presume a victory," I say.

Niall's beard shakes with laughter. "Yes, boy. I daresay I do."

"What is your offer?" Marcus asks.

"I offer you life. I offer you freedom. Leave your weapons and all supplies, except what you need for the journey. Take your men to Isca or Wenta. You'll be safe from me there."

"While you ravage Moridun and the coast."

The Wrath of the Iutes

"If I had wanted to raid the coast, I'd have done it from the sea," Niall replies. "I do not come to ravage and plunder. I come to conquer."

"You would *settle* at Moridun?" I ask, surprised.

"My people are already settled here," he replies, "even if they do not acknowledge my sovereignty over them. It is merely a change of a ruler."

"The Atecots are *not* your people," says Eochu. "You exiled us for worshipping the one True God."

"Those were decisions made by those who came before me," Niall says, waving his hand. "I would accept you and your God into my kingdom. You would no longer need to serve the Britons."

"The Britons welcomed us with open arms after we had to flee our home. You'll find no loyal subjects here," replies Eochu defiantly.

Niall merely smiles at him and turns his attention back to Marcus and me. "Those are my terms. I give you until morning to decide. Mind, though – either all of you go, or none at all. I will not let any more refugees or spies pass through our lines."

He waits for the *drui* to translate his words, then smacks his lips and all three of them turn back, without waiting for our answer.

They march slowly at first, in silence, until they reach within charging range, then they raise a shrill war cry – followed by a sudden and brutal assault along the entire length of the northern and eastern rampart.

None of the men gathered in the courtyard to hear Niall's offer voted to leave. Not the Atecots, fearing to fall under the rule of the pagan king. Not Ahes and her Armoricans, who remembered fighting the Scots like Niall for generations. Not even, to my surprise, my Iutes.

"We are warriors," said Aecba. "We fear no death. Wodan's table awaits us if we perish here."

"Princess Myrtle is only a few days' march away from here," added Raegen. "If we give up the fort without a fight, who's to say this… Niall won't march to where she is now?"

I wasn't sure of my own resolve. I believed Niall made a mistake not letting go anyone who was willing to leave. In this way, he made sure the decision of each of the warriors was influenced by those of their peers. Left alone with our thoughts, many of us would have taken his offer. Myself, perhaps, included.

Or maybe it was his plan all along. Maybe he *does* want to finish the campaign by slaughtering every single one of Wortigern's warriors, and burn us down with the fortress around us, especially the Atecots, to cement his rule over his new kingdom. And we just happened to be embroiled in this conflict by a stroke of bad fortune.

The Wrath of the Iutes

The presence of the *druis* in Niall's entourage makes me wonder if maybe there was more than just rational thought behind his decision. Maybe it's some heathen superstition; maybe the *druis* elders had read the best hour for the attack in the entrails of some poor animal, or saw it in a poison-induced vision, and told the chieftain to slaughter us all in sacrifice to some cruel Hibernian god…

As I watch the Scots approach, with a war song on their lips and the torches and weapons brandished in their hands, I recall what Wortigern told me just before he left for the ships.

"Nobody will remember this battle, boy," he said. "Not here in Britannia, at least. If you win, the chroniclers will note this as yet another Scots raid, one that came dangerously close to Moridun. And if you lose… you'll just be one more unnamed fort in the line of many that failed to stop Niall's conquest."

"If we lose, the Iutes will remember where their *aetheling* fell."

He chuckled. "Yes, perhaps. If anyone lives long enough to tell them the story."

I draw the sword and lean against the battlement. There will be no more arrows today, no javelins, no darts – just sword against axe, spear against shield, club against skull. I lock eyes with the Scot running straight for me, waving a small hatchet over his head. He leaps over the outer ditch, reaches the wall and starts climbing up the jagged stones. As soon as he's within my reach, I lunge over and stab him in the shoulder. He falls with a cry, only to be replaced by another warrior, indistinguishable from the previous. To my right, an assaulting Scot grabs one of the Atecot defenders by the tunic and pulls him down. They both fall back into the ditch, and I lose sight of them in the pile of mangled bodies beneath the wall.

I look wearily up. There's a dozen more men charging at me, lined up to take the place of each one I kill. I take a deep sigh. It's going to be a long day.

With a loud crash, a small section of the northern wall comes down under the weight of the enemy crawling over it. The Scots pour through it like water through a hole in a dyke. They throw their torches at a nearby hut; the thatch catches ablaze. We strike at the incursion from both sides – the Iutes and I from the right flank, Ahes and her Armoricans from the left. Somehow, with a fierce effort, we manage to contain the bulge and push the Scots back; they leave a dozen men lying dead in the fort's courtyard, in the dancing shadow of the burning hut. The Armoricans follow after them and fill the gap in the rampart with their shields and bodies. For a moment, the crisis is averted – but the fight takes too much of our strength, and no matter how valiantly the Armoricans fight, sooner or later, the Scots are going to push through the gap again.

But it's not all bad news. The breakthrough seems to have also used up some of the fighting strength of the enemy and is followed by a brief lull on the northern wall. I climb up onto the breastwork next to Marcus and take in the view on the river plain below.

The Wrath of the Iutes

"They have no reserve left," I note, studying the disposition of the enemy army before us.

"We haven't had a reserve since the assault started," Marcus replies bitterly, then adds, nodding in the direction of Niall's camp: "It is time."

"Are you sure?"

"We won't get another chance. Can you see him?"

I shield my eyes and look to where he's pointing. Niall, his *druis*, and some ten men of what must be his household guard, stand on top of a low spur rising from the northern slope towards the river, maybe three hundred feet away. For a brief while, I watch as he sends runners with orders to those fighting at the ramparts.

"I see him," I say. "And I see two lines of spearmen between him and us."

"Nobody said it would be easy."

We climb down and rush to the stables, where Marcus's *equites* and my Iutes are already waiting. This is a last-ditch plan, one that Marcus and I, inspired by our dawn sally, came up with when we realised that what was coming was likely our last stand. In the back of my head, I remember Donwen's plea; I can think of no other way to help her, if indeed it's still possible to help her at all.

"Ahes – what are you doing here?" the *Decurion* asks, seeing the Armorican princess tighten her saddle.

"What does it look like I'm doing?" she snaps back.

"We're riding for doom," Marcus tells her.

"We're all doomed anyway," she replies. "Better die out there on horseback than here, choking on smoke and blood."

"She's right," I say. When we first met, I thought Ahes was just a spoiled noble's daughter, treating our mission like an exotic trip, playing at being a warrior. But watching her during the siege, I've grown to respect her. Not strong enough to wield a spear or a sword with the skill of a trained warrior, she nonetheless proved herself talented with the darts and javelins; she killed at least four Scots in the early assaults, more than some of Marcus's men. "Let her come with us. One more lance can't harm us."

We all mount up – I ride one of the *equites'* warhorses again – and form into a thin wedge on the muster yard. At Marcus's signal, the northern gates swing open, and before the Scots outside realise what's happening, the Atecot guard storms outside to punch a hole in the enemy's line wide enough for us to ride through.

They fall by the dozens to mask our sally; when we pass, they stay behind to make sure the gate shuts safely behind them. It's a suicide stand, just like ours is – likely, a suicide charge – I glance back to see them mown down against the wall, though they fight like wild boars trapped by the baying hounds.

We hurtle down the slope and shatter the first line of spearmen in our way before they can set up – our sally takes

The Wrath of the Iutes

them by complete surprise; the second line tries to make a stand, but they, too, are too slow to stop us. No one can stand in the way of a wing of *equites* in full charge. Our lances break on their shields. The impact sends them flying. Within minutes, all that is left between us and Niall is a tight ring of his household guards and the *druis* elders, hidden behind a wall of large oval shields.

"Death!" Marcus raises a grim war cry, echoed by his men. "Donar!" my Iutes join them as we smash into the guard. They stand firm; these are no mere youths, or mercenaries. These must be the men with whom Niall started his mission to unite the Scots. Though we slay a few in that first strike, the rest of the ring holds fast, forcing us to pull away and turn around for another attack.

Through a gap in the Scots' ranks, my eyes meet Niall's. He stares at me in a proud, fearless challenge, with his hand on the pommel of the sword at his side. He makes no effort to prepare himself for a fight, certain that his guards will shield him from our assaults. His confidence unnerves me – as does the presence of another man next to him: a giant warrior, clad only in breeches and paint, holding a great two-handed sword. He looks like he could cut off a horse's head with one blow.

Marcus splits his force in two and strikes from both sides. Again, a few of Niall's guardsmen fall to our swords, but not enough to make a dent that would allow us to get closer to the Hibernian chieftain. We turn again, and again, gnawing away at the defenders, but now we're starting to lose men, too; five *equites* already lie at the foot of the spur, and Aecba's left side is covered in blood. Worse still, Niall's warriors fighting at the ramparts have noticed our attack and are running towards us in a great horde, to save their lord.

"We can't break through," I cry to Marcus.

"One last time," he shouts back. "One last charge!"

Just then, the wind brings the echo of a loud cry, coming from across the river. Most of the words are lost in the breeze, but I can make out a few: "…make way… arrow…clear shot…"

I look in the direction of the shout, but I can't see anything through the clump of low trees and bushes that shields the river shore from our view.

"Have you heard it?" I ask Ursula. "Or am I going mad?"

"I've heard it," she replies. "Was it Donwen?"

"I can't see – but if it's her, it might be our last chance."

"Last chance for what?"

"Follow me."

I split away from Marcus's main attack and, with the wedge of Iutes behind me, rush at Niall's wall of men from the north. The Scots guards, led by the giant swordsman, step forth with their shields raised to meet us.

"I will do it, *Hlaford*!" I hear Aecba cry as he spurs his pony to charge past me.

The Wrath of the Iutes

"Aecba, no – wait!"

But he doesn't listen – and I can see why; the gash in his side is deep and wide, the old wound torn apart; his guts fall out, trailing behind him. In a few moments he will be dead anyway. I don't know what reserves of strength are keeping him upright.

He doesn't charge head-on at the spears; instead, he turns at the last moment and leaps from the saddle at the giant. The swordsman holds fast, but Aecba tugs on his sword arm with all his remaining strength. I dismount and join him on the other side and, together, we finally pull the giant to the ground. Ursula storms after me in the gap we made, and the rest of the Iutes follow, cutting a wide path towards Niall.

"Back!" I manage a shout while wrestling with the swordsman. "Before you're cut off!"

I don't see what happens next – the giant throws Aecba aside, rolls me over and pushes my face into the mud. I struggle, but I can tell there's no way I could wrestle myself out of his iron grip. My sword lies just out of my reach – I try, but the giant grabs my arm and twists it. I hear the pony hooves stampede past me, one by one, until all are safely out of the noose of swords and shields tightening around them – and then, the unmistakable whooshing flutter of the long *druis* arrow, flying straight and true over my head.

The giant's grip on me slackens for a moment – just enough for me to free my arm, reach the sword, flip it in my hand and jab him in the stomach. It takes several long, agonising seconds, with my face still pressed in the dirt before he falls off me. I gasp for air before looking up to see what made the swordsman and the guards around me so distracted.

In the centre of the ring of shields, still surrounded by his best warriors, still flanked by his faithful *druis*, his hand still on the pommel of his sword, Niall stands upright, staring with his left eye towards the river, his mouth agape in surprise, his finger pointing at something only he can see.

His right eye is pierced through with the *drui* arrow, buried deep in his brain.

A rivulet of blood trickles slowly from the eye socket and from his mouth. He lets out a terrible, wordless groan – and crumples to the ground.

CHAPTER XVII
THE LAY OF FIANN

As I help Donwen climb out of the river, I notice she only has a single arrow left in the bag at her belt. Her tunic is torn on the side, revealing another fresh scar.

"Where are your men?" I ask.

"Gone," she replies simply. "But it was worth it."

She walks past the shocked Scots, reaches the body of their dead king and kneels down by him. Nobody disturbs her as she puts her hand on Niall's head, closes her eyes and whispers something in the old Briton tongue – a prayer? Or a curse?

All around us, those of Niall's men who heard the dire news are gathering in stunned silence at the foot of the mound where he fell. There are still small skirmishes along the fort's wall – the message hasn't yet reached everyone, but the battle is over. For now. The king's surviving guards surround his body with a circle of spears, just as they did moments ago when he was alive. One of the *druis* steps forward, spreads his arms and stares at us in morbid silence. None of the Scots dare to pass the line of his outstretched hands.

"We should get back," I say to Marcus. "They're all in a daze now, but it won't last long."

He nods and bids his soldiers pick up our fallen. Ubba raises Aecba's bloodied body and throws it over his saddle. We ride back to the fort in a quiet procession, passed by still more of Niall's warriors returning from the rampart. The silence is unnerving; I expected them to curse us, pelt us with abuse and dirt. Instead, it's as if with Niall's death, their spirits have also been crushed. They shamble past us with their heads down, stooping, dragging their spears behind them.

"We need to send a rider to Moridun, to tell them what happened," says Marcus when we reach the fort and shut the gates behind us. With the Scots returned to their camp, the way south is open again, though we can't know for how long.

"And what *are* we going to tell them?" I wonder. "All that's happened is that Niall's dead and we survived another day. His army's not going anywhere yet, and there's still enough of them left to defeat us and march on Demetia."

"I fought these barbarians enough times to know that if you cut off their head, the entire body withers. Drustan, come here!"

The young *eques* stands to attention.

"Go back to the harbour," Marcus tells him, "and tell *Comes* Agricola what you saw here. See if you can find out any news about the *Legatus* and his troops in the North while you're there."

Drustan nods swiftly, mounts up and storms out of the southern gate. Marcus then turns his attention, at last, to

The Wrath of the Iutes

Donwen. The weary *drui* leans on Ursula's shoulder, holding to her wounded side. Blood seeps through her fingers.

"You need this looked at," Marcus says. "I'll get my surgeon –"

"I know how to treat my own wounds, Roman," Donwen replies. "I just need hot water and some figwort."

"You'll find everything in Cado's tent. Once you're done, get back to me. I need to ask you a few questions."

"I don't take orders from you, city-dweller," she scoffs.

Marcus raises his hand in a commanding gesture, but I grab him by the wrist and pull his hand down.

"Come by the *Praetorium* – or what's left of it – whenever you're ready," I say, nodding at the ruined house. "We will drink heather wine and tell tales of glory."

She scoffs again, but softer this time, and with a half-smile.

"Give me an hour to patch up," she says. "I've heard good things about this heather wine, and I'm eager to try it."

"Whatever do we do with them?" asks Marcus, studying the plain below. The Scots camp remains silent; the men shuffle aimlessly from tent to tent, huddle around the fires, wash themselves in the river, or come up to the hill of their king's death, still protected by Niall's guard of the *druis*, to pay their respect.

They don't seem like an army eager to conquer new kingdoms anymore; more like a camp of refugees, stuck in a strange territory, not knowing whether to keep moving or go back home. But I don't believe Marcus's assessment. There's still life in this body, even if it is dormant now. Niall couldn't have commanded a warband this size himself. There must have been some hierarchy, other warchiefs ready to pick up the war horn. As soon as they decide among themselves which of them should do it, I fear the Scots will remember again why they came all the way here.

I look back at the fort's courtyard, where the soldiers are piling up the dead bodies. We can't bury them yet – the graveyard is outside the fort's walls, at the bottom of the eastern slope, too close to the enemy tents to risk getting out in case the Scots decide to strike again.

"Send them our food," I say.

"What?"

"Right now, they're confused and hungry. Tomorrow morning, they'll be even more hungry – and furious. They may not care for conquering Demetia anymore, but they know we have the food. We can either share it with them, or wait for them to take it themselves."

"There's not enough of it for all of them."

The Wrath of the Iutes

"Then we give as much as we can. Give them wood and oil for the pyre, and heather wine for the vigil. We will throw a great feast to mourn the death of their king. Celebrate the glory of their campaign."

"Celebrate – with these *heathens?*" A grimace of disgust mars Marcus's face for a moment.

"They're warriors, like you and I. They need to know they haven't come all this way for nothing."

"Well then maybe we should give them our gold and silver, too?" the *Decurion* scoffs.

"I was just about to propose that," I say. "Isn't this how you *wealas* deal with such things?"

"What do you mean?"

"Rome survives by paying off her enemies. Odowakr departed from Trever with ten wagons of gold, despite his defeat. It only makes sense."

Marcus sighs. "I'm sure Wortigern would've agreed with you, if he was here. He's always preferred diplomacy to war. Me, I'm just a soldier." He bites his lip and studies the enemy camp. "And as a soldier, I can see we have no chance of surviving another assault like the last one. Even without Niall in command."

"Then you agree?"

"It is as you say – they will get it all with or without our consent." He scratches his new face scar absentmindedly; blood from the torn scab oozes down his cheek. "We should go down there," he adds. "Tell them what we've decided before they find their resolve again. You, me, Eochu…"

"And Donwen," I say. "She will know how to talk to those *druis*."

In the darkness, beyond the circle of light beaming from the blazing pyre, the bard's wordless chant swells over the crackling of the flames. Donwen approaches the pyre, nocks her last arrow onto the bow, dips its tip in the bucket of molten tar and puts it to the flames. She aims the burning missile high and releases it in a slow, bright arc over our heads until it disappears with a hiss into the black ribbon of the river.

She is the last archer to do so, after all of Niall's companions and officers, as befits the one who shot the arrow that ended the great warchief's life. As the bard's chant descends from its booming heights, she bows down before the pyre and turns around to face Niall's chief *drui*. The robed elder steps forward and puts a heavy golden *torc* on Donwen's neck – the *torc* that belonged to Niall.

I understand these Hibernians – or Eriu, as they call themselves – and the way they think better than I do that of the *wealas*. They are heathen warriors, like the Iutes, Saxons or Franks. I know they bear Donwen no grudge. She slew their king fairly, in battle, through an admirable feat of martial

The Wrath of the Iutes

prowess. Clearly, it was the gods – the same gods Donwen worships: Toranis, Teutates and others, for, as the chief *druis* told me, they were once shared throughout both islands, even as far as Gaul – who decided the flight of her arrow. She deserves their respect as if she was one of their own.

"When we set forth to Britannia, I made the rite of oak and bull as I had before every campaign," the chief *druis* tells me later as we listen to the Scots bard tell the story of the warchief's life. "The blood spilled onto the sigils of otter and hawk."

"Transformation," Donwen explains.

"A *great* transformation." The *drui* nods. "We both knew what that meant. Niall would either become the greatest king the Eriu ever saw… Or he would die here."

"You knew – and still you came?"

"What kind of warchief would he be if fear of death stopped him from reaching for greatness?" He laughs and shakes his head sadly.

"Was his mother really a Saxon?" asks Ursula.

It is odd for us all to sit at the feast celebrating the man who was our mortal enemy. A day earlier, the warriors with whom we now share bread and wine – most of it from our own supplies – were eager to slay us all, to conquer the land we defended and to enslave its people. Now, they drink with us, sing with us the few songs all of us know and treat us no worse than as if we were a part of their army returned from some different mission.

Even the Atecots from the garrison forget their ancient hostilities for this one night and take part in the festivities, though I see them frown and grimace at the heathen rituals. With enough ale, they join their Hibernian brethren in songs and dances that are familiar to all of them.

"She was a slave of his father's wife," the *drui* replies. "Have you not heard the bard's song?"

"I do not understand your tongue."

"Chief Iwocat had four sons with his wife – and one with the slave… But it was the slave who became the *Rex*."

For a moment, I gaze silently at the blazing pyre. "My father was a slave, too," I say. "And now he's the king of the Iutes."

The *drui* stares at me in surprise. "How fitting that the two of you came to meet here, far away from each other's homeland."

"What will happen to Niall's kingdom now?" I ask.

"He has sons," the *drui* replies. "They will resolve the matter between themselves."

"Through war?"

The Wrath of the Iutes

"War, feats of strength, poetry contests… There are ways to decide these things." He sighs. "But it will be years before any of them gathers enough power to invade Britannia again."

"If there is still a Britannia left to invade by then," says Marcus ominously, and then hides his face in the goblet of ale.

Wary of the power of the Scots' heather wine, I leave the feasting, the singing and the dancing behind and descend to the river shore, to cool my head in the dark waters of the Teibi.

I find Ursula and Donwen there, sitting on a half-sunken tree trunk; Donwen has her arm around Ursula. Ursula lays her head on Donwen's shoulder. I sense this is an intimate moment, and I want to leave, but Donwen spots me and waves invitingly. I sit down on the trunk, a few feet away. Ursula takes my arm and pulls me closer.

"Ursula told me the truth about you two," says the *drui*.

"What truth?"

"About your wedlock."

"There was no wedlock. We were only pretending. The king died before he could pronounce us, and the gods –"

"You don't need the priests' and the gods' approval to be wedded. They are only there to bear witness to what's already in your hearts."

"He's a man," says Ursula. "He doesn't understand what's in his heart."

"And you do?" I ask, annoyed. I didn't come here to discuss the contents of my, or Ursula's heart; she is right – I don't know the extent of my feelings for her. Until she confronted me in Scillonia, I really believed we were only a couple of good friends. Have I been blind all those years – or did Ursula herself only realise the truth recently?

She scoffs but doesn't reply. We stare in silence at the dark, slow-moving waters of the Teibi.

"What are you going to do now?" Ursula asks, and after a moment's confusion I realise she's talking to Donwen. "Now that you're back… home?"

"Mona is my home – I know nothing about this place. I can't imagine settling down among the city-dwellers or these Christian Hibernians."

"What about your brother?" I remember the wounded boy. "Is he…?"

"I don't know. He didn't fight in the fortress. Some younger men stayed behind to guard the villages. He might still be alive."

I stand up and unfasten my sword belt.

The Wrath of the Iutes

"What are you doing?" asks Ursula.

"I was wondering what I've been carrying this thing all night for... Now I know. I think you should have this."

I present her with Caratacos's sword. For reasons I myself wasn't sure of, I'd decided it was a more suitable blade to carry during Niall's farewell than my Roman *spatha*. I also have Wortigern's diadem with me in the satchel – I've been carrying it with me everywhere ever since the *Dux* gave it to me, feeling it was too precious to risk falling into the wrong hands. As long as the battle lasted, I didn't need to worry about what do with it, other than keep it safe. Now, I had to make a decision. For a moment, I pondered giving it to Marcus – who better to deserve it than the victorious commander of the siege of *Cair* Wortigern? But if the *Dux* wanted to give his diadem to any Briton, he would've done so a long time ago. It seemed I really had to take it all the way back to Cantia – though I did not yet have a clear idea why.

She takes the old blade out of its sheath and stares at it in the dimming light of the pyre.

"It looks ancient and noble. We don't carry swords like it anymore. What is this thing?" she asks.

"It's the last sword of your last chieftain, Caratacos. I stole it from Hrodha's fort for Ouein, in exchange for your people's help."

"Why would Ouein want this old thing, after all this time?"

"He…" I glance at Ursula. "He believed himself Caratacos, reborn."

Donwen laughs bitterly. "No wonder he thought it was his destiny to lead us all into doom!" she says. "If he was Caratacos, then I must be Boudika herself!" She presses the weapon in my hand. "Keep the damn sword. I don't want it."

"But you're the last *druis*," I protest, handing it back to her. "If not you, then who would –"

"The *druis* are no more. I'm just Donwen of Red Stone Island."

"Then… What should I do with it?"

She shrugs. "What did Elder Ouein – I'm sorry, *Caratacos*," she corrects herself mockingly, "tell you?"

"He said… He said the sword should help keep the memory of your people."

She ponders the blade for a moment longer and then, before either of us can stop her, lobs it into the river. The sword splashes in the middle of the deepest current and sinks without a trace.

"If my people will be remembered at all, it will be by their deeds and their songs, not by some ancient trinkets of failed chieftains," she declares as I stare, dumbfounded, at the dark, slow-moving river. "Thank you, Octa," she adds. "My mind is much clearer now. I know what I should do."

The Wrath of the Iutes

"I don't understand."

"I will go back to Mona. Find those who survived – the Northerners couldn't have killed us all off – and then we'll go into hiding. Vanish in the mountains and in the forests. We will recede from the world; we will become shadows, mysterious figures, stories told to children by the burning hearth, in winter. We will become like the folk who built the stone tombs. Not even a memory."

She asks us to leave her by the riverside, to contemplate this strange new future of her kindred. As we return to the feast, Ursula grasps my hand tightly.

"I don't want to fade away," she says.

"What are you talking about?"

"Can't you see? All the ancient tribes of this island are disappearing into the mists of the past, one by one. The stone builders. The Scillonians. The *druis* of Mona. Not even songs remain. And I know my people will be next. Already Cantia is half empty, with all the nobles leaving for Armorica. Wind blows dust through the streets and markets of Dorowern, where there were once crowds."

I remember my wheat fire vision – and Wortigern's words, about the Britons dreading the passage of time. I tell her the same thing the *Dux* then told me – the same thing Rav Asher said in Coln.

"You can't stop the river from flowing."

[426]

"This is not what I want to hear right now."

"But it's the truth." I stop and turn to her. "Is this why you want to marry me? To turn yourself into a Iute? To become one of the new people, a part of the new song of Britannia?"

She lets go of my hand. Her fingers clutch into a fist, but she stops short of hitting me.

"How are you always finding the worst possible thing to say?"

"I don't understand…"

"I guess I *was* wrong about you, after all. About us."

"Ursula —"

"No, it's fine." She raises her hand and steps back into the shadow. "We can remain just friends if that's what you want. I will not humiliate myself with this talk of wedlock anymore — not until you grow up enough to take it seriously."

She turns away and, ignoring my calls, runs off back to the river shore — back to Donwen.

In the morning, before most of the men in the fort and the Scots camp even wake after the feast, Drustan returns from Moridun. He's not alone — riding behind him, in a small two-wheeled cart, are Warus and one of Wortigern's Atecot

The Wrath of the Iutes

officers, a young *Decurion* named Fiann; he wears a patch over his left eye, and his right arm is a mere stump, swaddled in cloth.

I shake Marcus awake. Wincing and rubbing his brow, he follows me into the courtyard as the cart rattles through the southern gate, where Eochu and a huddle of Atecots already eagerly await the news of their brethren.

"How many survived?" they clamour. "What about the *Seahorse*? Does Wortigern live?"

"Leave the poor men alone," Marcus says. "Let them breathe." His soldiers step in to push the crowding Atecots away from the cart and make a corridor for the two men, leading to the *Praetorium*. Most of the damage from the fallen roof has been cleared up, but the dining hall now has neither a ceiling nor a table; what's left is enough for a few of us to sit around the hearth and listen to the survivors' tale.

There's only one question that we want them to answer first, though we all guess the answer.

"Wortigern?" I ask.

"Last I saw him was three days ago, when he led one final assault on the walls of Cunedag's fortress," replies Warus. "By then, less than twenty men remained of the original force."

"He stormed the walls at Forks with just twenty men?"

"He gathered some support from the local villages: Laigin settlers who didn't like the idea of being ruled by the Northerners," adds Fiann. "But they didn't last long."

"Long enough to put fear of God into Niall and Cunedag," says Eochu with a satisfied smile. "Then all who went with Wortigern are dead, just as we expected."

"Not all," Warus interjects. "A few managed to flee back to the safety of our ships – and Cunedag took a few more alive, as hostages."

"Hostages?" Marcus exclaims. "What for?"

"To negotiate peace," I explain. "Cunedag doesn't want war with Ambrosius – he just wants to be left alone in his land."

"How do you know?" Marcus gives me a suspicious look. "Have you two discussed this when you were in the North?"

"No, we haven't," I reply forcefully. "But I understand how he thinks. It's all we ever want from you Britons. A land to settle, and to rule for ourselves."

"Ambrosius will never agree to something like this. Another foe living on his frontier…"

"He doesn't have to be your foe. I wouldn't be surprised if Cunedag offered to still protect your borders and shores from the Scots, like we Iutes do in Cantia."

The Wrath of the Iutes

"There will be no negotiations as long as he holds my men captive," says Eochu.

"Not only your men, Atecot," says Warus. "A few of your *equites* are there, too, *Decurion*, from the patrols caught by Niall. And your mercenary friend Mullo," he adds, turning to me.

"How do you know?" I ask. "Have you seen them?"

"I have," says Fiann. "Cunedag showed us to them before the last assault, trying to stop us from throwing our lives away. But Wortigern was unmoved. He said he wasn't there to negotiate — he was there to kill Cunedag, or die trying."

"He couldn't live with Cunedag's betrayal," Eochu muses.

"One too many," I say. For all his wisdom, Wortigern kept choosing the wrong people to trust. Even my father eventually decided to carve a future of his own, not the one Wortigern had planned for him…

"How did *you* survive that last assault?" Marcus, still suspicious, asks the Atecot officer.

"I wasn't there. The *Legatus* sent me and my men to defend the ships, in case Cunedag tried to take them over."

"The Scots attacked us in boats," adds Warus. "If it wasn't for Fiann here, they would've overrun us. The *Seahorse* was damaged too badly to return — they're hiding in a cove on the western coast, trying to repair the ship with what they have."

I scratch the tip of my nose. "Then, neither of you saw Wortigern fall."

The two men admit I'm right. "But there's no way he could have…" Fiann starts.

"If Cunedag captured him alive, he'd have the best hostage he could've ever hoped for," says Marcus. "We can't let him get away with this."

"There's little we can do," says Eochu. "We don't have nearly enough force left to bring war to Cunedag without Wortigern — and in case you forgot, there's still an entire Scots army between us and him…"

His calm, but firm words cool everyone down. I can see why Wortigern chose this man to be his *Praetor*. It's true: the anger of Niall's warband may have been placated by the funeral feast, but we still don't know what their next move will be. They have not yet begun to make any preparations for the long march back North — and though the *druis* elder assured us they must, eventually, return to Hibernia for the choosing of the new king, we can't possibly leave the fort empty with the hundreds of Scots warriors still camping at its doorstep.

An inkling of an idea ignites in my mind. I stand up. The eyes of everyone turn to me in surprise.

"I think I know how to cook both of these stews in one pot," I say.

The Wrath of the Iutes

"Have you seen Donwen anywhere?"

"She's gone."

Ursula looks up from her bowl of potage and brushes her hair from her forehead. A squiggle of blue pigment marks her right cheek, just below the eye, drawn to conceal one of the fresh scars she gained in the siege.

"She marked you," I note.

She runs her finger along the pattern. "Briton warriors of old painted each of their scars this way. Donwen only had the time to do this one before she left."

"It's not permanent, is it?"

"The rains will wash it away," she says glumly. "What did you need her for?"

"I want to speak to that *druis* elder again. I suppose I will have to manage on my own."

"I'll come with you." She pushes the bowl away and reaches for the sword belt.

"Are you sure?"

She puts on the boots and the cloak and leaves the tent without replying.

"Listen," I start as we walk down the hill. "I – I've been thinking a lot all night."

"Have you now."

She marches quickly, in big strides, past the fort's forward guards, into the no-man's land between the walls and Niall's camp.

"It's not my fault, you know," I say, struggling to talk and keep up with her at the same time. "I never had anyone to speak to about… these matters. My mother died when I was a child. My father –" I slip in the mud. Ursula doesn't slow down, so I have to run a few steps to catch up. "– is a bitter old man, whose heart froze when he lost the only two women he ever loved… Will you please slow down?"

The Scots guards stop us at the border of their camp. Last night's friendliness is gone with the last vapours of the heather wine. I tell them we have to see the elder *druis* urgently. They command us to wait while one of them goes to fetch him.

"It's easier for you women," I continue my pleading with Ursula. "You have someone to talk to *all* the time. Even when you don't know each other. You have your Basinas, your Donwens, even when that Scillonian woman took you captive, you somehow managed to strike a connection with her… The only one I could talk to was Silvia, and even she…"

"Who in Hell is *Silvia?* Wait – you talked about *us* with that whore?"

"She used to be a courtesan –" I start, then stop, seeing Ursula's furious stare. "It doesn't matter. She didn't help me

The Wrath of the Iutes

— and she was my only chance. Do you think I could ever discuss my feelings with someone like Audulf or Seawine? All *we* can talk about is hunting, fighting and humping."

"You have me."

"I can't talk to you about… you. It wouldn't be fair."

The guard returns and takes us to the smouldering funeral pyre. The *drui* finishes brushing his king's ashes into a large, squat clay urn. All around us, the Scots warriors are packing their bags, rolling their tents, loading their carts; the one man keeping still among all this activity is the one sitting on a folding bronze stool at the foot of the pyre, plucking at the horsehair strings of his ten-string lyre, mumbling to himself and wincing from time to time. I recognise him as Colla the Bard – the poet who sang the lay of Niall's life at the funeral feast.

"Greetings, Octa, son of Aeric," the *drui* bows. "You've come to bid us farewell?"

"Something like that. Why is your bard so vexed? I thought Niall's song was already written."

The *drui* chuckles. "Our sister from Mona passed by this morning. She requested that the song did not mention her as Niall's slayer – and we agreed to respect her wish."

I glance at Ursula. "She was being serious about fading away even from song, then… Who will replace her?"

"I leave that up to Colla. By the laws of poetry, I imagine Eochu would be the most suitable kingslayer – one Hibernian killing another in a distant land." He puts a lid on the urn and steps back as the servants take it away to be sealed with beeswax. "Now, what is it that you wanted?"

"Tell me, elder," I start, "how are you planning to return to your country?"

"The same way we came. Up the Roman road, and back to Mona – in a hurry. The food you gave us will only last a few days. Why do you ask?"

"Is the way clear for you?"

He tilts his head and narrows his eyes. "Why the concern, warrior?"

"We would prefer it if you didn't suddenly find a reason to come back."

"You... know something?"

"You don't?"

"Let us not play games, warrior. I admit, with all the... disruption brought onto our lines by the *druis* of Mona and your *Legatus*, we received little news from our rearguard."

"I feared so."

"Why? What happened?"

The Wrath of the Iutes

I invite him to sit down. A servant brings us furs to cover the wet grass.

"One of the ships we sent to fight the treacherous Cunedag returned from Moridun last night," I say. "Wortigern lost – of course. There was never any hope, not after we found out Cunedag recaptured Segont…"

Ursula gives me a sharp look.

"Segont? Impossible," the *drui* scoffs. "We would know by now."

"You just admitted you had no news from the North."

"Why would Cunedag do that? He's been nothing but a good ally."

"He was a good ally to Wortigern, too, until he decided to change sides. How can you trust a man who found it so easy to betray his old friend?" I shrug. "You can wait here to verify the truth of my words – knowing that every day of delay brings closer the threat of starvation to your army, and we have no more provisions to give – or you can trust me… And help me."

"*Help* you? In what way?"

"If Cunedag decided to make enemies of us both, it only makes sense for us to join our forces against him. We would march with you – the Atecots, Marcus's cavalry… You may have the numbers, but we know how to conquer our own forts. Together, I'm sure we can destroy him – and once we do, you'll be able to go home in peace."

He tugs at his beard in thought.

"What makes you think we need your help in dealing with the Northerner? We already took Segont from you once."

"You never really *took* Segont, though, did you? The rumours were false. I've seen you in a siege. Not even with an army twice your size could you have taken a fortress like Segont in such a short time. Cunedag *gave* it to you. Now he has simply taken it back."

"No matter. We have nothing to fear from Cunedag and his Northern dogs."

"As you wish, elder. I'm sure you know better than I do what your army's capable of."

I stand up and bid him farewell.

"Wait." He raises his hand. "Our help does not come cheap."

"Of course. What's your price?"

"Come back later today. I will have to discuss this with other *druis* and the clan chiefs."

We leave the camp in a hurry. As soon as we find ourselves out of sight of the Scots guards, I stagger and sway

The Wrath of the Iutes

into Ursula's supporting arms. She holds me up as we pass through the gate.

"I thought I was going to faint, or retch, or both," I say. "My hands are still trembling."

"How did you know Cunedag took Segont?" she asks.

She puts me in the wall's shadow and calls for water.

"I didn't," I say. "I guessed."

"You *guessed?*"

"I may well be wrong. But I tried to think of what my father would do in Cunedag's place – and this is exactly what he'd have done."

"Why? Why betray another ally and risk the wrath of an entire Hibernian army?"

"Because I believe Cunedag still wants to be a good neighbour to the Britons. If he destroys the returning Scots, he not only takes their plunder and slaves – he will prove he can still protect Ambrosius's border, even if he's no longer taking orders from Ambrosius's generals."

"He still has the hostages."

"I'm hoping facing our combined armies will persuade him to release them. The Scots won't care for our hostages – he will have no leverage over them."

"And if you're wrong? If he holds to his truce with the Scots, if Segont is still in Hibernian hands and all of your promises turn out to be lies?"

"Then we'll perish in some mountain valley, fighting both Cunedag's and the dead king's warriors. Not the worst way to go, is it?" I smile weakly.

CHAPTER XVIII
THE LAY OF CUNEDAG

I've been holding my breath for the past three days. I only let out a sigh of relief when Scots riders return from the forward patrol with the news we've all been waiting for: Cunedag holds Segont.

"Well done," says Marcus when we gather in the evening to discuss the situation. "Your wager paid off. It seems you barbarians really *do* all think alike."

We set our camp in front of the Scots army: Niall's warchiefs did not trust us enough to have us behind them, wary of finding themselves in the exact same pincer they'd avoided through Cunedag's betrayal. Needless to say, we didn't appreciate our position either – it would've been all too easy for the two erstwhile allies to crush us between them. But we are fast-moving, and our Laigin guides know the local mountains better than the Scots, so the only danger we truly face is being forced to run off into the woods... At least as long as we don't get too close to one of Cunedag's forts.

"What now?" asks Ursula. She's the only one I asked to come with me on this expedition. Before leaving *Cair* Wortigern, I released Seawine and the other Iutes from their duty. I could no longer bring myself to ask them to follow me on yet another campaign. This wasn't their war; it wasn't my war, either – but I felt obliged to do everything in my power to either save Wortigern and his men, or make sure their lives were not given in vain.

"Take this," I said, giving the satchel with the *Dux*'s diadem to Seawine. "Keep it safe. If I fail to return, make your way back to Cantia and give it to my father."

"What is it?"

"To us – nothing. But to the people of this land, it could bring untold chaos, maybe even another war."

He weighed the bag curiously in his hands. "It doesn't feel any heavier than an armband," he notes, amused. "I hope you do come back, *aetheling*. I don't think I could explain to your father why I brought him this trinket instead of his son."

"Oh, he'll understand when he sees this."

It is for my father's sake that I'm joining this march – for the sake of his friendship with Wortigern, his love of Rhedwyn, for everything he once wanted to achieve, before the events of Wortimer's War turned him into the man he is now: an alliance between the Iutes and the Britons, a new future for Britannia…

"Octa?" Ursula repeats her question. "What now?"

I look up and stare at everyone gathered around me. I can see them guessing, wondering if they made a right decision to trust me with their lives and those of their warriors. Each of them has a different reason to be here. Marcus's is the most straightforward – he's here to fight for his commander, for his land, for his people. To him, Cunedag is a mere heathen traitor who needs to be punished; to him, this is just the continuation of the war he'd always been fighting: the war

The Wrath of the Iutes

against barbarians encroaching on his homeland's borders. If it means he dies here, so be it.

Next to him sits Ahes, still nominally leading her band of Armoricans, though it's old Warus who commands the men now, to the best of his abilities. Most of the hostages in Cunedag's keep are her people, but something tells me she's not coming with us just out of a desire to free them: she sits next to Marcus, her knee meeting his knee, her shoulder joined with his, her eyes barely aimed at anyone or anything else than the *Decurion*'s roughly chiselled face.

Praetor Eochu looks at all of us with a gloomy, dispirited expression. He's left a handful of warriors to guard the fort – helped in this task by my Iutes, for a while at least – and gathered a couple of *centuries* of Atecots to join us on the march, but I know he has little faith in the success of our endeavour. I spoke to him, briefly, last night; the loss of the northern frontier, the severe casualties his troops suffered during the siege and the likely death of Wortigern all but broke his spirit. Only Niall's death and the withdrawal of the Scots gave him some hope – though not for long. "We may have halted the flood for a while," he told me. "But it is as the *Legatus* said – we have no strength to hold it back forever."

The last of this small war council is Fiann, the young officer. I know little of him – as far as I can tell, he and a handful of other survivors from the battle at the Forks are only with us to avenge their fallen kin, or die trying.

Apart from Ahes, I am the youngest here, and the least experienced in matters of war – and yet, for the moment, they're all waiting for my word. This march was my idea, after all; I am the only one of them who seems to know how heathen warlords think, and so far, all my guesses have proven correct. I imagine they're hoping I have some other insight into Cunedag's mind, some secret strategy known only to us barbarians. I clear my throat, knowing what I'm about to say will only disappoint some of them, anger the others and confuse and surprise everyone.

"Now," I say, standing up and taking a long pause for effect, "I will go to speak with Cunedag."

He meets us halfway up the slope of the Forks, accompanied by a retinue of six warriors – two more than our company, made up of myself, Ursula, and the two faithful Iutes, Hleo and Haering, who alone chose to follow us north rather than stay with Seawine.

"I knew I'd see you again, *aetheling*," says Cunedag. "And that when I did, it would be in disagreeable circumstances."

"The disagreeableness is all of your doing," I note.

"I will not deny it. If only there was another way…" He smiles, sadly, and looks to the west, where the mountain mist shrouds the road to Segont. "I suppose you're here to talk about the army heading right now towards my forts."

"*Your* forts?" I scoff. "The Romans built and manned them. The Britons maintained them for generations."

The Wrath of the Iutes

"And then they abandoned them for generations more," says Cunedag. "My kin were the first to hold this frontier in a century. Have you heard of the concept of *usucapio* – ownership through possession? Even by Imperial Law these forts are now ours."

"I studied Imperial Law under Bishop Fastidius," I say, "and I know you cannot invoke *usucapio* when you take something by force. But it matters not. I am not here to discuss what belongs to whom. I am only here to demand the release of hostages."

"And why, pray, should I do that?"

I point towards Segont. "Right now, nearly a thousand men prepare to lay siege to your fortress. Only a few of them care at all about your hostages – the Atecots and Marcus's *equites*…"

"And yourself."

"I'm only here for Mullo. And Wortigern – I presume he still lives?"

"Not for want of trying." Cunedag winces. "The old man all but threw himself on our spears. I lost four warriors just trying to pin him to the ground." He looks to Ursula, then back to me. "If I gave you back your mercenary and the old *Dux* – would you go home?"

I furrow my brow in surprise. "You would release Wortigern – and lose all the leverage?"

[444]

James Calbraith

He shrugs.

"Capturing him alive was merely an accident. I already have more hostages than I could possibly need to convince the Britons to sit down for talks. And as for the Scots… If I didn't think I could handle a handful of leaderless, half-starved pirates, I wouldn't be risking their wrath like this."

"I…" I search for words. "Why do you need *me* gone? It is not my presence that should trouble you. There's an entire army here, and I'm just one man…"

"A rather bothersome man. I understand it is you who is behind this unlikely alliance of the Scots and the Britons that threatens my domain. And you're the son of someone I once called a friend. It would be easier for me to wage this war if I didn't have to look out for you on the battlefield."

"Octa…" Ursula says quietly. She lays her hand on my shoulder.

"What do you think?" I ask.

"Isn't this what we came here for?" she says. "You would fulfil your duty as a warrior, and as a friend. Nobody would expect anything more from you."

"Then you, too, would want us to go back."

"Doesn't your father need you more than these Britons or Hibernians right now, *aetheling*?" Cunedag asks.

"How do you know about that?"

The Wrath of the Iutes

He looks at me mockingly, and I remember he would have had plenty chances to speak to Wortigern about what the *Dux* knew of what went on in other parts of Britannia.

"Octa – do you know what he's talking about?" Ursula asks. "You've had news from Cantia?"

Cunedag laughs. "You haven't told them? You'd keep the war a secret? Did you fear that if your men found out the truth, they'd never have agreed to stay here and fight for the – what you fair-hairs call us – *wealas*?" He turns to Ursula. "Explain me this, Briton shieldmaiden. As we speak, *Rex* Aeric is waging a losing war against the Saxons – and meanwhile, this young *aetheling* wastes time protecting a distant border of the people his father, no more than six years ago, considered his deadliest enemies. Why would he do that? Does he love Ambrosius and Wortigern more than his own family?"

"He did it because I asked him to do it," says Ursula, firmly, surprising both of us. "I wanted to see more of the world than I ever could have if I was stuck in Cantia. I wanted more glory than I would have ever won fighting sea raiders and forest bandits."

"And now?" I ask. "Is your lust for wander and glory satisfied?"

"I've seen all there is to see here," she replies. "And a war with the Saxons is a worthy cause to return to. I can't believe you'd hide Aelle's attack from us – from *me*. Did you think you couldn't trust me?"

[446]

Cunedag chuckles. "Calm yourself, girl. Neither you nor Octa are on trial here. I would have done the same in his place – indeed, I *have* done the same. I joined Drust for the exact same reasons as you, even when my people were dying from famine and wars with their neighbours. But, isn't it time for your adventures to finish?" He sweeps his arm towards the coast. "I could have one of my boats send all of you to Moridun today. Of course, you would have to take Wortigern with you – maybe back to Londin?"

"You'd be making a mistake sending him away – Wortigern is the only Briton who could try to convince others to listen to your demands."

"Wortigern already gave me all that was in his power to give. The rest, I will have to take with my own hands – just like your father did."

I look to the east; the wind scatters the clouds and fog, revealing the peaks of the Oriri and the long arc of the coast, a golden crescent bending gently northwards, towards Mona.

Having traversed this bleak landscape back and forth, I can't imagine many Britons willing to give their lives for it. There are no walled towns here, no fertile land for their *villas*, no resources worth speaking of – I heard there were great lead and copper mines beyond the mountains, but those lie a few days east, safe, for now, behind another line of forts held by Ambrosius's brother Utir – and only a few roads, all leading nowhere but Mona. Cunedag proved his worth as an ally time and time again; choosing to fight him over these barren rocks, denying him the rule over the land his people bought with their own blood, could only have been a matter

The Wrath of the Iutes

of stubborn honour and prejudice for Ambrosius and his courtiers, the same prejudice which denied the Iutes and Saxons the right to settle under their own chieftains for so long.

And Cunedag isn't even a true barbarian. His ancestors were Roman officers, guarding the northern frontier just like he is now. His people are of this island, merely of the wrong side of the Aelian Wall. I can see why he believes he deserves the rule of Wened – and I can find nothing wrong with his belief.

"My father may have fought the Britons once," I start slowly, "but we are good neighbours now, and it's important that we stay so – even more now with the growing threat from the Saxons to all of us. And although Ambrosius's court is far away, he exerts powerful influence in Londin. If…" I stutter. "If I betray them here, they won't forget it anytime soon."

Cunedag winces and nods. "I understand. But would you really risk even Wortigern's life just to stay friends with the Britons?"

"And would you really kill him?"

"If I saw no choice. Even he agreed it was the only prudent course of action, under the circumstances."

"Then you will not release any other hostages?"

[448]

"I will not. Unless Marcus and Eochu stand back from Segont and leave the Scots for me to deal with. I'd make sure no pirate king would ever dare to land here again."

"I will relay your words to the *Decurion* – but I fear threatening him like this will only inflame his pride."

Sadness fills his eyes as he bids us farewell. We both know it would be best for all if the Britons gave in to his demand. If they did, the only real casualty would be their pride. In a war that will inevitably result from their stubbornness, many good men are going to fall, men needed to guard this land from future invaders, men who until a few weeks ago were friends and allies.

Marcus puts his hand to his chest, then raises it and waggles his index finger twice. Two men split from the group and skulk away among the trees, in the direction of the walls of Segont. In the dark, the line of the rampart is marked by a line of burning braziers – one in each corner, two on the towers over the gatehouse, and a couple more on each wing of the rampart between. Segont is a small fort by the standards of Saxon Shore or Gaul, but it is a colossus here in Wened. When it was first built, it would have had enough space for two full cohorts of *auxilia*, and if it was properly manned and maintained, our army couldn't even dream of conquering it without siege machines. Even now, with the garrison of Northerners maybe a third of what it should be, it's clear Niall's warriors only captured the fort so swiftly and unexpectedly through Cunedag's treachery.

The Wrath of the Iutes

Without it – and without us – they would now be throwing themselves in wave after wave at the tall ramparts, in futile hope of breaking through not just to the Narrows on the fort's other side, but to the food and other supplies stored within. Hunger is now as much of a threat to us as Cunedag's warriors. The Atecots and the Britons still carry a few days' rations each in their travelling sacks, but we are forced to eat it out of sight of the Scots, so as not to provoke them with our full bellies. These, too, will run out in a couple of days, and if we are forced to stay here that long, we'll also be facing starvation.

Though they never had the opportunity to do so before, Marcus's men know how to take a Roman-built fort, especially one in such disrepair as Segont. The original gates have long rotted away, replaced by simple barricades of logs and boulders, with one narrow gap in each opening in place of the postern door. The triple earthen banks once surrounding the walls have long ago eroded into little more than ripples in the ground, and silt and dust fills out the defensive ditches. Three of the four corner towers has crumbled into piles of stone and powdered brick – but the one that remains, guarding the south-eastern direction from which we will launch our assault, is still topped with a *ballista*, and from what Marcus tells me, Cunedag's men know how to use it; an attack by day will easily turn into a massacre.

This is why we've come here in the middle of the night. We reach the edge of the sparse forest surrounding the fort from the south, and lie low in the tall grass, with the rest of the cavalry wing to our left and right. One of the two Atecot *centuriae* awaits their turn behind us, hiding in the wood; the other one stands with the Scots army on the sand ridge overlooking the fortress from the east.

That we were all able to get this close to the fort's wall from the south is another proof of how decrepit Segont's defences have become. Back in the Roman days, we would have been stopped by the watchtowers and barricades guarding the crossing on the River Segont, which flows a short distance south of the fort's walls. We've been expecting to at least stumble on some more of Cunedag's bands coming our way from Gangania — but so far, other than a few patrols examining our position from a distance, the Wotadin seem to be holding back from attacking us, waiting for the Scots to bleed themselves out on the fort's defences.

The final pair of soldiers departs on the *Decurion*'s command, then Marcus nods at me and Ursula. "Follow me," he says. "Stay quiet."

We half-crawl, half-leap through the final stretch, over the ditches and the earth banks, and reach the wall. Not repaired in a generation, it's full of holes, cracks and gaps, making for an easy climb, even in the darkness.

Hanging on with my fingers, I peek over the battlement to see where the light of the nearest brazier loses its fight with the night. I leap over and creep into the shadow. Ursula lands on the rampart next to me, as quiet as a cat. Somewhere along the way, we lost sight of Marcus, but we don't need him with us. We sneak towards the three warriors guarding the brazier. They know something's amiss, and strain to gaze into the darkness around the fort — but in doing so, they fail to spot what's behind them.

The Wrath of the Iutes

I draw my sword from the well-oiled sheath, noiselessly. I leap at the nearest of the guards and pierce him through the back. Ursula grasps the man beside me and slices his neck with the long knife. The third one struggles to draw his sword; I grab him by the tunic, and we wrestle for a few moments before I trip him and throw him over the rampart.

One by one, the braziers on the walls around us vanish. A shrill whistle rings out in the darkness. I can't see them in the shadows, but I know this is a signal for the *equites* remaining outside to launch from their hiding places and rush towards the southern gatehouse. Ursula and I leap down onto the courtyard to join the others at the gate. Marcus is here, too, slashing and thrusting his cavalry sword, downing one foe after another. Pushed from both sides, the gate guards stand little chance, and within moments we reach the gap in the barricade. I help Marcus and Drustan throw down the great oak trunk that forms the main barrier; we all stream out through the gap, pursued by the surviving guards – who run straight onto the swords of the *equites* and Armoricans waiting outside. Ahes is here, too, lobbing *plumbatas* at Cunedag's men with the skill and daring of a seasoned Legionnaire.

Having dealt with the gate guards, Marcus orders his men back, away from the wall, to make way for the first of the Atecot *centuriae*. Eochu's warriors strike at the barricade and crawl all over it, but the Northerners, having shaken off the initial surprise, hold fast. It's no surprise Cunedag managed to hold the frontier for so long – the men defending Segont are no green youths; our bold attack shocked them at first, and opened the gate for the next wave of the assault, but still they managed to regroup just in time to push the Atecots back.

The *Decurion* reaches for his horn. A three-note call is a sign for the Scots. They pour down the slope of the ridge and smash against the gate like a rolling wave against the cliff. Only the first line of the assault carried torches, which most of them dropped when they reached the rampart, so I can scarcely tell what's going on, but from what I can gather the Scots army has split into bands, each led by one of Niall's former subordinates. The difference between this unruly mob and what Niall's command had managed to carve out of them is stark. Where Niall would've had them climb the walls from all directions, to stretch the defenders thin, the warchiefs are throwing their men at the one narrow opening Marcus and the Atecots punched in the gatehouse.

"Shouldn't we help them?" I remark to Marcus.

He winces. "I've done all I could. I opened the damn gate for them! If they can't make use of it, I'm not going to waste men showing them how to wage a war."

It takes more than an hour of bloody fighting for the Scots to finally break into the fort. In an instant, all the other warriors, trying to climb over the walls or find their way through the gates on the other sides, rush to make use of the single breach. Soon, fires break out inside the fort, illuminating the gory scene. The scene of triumph that turns into a rout as the Scots, rather than continue pouring inside, suddenly turn and surge out in panic. As they fan out into the river valley, Marcus curses, mounts up and rides back towards the fort, calling on his men and Eochu to follow after him.

We punch into the flank of the pursuing Wotadins, just as they emerge from the fortress chasing after the fleeing Scots.

The Wrath of the Iutes

The mere sight of our mounts, in the flickering light of the flaming roofs, is enough to force them back inside; they have no desire to die trampled outside the safety of their walls. They are satisfied to have pushed back the night assault.

Still furious, Marcus rides up to the Scots camp, straight to the *druis* elder's tent.

"What happened?" he demands, but the *drui* is as confused and surprised by the developments on the battlefield as we are. As the survivors pour back into the camp, their broken-up sentences begin to form a dreadful story.

Once they swarmed inside the fort, the Scots saw the gates of the granary and the supply stores wide open; baskets of freshly baked bread and cheese, barrels of salted meat and ale waiting for them, as if in an invitation to a feast. The starving warriors forgot all about the battle and rushed to grab as much of the food as they could; brawls erupted between them, even as the Wotadins gathered on the courtyard and struck them from the flanks and back. Before long, dozens of Niall's warriors lay dead, and the rest were desperately seeking a way out from the ever-tightening loop.

"Count your men, *drui*," Marcus says. "Let me know how costly this disaster was for you. Hope the ones who survive at least managed to feed themselves before fleeing. On the bright side, you now have fewer mouths to feed," he adds dryly.

"Have we lost, then?" asks Ahes when we return to our own tents.

"Not yet," Marcus replies. "The siege is far from over – but we will have to wait until morning, and in the morning Cunedag is bound to finally send reinforcements."

"Maybe it's time to consider his proposal," I say.

"I will not yield to a barbarian while there's still a chance of victory, *aetheling*."

In the morning, Marcus sends out patrols onto the roads leading to Segont. Ursula and I ride out in the direction of the Forks. Hleo and Haering bounce miserably behind us on two mules, saved from slaughter by our timely victory over Niall. The pony I'm riding now belonged to Aecba – who rests in a hero's grave in the centre of *Cair* Wortigern's graveyard. This is the second time I have taken a mount from one of my fallen men; I try not to think how inauspicious an augury it might seem.

In place of Cunedag's relief army, we spot only a single horse, mounted by two men, appearing out of the fog. As we trot carefully closer, I see that the rider in front is none other than Mullo. The man behind him rests motionless, his hands tied over Mullo's waist, his face hidden in the Legionnaire's back.

We meet in the middle of the ford. I help Mullo climb down from the saddle – he's weak and weary; his face is covered with bloody grime. Ursula reaches for the other man. As he slumps into her hands, Ursula cries out.

The Wrath of the Iutes

"*Dux* Wortigern!"

At first, it looks like he's fainted from the long ride, but one glimpse of his pale-grey face and milky, unseeing eyes tells me he's been dead for hours — and that's even before I notice the deep red horizontal scars on his wrists.

"Wodan's beard…" I whisper. "Has Cunedag tortured him?"

"Cunedag hasn't touched a hair on Wortigern's head," says Mullo. "It was all the *Legatus*'s doing. He had us run him a hot bath, and then he slit his wrists, like the Roman sages of old. When Cunedag learned of this, he put me on this horse and told me to ride to Segont."

"What about his army?" I ask.

"They're coming," he replies. "They can't be more than a couple of hours behind me."

"What does it all mean, Octa?" Ursula asks; her voice trembles with unease, as does mine when I answer.

"It's a message. For me. For us. He's telling us to go home." I help her lay Wortigern down on a dry patch on the muddy roadside. His body is light and frail in death; it little resembles the mighty warrior and great commander that I spoke to just a few weeks ago.

"We will have to bury him here," I decide.

"What? Why?"

"I can't let Marcus see him like this. Wortigern wouldn't want this, either. It would only spur the *Decurion* and his men to do something rash and unnecessary. Hleo, Haering, help me."

The two Iutes pick up the tools from their saddle bags: a latrine-digging shovel and a tree-felling hatchet, and begin the hard work. The soil this close to the river is soft and moist; it's not long before they manage a hole deep enough for the *Dux*'s body while Ursula and I search the riverbank for boulders with which to pile a small cairn over the grave.

"What are you going to tell Marcus?" she asks as we carry a large flat stone, so heavy it takes both of us to lift it, towards the gravesite.

"It's Mullo who will do the talking –" I start to explain the plan that began forming in my head almost as soon as I saw Wortigern's dead body. "Wait!" I cry, seeing Hleo and Haering hold the *Dux*'s corpse over the hole they just dug. "Show some respect, by the gods."

I take Wortigern's hand and remove the seal ring from his finger. I nod, and the two Iutes lay him carefully into the ground.

"This doesn't seem like a tomb worthy of such a great man," says Ursula.

"His body is only an empty shell now," I say, remembering the teachings of Elder Ouein. I find it fitting that a man who gave his life fighting for this remote fringe of Britannia should be buried in the manner of its eldest

The Wrath of the Iutes

inhabitants. "Wherever his spirit has gone, it will have no need for ceremonies."

"There is one ceremony his soul *will* need," says Ursula.

She kneels down by the side of the grave and raises her hands to the sky. Mullo joins her. Reluctantly, I bend my knees as well. To my surprise, as Ursula recites a prayer for the *Dux*'s soul, I feel heavy tears roll down my face.

"Let me hear it one more time," Marcus says, rubbing his frowning brow. "What did the *Legatus* tell you, exactly?"

Mullo gives me a quick glance, and I reply with a nod.

"He orders you and Eochu to retreat back to *Cair* Wortigern, and leave the Scots to Cunedag. He wants Ambrosius to send a delegation to discuss the settlement."

"And the hostages?"

"They will be released once the fighting here is over. Cunedag says it's too dangerous for them here right now, with the Scots still at large."

"That does make sense," I note. "Who knows if the Scots will keep to our alliance once they capture Segont."

Marcus rolls Wortigern's signet ring in his fingers, and raises it to the sun.

"And he couldn't come here tell us this himself?"

"His injuries from the battle are too grave for him to move," Mullo says. "I doubt he'll live until Sunday."

I can see in his eyes he's not comfortable with all this lying. As I explained to him along the way what he was supposed to tell Marcus, I had to remember how unfamiliar he, a Legionnaire from Gaul, was with Britannia and its convoluted politics. He had no reason to trust me over the *Decurion*, Cunedag or Eochu. All that I had on my side was the unlikely friendship he struck with Wortigern in Cunedag's captivity. The *Dux* told him to listen to me over anyone else; I had to believe that was enough.

"I just wish we had something more to go on than just your words and this ring," says Marcus. "A letter, at least. A seal." He turns to me. "What do you think about all this, Octa?"

I lick my lips. "It does sound like something the *Dux* would say. You know he would've preferred this conflict to end in peace – and the Scots' demise."

"I suppose so." Marcus nods.

"And really, is this land worth us dying for?" I ask, and look to the mist-shrouded peaks looming over the Segont plain. "Are these *Scots* worth dying for? I came here to fight Niall's warriors, not help them go back home – certainly not die in their defence."

"It was your idea in the first place."

The Wrath of the Iutes

"Only because I thought it was the only way to free Wortigern and the other hostages. Now that we've accomplished that, what more reason do we have to stay here?"

"I would've trusted Cunedag more if he hadn't betrayed us once already. The only guarantee I have is his word, and it's worth less than a dog's turd after what he's done to the *Dux*."

"And yet, Wortigern seems to trust him."

"And that's the only reason why I'm still considering this proposal. If I could talk to the *Legatus* myself…"

Marcus rubs his chin in thought; just then, war horns ring out all along the eastern ridge. We rush out of the tent to see the Scots renew their assault.

"I told them to wait for my signal!" Marcus clenches his fists in futile anger. "What do they think they're doing?"

"Seems to me, they think they can take the fort without us," says Mullo.

The warriors attack the walls in an even more chaotic manner than at night, leaping, climbing, throwing themselves at the gates. Some of them rush past the fort altogether, in an attempt to reach the boats on the beach and cross the Narrows without having to deal with Segont's garrison at all.

Soon, the reason for their urgency becomes clear: several hundred men climb the dune ridge, just behind the Scots camp. In the sea breeze, their banners unfurl – silver hound heads on black cloth. The sound of their war trumpets shatters the sky.

There are still enough of us and the Scots to make this an even battle; two hundred Atecots, less a dozen or so fallen in the night battle, are waiting in the wood for the *Decurion*'s command to throw themselves on Cunedag's narrow flank. The *equites* are ready to charge into their rear. A commander as skilled as Marcus could turn this around, even if the Scots warchiefs were only interested in running away to Mona. But he and I both know: even if we win, the victory would be a bloody one – and for Cunedag, a mere setback, rather than an outright defeat.

"If we are destroyed here, there will be nothing standing between either of those armies and Moridun," says Eochu.

Marcus stares at the Wotadin line; mail coats shimmer under their cloaks in the noon sun, spears and swords gleam silver. They look a lot more like a regular army of a civilised allied ruler than the disordered, hungry mob, desperately struggling to overrun the fortress below. I'm sure Marcus must be aware of the contrast. What is he waiting for? For that matter, what is *Cunedag* waiting for? His warriors still haven't moved from the ridge, even as the Scots threaten to breach the makeshift barricade in the southern gate. He knows we're here – he must be giving the *Decurion* time to make a decision…

"Call the retreat," Marcus announces, at last. "Break the camp. We're going home. Let these damn barbarians sort it out between themselves."

The Wrath of the Iutes

CHAPTER XIX
THE LAY OF AMBROSIUS

The *Maegwind* hobbles into the harbour, its one surviving sail fluttering, powerless, in the mild breeze. The Armorican crew had little time to repair the damage from the battle in the North, but it was enough to carry us eastwards along Demetia's coast, to the harbour at Isca.

After weeks spent roaming through the sparse countryside of Armorica and bleak desolation of Wened, Isca's harbour is a stunning, and welcome, sight. A huge square of whitewashed stone surrounds the inner basin, its three sides crowded with piers and wharves. Up close, I can see the inevitable damage of the years – the peeled-off plaster, the weathered concrete, the crumbled pillars; there's no roof over any of the *porticoes*, and more than a half of the original piers rotted away in the tide, leaving only twin rows of timber poles in their wake. The harbour is quiet and empty for its size, with only a few ancient-looking merchant ships and some fishing boats bobbing gently on the waves.

The town that looms over the harbour was once a Legion's fortress, one that controlled the entire territory from here to Mona. It was big enough to hold five thousand men and everything they needed for a comfortable life, including yet another amphitheatre, a bright circle of gleaming stone between the harbour and the fort's walls – but judging by the scarce presence of guards in the harbour, and the abandoned *porticoes* where once would stand dozens of market stalls

The Wrath of the Iutes

offering all sorts of goods to the locals and visitors alike, Isca itself remains as silent and empty as it had been the day after the Legions left Britannia. The only human activity I can spot is in the remains of the small town that grew up around its southern gate.

"We must be close to Corin now," says Ursula. "And this place looks just as bad as Dorowern. Where are Ambrosius's riches we've heard so much about? Where are the marble avenues, the theatres, the bath houses?"

"It's only a military port," I say. "And without the Legion's presence, it's hardly worth the upkeep. A city like Corin must be in better shape than this."

We sail up to the salt-ravaged oak boards of the largest wharf, and the *Maegwind*'s crew descends to moor us to the wooden posts.

"Then it's really over?" Seawine asks. "We're going home?"

"You'll need to get a ferry over to Abonae, to mount the Londin highway," Warus tells us. "I don't know how long it will take you to reach it from there – on the old maps it's marked as one week, but that was when the roads were properly maintained, and all the bridges still stood…"

"It's fine, Captain," I say. "Past Callew we'll be in Wortigern's old domain – and that's as good as home. Thank you for getting us all the way here."

"I wish I could go with you," says Ahes, staring longingly over the roofless walls of the harbour towards Isca's rampart. "There's still so much I haven't seen in Britannia."

"The war with the Scots is over, my lady," old Warus reminds her. "And the *Decurion* told us we are no longer needed. Your father will be most anxious for our return."

Ahes's eyes mist over when Warus mentions Marcus's name. She faces him in a huff. "I bet my father hasn't even noticed I'm gone. We're going back only because the winter is coming, and I don't want you trapped here for my sake. But —" She turns back to me. "I promise I'll be back as soon as I can."

I smile. "It's not to me you're promising this, are you? I'll be on the other side of the island by then. But I'm certain Marcus will be waiting keenly for your return."

I bow and move towards the ship's stern, where Ursula watches the small crowd gathered on the wharf, waiting to board as soon as my men make space for them. These are refugees from *Cair* Wortigern and the surrounding farms, eager to come back to their homes even before finding out if the war with the Scots is over. We haven't yet heard any news from Segont, good or bad — but these folk are too impatient to wait, and have been gathering in the harbour ever since they heard of Niall's death. Since the *Maegwind* will be stopping at Moridun on its long way back to Armorica, Warus agreed to take some of them along.

"I don't see her," says Ursula nervously. "She's not here."

The Wrath of the Iutes

"Maybe she's fallen ill?" I propose.

"Or maybe they took her away."

"As would be their right," I note, assuming by "they" she means Ambrosius and his court nobles. "Don't worry." I put my arm around her shoulder gently. I wait for a rebuke, and when it doesn't come, I pull her closer. "We'll check in the fort. Whatever happened, we'll find out shortly."

"Stay here," I tell Seawine and the other Iutes, just before we enter Isca's gates. "I imagine they don't see many fair-hairs here, especially armed and mounted. Let's not make these people any more anxious than they already are. They've only just learned they won't have to fight the Scots."

Seawine nods with an upset grimace. "Just make sure the princess is fine."

"When are you going to tell them?" Ursula asks when we are beyond the gate. The guards let us through only after we show them the pass Marcus gave us to ensure a swift and unperturbed passage through Ambrosius's domain – the only way a troop of Iute cavalry could march down the Londin highway without raising alarm in every fort or watchtower along the way.

"I don't know that I'll tell them at all," I admit. "There's no reason for any of them to suspect Wortigern had any news from Cantia. Hopefully by the time we reach Robriwis, all the fighting will be over, at least for the winter."

"If you don't tell them by the time we reach Callew, I will."

I stop. We're in the middle of the main avenue – if this was Londin, somebody would bump into me right now and shower me with abuse; but I count only three other people on the entire street here: a plain-clothed woman, hurrying home with an *amphora* on her head, a soldier standing guard before some storehouse, and an old shepherd, sitting under the ruined wall of what was once the Legion's bath house, but is now a cow barn. None of these people pay the least attention to us.

"Why?" I ask.

"Don't you think they deserve to know the truth? Seawine is not just your soldier – after all we've been through together, he's our friend. If he finds out you've been hiding this from him, he will start to wonder what else you're hiding. And you need his trust if you want to make him lead your *Hiréd* one day."

"What makes you think I'd do that?"

She rolls her eyes. "I know you better than anyone, Octa. You will need your own guard as the *aetheling*, and who better to command it than Seawine?"

We reach the main crossroad. The *Principia* building, like in so many other forts, has been dismantled to make way for a small market square, so we walk up to the *Praetorium* instead, still a substantial building, taking up an entire quarter of this side of the fort – it's the size of a *domus* of a small *villa*. Most

The Wrath of the Iutes

of it is populated by Gaulish fowl, ducks and a few goats. The once-broad entrance to the *atrium* is blocked off to keep the livestock inside, leaving only a gap narrow enough for a single cart. Only the southern wing still stands untouched, guarded by four bored spearmen.

"You left the girl here?" I ask. "Niall would've razed this place in a day."

"There were more soldiers when I was here," she says. "They must've been called off when they heard the Scots retreated."

"We're here to see the *Praetor*," I announce to the guards.

"He's asleep," the guard says. "He won't be in a good mood if you disturb him."

"I couldn't give a mule's arse about his mood," I snarl. "I marched from Moridun to Segont and back again to protect his ducks and goats. I speak for Wortigern. He will see me."

The guards look at each other, my outburst shaking them from their lazy stupor; one of them rushes into the building, to warn the *Praetor*. I ignore the other one's protests and barge into the dark, stuffy corridor. I brush aside the dust and cobwebs and cough; the place hasn't been cleaned in years.

"*Domna* Madron?" calls Ursula. "Are you there, child?"

The little girl runs out from one of the rooms and throws herself into Ursula's arms.

"Are you taking me back to *Avus*?" she asks.

Ursula looks to me. We haven't yet discussed what we are going to do with the girl, though the most likely solution I considered was sending her into Marcus's care.

"You're not taking her anywhere," a nasal, high, somewhat whiny voice interrupts us. The man I guess to be the *Praetor* emerges from his study. In the daylight beaming from the room, his body throws a fat shadow on the wall of the corridor. He sniffs and scratches himself before inviting us inside.

The study is also his bedroom – or rather, his bedroom is also his study, as a four-post oaken bed takes up most of the space. A naked girl lies in the bed, half-covered with a stained blanket. I notice her hair is dyed red. She giggles at me when we enter. The *Praetor* grunts at her, and she runs off, covering herself only with the blanket.

He's an ugly man, with small eyes and a face like a rotting pear, topped with a brush of light brown hair. His fingers are heavy with rings, and the tunic he wears is embroidered with golden thread. A red-lined cloak lies thrown over the chair by the desk.

"Who in Hell are you?" he asks. He looks at Ursula. "You, I've seen here before."

"I was the one who brought the girl from *Cair Wortigern*," Ursula replies. Madron hides behind her. "And now I'm taking her back."

The Wrath of the Iutes

"Did the *Legatus* send you?" he asks, but before we can answer, he waves his hand. "Never mind. His will doesn't stretch to Isca. He's made a mistake letting the girl out of his sight." He chuckles.

I step forward. My hand hovers over the pommel of my *spatha*.

"What do you mean?"

He notices the threat and nods at someone behind me. Two guards enter the room. One of them grabs me by the arms.

"*Dux* Ambrosius is coming to pick her up tomorrow. She will live in the palace in Corin, as she should have all those years."

"No!" Madron cries out and clutches on to Ursula's breeches. "I don't want to!"

"This is against her family's wishes," I say. "Not just her grandfather's. The girl is ours."

"She doesn't have any other family, unless you count those barbarian…"

He stares at me closer. My red hair must have thrown him at first, and only now does he notice my barbarian features and clothes. He yelps and steps back.

"You're one of *them*!"

He grunts at the guards again; I can see their consternation – there are only two of them, and if one of them lets me go to take care of Ursula and Madron, I'll be able to overpower the other one with ease. They've heard my boasts at the door – they know I'm a veteran, a hardened soldier, whereas the worst they ever had to deal with were some rioting sailors in the harbour.

"Guards!" the *Praetor* cries in a panicked voice. "Help! Attack! Barbarians!" A small *pugio* dagger appears in his hand, but instead of using it on us, he cowers behind his desk. I hear a few more men running towards us down the corridor.

I sense the guard loosen his grip on me as fear takes the better of him; I twist myself out of his grasp and throw him against the wall. I grab Ursula and pull her out of the room.

"We'll be back," I warn the *Praetor*. "We'll be back," I promise Madron as the guards grab the weeping girl and carry her away.

There is no tavern in the harbour, or in the settlement sprawling between it and the fort, but there's enough space among the marble pillars of the crumbling *portico* surrounding the basin for us to set up our tents. At dusk, we gather on the paved square which once served as a fish market, to eat a small farewell *cena* with Ahes and her Armoricans, before *Maegwind* sails west for the final time, burdened with the returning refugees.

The Wrath of the Iutes

The *Praetor*, it seems, was satisfied with running the two of us out of the town; we set up a few guards on the approach to the harbour, by the abandoned amphitheatre, but they soon grow bored with their duty, and I pull them back to the warmth of our campfires. There's no pursuit coming, no soldiers even bother to check on what we're up to in the harbour, no *vigiles* disturb our feast.

"I don't think he took us seriously," I note to Ursula, pointing towards the fort's silent walls with a hand holding a mug of warm ale.

"Should he have?" she asks. "What are we going to do? We can't defeat an entire fortress garrison."

"Maybe we won't have to. I think I have a plan."

"Even if this plan of yours succeeds, then what? Do we fight Ambrosius, too?"

"Would you rather leave Madron in their hands?"

"No." There's this brutal coldness in her voice again that returns every time we talk about anything that might threaten the girl. "We promised we would get her out of there, and we will do just that. But I still don't know what the next part of your plan is. Take her to Marcus? The only ship that we could use is leaving tomorrow morning. Ride to Cantia? We would have to cross the breadth of Ambrosius's domain, with his entire army in pursuit."

"We'll figure it out. We always do."

"I hope so. Because I'd hate to see anything happen to that little girl."

I sip my ale and watch Ahes walking slowly towards us; she stops by every Iute she passes and exchanges a few words with them, before moving on.

"You've really grown fond of the child, haven't you?" I ask.

"There's something about her… I can't quite say what." She smiles. "Somehow, she reminds me of the younger you."

"Me?" I almost spit out the ale. "Well, she *is* a half-Iute, like me," I note. "Maybe that's why."

"Don't you hate that she's Wortimer's daughter?"

I shrug. "We don't choose our parents. I pray that she only took after her mother in character."

"How much do you know of this Rhedwyn?"

"I know that she was the woman my father loved above all others – including my mother. I know a mere mention of her name roused the blood of my men. There is no woman who's sung about more in the songs of the *scops*." I slurp out the last of the ale and throw the mug into the bushes. It rattles on some stone pavement, hidden beyond the ferns. "I imagine someone like Queen Basina when I think of her – but of course, I only know her from stories and poems."

"Who are you talking about?"

The Wrath of the Iutes

Ahes finally makes her way to us and sits beside Ursula.

"*Domna* Madron's mother," Ursula explains.

"Oh." Ahes stares into the campfire for a moment, not certain how to join the conversation on the topic she knows nothing about, then decides to ignore it altogether. "I came to say goodbye."

"Already?"

"I'm tired – I'll be going to sleep soon. And we leave at first tide tomorrow, so we may not get a chance to speak again."

"I'm sure this won't be our last meeting," says Ursula with a warm smile. "I don't think we'll be stopping our journeys any time soon – we're bound to visit Armorica again one day."

Ahes stares at the two of us with bright eyes and a broad beam.

"What is it?" asks Ursula.

"I just hope to find one day someone who will love me like you two love each other," says Ahes.

Ursula and I stare at each other. She's the first to look away. Her unexpected awkwardness makes me finally realise something I've been missing all these weeks.

Behind all her brashness, despite all the airs she puts on, she is just as lost and confused about her feelings as I am. She never expected to fall for a man – any man; and I never expected for our friendship to grow into anything more.

"Are you alright, Octa?" Ahes asks, worried.

I rub my eyes and shake my head. "I'm fine, I just…"

I reach my arm around Ursula and pull her closer.

"What's wrong?" she asks, sensing a shift in my mood.

"I just want you to know that… whatever you decide, whenever you're ready – I'm here for you."

"Whatever brought this on?" she asks. Her voice is soft, tinged with worry and amused curiosity.

"I just remembered something. It doesn't matter. What matters is that you don't owe me anything. Not as a friend, not as a wife. Silvia was wrong."

"Who's Silvia?" asks Ahes, but Ursula frowns and shakes her head at her, then nods at me to continue.

"I don't care how things were done before," I say. "This is a new world. A new Britannia. The old order is gone. Rome is gone. The *Dux* is gone. We can do whatever we want."

Ursula looks away, towards the sea, gleaming with stars.

"I don't… I don't yet know what I want."

The Wrath of the Iutes

"Neither do I. And that's fine. We'll figure it out as we go along."

She smiles and, at last, for the first time in a long while, returns my embrace.

"I'm glad you two finally made up," Ahes says. "I've only known you for a few weeks, but I already feel like you're my friends, and I hated to see you argue."

"Friends argue," says Ursula, still smiling. "It's because we're not afraid to tell each other the truth, however harsh."

I clear my throat, yawn and stretch my arms. I groan at the various shoots and bursts of pain this causes. "I think I'll be going to bed early, too," I say. "I feel as if the burden of all the fighting and marching is finally coming down on me."

"We still have a long way to go," Ursula reminds me. "And — we still need to figure out what to do about Madron."

"I know, but whatever happens, we're finally on our way home. It's different than riding towards some unknown battlefield."

"Before you go," Ahes says, "I just want you to know how grateful I am."

"For what?" asks Ursula.

"For all of this." Ahes waves towards the sea. "For showing me the world beyond Armorica."

[476]

"You haven't seen much outside the grim mountains and barren hills of Wened," I say.

"It was enough. For now. One day, I will sail again, and see all there is to see, I just know it – my father can't keep me forever, now that I know how easy it is to flee his domain. Maybe one day I'll even visit you in Cantia!"

Ursula chuckles. "You caught it too, hmm?" She sighs. "Be careful. It's like a sickness of the soul. I don't know how long we will be able to stay in Cantia ourselves, once we rest and heal after this year's adventures."

"I don't know if one winter will be enough," I say. "Right now, all I want is to lie down in my bed at Rutubi with a jug of warm Iutish ale – and not come out until Easter."

Ahes stands up. "I have to go now. Thank you both, once again. For everything."

She leans down to embrace and kiss Ursula on the cheek. She then does the same to me – and kisses me on the lips, ever so briefly, before turning swiftly back – but not swiftly enough that I don't see the tear gleaming in her eye.

"I have no idea what they all see in you," says Ursula, watching the princess walk away towards the *Maegwind*, bobbing silently on the dark water. She then hugs me again. "I really don't."

The Wrath of the Iutes

"We should've stormed that place yesterday," Seawine seethes. "Before they were ready."

"It doesn't matter how ready they are, they're no match for us," I reply. "I needed to make sure that the *Praetor* wasn't lying, and Ambrosius is really coming here."

Seawine, Ursula and I are set up in hiding in what remains of an ancient shrine on the side of a crossroad; one road is the Roman highway to Corin, the other is a gravel path used by local village folk, which leads first into the graveyard hidden in the sandy hills and marshes, before snaking back along the river towards Isca. The rest of my men wait for orders in the ruins of Isca's amphitheatre.

"Why can't we just take the girl and run away?" Seawine asks.

Two horsemen appear on the road and pass us by in a slow trot. They're wearing *equites* capes and Legionnaire helmets – they must be the vanguard of the approaching procession. I look for markings on their capes and shields; one of them is wearing an Imperial Eagle, but the other one's shield is so old and tattered, no mark can be clearly seen.

"And ride across Ambrosius's domain as fugitives, with his entire army on our backs?" I shake my head. "Remember, we have to get her back to Cantia somehow."

A carriage shimmers in the haze, accompanied by a troop of maybe twenty soldiers – not a substantial escort, considering not even a week has passed since Niall threatened to overrun the neighbouring Demetia. I can't imagine my father travelling with so few men so near a war frontier; indeed, I can't see him travel like this around Cantia even in peace. If this really is Ambrosius, he must be in a real hurry to get here.

"We should go," urges Ursula. "Or we're going to lose them."

Seawine sets off back down the gravel path to reach the Iutes in the amphitheatre while Ursula and I rush after the two *equites*. They let us get close without suspecting anything – they have no reason to fear an ambush here, and certainly not from just two pony riders. One of them even nods and smiles at me as I ride up to his side, but his smile turns to shock when I grab his reins and draw my sword. Ursula leaps on the other rider's horse and pulls him off of the saddle.

"What the –" the *eques* starts, but the sword's point pressing at his heart silences him.

"Down," I command.

With the two riders on the ground, I turn the horses around and slap both on the rear with the flat of my sword, launching them back where they came from.

"I need your cloak, your helmet and your shield," I order the *eques*. Ursula tears the cloak off of her man without a word. We lead them both to a small birch tree on the side of the road, and we tie them up with their sword belts.

The Wrath of the Iutes

"Who are you?" the *eques* demands, watching me put on his Imperial Eagle cloak and bronze helmet; it's a little too big for me, but I hope the guards at the gate won't notice.

"Someone who's tied you up instead of killing you outright. Remember that."

"The *Dux* is coming right after us with his best warriors," he says.

"Tell him I'm looking forward to meeting him."

"You'll pay for this!"

I give him a weary look, then cut off a piece of his tunic sleeve, roll it into a ball and shove it in his mouth.

We enter the fort through the northern gate, unperturbed. The guards here let us pass with a wave; the *Praetor* did not think to strengthen the defences on this side. Only once we reach the southern gate do I notice some changes resulting from our arrival. The guard is stronger than it was yesterday, and the main gate is closed shut, with only the postern door opening from time to time to let in the passing townsfolk.

We halt in the shadow of the eaves of the old barracks, a block away from the gate, and study the soldiers. I notice a tall, balding man in an old *centurion*'s cloak, sun-bleached from its original crimson into a pale pink, and a sculpted breastplate that must remember the days when the

Legionnaires still lived here, leaning on a spear and watching lazily the men passing through the postern.

"This one must be the commander," I say, pointing him out to Ursula.

I spur the pony to a charge. As we approach, the *centurion* spots us, grabs his spear and points it at me. I leap from the saddle and roll on the ground under the spear's blade, and kick his legs from under him, just as Ursula tramples another guard under the hooves of her pony. I wrestle with the commander in the dirt; I underestimated his skill and determination: with a few grapples, he overpowers me and throws me over his head. I land painfully on my back, then swiftly roll over and leap up, drawing my knife. In the corner of my eye, I glance Ursula club the third guard on the head with the pommel of her sword, then grab and push him against the wall. I spot a fourth soldier behind her, but I have no time to warn her when the *centurion* rushes at me with his short sword drawn. In desperation, I grab a handful of dust and throw it in his eyes, then charge at him with my head down. I ram him in the chest and throw him to the ground again, then punch him a couple of times in the face with a fist wrapped around the knife's hilt, until his nose is a bloody pulp and he's too dazed to fight back. I lift him up with the knife pressed to his throat.

"Stand back!" I cry at the soldier who was ready to pounce on Ursula from behind. "Drop your sword! And you," I order the *centurion*, "tell them to open that gate!"

He hesitates and protests – I push the blade, drawing blood.

The Wrath of the Iutes

"We both know there's nothing in this place worth your life," I say. "Certainly not that lump of fat in the *Praetorium*."

He nods at the guard held by Ursula. The soldier unfastens the chain and removes the thick wooden beam holding the gate shut. His companion lifts himself off the ground and throws the gate open. Moments later, my Iutes storm through, all seven of them, even Hleo and Haering, bobbing at the back on their mules.

I release the *centurion* and mount up. He calls the alarm, but I don't care anymore — there's no one here who can stop us now that we're all inside. I lead my men down the main road, across the market and to the *Praetorium*. The *Praetor*'s guards mount a feeble defence at the building's entrance, but we burst through their line without stopping, throwing them to the sides. Someone shuts the *Praetorium*'s door just before I reach it; Ubba and Raegen attack it with hatchets. Within seconds, we break through inside.

"Find the girl," I call to Ursula, who rushes down the corridor, followed by Seawine, while the rest of us get to work setting up barricades from an overturned wagon, crates, barrels and other assorted waste: one across the entrance to the *atrium*, the other at the door to the main hallway.

The *Praetor*'s remaining guards watch all this from a safe distance, spears at the ready in their trembling hands. Our raid must seem to them like an invasion of the Huns: the worst, most violent thing to have happened to this sleepy town in a generation. Without the *Praetor*'s orders, they are too confused and frightened to stop us fortifying the house. At last, the *centurion* from the southern gate catches up to us

[482]

and begins to bring some order and discipline to his soldiers; but by then, we've managed to build a solid barrier across the courtyard, one that would clearly cost the lives of several of his men to breach, and he's still hesitant to risk them in exchange for the *Praetor*'s safety.

Ursula brings out the girl, the *Praetor* – and two more guards, who were hiding somewhere inside. I release them, after stripping them of weapons and armour.

"Go, welcome your *Dux* to Isca," I command them. "And tell him this fort now belongs to Octa, son of Aeric."

"Octa, son of Aeric. How much you've grown."

"And you, *Dux*, haven't changed a bit."

Standing on the other side of the overturned wagon is another man I haven't seen since that fateful day six years ago, when he and Wortigern brought me and the little girl, then still known only as Myrtle, to the Eobbasfleot battlefield. *Dux* Ambrosius has maybe a few more grey hairs, a few more wrinkles, the richly embroidered tunic is wrapped more tightly around his midriff, but he hasn't aged anywhere near as much as Wortigern over these passing years. It is a cold day – he wears a thick purple cloak and a grey woollen hat with the pattern imitating the *Dux*'s circlet on his head.

"I have to admit, I don't quite understand your plan, *aetheling*," he says, looking at the barrier between us and my men, hiding behind shields. "You are trapped inside my

The Wrath of the Iutes

Praetor's house, within the walls of my fort, surrounded by my guards. It is only through my respect to your father that I haven't yet ordered to set fire to this place."

"And burn down the *Praetor* and *Domna* Madron with us? I don't think so."

He chuckles. "Don't tell Lucius, but he's not worth to me as much as he might think. As for the girl…" He scratches his brow under his hat. "What is it that you want with her? Why are you even here? Did Wortigern send you?"

"Wortigern…" I hesitate. His soldiers stand just a few feet behind. "It's cold out here – would you like to continue this conversation inside?"

He glances over his shoulder, then back at my Iutes. "You give your word no harm will come to me and my men?"

"As long as you give me yours."

He nods and waves at the soldiers to step back. Seawine and I push away a large crate, and I help Ambrosius climb over the barricade. We enter the *Praetorium*, and I lead him to the study. I order one of the servants to bring us wine from the *Praetor*'s cellar, then ask everyone but Ursula to leave the two of us alone.

"Wortigern's dead," I say when the wine arrives.

"Are you sure?" Ambrosius eyes me suspiciously. "We heard rumours, but nothing certain…"

"He died in my arms," I say. "I buried him myself. Nobody else yet knows about it except my men – and now yourself."

Ambrosius's face turns grey. He rubs his eyes.

"How did he die?"

"From wounds he suffered in battle with Cunedag," I say. I can tell he senses I'm lying, but he can't guess why I would bother inventing a story about something so obvious.

"So it wasn't him who sent you here?" he asks after a pause.

"In a way, he did," I reply and reach for my satchel. "He gave me this before going North. I assume you understand its significance better than anyone."

He touches the satchel first, trying to guess its content with his fingers, before opening it gingerly, as if expecting a snake to leap out from inside.

He takes out the *Dux*'s diadem with a frown. Ursula gasps – this is the first she's seen it, but even she recognises it from the stories her parents told her.

"So, he chose you as his successor," Ambrosius says. "I suppose it made sense in his age-addled mind. Or did he confuse you with your father?" He shakes his head, then the frown on his face deepens. "This is curious."

"What is it?"

The Wrath of the Iutes

"Why is this stone new?" he asks, pointing to a rectangular sapphire in the front of the diadem.

"I don't know. Maybe the old one fell out."

"And Wortigern would have wasted resources to get it fixed, just to keep it in the chest?" He bites his lip and scratches at the sapphire. The stone – or rather, as I see now, a thin piece of blue glass – pops out, revealing a piece of paper folded behind it. Ambrosius unfolds it before I can reach for it, and stares at it with a confused frown.

"Do you recognise these symbols?" he asks, showing me the paper.

"These are the magic runes of our people," I reply, astonished. "Only the priests and some elders know how to put these to paper."

"Then I assume the message was meant for you."

My father must have taught Wortigern the runes during the years they wrote to each other from one side of Britannia to the other. I struggle with the symbols myself, but fortunately, the *Dux* was as bad at writing them as I am at reading, and made sure the three lines were easy to decipher by someone as uninitiated as myself:

Ask your father about his secret

Myrtle is more important than you think

[486]

James Calbraith

Make sure no harm comes to her

"What does it say?" asks Ambrosius.

"If he wanted you to know, he'd have written it in Latin," I reply, still pondering the message. "But it tells me to keep *Domna* Madron safe, which I was going to anyway."

"So you're now not just Wortigern's heir, but some kind of guardian for the girl, too?" he scoffs. "Don't you think that's putting too much burden on someone so young?"

"We have more right to her than you, or anyone else here," says Ursula. "The Iutes are her only surviving kin."

"Just because her mother was a barbarian wench, doesn't make the girl one of them," Ambrosius snarls. "I was at her baptism. She is Madron, daughter of *Dux* Wortimer, not Myrtle, daughter of Rhedwyn. She is as Briton as you or I." He points at Ursula. "I can tell by your speech you're an educated girl. You know our laws. The Iutes have no right to take her from us."

"*Us?*" I ask. "You only want her for the standing you think she'd bring to your court. Wortigern kept her away from you for a reason."

Ambrosius takes a long sip of the wine, then looks at the flask. "I sent Lucius this bottle," he notes. "You're making the same mistake as your father once did. You think just

The Wrath of the Iutes

because I am a shrewd and wise ruler of my people, I must wish everyone else harm."

"I don't think this at all." I shrug. "But I know you don't care for Myrtle any more than you care for this diadem. She is just a tool for you."

"A means to a worthy end." Ambrosius nods. "Wouldn't you like to hear *what* I need her for, before deciding what to do with her?"

"Lord's wounds, she's just a six-year-old girl with no family!" Ursula exclaims, banging her fist on the table. "She's not a warship or a wing of cavalry for you to play with!"

"No. She's much more than that," says Ambrosius.

I take Ursula's hand and urge her to calm down. "The *Dux* is right. We should hear him out. Maybe he'll surprise me and propose something other than just marrying Madron off to his wealthiest courtier."

Ambrosius chuckles. "If I didn't know you were Ash's son, I would've guessed now." He leans back in the chair. "None of my courtiers deserves the girl's hand. I know that; Wortigern knew that. If I thought otherwise, I would've taken her from him a long time ago."

"Who, then?"

"My son, Honorius."

Ursula and I stare at each other in silence.

[488]

"I didn't even know he had a son," I whisper in Iutish.

"What does it mean?" she replies. "What's his plan?"

"I have no idea. But it doesn't sound as bad as I feared it would."

"I never managed to convince Wortigern to this plan," Ambrosius says with a curious glint in his eye, which makes me suspect he understood our exchange. "To this day, I don't know why. But think about it, if you will – the two great ruling houses, joined. Britannia as one under their rule. The blood of heathens and the blood of Imperators. What a powerful union it would be!"

"Almost too powerful," I murmur. "I can see why Wortigern wasn't keen on this idea. With him gone, you would be the only one who controls that wedlock – and that bloodline."

And with Roman Britannia again under one rule, what future for the barbarians – for Iutes, Saxons, Angles in the North? What of the fragile peace? As long as the *wealas* provinces remained disunited and torn, there was space for us to expand into. With them joined together, would they not grow strong enough to face us again?

I'm certain my father would've disapproved of Ambrosius's ambition, even if it meant a half-Iutish princess sitting by the side of Britannia's ruler. If he corresponded with Wortigern often enough to have taught him the runes, he would know all about the *Dux*'s plans concerning the girl, born of the woman he once so loved.

The Wrath of the Iutes

But I am neither my father nor Wortigern; and, by the will of the Fates, it is up to me now to make the decision.

"How old is your son?" I ask the *Dux*.

"Nine."

"Then it is years before we can talk of wedlock." I take a sip of the wine. "I gather my word is not completely worthless here, or else you wouldn't agree to cross the barricade. How far would you be willing to extend this trust?"

"That depends." He grows instantly suspicious. "What did you have in mind?"

"The greatest gift my father ever gave me," I start slowly, staring into the wine cup, "was giving me freedom in whatever I did."

"I sense more than a hint of Pelagian doctrine," Ambrosius notes with a scowl. "Your father was raised among the heretics, from what I remember. It's a fine idea, free will. It's what separates us from dumb beasts. But we live in the real world, bound by real duties and obligations. None of us is truly free to do what we want."

"I was. My father made good on his promise, though I could see it pained him. I was free to choose my future, whether as an *aetheling*, a warrior, a scholar, or whoever else I wanted to be. It's how I was able to go fighting in Gaul, and it's how I ended up here."

"You are just a child," Ambrosius says and waves dismissively.

"So is Madron," says Ursula.

"She is too young to make this kind of choice!" Ambrosius exclaims.

"I agree," I say. "And now that her grandfather is gone, she no longer has anyone who could make the choice for her. This is why I propose to take her to Londin, and place her in Bishop Fastidius's care, as I once was placed. When the time comes for her to decide, you would come to Londin with your son and seek her hand, as is the Roman custom. It would be her choice, and her choice alone – and I swear my father and the bishop would honour it."

"And in the meantime, you would fill her head with all sorts of stories, songs and ideas, so that she'd never even think of marrying my son."

"You wouldn't trust the Bishop of Londin? You and Germanus put him there yourselves."

"And I've regretted it ever since. He's as much of a heretic as every other Easterner of his generation."

"I know you're an honest man, *Dux*," says Ursula. "And you know it's a fair proposal. The children are too young to be wedded, according to our and the Church's laws. You'd have to keep her locked up in your palace until she's of age, with all those nobles circling around her like ravens… Or

The Wrath of the Iutes

she'd be safe and away in Londin, behind the cathedral walls."

Ambrosius scratches his chin. "I admit, I see some merit in what you propose... But how do I know you won't just steal her from me and lock her up in your father's mead hall, or wherever it is you heathens keep prisoners?"

"This is why I mentioned trust."

"Trust is not enough. Don't you barbarians have some kind of ritual involving blood and demons for this occasion?"

"I would swear an *ath* on this, yes." I nod. "Though I'm surprised you've heard of it."

"Wortigern amused me with tales of his heathen friends," he replies, then points at Ursula. "You, girl. I know nothing about you. Why are you here? Are you his consort?"

"For the purposes of this meeting, she's my second in command," I reply.

"I can see you are of Briton blood — but are you civilised, or one of those half-barbarians from beyond the Wall?"

"I am daughter of Adminia, Councillor of Dorowern," Ursula says proudly. "And I would swear on the Scripture, if that satisfies you."

He scratches his chin again. Flakes of skin drop into his wine.

"It would be six years before they're both of age," he says. "Six long years."

"Where better to spend them than studying the Scriptures under Bishop Fastidius's tutelage?"

He scoffs. "This is exactly what I'm talking about. I don't need you putting all this knowledge into my daughter-in-law's head. She only needs to know how to raise heirs for my son, not how to read, write and, Lord forbid, think for herself. Still, you have made your case well... I've heard enough!"

He claps his hands. His soldiers enter the room, swords drawn. One of them throws Seawine to the floor.

"Madron!" exclaims Ursula. She leaps from the chair, only to be halted by one of Ambrosius's men in the door.

"She's in her room, undisturbed," the *Dux* says, once Ursula is forced to sit back down. "Did you really think you could have outsmarted me, boy? I could have taken the girl from you at any moment – but I wanted to hear you out, first. As it happens, your proposal solves a few of my problems, so I'm willing to consider it. On two conditions. Will you hear them?"

"Doesn't seem like we have much choice," I say.

"Smart." He smiles and bends one finger. "My man in Londin, Riotham, will have unhindered access to the girl, to report on her well-being."

"I see no problem with that."

The Wrath of the Iutes

He bends the second finger. "In a year from now, when Myrtle is of the right age, I will come to Londin with my son, and meet with whoever you've sorted out to be her legal guardian by then, and we will have ourselves a *Sponsalia*. A feast of betrothal." He raises his hand. "I know, I know – at first sight, this doesn't seem to match to what you had in mind. But the old laws are clear. A *Sponsalia* can be voided at will by either of the couple – and I promise I will respect the girl's choice if she were to change her mind in these six years."

"Why do you need this, then?" asks Ursula.

"I have to show *something* to placate the nobles. My domain suffered quite a few setbacks in recent years, as I'm sure you're aware. If I can buy six years of peace for one promise neither of us intends to keep, isn't it a good deal?"

I cover my mouth and whisper to Ursula in Iutish – almost certain now that Ambrosius might understand some of it after all: "I sense a trap."

"It might be – but what can we do? At least this way we'll have Madron with us – and a year to prepare for whatever may come."

I turn back to the *Dux*. "Fine. You will have all that. Now let us see if the girl's alright before we swear on our deal."

"Of course she's alright," Ambrosius scoffs. "I'm not a monster. Go, take her. I'm not good with small children, anyway. And as for this…" He turns the diadem in his hands

[494]

before throwing it to me. "Ah, take it, too. One day it will make a fine dowry."

The Wrath of the Iutes

CHAPTER XX
THE LAY OF AUDULF

A skein of grey geese flies over our heads and lands in a marsh on the southern side of the road, joining their brethren in a loud, proud honking chorus.

"The winter is nigh," I note to Ursula and tighten the cloak's collar. There are scarcely any leaves left in the ash trees, and the tops of the hills were dusted with hoar in the morning. "We've been away for so long."

"Too long," says Seawine, riding to my left. "I never thought I'd miss the sight of these Downs."

The road snakes up the northern slope of the Downs and climbs over the weathered terraced fields onto the brow of the hills. We're taking the ancient sacred ridgeway to Dorowern: I decided to leave the Roman highways in Callew, after we bid farewell to the armed escort Ambrosius gave us as guides across his domain. I don't want to enter Londin with Madron in tow just yet – she rides in a small, two-horse carriage in the middle of our procession, driven by Hleo and with Haering keeping her company inside. I wouldn't feel able to guarantee her safety in the big city, with just our handful of Iutes. Too many people in the capital remember her father – and her grandfather. First, we must reach the shelter of Cantia.

The Wrath of the Iutes

"We're not home yet," I say. To our south, the first reaches of Andreda forest loom in a dark band, and beyond it, the land of Aelle's Saxons. I haven't heard any solid news from Cantia since the conversation with Wortigern. I don't even know if it's safe for us to be on this track. The few rumours I overheard in a tavern in Callew mentioned some new bands roaming the woods and threatening the merchants on the road to New Port, but those would be further east, away from Londin and near the burning border with Cantia.

I spur the pony to a trot, and others do the same. The carriage bounces and rattles on the uneven dirt road; Hleo's only driving experience until now has been taking a fish wain to the Briton market on Wecta. I feel sorry for Madron, trapped inside the leaping box, but I feel we need to get out of sight of Andreda as fast as possible, even if it means some discomfort for our precious passenger.

I wonder how much the girl understands of what's happening to her. We told her that her grandfather fell in battle, and when she stopped crying, we explained we were taking her to her mother's family; but she never had any contact with the Iutes before, and couldn't possibly have the grasp of distances involved in our travel. Other than the journey she was taken on by Wortigern to Eobbasfleot, which she would have been too young to remember, her short life was limited to the few towns and forts in Ambrosius's domain. For the first couple of days she kept asking if we were there yet; after Callew, she must've realised the journey was going to be longer than any she'd ever undertaken, and since then, she has sulked in desperate silence inside the carriage.

I keep thinking about the "secret" Wortigern mentioned in his message. My father keeps many secrets, no doubt. There are things he did in his youth, especially during the war with Wortimer, that he never talks about, even with me. But I can't think of anything that would have to do with Madron. I already know that he helped Rhedwyn poison Wortimer, and that Rhedwyn died in the attempt – something I don't think anyone else knows, except his brother, the bishop. What else could it be? The mystery sounds ominous and makes me only more anxious about our return to Cantia.

Shortly before nightfall, we reach a crossroads with the Roman highway to New Port, with a crumbled ruin in the north-west corner. Though I've never been here before, I recognise the place from my father's stories. There was a bloody battle here, many years ago, between a detachment of Wortigern's soldiers and a mob of serf rebels; years later, Bishop Germanus conducted here a great mass, before marching on Londin with the army of his followers. Crucially, however, the crossroads is the border of the Saxon territory, and I'm glad to see it empty when we arrive. If Aelle's bands were to stage an ambush, this would be the perfect place. Any further north, and they'd be risking stumbling onto the Londin guards and needlessly risking igniting a conflict with the Britons.

The *wealas*, I tell myself. I must start thinking of them like this again, now that we're coming back home. No longer allies, no longer masters for whom we do mercenary work – the purse filled with silver coins jangles at my waist, and at the waists of all my men, a payment Ambrosius reluctantly rewarded us with for our services in defence of his border; here, they are our neighbours, sometimes friends, but mostly,

The Wrath of the Iutes

strangers, locked in an uneasy truce, hiding from us behind the walls of their cities.

"We need to find somewhere for the night," says Ursula.

"I know just the place."

I lead them up the New Port road, and after a couple of miles we turn onto another trail, winding up a narrow ravine. The carriage struggles to climb the track, but there's enough space here for an oxcart, and before long we reach the flattened summit and a scorched shell of what was once a large stone building.

"Did you know it would be like this?" asks Ursula.

"I feared so. It's still tragic to see it so thoroughly destroyed."

"What is this place?"

"This used to be Verica's inn. My father was very fond of it. While it stood, it was the first, or last vestige of civilisation before his home at Ariminum, depending on which way you went."

It's impossible now to tell which of the recent wars or passing bands burned the place almost to the ground. We find some unidentifiable human and animal remains still scattered around the shattered ruin, and we have to clean them up before I allow Ursula to take Myrtle out of her carriage and take her to the first of the tents we set up within the blackened walls.

[500]

James Calbraith

"Put a watchman on the path," I command Seawine. "There's a narrowing where a barrier used to be."

"Do you expect trouble? In this desolate place?"

"I hope not – but we don't know what's been going on in these parts while we were away. We can't be too careful."

Seawine wakes me up, shining an oil lamp in my face. I push it aside and rub my eyes.

"What is it?"

"Ubba says he spotted some movement in the rocks."

"Wolves?"

"Bigger."

I shake Ursula awake and we clamber outside. I look at the sky – the dawn is creeping slowly over the hills on the other side of the Roman road. I can feel the wind freezing droplets of dew on my unshaven face.

"If it's the bandits, they won't strike until it's bright enough," I say. "We have some time to prepare. Ursula, get the girl, keep her quiet. There should be a hidden path back to the highway somewhere behind these rocks." I turn back to Seawine. "Hleo and Haering will ride south in the carriage, as decoy. If there are too many of them, leave the carriage

The Wrath of the Iutes

and hide. The rest of you, wait until the first light then follow after me and Ursula."

"And where are we going?"

"North. To Beaddingatun, if anything's left of it – or Ariminum, if not."

Seawine frowns. "Why wouldn't there be?"

I bite my tongue. I still haven't told him about Aelle's attacks on the Iute frontier. Beaddingatun is no longer just a Iute village, and it lies beyond the borders of my father's realm, but it was always exposed to enemies coming from both north and south – it was among the first settlements to be razed by Wortimer's bloodthirsty roughs, and I wouldn't be surprised if it fell prey to Aelle's "forest bandits" just because it was in the way.

"You never know, a lot may have happened while we were away," I say, disguising my unease with a shrug. "Get your things. And be quick about it."

I'm relieved to discover the passage my father mentioned using when he was spying on the forest bandits, many years ago, is still there; it's steep and narrow, slippery in the frost, fit more for mountain goats than ponies. I'm not yet as used to Aecba's mount as I was to the one I abandoned in the North. It spits and nickers in annoyance every time it slips on the rocks, but it plods on in the darkness. I glance back. Madron sits on the back of Ursula's pony, clutching on to the mane in utter silence, staring grimly ahead. She may not know where she is or why, but she senses the seriousness of our situation. Wortigern prepared her well for a life of danger.

We reach the Roman road just as the first rays of the sun illuminate the paving stones. I glance to the south and see silhouettes of two horsemen waiting at the foot of the hill, at the entrance to the inn road.

"They haven't spotted us yet," I whisper to Ursula. "Trot slowly, but be ready to gallop on my signal."

She nods and mounts up behind Madron. We make a few hundred feet before I glance back and notice one of the riders pointing us out to the other.

"Now!" I cry. We launch into a gallop. The ponies neigh and groan, shod for charging on dirt and mud rather than over stone pavement. It's almost ten miles from here to Ariminum; the mounts can't possibly run the entire distance. I only hope we will manage to create enough of a gap between us and our pursuers for them to lose interest – if they are indeed just random bandits, seeking easy prey. If they're Aelle's men, they will not let us go without a fight. They might not know who we are, or why we are travelling down this highway, but they'll know we're Iutes, or their allies, just from the fact we ride the moor ponies.

I glance back again. The hunters slow down, then turn back. They must have spotted the carriage coming down the path, a more worthy prize than two lonely riders.

"Ride on to Ariminum," I tell Ursula. "Don't stop until you get there. I'll go check on the others."

The Wrath of the Iutes

"And where is this 'Ariminum'?"

Her question gives me pause. Of course, why would she know the location of some small *villa* on the New Port road? It was only ever important to my father and his family. I'm not even sure if I still remember how to get there myself…

"Turn left just before Saffron Valley," I tell her. "Onto the road to Beaddingatun. Ariminum is the *villa* across the river from there."

"Be careful," she says and launches into a steady canter. I turn around and ride back towards Verica's. Before long, I reach what appears to be a chaotic brawl between Seawine and his Iutes on one side, and several warriors on the other, fighting on foot with spears, clubs and knives. More men are running and riding from the south – they will have discovered by now that the carriage was a mere bait.

I swerve to the muddy roadside to let the dirt dampen my hoof beats, and lower myself to a charge. I ride right up to one of the two horsemen and slash him across the back with the lance. The other one turns to face me; he raises a round, painted shield and deflects my lance deftly, confirming he's not just some forest bandit. These are Aelle's men, no doubt; they're well trained, though not as battle-hardened as my Iutes. Two are dead already, lying face down in the ditch. I let go of the lance and strike again at the rider with the sword, cutting just below the shield. He yelps, drops the shield and swings his axe inches from my face. I sway back, slash upwards and sever his arm right off. I kick his side, and he falls off the horse with a cry.

"Where's Hleo and Haering?" I ask Seawine.

"Lost sight of them when the carriage flipped."

"Flipped?"

"Haering took a turn too fast."

He parries a falling knife blade. It slips off his sword and cuts a deep groove down his forearm. I punch the enemy with the pommel, grab him by the tunic and throw him to the ground, where my pony kicks his head in.

"There's more!" cries Ubba and points further up the road. I count at least half a dozen warriors approaching on small forest ponies. Together with the Saxons still alive around us, they will outnumber us two to one. Where are they all coming from? This can't be an accident – we must have been followed by this band since nearing Andreda. Is it possible that Aelle knew we were here? Perhaps Ambrosius betrayed us, after all – and decided to use Aelle's hands to get rid of me and take Madron back for himself…

"Save yourself, *aetheling*," says Seawine. "We'll hold them back."

"This isn't about me anymore," I tell him. "We can't let them chase after Ursula and the princess."

I plunge my sword into the skull of another Saxon and realise the leg of my breeches is cold and wet. My left leg is going quickly numb. A random stab - when did that happen? Doesn't matter. As long as I can hold the sword…

The Wrath of the Iutes

There's one last thing that can help me. I reach for the flask at my side. Henbane – I've been carrying it for so long, I almost forgot I had it. I uncork it, and the strong smell hits my nostrils like a fist. The liquid inside is thick, viscous; I don't know if, after all this time, it will work as intended, or just send me retching, but I have to try. I close my eyes and pour it down my throat.

"Line up!" I call. I need to bring some order to this fight before I succumb to the henbane. "Seawine, go left. Raegen, Acha, to the right." I wait for Ubba to finish off his opponent. He's bleeding from cuts to his legs and sides, as is his pony. I tell him to ride onwards, try to reach Ursula or Beaddingatun, if he can; he won't be able to hold the line with us for long anyway.

The Saxon riders form a wedge, though it's more loose and unsteady than the ones my Iutes are capable of. It's as if they're aware of the need of formation, but haven't been trained to perform it. This is our chance. I pull back, taking Raegen with me; it's a small gap, but I hope it's enough to lure the enemy into the trap.

The six-man wedge strikes our four-strong line and immediately falls apart. There are no more manoeuvres left; it's sword against shield and axe against lance, and my men and I are already weary with the battle that's taken too much of our time and effort.

I feel anger rising within me like fire in the wind – or maybe it's just the henbane? We're so close to home, having fought and travelled for so long, across the Empire, across Britannia; too close to be killed now by some Saxons who don't even know why they were told to fight us. I let the wrath burn in my blood and power my sword arm. My pony rears and as it drops, I hack at the nearest Saxon as if he was a wooden target dummy. Blood from his shoulder spurts in my eyes. I slash again, striking his helmet. The weapon almost flies from my hand; the helmet bursts in two, as does the skull underneath it. The warrior falls silent and dead mid-cry.

I feel a strange, numb sensation in my thigh. I look down – one of the Saxon riders, whom I thought dead already, managed to crawl under my mount and pierce me with a spear. The henbane numbs the pain, but can't stem the blood flow. Now I'm wounded in both legs, and I feel my grip on the pony's flanks weaken.

A Saxon perishes under my pony's hooves for the second time. Another rider appears in his place. I whirl the sword with both hands. The blade cuts the enemy's shield in half; the blow smashes the bone in his arm into pieces. My stomach churns; dark spots appear before my eyes. I taste blood and bile in my mouth – I must've bitten my tongue in the heat of the fight, but I feel nothing.

"North!" cries Raegen. I turn in the direction he's pointing, and my heart sinks. More riders, flying towards us, capes fluttering in the northern wind. We're trapped; worse still, if they're coming from the north, it means they got Ursula already…

"Pull back!" I call. "Each to their own!"

We tear away from the six Saxons – four now left, but at the cost of more injuries to my men – and ride off to meet

The Wrath of the Iutes

the new threat. I see no chance of us all surviving, but the Roman road is long and wide, and maybe one or two of us will manage to break through to seek safety… If there is any safety to seek out.

There's something odd about these new riders. Two of them, riding in front, are wearing what looks like bearskin cloaks. The others don silver mail shirts under long black capes. A pattern in white thread flashes on the capes, but I can't yet see what it is. They ride well, at least the two bearskins in front, better than any of the Saxons we just fought. Are these Aelle's own guards, or some secret cavalry unit he's been training for the war with my father?

I have no strength to raise the sword – if I let go of the reins, I will fall off the pony. There's just enough of the henbane left surging within me to keep me conscious, despite the blood loss. Seawine, riding to my left, draws his weapon, but his hand is shaking. Raegen and Acha drift to the right edge of the road, hoping to stretch the enemy line. But all of this is in vain – we're outnumbered and, with the arrival of new riders, outmatched… I brace myself for a strike.

The caped riders storm past us, lances down, and keep on charging – towards the Saxons. The two men in bearskin cloaks halt at my side. One of them grabs my pony's reins – the other holds me up just as I start to sway from the saddle. I stare at them, but with eyes blurry from sweat and blood, I can't quite see their faces.

"*Aetheling!*" the one to my right exclaims. "It really is you!"

The voice sounds familiar – it's a Iute, alright, but who…?

"Get on my pony, Octa," says the other. "By Donar's hammer, you look almost as bad as I did after Trever. Let's get you to a healer!"

This one, at last, I recognise – it would be impossible not to – but I still can't quite believe it. I wipe my eyes and take another look at my rescuers.

"Audulf!" I cry out. "Colswine! What are you doing here?"

"We? We were just out on patrol – we heard a large Saxon band was roaming near Verica's. The better question is, what are *you* doing here? We thought you were still in Gaul!"

"We have a lot to talk about," says Seawine. "But first, have you seen Ursula – and the little girl with her?"

Audulf and Colswine look at each other. "So it *was* her! She rode past us without stopping. I don't know where she'd be by now."

"But I do," I say. I glance back, but I can't see anyone fighting anymore – Audulf's Iutes must have routed the Saxons, and are now in pursuit. "Take us to my father's place. It's a *villa*, just off –"

"You mean Ariminum?" asks Audulf. "Certainly. That's just where we set up our camp."

The Wrath of the Iutes

"Why not Beaddingatun?" asks Seawine.

Audulf gives him a surly, heavy stare.

"We *do* have a lot to talk about," he says, then, noticing my pony, he asks: "Isn't this Aecba's mount?"

We reach the fork in the muddy road – the path north leads to the *villa*; the southern branch will take us to Beaddingatun.

I order the wounded to be taken to Ariminum, but I tell Audulf to show me the village first.

"Are you sure? You're still bleeding."

"It won't take long."

The village is not as badly damaged as I feared. Maybe a third of the huts have been burnt down, most of them on the southern outskirts. Beaddingatun had grown swiftly since its first destruction in Wortimer's War – it is now as much a Briton village as it is a Iutish one, with peasants having moved here from Saffron Valley and other smaller settlements, seeking safety in numbers and the low earthen wall the Iutes dug up around it. I notice the whitewashed stone chapel still stands intact on the village's eastern edge – another draw for the Briton settlers.

"The *wealas* suffered the most in the attack," says Audulf. "Our people had sense to flee into the woods when the Saxons came."

[510]

"Why have the Saxons done it?" asks Seawine. "And why did they attack us on that hill, in such great numbers?"

Audulf looks at him, surprised. "You mean you don't know about the war?"

"The war?" Seawine turns to me. "Octa, have you heard anything about this?"

I wince. "I've heard some rumours in Callew… Didn't want to worry you needlessly."

"It's all over now, anyway," says Audulf. "For the winter, at least. Aelle struck here first," he adds, nodding at the village. "He tried to draw us out across the Medu before assaulting Robriwis."

"I assume we won," I say. "Seeing as you're here."

"Your father pushed them back eventually," he replies. "But I wasn't there to see it. I was still recuperating at Rutubi when the news came of the Saxon retreat. You'll have to ask him about it yourself."

"I've seen enough here," I say. Pain runs through my left leg again; I do need this wound looked after – one of Audulf's men wrapped it roughly, but we had no time to treat it properly. The last thing I want so close to home is to lose a limb due to some random Saxon's dirty blade.

"Those men who rode with you," I ask as we turn back towards Ariminum, "you've trained them yourself?"

The Wrath of the Iutes

"As well as I could. Many youths were eager to join our ranks, after hearing of our adventures in Gaul. I selected a few – the others are waiting to start their training on your return."

"I see you've decided to keep the bearskins," I note.

He chuckles. "These are new ones, actually. I saw a pile of them at the Dorowern market. It terrifies the Saxons, especially those who fought at Trever. If we had enough, I'd dress all my men in them."

"Instead, you have them wear these black capes with… what is it?"

"A white horse. Like Odo's cavalry used to wear."

I smile. "Good idea. After all, we'd never have managed to achieve anything if it wasn't for Odo's teachings. Have you told him of this?"

Audulf's face darkens.

"What is it?"

"I'm sorry – I forgot you were away. Somehow, I thought you knew."

"Knew what?"

"Odo died last month. This cold weather got to him. We just got the news before setting out on this patrol. He dines with Wodan now."

James Calbraith

I halt and look to the whitewashed chapel. Odo was a Christian, but something tells me he wouldn't have minded Audulf's heartfelt tribute.

I don't expect to find any trace of my father or his family in the *villa*. The property now belongs to the Church, and what is left of it – an old wood mill on the Loudborne, a few small plots of lavender and saffron, and a riverside pasture shared with the neighbouring villages – is run by a local priest in the name of Bishop Fastidius. Even Paulinus, the ancient priest who taught my father to read and write, and was seemingly immortal, judging by how often my father mentioned meeting him, is gone now – either dead or retired somewhere where he wouldn't have to face the painful memories.

So it's quite a surprise when one of the older groundskeepers approaches me as I step out of the *domus* – for the first time in two days, now that my leg has begun to heal – studies my face carefully, and says:

"You look just like your mother."

He's my father's age – but the years of hard, physical work have made him look older, his back slightly bent, his fingers darkened and twisted. His once black hair is powdered white. A scar runs across his left eye – not from a weapon, but from some animal's claw.

"You knew my mother?"

The Wrath of the Iutes

He chuckles. "I knew all of them. Ash, Eadgith and I were play friends. Even Bishop Fastidius – though he was just young master Fastid, then. I'm Vatto," he introduces himself. "The last of 'Ash's Saxons'."

"Vatto! I've heard of you. The gardener's hand, right?"

"Master groundskeeper now," he says. "For what it's worth. There's no garden to keep anymore, just a vegetable patch for the priest's kitchen." He wipes his hands on his apron. "I'm sorry about your mother."

"Thank you."

"I don't know why she didn't just come back here after the war." He shakes his head. "I'm sure Fastid – I mean, His Grace – wouldn't mind her living in the *villa*. We could have used a good blacksmith."

"She didn't want to live among the *wealas* after what they did to us in the war."

Vatto winces. "Those were Wortimer's bandits. We honest Britons had nothing to do with all that violence."

"Yet you did nothing to stop him."

"I know nothing about that, young master." He smiles apologetically and wipes his hands on his apron. He's vaguely aware of my position – the Iute warriors gathered on the grounds of the *villa* salute me when they pass by – but he still sees me just as his old friend's son, even if that old friend grew from a boy running around cow pasture with wooden sword to a Councillor in Londin, and then, inexplicably, a king of a barbarian tribe. "I'm just a groundskeeper. It's just that sometimes... I wish they were all still here. Ash, Eadgith, Gleva, Bana, Acha... Playing at war instead of waging wars. Feasting, hunting, humping in the woods... Life was simpler back then."

"Everything changes."

"So it does, young master. So it does. As a gardener, I know it best. A seed grows into a tree, the tree withers and falls to feed another tree." He smiles again and bows. "It was good to finally see you, boy." He pats me awkwardly on the shoulder, then turns around, bent even more, and goes back to hoeing his vegetables.

Just then, some new riders enter through the remains of the gate, returning from another patrol. They bring news – and our two missing Iutes, Hleo and Haering. They're covered in mud, but appear unharmed.

"We hid in a ditch by the old barrows," says Hleo. "We thought we were the only ones who survived!"

"The Saxons are gathering again, in the ruin at the crossroad," says one of the riders.

"Would they dare attack the *villa*?" I ask Audulf.

"I doubt Aelle wants to risk the bishop's wrath – even when they struck at Beaddingatun, they made sure not to harm anyone here. But they'll be waiting for us on the road, if we don't hurry."

The Wrath of the Iutes

"Then it's time for us to leave. Gather everyone who can still ride, leave the rest in the *domus* – they'll take good care of them here. Seawine, Ursula!" I cry. "Prepare a wagon for Madron. We're going home!"

The embrace is long, tight – and uncomfortable. I can't remember the last time my father hugged me like this. A pat on the shoulder, a slap on the back, a smile and a nod were the usual expressions of fatherly love I would expect from him. I don't quite know how to react. I breathe in the heavy smell of leather, fur and sweat from the collar of his cloak, and tap him on the sides. He steps back and makes way for Betula. Her one-armed hug is short, strong, soldierly.

Father leans down and rustles Madron's hair. "It really is you," he muses. "*Madron*, huh. A good name."

"Wortigern chose it himself," I tell him.

I can tell he's looking for some semblance of his beloved Rhedwyn in the girl's face. Judging by the wistful, forlorn smile, he must have found it. He stands back up.

"You must have so many stories," he says. "I can't wait to hear them."

"And I can't wait to hear yours," I reply. "I was so worried when I heard of the war."

"Not worried enough to ride to our help."

"You know we were too far to do anything... How did you beat Aelle? He's not someone who would have come all this way if he wasn't certain of victory."

The forlorn smile turns to a mischievous one. "Don't underestimate your king, son. It's the same mistake Aelle made. Come, I'll show you something."

He leads me up the stairs to the top of the rampart. I am now familiar enough with sieges to recognise traces of one on the blood-splattered walls of the fortress and in the burnt-out buildings in the courtyard. The village that once spilt outside the walls is all but gone, torched down and razed by the besieging forces, though I see some of the village folk are already returning, rising tents and simple huts in place of their scorched houses. Judging by the amount of damage to the fortress and how widespread the destruction around it is, Aelle must've brought at least a thousand warriors to the field, if not more. The battle here was the same size as that at *Cair Wortigern*.

We climb to the top of the gate tower, and I stop, astonished, at the sight of a massive device of roughly hewn timber, iron beams, twisted ropes and pulleys. I remember the schematics of one just like it in one of the volumes I got from Rav Asher in Trever...

"An *onager*!" I exclaim.

"I believe that's what it's called, yes." My father nods and pats the machine on the frame. "We built it according to the books you gave Betula in Gaul. It wasn't an easy feat – even with some help from the Briton craftsmen, and Fastidius's

The Wrath of the Iutes

translations. This is the third one we tried, and the only one that didn't fall apart on the first shot... But once we got it going, you could almost see the courage in the Saxon hearts melt away like spring snow." He chuckles.

"I don't think I've ever seen you in such a good mood," I note.

"It was a fine battle," he replies. "One the likes of which this land hasn't seen since Eobbasfleot. It made me feel young again – and *useful*. Before Aelle struck, I was beginning to wonder what even the point was of being a *Rex*. You should've seen..." He chuckles. "But then, you've seen plenty more in your travels than this. Come, we will prepare the feast."

"Father, I..."

He pauses. "Or are you still tired? Of course, you've only just arrived – and your injuries haven't healed yet. We can do it when you're ready."

"It's not that. I – I need to ask you something."

I dig into my satchel and present him with Wortigern's diadem.

"He wanted me to bring this to you," I say.

He picks the trinket up and raises it to the dim sunlight. "I did wonder what was going to happen to it after his death... First Myrtle, and now the *Dux*'s diadem." He smacks his lips. "Wortigern, you old fox. Why did you send all your old trouble my way? What am I supposed to do with all of this?"

"There's more." I show him the note in the Iutish runes. "Do you know what he could've meant? What is this *secret*?"

I have never seen his face go through so many emotions so quickly. It turns from joy to grief, then to anger as he crumples the note in his hand and slams his fist against the frame of the siege engine. He calms down only when he sees in my eyes the fear provoked by his sudden fury.

He rubs his eyes, takes a deep breath and puts his hand on my shoulder.

"I suppose I would have had to tell you this anyway, now that the girl is here."

"What do you mean?"

"Myrtle…" He takes another breath. He pretends to be composed now, but his face is the same colour as the stones in the rampart behind him, and the hand on my shoulder trembles. I fear for his heart. "*Domna* Madron is your cousin. And not like Haesta was Hengist's cousin, some distant relative from the same clan. She is the daughter of your father's sister. Your flesh and blood."

"But I don't have an aunt." I scratch my head in confusion. "Eadgith had no siblings, and you're my only…"

It is now my turn to go grey-faced.

The Wrath of the Iutes

"Rhedwyn."

"We were both children of Eobba, the third chieftain, the one who perished on the whale road with his entire clan. We had no way of knowing. I was a slaveling with no name, she – a princess of the Iutes." He leans against the wall. "I only found out about it just before we were supposed to be finally wedded. And then… Everything fell apart. Wortimer, the war… It took me years to come to terms with what happened – and now you have brought it all back…" He shakes his head. "I don't know why Wortigern insisted that I tell you this. It changes nothing."

I reel from the revelation. Suddenly, everything about my father becomes clear: his melancholy bouts, his grim demeanour… I can't even begin to imagine what he must have gone through. To find out he had a sister – to lose a lover – and then, to lose them both in such a tragic manner… I can't even begin to comprehend what it must have been like.

"Does – does anyone else know?"

"No one who lives. Other than Wortigern, I only told Hengist. This is why he agreed to let me have me the *Drihten*'s circlet so easily – he knew it should've been mine all along, as Eobba's heir… And Rhedwyn herself, of course."

"Maybe that's why."

"That's why – what?"

"Wortigern knew that, with his death, you'd be the only one left with this burden. Now we share it — you're no longer alone."

He smiles, sadly. "Yes, perhaps you're right." He touches his chest. "I do feel a certain relief… I kept it all inside for too long. Besides, it helps to avoid certain… misunderstandings when Madron grows older."

"Father!" I cry out in outrage. "She's only six years old!"

"She'll be sixteen before you know it. And I can tell she'll be just as beautiful as her mother." He gives me a sharp look. "But then, your heart is already taken, is it not? You and Ursula — I've seen you together. After everything you've been through, you must have…"

"I — I don't know about that, Father. I'm not sure. It's… not that simple."

He smiles. "Nothing is ever simple at your age, boy. Especially the matters of the heart. Let us go back to the mead hall. I have this rare drink from Gaul — they call it *sicera*. We'll open a barrel, and you'll tell me all about your troubles."

TO BE CONCLUDED IN THE SONG OF OCTA, BOOK THREE: THE CROWN OF THE IUTES

The Wrath of the Iutes

HISTORICAL NOTE

The deeper we go into the fifth century, the further away we find ourselves from written history, and nearer myth. What we know of Britain of that age comes not from the chronicles or letters, but from legends, told centuries later in the mountain courts of the Welsh warlords. We enter the world of Cunedda the Hound, founder of Gwynedd, brought by Vortigern to defend the northern reaches of Wales from the Scots and the Picts; of Madrun, or St. Materiana, Vortigern's granddaughter, who stands at the root of every Welsh dynasty's family tree; and of Niall of Seven Hostages, the Irish warlord, mysteriously slain on an expedition to Britain. The world of the first, legendary, kings of Armorica, like Gradlon and Budic, who started the long process of turning the province into Brittany, a colony of Britons. And of King Marcus of Cornwall, his nephew Tristan, and the eternal myth of their love for Iseuld. This book is largely set in how I imagine this mist-shrouded world to look like.

That the druids of Gaul and Britain believed in some sort of reincarnation, the so-called "Pythagorean doctrine", was noted by ancient writers and historians since Julius Caesar. Of course, the Romans were unreliable narrators, and we can't be sure that they truly understood the nuances of philosophy of the people they were only interested in conquering and destroying.

As for Emperor Majorian and his war against the Goths, it was a resounding success. Theodoric II was roundly defeated at Arelate, and forced to abandon Septimania and Hispania to the Romans. The Burgundians were subdued, Lugdunum was taken, and for a while it seemed that the Western Empire was well on its way to regain most of its land and power…